"The writing is [illegible] trapped inside his head with n[illegible] how much we really know abo[illegible] [illegible]ch we choose not to see. It's s[illegible] [illegible]e in the best possible way. O[illegible] [illegible]ers I've read in years."

— Beta Reader, Los Angeles

"Chilling in its restraint and brutal in its precision. Your Driver's Arrived doesn't rely on shock value—it lets the silence do the screaming. Eric is the kind of character you'll think about every time you get in a stranger's car. Terrifying because it feels so real."

— Claire Jensen, Early Reader

"Nicora masterfully walks the line between confession and manipulation. You don't just read Your Driver's Arrived—you become complicit. It's a psychological thriller that makes you question your own instincts, and by the end, you're not sure whether you were listening to a killer... or agreeing with him."

— Eli Mercer, Fiction Editor, LitQuarterly

YOUR DRIVER'S ARRIVED

YOUR DRIVER'S ARRIVED

Psychological Thriller

by

Mark Nicora

This is a work of fiction. Names, characters, places, and incidents either are the product of the author's imagination or are used fictitiously. Any resemblance to actual persons, living or dead, events, or locales is entirely coincidental.

The Library of Congress has cataloged the edition as follows:
Name: Nicora, Mark, author
Title: Your Driver's Arrived
Description: First Edition
Identifiers: TXu 2-481-185
Subjects: Thriller (Fiction)
ISBN : 979-8-234-00214-3

To those who stood beside me in the shadows—
your insight, your honesty, and your steady presence carried this story forward.

This book is ours.

You know who you are.

PROLOGUE

WE LIVE OUR LIVES IN the now. Instant gratification reigns supreme—from same-day delivery to on-demand entertainment, our world prioritizes convenience over substance, efficiency over connection. Eyes locked on screens, we scroll endlessly, curating digital personas while real-life interactions wither. We share moments but rarely experience them, trading authenticity for algorithms.

So what's the problem? This is the way of the future, right?

Maybe. But what if technology isn't just a tool for convenience? What if it's something more insidious? A weapon. A mask. An opportunity for killing.

Because when the whole world is watching, sometimes, no one really sees at all.

Your Driver's Arrived is the disturbing story and the likely confessions of a tormented man, Eric Sutton.

Eric could be anyone. The friendly neighbor who waves as he mows his lawn. The devoted husband who never forgets his wife's favorite flowers, or the proud father who cheers the loudest at his daughter's ballet recital.

To those who know him, Eric is a good man—dependable, kind, the sort of person who would drop everything to help a friend in need. He has built a life most would envy: a stable career, a beautiful home, a family he cherishes.

But Eric has a secret.

Beneath the mask of normalcy, beneath the warm smiles and steady hands, lurks something far darker. A hunger. A need. A relentless obsession.

For Killing.

But he isn't the monster lurking in the shadows. He isn't the stranger you cross the street to avoid. Eric has spent years perfecting the balance, of living two lives—one as the perfect family man, the other as a predator hidden in plain sight. His methods are calculated, his actions precise. And his cover? Flawless.

Told in his own words, Eric—whose name has been changed to protect his family—peels back the layers of his own darkness, examining every detail of what he's done, searching to relieve the guilt and more importantly find the answer to the one question that haunts him: *Why?*

His voice is eerily calm, his actions disturbingly methodical. Emotion does not cloud his confessions, making it difficult to see him as anything other than a force of nature—cold, detached, inevitable. And yet, beneath the surface, there is something unsettlingly human about him. A flicker of goodness. A thread of logic so twisted yet clear that it compels us to listen, to understand, maybe even to empathize.

But understanding Eric comes at a cost. His story is not just a glimpse into the mind of a predator—it is a reflection of the world we navigate every day, the silent risks we take without a second thought.

And no matter what we think of him, his confessions force us to confront an uncomfortable truth: we slip into the back seats of ride-share cars, trusting without question, believing we will arrive safely at our destination.

But what if we don't?

Chapter 1

CREATION

ARE SERIAL KILERS BORN destined to become what they are, or is there a moment—an event, a trigger—that awakens something dark within them? Charles Manson, Jeffrey Dahmer, John Wayne Gacy, and Ted Bundy were once just normal children, living lives that, for a time, looked no different from my own. They had families, friends, childhood memories. And yet, somewhere along the way, something shifted.

Movies, books, and documentaries attempt to weave explanations, giving us reasons—trauma, neglect, abuse, mental illness. Maybe we create these stories out of fear, a desperate need to understand the unthinkable. After all, if we can pinpoint the cause, we can pretend it's something we can prevent. Because the alternative is terrifying: that sometimes, there is no reason. That darkness exists without explanation.

Lately, I find myself reflecting—not just on what I've done, but on the path that led me here. The guilt is creeping in, a slow and steady pressure that I can't ignore. Maybe I'm tired—tired of running, tired of the chase. Maybe that's why I'm writing this down, knowing that putting my thoughts into words might mean risking everything.

But my struggle isn't just about why I continue to do the things I do. It's about why I *enjoy* them so much. The thrill, the rush, the euphoric high—sensations that shouldn't feel so intoxicating, yet they do.

I don't see myself as a serial killer. And while I take responsibility for what I've done, I know I'm not the only one to blame. This isn't denial—I own my actions. But I didn't arrive here alone.

I know most of you will read this and see a monster. A killer. Someone no different from those whose names fill the pages of history's darkest stories. And like them, I wonder: how will the world explain me? How will they justify what I've done? And ultimately, how will I be remembered.

But there's still a part of me that clings to hope. Hope that I can break free from this cycle. Hope that, before someone else has to try and explain me,

I can find a way to stop myself.

LOOKING BACK, MY CHILDHOOD was pretty normal—mostly uneventful, but in the best way possible. I grew up in a small midwest town in Ohio, a place called Warren. My parents both worked hard. Dad was a controller at a hospital, and my Mother worked as a secretary at the local steel mill. We weren't rich, but we had a nice home in a nice neighborhood. Mom always said we lived on the "*good side*" of town, as if that distinction really meant something.

I was the youngest, with three older sisters. We got along for the most part, though there were plenty of arguments—but nothing out of the ordinary for siblings. What stands out most about my family growing up wasn't the fights or the mundane routine, but the traditions. Every holiday was celebrated but Christmas was always special. No matter what, we made it a big event with an abundance of decorations, presents stacked under the tree, and the house filled with warmth and laughter.

But more than the holidays, it was dinner that defined us most. Every single night, no matter what—sports, dance, school activities—we all sat at the table together. It wasn't just about eating; it was about being a family. We'd all pitch in to cook, and after the meal, we cleaned up together. It was a ritual, something that grounded us.

Weekends had their own rhythm. Friday or Saturday nights, I was usually at a friend's house, while my parents entertained guests or went out on the town to dinner. But Sundays? Sundays were sacred. Mornings were reserved for church, and afternoons meant big family dinners in the dining room with the fancy china. The kind of meals that felt like an event, where extended family gathered and conversations stretched late into the evening. And lastly, without fail, every year, we spent two full weeks on a family vacation. No exceptions. Vacations weren't elaborate, mostly camping but it was time together and there were always a lot of laughs and stories to share.

Summertime at our house was something else entirely. We were the only family in town with a built-in pool, which made our backyard the place to be. That pool was my golden ticket to popularity. Every day I could count on, no less than three or four girls asking if they could come over to tan poolside, which, in turn, attracted my guy friends to want to come over. Of course, my parents weren't keen on turning our backyard into a full-blown public pool, so they limited the number of people I could invite. That just meant my friends had to get creative—offering to bring pizza, burgers, or drinks in exchange for an invite. It was a fair trade.

And so this was my life, as I remember it all through high school. Thinking back now, life growing up was good. Really good.

Like a fork in the road, after graduation, I packed my bags and set off for a new adventure. My friends and I had chosen The Ohio State University, full of energy, excitement, and endless possibilities. We found a place off-campus—a modest apartment on Lane Ave, that quickly became the center of our new world. Late nights, laughter, and the buzz of freedom filled the air.

Growing up, I had watched my parents host lavish parties, their home always alive with music, drinks, food and conversation. It must have rubbed off on me because, before long, life at college became one party after another. Weekends blurred into weekdays, and textbooks often took a backseat to late-night gatherings.

But beneath the fun, something gnawed at me. Like many students, I wasn't sure what I truly wanted to do. My classes felt directionless, my ambitions undefined and by the end of my third year, I knew I needed a change—something drastic. I had read an article about the steps needed to become a millionaire in life. At the top of the list was spending time in the military, a branch with strict discipline and traditions. So at the dismay of my parents, friends and girlfriend at the time, I dropped out of school and

I joined the Marines.

BOOT CAMP AT PARRIS ISLAND was like stepping into another world. The moment I arrived, the heat pressed against me like a weight, and the drill instructors wasted no time making it clear—I was no longer in my comfortable Midwest town.

I felt like Chris from the movie *Platoon*, thrown into something far bigger and harsher than I had imagined. In my letters home, I admitted more than once those first few weeks that I might have made a mistake coming here. The reality of my decision hit me hard. The structure, the discipline, the relentless pace—it was nothing like the carefree life I had known.

For the first time, I truly appreciated all that I had growing up. The home-cooked meals, the laughter around the dinner table, the stability of my childhood—all of it seemed like a dream from another lifetime.

It's safe to say that by the third week at boot camp, I still may not have known what I wanted to do with my life. But one thing had become clear—this wasn't it.

Nevertheless, I gave 110%, pushing myself through every challenge they threw at me. But in the back of my mind, I held onto a promise: When my service was done, I was going back to college. This time, I would finish what I started.

But that was going to have to wait for six years, six long years. That's how long I had signed up for. It sounded like an eternity. I had to keep my head in the game so I made a promise to myself—every challenge would be an adventure, every obstacle a lesson. If I was going to do this, I was going to make the most of it.

Surprisingly enough by week seven, I had settled into the Marine regiment. Truth be told, I was starting to enjoy the discipline and the day to day routine—two things that had been sorely lacking in my college years. The structure, the order, the relentless push to be better than the day before—it was beginning to shape me in ways I hadn't expected.

Marine Corps boot camp is divided into four phases, and by phase three, we found ourselves on the rifle range. This was new territory for me. Before joining the Marines, I had never held a gun, let alone fired one. My only exposure to firearms had been through movies, where heroes shot with precision while barely looking down the sights. In reality, the idea of handling a real weapon made me uneasy. After all, I grew up in the Midwest but we lived in the city. My dad, friends we didn't hunt. We didn't even have BB guns growing up.

Thankfully the instructors were relentless and thorough. They broke everything down to the fundamentals—breathing, aiming, squeezing the trigger—not yanking it like in the movies. Looking back, I think my inexperience was an advantage. Unlike others who had shot before or hunted, I had no bad habits to unlearn. I absorbed every lesson, followed instructions to the letter—not out of confidence, but out of sheer fear of messing up. I had no intention of accidentally shooting myself or someone else for that matter.

And then, after days of listening and practice something remarkable happened. It all came together and worked.

Before long the rigorous training of the weapon was over, the moment of truth arrived—qualification day. We were given 35 rounds to hit targets at varying distances: 200 yards, 300 yards, and a daunting 500-yard mark. A perfect score was 350 points. To pass, and not have to go through training again, you needed a score of at least 250 to earn the title of Marksman. At 280, you'd be a Sharpshooter, and at 305, an Expert.

Sixty of us stepped up to qualify that day. One by one, we all took turns aiming and firing for the best score possible. When it was my turn, I blocked everything out—no nerves, no distractions. Just the target, my rifle, and the rhythmic cadence of my breathing and simply relied on what I was taught,

When the final scores were posted, 340 points, a near perfect score.

Out of sixty recruits, I was the only one to achieve it.

Obviously excited and proud but something in me shifted that day too. I guess it was subconscious but I came to understand the rifle had become an extension of my body, the act of firing almost instinctual, precise in a way that unsettled me. This wasn't just skill —it was something deeper, something I hadn't known was there, waiting to be uncovered.

That moment altered the trajectory of my life. Not just because I had excelled, but because I had glimpsed a part of myself I could never unsee.

Five years and forty-five weeks remained on my Marine Corps contract. And I would spend every one of them proving what I had or would become.

AFTER BOOT CAMP, I received my first orders: an infantry unit stationed at Camp Lejeune, North Carolina. It was a new beginning, a new challenge, but I had no idea just how quickly my path would take a turn.

Not long after checking in, I was approached—handpicked, really. My rifle scores in boot camp had caught someone's attention, and with little more than a suggestion that felt more like an order, I was urged to consider Scout Sniper School.

I didn't hesitate. My newfound love for shooting made the decision easy.

For the next ten weeks, I trained at Camp Geiger, absorbing everything there was to know about precision shooting. The lessons went far beyond simply aiming and firing. We studied the science of the shot—how wind, weather, even the curvature of the earth affected a bullet's trajectory. We learned how glass—rifle scopes, windows, even the moisture in the air—could change the path of a round. Every variable had to be accounted for, every movement calculated.

Then, once again, came qualification day. The final test. Targets set at distances most shooters never even attempt—300, 500, 600, 700, 800, 900, and the daunting 1,000-yard line. A single pull of the trigger had to be perfect.

The pass rate was brutal—only 40% of us would make it.

I was one them.

At the time, I thought it was just another accomplishment, another box checked off in my career. I had no idea how much it would change the course of my life, forever.

Upon graduating from Scout Sniper School, I was quickly assigned to my first combat infantry unit, the 3rd Battalion, 8th Marines. Six of us were assigned to the Intel Division (S-2) of H&S Company. Together, we made up two cells, or teams. In my cell, I was the primary weapons operator, Damien Locke was our flanker, and Owen Tate was our spotter. Over the next four years, I would serve alongside these men, forging a bond that would last a lifetime, especially with Owen, who would become my closest friend.

Movies glamorize the life of a serviceman, and even more so the life of a sniper. They portray us as constantly on call, fearless, prepared, and capable of adapting to any situation. While I have no doubt there are sniper cells out there that embody those qualities, during peacetime, we were not one of them. Our days were primarily filled with training, hiking, cleaning weapons, and standing guard over already well-secured areas. But those days also gave us the opportunity to learn each other's secrets, fears, loves, likes, and intimate stories. Owen and I formed a bond quickly. We enjoyed each other's company, appreciated each other's sense of humor, and knew from the beginning that we would remain friends well beyond our time in the Corps.

As luck would have it, in the late '80s, a civil-war uprising began in Somalia and prompted our unit's deployment to the U.S. Embassy. Our mission, to provide security, evacuate the embassy, guard the facility, and conduct daily patrols through the local village.

Despite the obvious dangers associated, I was actually excited about the opportunity to go into combat, to put my training to the test, and to prove to myself who I was and what I was capable of doing.

Owen and I, to my chagrin, spent countless hours on patrols, standing watch at posts, and running drills, yet we never got the chance to truly put our skills to the test. The monotony of it all left us restless, and more than once, we found ourselves speculating about the "*what-ifs*."

"*What if something actually happened?*" we'd ask. "*What if we finally saw some real action?*"

Sometimes, in the lull of another uneventful shift, we'd joke about taking a shot at an enemy soldier and simply claim we panicked, that it was just an honest mistake. Other times, we'd take it further, concocting elaborate cover-up stories—maybe we'd say the guy was reaching for a weapon, or that he looked like he was signaling to someone. We'd run through the details, testing out different versions and refining the narrative like it was some kind of strategy game. Of course, we never did it. But those conversations—those dark, ridiculous hypotheticals—kept us entertained for hours, helping to pass the time in a world where - waiting felt like half the battle.

AUGUST 2ND THE UNPRECEDENTED and unexpected happened. The country of Iraq invaded Kuwait. It was a move that at the time shocked the world and on August 4th, after nine long months in Somalia, we finally received orders. We were heading to the Middle East, where action was all but certain.

For eleven days, we drifted across the ocean aboard the USS WASP, anticipation burning. The journey was slow, agonizing, and every moment was spent wondering when we'd finally get our shot. We were flown ashore in a C46 helicopter, the scent of war greeted us—thick smoke rising in the distance, black columns marking the remnants of an obvious ongoing skirmish. The distant rattle of gunfire was enticing. Owen and I exchanged a glance, a knowing smile passing between us. This was it. This was our chance.

We were instantly assigned to CSSD-21, Combat Service Support Detachment, out of Cherry Point, North Carolina. The name alone had weight—it spoke of something important, something vital. It sounded like we would be the primary support sniper team, the hidden shadows delivering death from a distance. We had purpose.

The next two weeks were spent adjusting to our new surroundings. Most nights, sirens echoed through our base camp, the distant crack of rifle fire keeping us awake, not out of fear but anticipation of what was to come. Owen and I no longer spoke of Somalia, of wasted time and missed opportunities. Instead, we discussed the missions that lay ahead, the process we would follow.

Upon checking in, we were each handed a deck of cards—photos of our primary and secondary targets printed onto their surfaces. We memorized them, studied them obsessively, often betting on how many we'd take down when the time came.

Finally, by day fifteen, Damien had arrived, completing our team. With all three of us back together, we were certain we'd be the first ones called, the first ones sent into the chaos. But reality was far crueler than we had imagined.

The truth came like a gut punch: CSSD-21 was an AirWing division, not an infantry combat unit. Our mission was simple, pathetic, and once again a waste of skill and time—guard the planes. For four endless months, we patrolled the airfield, rifles slung over our shoulders, our fingers itching for a trigger pull that would never come. The ongoing sirens, and every distant shot, was a taunt, a reminder of what we would never have.

Time passed, albeit slowly and somehow we survived the boredom. For me, my service was nearly over, and I was making plans for the next chapter—school, a steady job, a girlfriend, a normal life.

I never regretted my time in the Marines, but I do regret the lack of a defining moment. I had trained, prepared, lived for the possibility of having to take a life, that feeling of having that power in my hands. And yet, that moment never came. It gnawed at me, an absence that festered. The thoughts have been there since the first day of sniper school, a quiet, insidious whisper in the back of my mind: *What would it feel like to have that much power over another?* I was ready. I was mentally strong. And most importantly, I was willing. But I never got the chance.

There was an unsettling emptiness in that knowledge, a hollow space where something—someone—should have been.

Looking back, as twisted as it sounds, I wish I had been given the chance. The chance to take the life of another, 2, 3, 10 individuals. The number doesn't matter just knowing I did what I was meant to do, trained to do and capable of doing. If I had been able to kill in a controlled environment, under orders, maybe… maybe I wouldn't feel this way now. Maybe I wouldn't have done the things I did.

Maybe I wouldn't still hunger for it.

Chapter 2

AWAKENING

AS EXPECTED, THE NEXT FEW YEARS unfolded just as I had imagined. I returned to Ohio State, graduated, and landed a coveted job in medical device sales. The career was promising, the money was good, and, most importantly, I met Denise—the kind of woman who made life feel perfectly aligned. Smart, ambitious, and effortlessly captivating, she was everything I could have hoped for. She stood at 5'10", with a presence that turned heads without meaning to. Her blonde hair framed a face that somehow made sense of everything—clear blue eyes that held both warmth and curiosity, a light dusting of freckles across her nose, and a smile that could stop time when it landed on you. Denise never tried to be sexy. It was just in the way she moved, the softness in her voice, the way she'd lean against the counter late at night with a glass of wine, wearing one of my shirts and nothing else. She was home and electricity all at once.

Owen and I remained as close as ever. We even shared an apartment for awhile during my last year of school, slipping seamlessly back into the camaraderie we had forged years earlier. But as life progressed, so did I. Denise and I moved in together, though my friendship with Owen never faltered. Drinks after work, the occasional round of golf, and our unbreakable tradition—Saturday football. It was a simple, structured existence. Everything was falling into place.

Then, almost as quickly as it had come together, life took a turn. An unexpected opportunity arose for Denise—one she couldn't refuse. A year in Copenhagen for work. It was meant to be temporary, an adventure, and without hesitation, I chose to go with her. Our bohemian phase, as Denise liked to call it. Bikes, bread, and late-night talks about nothing.

At first, the move was exhilarating. The canals, the history, the culture—I immersed myself in it all. But excitement has an expiration date, and mine came swiftly. Unlike Denise, who was consumed by her job, I had nothing but time. Too much time. The museums and landmarks lost their charm within weeks. The city, so vibrant and alive, became a backdrop to my growing restlessness.

By the third month, I found myself pacing through unfamiliar streets, searching for something I couldn't quite name. By the fourth, I had exhausted every distraction and began retreating into my own mind. Memories of the past surfaced—some welcome, others less so. And then, by the fifth month, my thoughts became darker, more consuming. I found myself fixated once again on that one missed opportunity. The one that had lingered in the shadows of my mind since my time in the service. The kill I could have made. The kill I should have made.

And, perhaps, the one I still could.

Over the next few days and weeks, my thoughts shifted—morphing from curiosity to obsession. The idle boredom that had once plagued me was now replaced with something far more consuming. I didn't just wonder what it would be like to kill again—I imagined it, constructed it, refined it.

I played out scenarios in my mind, each one sharper, more precise than the last. The logistics, the execution, the aftermath. I examined every angle, every possibility. What I would do. How I would do it. How I would get away with it.

And the more I thought about it, the more I knew—this wasn't just a passing fixation. It was inevitable.

Not only could I kill.

I would.

And,

I would do it flawlessly.

THERE'S A LINE FROM BODY HEAT that Owen used to quote all the time:

"Anytime you try a decent crime, you got fifty ways you can fuck it up. If you can think of twenty-five of them, you're a genius. And you ain't no genius."

Teddy Lewis, the bomb maker in the movie, was making a simple but crucial point—no matter how much you plan, no matter how many precautions you take, you're still only accounting for half the ways things can go sideways. The rest? Well, that's what gets people caught.

I never claimed to be a genius, but I did consider myself smarter than most. Smart enough to know that most crimes—especially murder—happen in the heat of the moment, sloppy, unplanned, driven by rage or desperation. That's why they unravel so quickly. But I had no intention of making those mistakes. My crime wouldn't be impulsive. It would be calculated.

And besides, I believed something even more absolute than Teddy Lewis's rule. Michael Corleone said it best:

"If anything in life is certain, if history has taught us anything, it's that you can kill anyone."

That was my truth. That was the philosophy I held above all else.

And I had time—seven months left in Copenhagen. Seven months to map out every angle, to research, to anticipate what others might miss. Seven months to uncover the other twenty-five ways things could go wrong.

But time wasn't my only advantage. I had something even more valuable: Owen.

He would be my test. The moment I told him what I was thinking, one of two things would happen. Either he'd call me insane, talk me down, insist I get help. Or, he'd do what he'd always done—he'd have my back. Just like in the service, when things got messy and we needed each other the most. If he was in, then I knew—without a shadow of a doubt—that we could pull this off.

Either way, I was ready for the answer.

But that answer would have to wait. I was smart enough to know this wasn't a conversation to be had over international phone lines, and a letter? Too risky. Too many ways it could be intercepted, misdelivered, or worse—left lying around for prying eyes. That's how people get caught. No, this conversation would have to happen face-to-face when I was back in the States. Until then, I had work to do.

For the next seven months, my days were dedicated to planning—methodically, obsessively. I mapped out potential targets, studied locations, dissected the best means to commit the act. Every scenario came with a web of risks, so I examined every angle, trying to anticipate what could go wrong before it ever had a chance to. Mistakes weren't an option.

And then, there were the nights.

Denise and I had fallen into a comfortable rhythm, a routine that felt effortless. We had dinner together each evening, talking about her day, her work, the little things that made up her world. Afterward, we'd settle in to watch one of the few English-speaking shows on Dutch television, our time together quiet and easy. We were building something real, something solid. And yet, there was a part of me I knew I could never share with her.

I didn't just want to protect her—I *needed* to. If this plan ever came to fruition, the last thing I wanted was for Denise to be caught in the fallout. The less she knew, the safer she'd be. Complete deniability.

That left me with only one person I could count on, and even then, I wasn't sure. Owen had always been there, had always had my back. But there was a difference between covering for me in the service and this. This was something else entirely. There was a chance he'd tell me I'd lost my mind. There was an even bigger chance he'd want no part of it.

And yet, deep down, I knew—if I could get him to see the logic, the precision, the *certainty* of it all—he'd understand. If anyone would, it was Owen.

BEING ON YOUR OWN in a foreign country had been an adventure—at least in the beginning. The thrill of a new place, the unfamiliar streets, the novelty of a different culture. But by our eighth month in

Copenhagen, that excitement had started to wear thin, replaced by a slow, creeping fatigue.

The weather didn't help. I'm sure Copenhagen has its fair share of pleasant days, but we hadn't seen many of them. For the most part, it had been cold, damp, and endlessly gray. The kind of chill that seeped into your bones and never quite left, no matter how many layers you wore. Rain was a constant companion, drizzling, misting, or outright pouring. At first, we laughed it off, chalking it up to part of the experience, but by the time June rolled around, the novelty had worn off. We missed the sun.

Then, as if fate had been listening, Denise got word that her assignment had been cut short—three months earlier than expected. Just like that, after nine months, our time in Copenhagen was coming to an end. And truth be told, neither of us minded.

Sure, there were things we'd miss—the charm of the canals, the quiet hum of the city at night, the little café on the corner where we'd become regulars. But the idea of heading home, of trading the damp chill for something familiar, something *ours*, felt like a relief.

And for me, it meant something else entirely. It meant,

I was finally going to have that conversation with Owen.

WITHIN A WEEK OF being back in Ohio, Denise and I had settled effortlessly into our old routine, as if Copenhagen had been nothing more than a long, extended dream. She returned to her old office, slipping back into the rhythm of her work, while I started fresh at a new company, tasked with overseeing their national sales team. The transition was smooth, almost too smooth—like slipping into a familiar but slightly worn suit. The kind that fits well enough but still reminds you that time has passed.

For nearly a month, I avoided making the call. Maybe it was caution. Maybe it was hesitation. Or maybe, deep down, it was the gnawing fear that things between Owen and me had changed. That the bond we'd built, the trust we'd forged through years of service and shared secrets, had somehow eroded. That he'd hear me out and decide he wanted nothing to do with me.

But I couldn't wait forever.

Late on a Friday night, after Denise had gone to bed and the house had settled into a heavy silence, I finally picked up the phone. The line rang twice before Owen answered, his voice familiar but carrying that slight edge of suspicion that comes when someone hasn't heard from you in a while.

We eased into small talk—how was work, how was life, how had the last year treated him? The words came easy enough, but there was an unspoken weight beneath them. He had to be wondering why I was calling after all this time.

After a few minutes, I cut to the point.

"You free for dinner one night next week?"

A pause. Just long enough to make me wonder what was going through his head.

Then, his voice, steady as ever. *"Yeah. Name the time and place."*

And just like that, the first step had been taken.

I HAD TOLD DENISE that Owen was coming over for dinner, mentioning that he needed to talk through some personal "*issue*" with me. As expected, she understood without question and made plans for a night out with the girls. Dinner and drinks with them meant I'd have the entire evening to have the conversation I had been turning over in my mind for days.

For nearly a week, I had been running through different ways to bring it up, debating the right approach, preparing for every possible reaction—especially the worst ones. Would he laugh it off? Get pissed? Walk out and never look back? I had no way of knowing, but I had to find out.

Denise left right on time at 5:30 P.M.. Owen pulled up at six, and by 6:15p.m., the pizza and wings had arrived, and a case of beer was chilling in the fridge. We eased into the night, kicking back with food and drinks, catching up on everything that had happened since we last saw each other.

Owen was doing well—better than well. He was on the verge of getting married, something I hadn't quiet expected, and had just started a new job. He seemed indifferent about it, shrugging as he took a sip of his beer.

"*Probably temporary,*" he admitted. "*Pays the bills, but I don't see myself staying.*"

Typical Owen. Never one to get too comfortable, always looking ahead to the next thing.

I nodded, half-listening, half-waiting for the right moment. The moment to shift the conversation, to put *everything* on the table.

And that moment was coming fast.

I knew Denise would be home around nine. Even on a night out with the girls, she was never out late. That was just who she was—responsible, predictable. The kind of person who had her life in perfect order. The kind of person who would never, *ever* understand what I was about to say.

It was close to 8:30p.m., and Owen and I had just about polished off a twelve-pack of Coors Light. We weren't drunk, not really, just loose enough for the conversation to flow without hesitation. Loose enough that I knew if I was ever going to say what I had been holding onto for months, *now* was the time.

I stood up, headed to the fridge for another round. As I pulled the door shut, I took a breath, caught my own reflection in the stainless steel. *Say it.* I told myself. *Now is the time.*

Walking back into the living room, I handed Owen his beer, heart pounding. Before I could even sit down, he looked me dead in the eye and said,

"*Okay... what the fuck is going on? What do you want to tell me?*"

The words hit me like a gut punch. My stomach twisted, my throat dry. He *knew*. Maybe not the details, maybe not the weight of it all, but he *knew*.

I must've looked like a deer in headlights, but there was no turning back now. I sat down, exhaled, and finally said the words that had been circling my mind for months.

"*Remember when we were in the Marines and used to think about killing someone?*"

No hesitation. Not even a blink.

"*Yeah.*"

That one syllable sent a shiver through me. Not because I was surprised by his answer, but because I knew what it meant. I knew he wasn't dismissing it as drunken nostalgia or some half-assed joke. He was listening. *Really* listening.

I swallowed hard and pressed on.

"*Well, here's the thing. I know we're not in the military anymore, and I know the risks are a hundred times what they were in combat, but...*" I hesitated, choosing my words carefully. "*I've still—after all these years—kinda... kinda still been thinking about it. A lot. To the point where I've even planned how I'd do it. How I'd get away with it.*"

And there it was. The truth, hanging in the air between us, waiting to be judged.

A dozen scenarios had played out in my mind before this conversation. Owen laughing it off. Owen getting pissed. Owen telling me I'd lost my fucking mind. I had even considered retracting, waving it away with a nervous chuckle—*Just kidding, man.* But before I could backpedal, he responded.

"*Who's the target?*"

My breath caught in my chest.

Shock. Excitement. Caution. All tangled together.

Was he baiting me? Testing to see how deep the madness went? Or was he *in*?

I let out a short laugh, trying to gauge his tone. I needed to be careful. I needed to *know*. So I waved a hand, playing it off. "*No one specifically... it's just a thought. An idea. That's why I wanted to talk to you.*"

Owen studied me, his expression unreadable. Then, casually, he popped open his beer, leaned back into the couch like we were just two guys talking about football. "*Does Denise know about this?*"

"*Of course not.*" I shook my head. "*I could never tell her. She'd never understand.*" I met his gaze. "*But you—you've been there. You get it, right?*"

For a moment, he just watched me. No immediate reaction, no quick dismissal. Just consideration. Then, with a small smirk, he exhaled and said, "*You know what I'm gonna say, right?*"

At first, I wasn't sure, but then it hit me. The grin, the knowing look.

I rolled my eyes, smirking back. "Yeah, yeah, yeah... *You try a crime, you'll fuck it up, and blah, blah, blah.*"

And just like that, the tension cracked. We both started laughing, not the kind of laughter that comes from something funny, but the kind that comes from *understanding*.

In that moment, I knew.

I had found the one person I could trust. The one person who wouldn't judge, who wouldn't run. The one person who, if I played this right, might actually *help me*.

The room shifted. The air between us changed.

Owen took another sip of his beer, then leaned forward, his voice quieter now, steadier.

"*I know you've had a lot of time to think about this," he said. "So what's the plan?*"

And just like that, we were no longer just two old friends catching up.

We were something else entirely.

WE SPENT THE REST OF the evening diving deep into the details—scouting potential locations, weighing different methods, and breaking down every possible risk. This wasn't idle talk; it was calculated, meticulous, the kind of planning only two people with military precision could execute. And by the time the night was over, one thing was clear—Owen wasn't just willing to help. He was *excited.*

There was one condition, though. It had to be a rifle shot. That was our expertise, our training. Anything else would dilute the purpose, take away from what I/we were trying to accomplish. This wasn't about improvisation or reckless impulse—it was about skill, control, and executing something with absolute precision. The air between us felt charged, humming with anticipation, like we were on the verge of the most exhilarating mission of our lives.

Just as we were wrapping up, headlights swept across the window—Denise was home. Owen stood, stretching, the weight of our conversation slipping away as if it had never happened. The moment she walked through the door, her face lit up at the sight of him.

"*Owen!*" she said, wrapping him in a warm hug.

They had always been close—years of shared history, late nights, and memories from a time when life had been simpler. Their reunion was effortless, natural. A quick exchange of laughter and stories, a welcome contrast to the intensity of the past few hours. Watching them, it was almost as if nothing had changed. *Almost.*

As Owen stepped outside, he gave me a final glance—no words, just a look that said, *We'll talk soon.* I gave a subtle nod in return.

When I closed the door behind him, I felt it. Relief. Satisfaction. The hardest part was over. Now, the real work—the *fun* part—could begin.

And maybe it was just the rush of the night still coursing through me, but something else shifted. Denise and I felt… better. Closer. I don't know if she sensed the change in me, the new energy, the renewed purpose. She never asked questions, never pressed for details, but she noticed. From that night on, I was lighter. More present. More *alive.*

For the first time in a long time, I felt like I had something to look forward to.

Thirty days after my conversation with Owen, life threw me a curveball. A transfer. Work needed me in Minneapolis, Minnesota—indefinitely.

Even though Denise was able to work from home there, the news still hit hard. We had roots here. A life. And just as I was beginning the planning phase with Owen—what I *knew* would be the most thrilling experience of my existence—this opportunity landed in my lap. A career move I couldn't afford to turn down. More money, more responsibility, a major step up.

But the timing was infuriating. Minneapolis was far. Too far. And I had no idea how it would affect everything Owen and I had set in motion. Still, there was no real choice to make. Within two weeks, we packed up our lives, said goodbye to everything and everyone we knew, and set off into the unknown.

On a dark Friday night, Denise and I loaded the car and began the long, grueling drive to Minnesota.

As we crossed the state line, snow dusted the pavement, the highway stretching endlessly before us. I had no idea then that Minneapolis wouldn't be a setback. It would be a *gift.*

The perfect place for what I had in mind.

Chapter 3

POINT OF NO RETURN

WE MOVED TO A QUITE SUBURB of Minneapolis—Eden Prairie. The kind of place where nothing exciting ever really happens. The streets were clean, the neighborhoods well-kept, and the people? Friendly, welcoming, the type who waved when you passed by and left their doors unlocked without a second thought. It was the perfect place to live, the kind of town where kids rode their bikes until sunset and families gathered for backyard barbecues on the weekends. For Denise and me, it was exactly what we needed—safe, comfortable, and stable.

But for me, Minnesota was something more.

Known as the land of 10,000 lakes, Minnesota had another reputation—hunting. Duck, pheasant, squirrel, and, more importantly, deer. The state was a hunter's paradise, and in some areas, the sound of gunfire wasn't just expected—it was normal. Year-round hunting meant that the occasional crack of a rifle barely registered in the back of anyone's mind. It was part of life, background noise, like the hum of traffic in a big city.

Denise and I had only been in town a few months, but already, we had tuned it out. The first time we heard a gunshot at dusk, she'd glanced up for half a second before returning to whatever book she was reading. I had done the same. No concern, no second thought. It was just another evening in Minnesota.

It wasn't until one night, after a long day of work, that the realization truly hit me. We were sitting on the back porch, sharing a bottle of wine under the soft glow of our patio lights. The wind rustled through the trees, the distant hum of crickets filling the space between us. And then—**crack**—a shot echoed through the night. Neither of us flinched. Neither of us commented on it. We simply sipped our wine, as if nothing had happened.

That's when it struck me. This wasn't just an open acceptance of gunfire—it was complete indifference. In another part of the country, a single gunshot would set off alarm bells, send people scrambling to call the police. But here? Here, it blended into the landscape, unnoticed and unimportant.

And in that moment, a thought settled in my mind, chilling and undeniable. If someone wanted to take the perfect shot—the kind that mattered, the kind that ended a life—this was the place to do it.

The next morning, I was on the phone with Owen. By now, we had developed a code—nothing too elaborate, just enough to ensure that if anyone happened to be listening, they'd have no clue what we were actually talking about. It was a habit we had picked up over the years, a skill sharpened in the Marines when operational security was drilled into our heads. Even now, in civilian life, old habits died hard. Our call was short but the message was clear, Owen would be coming for a visit.

It had been over two months since our last conversation over dinner, and in that time Owen and I had each gone out and purchased an AR-15. It wasn't quite the M40A6 sniper rifle we had trained on, but it was damn near identical to the M16A2, our standard-issue rifle in the Corps. The AR-15 had everything we needed—a familiar feel, reliable performance, and a maximum effective range of 550 yards for an individual target. More than adequate for what we had in mind.

Denise was oblivious to my purchase. As I'd mentioned before, protecting her was my top priority. She never knew me as a gun owner, and she certainly didn't approve of firearms. Telling her about the rifle would have been pointless—just a guaranteed way to spark a two- or three-day argument that would go absolutely nowhere. Instead, I kept it out of sight, locked away in a storage facility I had rented. Officially, the unit was for household goods—things we didn't have space for but weren't ready to get rid of. Work was even covering the cost, which made it all the more convenient.

Owen's flight arrived on Saturday. I picked him up at the airport, and as soon as he threw his bag in the backseat, he turned to me with a knowing smirk.

"*So, what's Denise think about you owning a gun?*" he asked casually.

I hesitated for half a second, then shrugged. "*Uh... she doesn't know,*" I admitted. "*I keep it in a storage locker, you know, to protect her.*"

Owen raised an eyebrow, amused. "*Right. To protect her.*" He let the words hang in the air for a moment, then leaned back in his seat. "*Well, maybe we should stop by that locker before we head to the house.*"

I nodded, gripping the wheel a little tighter. "*Yeah, OK*" I said and we proceeded to the unit.

I parked the car in front of my storage unit—9077—a nondescript metal door among hundreds just like it. The facility was quiet, the occasional hum of a passing car the only sign of life. Owen and I stepped out, and I unlocked the unit, pulling up the door with a metallic clatter. The air inside was stale, filled with the scent of dust and cardboard.

"*Let me see the weapon,*" Owen said, his voice even, almost casual.

I hesitated for just a moment before moving toward the back of the unit. Stacked boxes concealed the case, exactly as I had left it. I shifted them aside, revealing the black hard-shell container beneath. Lifting the lid, I pulled out the AR-15. The weight of it in my hands was familiar, reassuring.

Owen extended his hand, taking the rifle from me. He examined it closely, rolling it in his grip, checking the sights, the feel. He didn't say anything, just nodded slightly before handing it back. Then, without a word, he turned and walked back to the car.

A minute later, he returned carrying an odd-shaped bag. I opened my mouth to ask about it, but before I could speak, he was already unzipping it.

Inside was a rifle barrel—an exact duplicate of the one attached to my AR-15.

"*Take this,*" he said, his tone firm. "*Swap it with yours.*"

I blinked. "*What?*"

But even as the question left my lips, I understood. The pieces clicked into place before he even spoke again.

"*After we do this, we'll switch them back,*" Owen explained. "*If anything ever comes of this, if the rifle is ever questioned, forensics won't match up. They'll have no case.*"

I stared at him, my mind catching up to the brilliance of his plan. He had thought of something I hadn't—an extra layer of security, a safeguard. If this was going to happen, it needed to be airtight. And this? This was the first step in making sure it was.

A strange sense of calm settled over me. Not excitement, not fear—just certainty. I had chosen the right person for this. We weren't just talking anymore. This was real.

Without another word, we got to work. The barrel swap was quick, efficient. No hesitation, no unnecessary conversation. When it was done, we packed everything up, closed the storage unit, and got back in the car headed for home.

The rest of the weekend played out as if nothing had changed.

Denise, Owen, and I spent our time like old friends reunited—laughing over stories, indulging in too much alcohol, letting nostalgia wrap around us like a warm blanket. Owen and I never mentioned our plans again, never even hinted at them. Not with Denise around. That was an unspoken rule—one that needed no discussion.

By Monday morning, everything felt normal. Like clockwork, Denise left for work at 8:30 a.m. sharp.

By 8:45 a.m., Owen and I were on our second cup of coffee, seated at the kitchen table. The air between us was different now. No more small talk, no more distractions.

It was time to work out the details.

IF THE MARINE CORPS taught us anything, it was to keep it simple—no overcomplicating the mission, no unnecessary risks. The plan needed to be clean, efficient, and untraceable. We mutually agreed on the plan.

The core of it was straightforward:

A remote location—somewhere isolated, but not suspiciously so.

A random target—no connection, no pattern, just an unlucky stranger.

A solid alibi for Denise—one that would hold up under scrutiny, ensuring that if she were ever questioned, her timeline would match exactly with when Owen and I were gone.

First, finding the perfect spot.

Living in a suburb of Minneapolis made it easy to find a convenient yet secluded location. That morning, Owen and I set out scouting. Just outside our home development was Baker Road, a quiet stretch of road leading north. We followed it all the way to Minnetonka Boulevard, where it dead-ended. From there, a quick left onto Minnetonka and an immediate right onto McGirley Road put us deep into preserve land, east of Lower Lake.

As soon as we arrived, we both knew—this was it.

The spot was ideal:

Close enough to home that we could be back quickly, ensuring our alibi held up.

Remote enough that traffic was minimal, limiting potential witnesses.

Common for hunting, meaning that even if someone did hear a gunshot, no one would think twice about it.

We spent the next half-hour assessing the terrain. Just off the road was an open field, providing over 1,000 yards of clear visibility. Perfect for a precision shot. From that distance, there'd be no muzzle flash, no immediate direction for anyone to look.

There was a traffic light—one of the few on this stretch of road—situated at the crest of a small hill. That was key. A car stopped at the light would be a stationary, easy target.

An unexpected added bonus, the hill itself—a natural advantage we hadn't even considered at first.

Drivers don't bother putting their car in park while waiting at a red light. Which meant that, once the target was hit, their foot would inevitably slip off the brake. The car would roll forward, coast down the incline, and veer off the road—likely ending up in one of the large ravines that flanked both sides of the road.

This was a major advantage:

The trajectory of the bullet would be nearly impossible to determine. A moving car, rolling uncontrolled, would make it significantly harder for forensics to pinpoint the exact angle of impact.

The final location of the vehicle would add further confusion. Investigators would have no clear starting point—no way to tell where the shot had originated.

The isolation of the area meant that the body might not be found for hours—possibly even a full day.

And with cold night air, time of death would be much harder to establish.

By the time Owen and I had finished walking the area, there was no question.

This was the spot.

THE NEXT STEP WAS ensuring complete randomness in choosing the target. Owen had dozens of ideas—hair color, gender, type of car, even something as specific as bumper stickers. He ran through them rapidly, rattling off qualifiers that, to him, would add an extra layer of control over the situation. But the more he talked, the more complicated it all started to feel. Maybe it was the nerves, maybe the sheer weight of what we were about to do, but I couldn't shake the feeling that his plan was too meticulous, too contrived.

Besides, how realistic was it to find a car that met all these criteria on a deserted road at just the right moment? The more conditions we added, the longer we'd have to wait for the perfect victim. The longer we waited, the higher the risk.

I suggested something simpler—something truly random, something that ensured no pattern could ever be established.

We'd roll a single six-sided die before leaving the house. If it landed on an even number, the target would be male; if it landed on an odd number, female.

To satisfy Owen's obsession with ensuring absolute randomness, I conceded to an extra rule: the number itself would determine the order. Rolling a 2 didn't just mean a male target—it meant the second male target. A 5 wasn't just a female target; it was the fifth female target.

That was it. No personal preferences. No overthinking. Just fate in its simplest form.

There were two additional stipulations we mutually agreed upon:

No passengers—a single occupant only. Too many variables if there was someone else in the car.

No other cars nearby—the vehicle had to be sitting alone at the red light. No one behind them who could witness what happened.

The last piece of the plan was the alibi.

It was no secret that Owen and I enjoyed drinking together. It was a habit that came naturally, one that Denise never questioned. With so many bars close to the house, it was only logical that he and I would go out for a few drinks on his last night in town. It wouldn't raise a single red flag.

Owen was scheduled to fly out Saturday morning, so if we were going to do this, Friday night was our only option.

To further cement our cover, we needed to establish a pattern—one that would create confusion if investigators ever came around asking questions. Starting that very afternoon, we began frequenting different bars every afternoon while Denise was at work and some evenings, rotating between a handful of establishments. The goal was simple:

If police showed a photo of one of us to a bartender, their answer would be an automatic yes, confirming our presence.

By varying our routine, no one would remember exactly which night we had been there.

Paying exclusively in cash ensured there were no digital footprints—no receipts, no timestamps.

We wanted our presence to be noticed but not memorable. We were friendly but not loud, engaging but never doing anything that would land us in a distinct memory of any employees.

By the end of the week, we had successfully blended in.

Now, all that was left to do was wait for Friday night.

THURSDAY CAM QUICKLY, almost too quickly. The days leading up to it had dragged, but now that the moment was near, time seemed to accelerate, pulling me forward whether I was ready or not. And now, here I was, lying in bed next to Denise, staring at the ceiling, my mind a battlefield of thoughts, doubts, and justifications.

Her breathing was steady, soft, and rhythmic, a quiet reminder of the life we had built together. Each subtle movement—an unconscious stretch, the shift of her weight against the mattress—echoed in my mind like a warning. ***Turn back. It's not too late.***

I squeezed my eyes shut, trying to quiet the noise, to push aside the gnawing thoughts clawing at my resolve. Slowly, I forced myself to breathe, to slow my racing pulse, to regain the discipline that had been drilled into me. Compartmentalize. Control. Execute. The plan was set. Every detail had been scrutinized, every risk mitigated. There was nothing left to question.

But the mind doesn't stop. It replays the steps, over and over, like a film stuck on repeat. Did we miss something? What if something goes wrong? What if I hesitate?

Each doubt that rises is met with an answer, a rationalization. No mistakes have been made. Everything is in place. This is what you wanted. What you've waited for.

Then comes the doubt in myself, the one I can't rationalize away so easily. It starts as a whisper, a quiet tremor in the back of my mind. But the longer I lie there, the louder it grows, insistent and demanding. Can I actually pull the trigger? What if they look me in the eye? What if, in their last moment, I see a reflection of myself?

I turn my head slightly, watching the soft rise and fall of Denise's chest. If she knew—if she had even an inkling of what I was planning—would she still be lying there so peacefully? Would she still trust or love me?

A hollow feeling settles deep in my chest. I turn back to the ceiling, letting my focus shift, forcing the emotions away. Disconnected from the facts, don't think about it as murder. I remind myself what I had told Owen, what I've told myself since the beginning. Act as though this is just another mission. Detach. Focus on execution, not emotion. This is about control. The power to decide fate. The power to be who you were meant to be.

I wonder, vaguely, how others feel in these final hours before doing a crime or taking a life.

For some, maybe the adrenaline has already started—a slow burn that builds into an uncontrollable blaze. Maybe their hands tingle, their heartbeat pounds, sleep becomes impossible—not from fear, but from anticipation. Everything is heightened—every sound feels amplified, every movement deliberate. Time stretches, slows. Minutes feel like hours.

For others, maybe it's the opposite. Maybe there's a strange sense of normalcy, a dull numbness that keeps them moving through the motions. Brush teeth. Check phone. Turn off the lights. Lay down beside a loved one, pretending everything is the same. But beneath that calm exterior, there's an unnerving quiet—a storm waiting to break.

I lie still beside Denise, my mind bouncing between these extremes, trapped between a state of hyper-awareness and detachment. And then, somewhere in that haze, a realization takes hold, undeniable and absolute.

- After tomorrow, I will no longer be the same person.
- There will be no undoing this.
- This is the last night I go to bed without blood on my hands.

And as exhaustion finally drags me under, just before sleep claims me, one last thought lingers—clear, sharp, and inescapable.

Tomorrow, someone takes their last breath—and I will be the one to take it.

Chapter 4

ONE SHOT ONE K . . .

FRIDAY MORNING ARRIVED with a startling clarity, the kind that made the air seem electric with possibility. As soon as I opened my eyes, the world felt different—colors sharper, objects more defined, time itself stretching and slowing as if the universe had conspired to make me feel omniscient. A heightened awareness coursed through my veins, something I hadn't even experienced in the Marines. It was intoxicating. I felt superhuman.

The morning routine was normal enough. Denise, Owen, and I shared a quick breakfast, exchanging the kind of casual conversation that blurred the edges of reality, making the coming hours feel surreal. By 8:30 a.m., Denise left for work. Owen and I, however, had a different task ahead. A task we had planned, debated, perfected. We went to the locker, retrieved the rifle, and placed it along with a magazine of five rounds into the trunk of the car. Our destination was set—the field off McGirley Road.

We parked on the side of the road, careful, precise. Owen, ever the methodical spotter, raised the field scope and scanned the landscape. He located our vantage point: 400 yards away, an elevated position that provided a clear line of sight to the traffic light at the top of the hill—our potential target zone. The darkness of night would be our cloak; there was no need for additional concealment. The absence of brush or cover was a blessing. No disturbances. No mistakes. No Ghillie suits to explain away if questioned. We were set. All systems go. Now, all that remained was the roll of the die.

Owen, as my spotter, was in charge of rolling it. A simple act, something people did mindlessly every day in board games and casinos. But this? This was different. The anticipation was suffocating, thick as tar. The entire fate of a human life hung on this one small cube of plastic.

I watched as Owen picked it up, holding it for a moment, turning it over in his palm. A piece of molded resin, its edges pressing against his skin. The pause before he released it was agony, stretching time impossibly thin. Our breaths were shallow, our pulses steady, brimming with expectation.

Then, with a flick of his wrist, Owen let it go.

Chaos ensued. The die tumbled, bouncing unpredictably, spinning and flipping across the tabletop. My focus narrowed, blocking out everything except that tiny rolling object as it danced toward its final decision. Every ricochet tightened the coil in my chest.

And then—stillness.

The die landed. A single number stared back at us. A verdict issued by sheer, indifferent probability.

We exhaled in unison.

One.

A poetic beginning to an unthinkable chain of events. The first lone female—regardless of age or race—to stop at the traffic light would be our designated mark.

The day passed in a haze and Owen and I exchanged few if any words. Denise called around 4:15 p.m., letting us know she'd be late, grabbing dinner with a friend. We left a note for her, saying we'd be at Kona Grill at 7:30 P.M. if she wanted to join.

By 5:15 p.m., the sun had begun its descent. Owen turned to me, reading my thoughts before I could speak. "*You ready?*"

I nodded. Words were unnecessary now.

The drive was silent. Owen, ever the professional, calculated variables—humidity, wind direction, barometric pressure. These were the unseen factors that dictated a bullet's fate. Most people assumed the shooter was the architect of a kill, but no—the spotter crafted the shot. The shooter merely executed.

A mile and a half from the field, near Lower Lake, we pulled into a crowded parking lot. Commuters, hikers, hunters—no one noticed us. Just another pair of men heading to a deer stand. We hiked to our vantage point, unpacked the rifle, and lay prone, facing the intersection.

The wind was steady—a slight left-to-right drift, barely a factor. My breathing evened out. No trembling hands. No hesitation. I pressed my eye to the scope. The weight of the rifle against my shoulder was familiar, comforting.

Headlights approached the intersection. Owen's voice, low and steady, cut through the stillness.

"*Target acquired.*

Steady.

Aim.

Await verification."

The world narrowed to the scope. Crosshairs aligned just below the target's head which was nothing more than a blur. No guesswork. No adjustments. A perfect shot.

Then, softly:

"*Sight adjust. One click up.*"

I hesitated, and to myself thought;

What, why? Wind adjustments were horizontal. Vertical corrections were for miscalculations in distance or height—impossible for Owen. He didn't make mistakes.

"*Stand down,*" Owen said. "*Negative target.*"

I exhaled, my finger easing off the trigger. I turned to him, irritation flickering. "*What was with the one-click up?*"

Owen met my gaze, something close to embarrassment in his eyes. "*Forgot to account for the windshield. Needed the adjustment for the angle of the glass. I'm used to military vehicles—flat glass.*"

A small mistake, but one that could have cost us everything. Bullets react unpredictably to slanted glass. Had I fired, the shot could have dropped inches below its intended mark—potentially wounding rather than killing. A mistake that would have left too many questions, too many loose ends.

I returned to my position, eyeing the hilltop once more. "*Nice catch,*" I murmured.

We waited. The night stretched on, our patience unwavering, our resolve firm. The first female at the stoplight would be ours.

The die had spoken.

WITHIN TEN MINUTES, headlights once again approached the intersection. Without hesitation, I took aim and waited for Owen to give the word. The routine was the same as before, his voice a soft but deliberate whisper cutting through the stillness:

"*Target acquired.*

Steady.

Aim.

Await verification."

My breathing quickened, but only slightly, as I anticipated the next words. What seemed like five minutes was, in reality, only twenty seconds. Then, like a slow-motion sequence from a film, or a distant echo growing louder in a canyon, the words hung in the air:

"*Target verified...*"

And then:

"*Fire at will.*"

At first, I didn't see a face, just a simple patch of exposed skin in my rifle's sight. The woman wasn't real to me, not yet. She was just a silhouette, a target. My own heartbeat was the only sound I could register. I exhaled slowly and steadied my grip, fingers tightening in quiet inevitability. The traffic light was my ally, affording me the luxury of time—time to line up my shot, to ensure precision. It also gave me a brief moment to look at the life I was about to take.

She was beautiful. Young. Maybe twenty-three, twenty-six at most. Long, flowing blonde hair cascaded past her shoulders, her low-cut dress revealing a portion of her chest, an unintended but undeniable target. It was Friday night. She was likely on her way to a date or a night out with her friends, oblivious to the seconds ticking away. The red light gave her just enough time to check herself in the mirror, to adjust her makeup and hair, unaware that she had only moments left.

I'd imagined this moment for years—on long patrols, during training, even in my dreams. I thought I would feel something: hesitation, excitement, fear. But now, as I lay here with my finger resting lightly on the trigger, there was nothing. Just silence.

Then the light changed to green.

As if it were a signal, an order issued by fate itself, I pulled the trigger.

The suppressed rifle bucked against my shoulder. A sharp crack broke the stillness of the night. Through the scope, I watched her body jolt, a slight twist before she slumped toward the passenger seat. No scream. No dramatic final moment. Just a body. Moments ago, she had been a young woman with a future ahead of her. Now, she was gone.

I remained still, watching, waiting. My breath slow and measured. Just as expected, the car began rolling forward. Gravity carried it down the hill until it veered slightly to the right, coming to rest beneath a patch of evergreens—natural concealment that only worked in our favor.

When the car finally stopped, I refused to blink, my gaze locked onto the doors. I waited for any movement. A breath. A desperate push to escape. A last-ditch effort to survive.

Nothing.

Then, the whisper from Owen: "*Good shot. Confirm, target down.*"

And suddenly, the reality of what I had done came rushing in. No amount of training had prepared me for this moment. Everything felt distant, as if I were watching someone else's kill unfold through my own scope.

But the detachment was temporary. My mind cleared, my pulse caught up, and the tightness in my chest faded. I had done it. I had ended a life.

I'd made my first kill and inside I was alive.

Chapter 5

BACK TO REALITY

OWEN AND I STAYED prone in the open field a few moments longer, just enough time to be certain there were no lingering witnesses. The darkness and the slight curve of the road were on our side; any car cresting the hill would have its headlights plainly visible before it spotted us. Satisfied that we hadn't drawn attention, we gathered our gear and briskly made our way back to the car. The clock on the dashboard read 7:10 p.m., much earlier than expected. That extra twenty minutes meant we had time for a quick detour to the storage locker before heading to Kona Grill.

Once at the locker, we swapped the rifle barrels as planned. The movements were efficient, practiced. The new barrel clicked into place with a finality that felt both satisfying and chilling, a reminder of what we had just done. I slid my rifle into its case, then secured it behind a stack of battered cardboard boxes. As I flicked off the overhead light and locked the unit, it was as though I was sealing away any trace of the nights events. I glanced at Owen; he gave a slight nod, neither of us needing to speak.

The drive to Kona Grill felt almost surreal, as if someone had pressed "*play*" on a life that had been on pause. The city lights flitted by, neon signs and street lamps reflecting off the windshield. Despite the adrenaline still rushing beneath my skin, I felt an unsettling calm settle over me. By the time we walked into the restaurant, that calm morphed into something else: power. A surge of confidence flooded my veins, and I couldn't help but scan the dining room with a superior sort of detachment.

To everyone else, I was just another patron. If they only knew what I had done what I was capable of they'd recoil in horror. The idea was exhilarating. Denise arrived at around 8:20 p.m., a picture of normalcy, smiling from ear to ear as she greeted us. We hugged like old friends reuniting after a long day, even though we'd seen each other just this morning. Owen and I, two people who had committed an unspeakable crime earlier, managed to slip seamlessly into easy conversation. Our table was soon laden with chef rolls, sake, and a couple of craft cocktails to toast Owen's last night in town. It was almost haunting how little our recent deed showed on our faces. We joked about mundane topics; the new sushi menu, weekend plans, the traffic on I494 with a casualness that felt both exhilarating and disturbing.

I found myself half-listening to Denise's stories from work, all while a distant part of my mind replayed the moment of the shot, the recoil of the rifle, the finality of a life snuffed out. Yet neither Owen nor I betrayed any hint of guilt or tension; to an outside observer, it was a typical Friday night gathering of close friends. If Denise had looked closely, she might have noticed an edge in my gaze, the faint flicker of triumph that refused to fade. But she seemed content, smiling and laughing in the warm, dimly lit ambiance of Kona Grill. I matched her mood, savoring every bite of sushi, every sip of my drink, basking in the knowledge that I had committed the unthinkable and walked away without consequence. I glanced across the table at Owen, and he caught my eye, raising his glass in a silent toast. We clinked drinks, and in that private moment, I knew we were celebrating far more than just his last night in town. We were celebrating the successful execution of our darkest secret and the unfathomable thrill that came with it.

SATURDAY MORNING ARRIVED with a sort of muted anticipation. Owen and I were sitting at the kitchen table, sipping black coffee while the local news murmured from the TV. I'd told Denise we wanted to catch the traffic report before heading to the airport, but in truth, I was on high alert for any mention of last night's discovery by Lower Lake.

Nothing. Not a single story, no breaking news about a body found in a car. It seemed the incident hadn't caught the media's attention yet —or, at the very least, they weren't broadcasting it. Strange how silence could bring such a tangled mixture of relief and unease.

I wasn't the sort of killer who craved the spotlight. I'd studied enough serial killers to know that some among them reveled in the fame, wanting their names splashed across newspapers and TV screens. That wasn't me. I'd be perfectly content never hearing another word about it, especially if it meant staying off the authorities' radar.

By 11 a.m., the News cycle still hadn't mentioned any fatalities by the lake. It was time to drive Owen to the airport—a thirty-minute ride I'd been looking forward to, mostly because it gave us a chance to debrief in private. The memory of the kill still sat heavily in the background, and we hadn't had the opportunity to speak freely about it since last night.

We packed the car, loading Owen's luggage for his flight, and as I slid behind the wheel, I could feel questions forming on my tongue. Then Denise emerged from the house, casually announcing, "*Hey, my nail appointment got canceled, so I'll come with you guys!*"

For a split second, my mind whirred with ways to gracefully refuse her. But that would only raise suspicions. I forced an easy smile and waved her over. "*Sounds great,*" I said, keeping my voice bright and unconcerned. There would be no private conversation with Owen, not today. Maybe never.

As she settled into the back seat, I resigned myself to the idea that our shared secret would remain locked between us for now, unspoken and undeniable. And in that moment, as I pulled away from the curb, I realized this was my new reality: weaving the ordinary and the monstrous together, second by second, lie by lie.

THAT SATURDAY, AT PRECISELY 5:00 p.m., I finally caught wind of the story on the local evening news. It was nothing more than a brief mention—a single-sentence blurb accompanied by a grainy shot of a police cruiser parked near Lower Lake. "*The body of a young woman was found in her car,*" the news anchor announced, "*what appears to be a lone accident.*" There was no mention of gunshots, no discussion of foul play.

Outwardly, I didn't so much as blink. Inwardly, my mind kicked into overdrive, questions multiplying like a swarm of wasps. Were the police hiding information? Were they planning to spring this on us later, once they had proof? Would they show up at my doorstep, unannounced and ready to interrogate me?

I glanced at Denise, who was casually scrolling through a shopping app, none the wiser. A spike of fear lanced through me—I wanted no part of her in this, no risk of her getting caught in the crossfire if the authorities closed in.

For a dizzying moment, a dark panic seized me. The rational part of my brain peeled me away from the edge. We had been meticulous, I reminded myself. No loose ends, no evidence connecting us to the victim. Perhaps it was just lazy police work or incompetent reporting —the kind of half-baked coverage I'd come to expect from local news stations.

Over the next few days, my vigilance soared. I checked headlines on my phone every couple of hours, flipping between local channels to see if the story might flare up with some new insight. One week drained into another, with no fresh developments. Then another week, then four—and before long, six months had melted away.

The Minneapolis Police Departments clearance rate for homicides hovered around sixty percent. The grim truth was that the longer a case remained unsolved, the less likely it would ever be closed. In all likelihood, my victim—my first kill—would be condemned to the pile of unsolved tragedies, a supposed "*accident*" that gave the police no real starting point, no definable suspect, and certainly no trail leading to me. By the year's end, the investigation remained active only on paper, moved to the bottom of a detective's priority list and left to gather dust unless some miraculous new clue appeared.

I remember the moment it struck me: we'd done it. Owen and I had committed murder and skated away unscathed. That dawning realization filled me with an odd mix of triumph and relief, followed quickly by a chilling sense of acceptance. Over time, the fear of being caught slipped into the distant corners of my mind, replaced by a strange sense of pride.

Finally free from the constant dread of discovery, I began to revisit the events of that fateful night—my scope fixed on the target, the adrenaline, the quick flash of muzzle fire—in a twisted way, relishing the memory. Each time I felt the recoil in my imagination, a ripple of pleasure ran through me. I had discovered a power I never knew I craved. And what disturbed me - intrigued me the most, was how eagerly I yearned to feel it again.

BY JANUARY OF THAT YEAR, Denise and I finally decided to take the next step and get married. Our friends would say it was long overdue, and they were probably right. She was, and still is, the woman of my dreams—a beacon of kindness, patience, and everything that I wasn't. Sometimes, in my darker moments, I'd reassure myself that her sheer goodness outweighed whatever demons I harbored inside. It felt like a skewed equation, but it offered me a fragile sense of justification.

In the whirlwind of wedding planning, I was too busy with color schemes, guest lists, and travel arrangements to dwell on my inner turmoil. Thankfully, the voices in my head that whispered about planning another "*incident*" grew quieter amid the chaos. I still struggled to reconcile the truth of what I'd done. In my mind, calling it murder felt too real, too final, so I latched onto the idea that it was merely an "i*ncident,*" a small, selfish act that didn't define me. It was a term I could live with—a neat linguistic barrier between me and the true monsters roaming the world.

Once the wedding vows were exchanged and we embarked on our honeymoon, life took on a dreamlike quality. Then came another promotion at work, providing a fresh set of responsibilities and challenges. Before I knew it, we purchased a fixer-upper of a house, which ate up most of my free time with renovations, painting, and hauling debris to the curb. I tried to see it all as part of a stable, ordinary life—a life I had always fantasized about.

Denise's personal touches soon transformed that worn-down place into a warm, inviting home. She had a flair for interior design and an unending well of enthusiasm, which rubbed off on me in a way I didn't think possible. Days slipped into weeks, weeks into months. By the time our first anniversary rolled around, it felt simultaneously sudden and inevitable. We toasted our first year of marriage over a quiet dinner, discussing possible vacations, our plans for starting a family, and the prospect of building a real future. In hindsight, those were some of the best days of my life.

But routine has a way of unearthing old ghosts. As we fell into a predictable rhythm—weekday commutes, weekend errands, shared dinners—a subtle restlessness began to creep back into my thoughts. It was that itch of dormant energy, urging me to break the monotony.

The memory of that first kill, that rush of power, hadn't disappeared entirely. It just lay dormant, waiting.

When Denise told me she'd be out of town for a work conference, only two days, I found myself in a sudden vacuum of free time. A weekend alone. My first instinct was to call Owen, to finally reconnect and maybe, just maybe, talk about the night that had irrevocably changed both our lives. But the idea made my stomach twist. Better to let sleeping dogs lie, I reasoned. Why reawaken what we had left behind?

So, instead, I spent the evening indulging in a steak dinner at a quiet bistro and finishing off more wine than I typically allowed myself. By the time I got home, the house was silent, empty. The hush of the rooms echoed a loneliness I'd almost forgotten existed. I flipped on the TV, half-watching infomercials while my mind drifted into the past.

Suddenly, the realization surged over me like a tidal wave, almost knocking the breath from my lungs:

What exactly had I accomplished that night with Owen?

Yes, I had the initial idea—the concept of the kill—but in every other aspect, Owen had dominated. He chose the spot, he rolled the die that decided who would die, and he meticulously did the calculations that guaranteed our success. When I really examined it, my role felt almost secondary, like I'd just been the tool he needed to pull the trigger.

I had believed, for a time, that my act had sealed my place in some private pantheon of dread, but now it felt hollow. The more I thought about it, the angrier I became. Owen had overshadowed me, or so it seemed in that moment of bitter clarity. Could he have orchestrated everything just to gain his own twisted gratification? Maybe that explained why we hadn't spoken: he was basking in our secret, taking all the mental credit while I was left with the sleepless nights and smoldering resentment.

My head spun with these thoughts, too volatile to allow for any real sleep. I paced around the living room, consumed by a gnawing sense of being wronged, of having my triumph stolen. The anger churned into something more dangerous—a reckless determination. If Owen had stolen my glory, then I needed a new plan, one in which I could prove my cunning and capability from start to finish. No one else would dictate the outcome or take the credit.

That meant another kill.

The clarity of that realization sent a charge through my veins. I knew it was madness, but it also felt like liberation. This time, it would be my plan, my operation. No roll of the die, no spotter's calculations. Just me, the target, and the thrill I had been craving. As the idea solidified in my mind, that old surge of power returned. Even the memory of my dull, mundane chores faded into insignificance, replaced by the electric possibility of proving—if only to myself—that I could orchestrate every step, every detail, all on my own.

For better or worse, I had made my choice. And with it came the terrible knowledge that my life, and -

my soul, would never be the same.

Chapter 6

A TWISTED RESOLVE

THE MONTHS THAT FOLLOWED were deceptively calm. Denise and I were spending more time together, and the closeness between us always had a way of steadying my nerves. Physically, she grounded me; mentally, she was my safeguard, keeping me from spiraling too deep into my own impulses. Beneath our happy routines, though, my restless mind was stuck on one singular drive: planning. I'd done it once, and now I knew it was possible to do it again.

If there was one revelation I took from the last incident, it was that the real world didn't look anything like a neat, sixty-minute cop show. There would be no immediate swarm of top-tier detectives armed with cutting-edge forensics. Minneapolis's homicide unit might have bright minds on board, but it was still a numbers game—forty percent of homicides remained unsolved, including all those sloppy, easily traceable cases. I wasn't sloppy. I'd proven that.

This time, I was determined to cover every angle, refine every detail, and keep my actions to myself. I'd test my own capabilities and cunning all alone, leaving no chance for confusion over who orchestrated what. Just one more time, I told myself, and I could finally quit the incessant thoughts rattling around in my head. One more time, and I could be the devoted husband Denise deserved. The father my future child deserved.

It was a vow that settled over me like a dark cloud, a promise I'd make to the most corrupted parts of myself. Each day, I rehearsed scenarios in my head: time frames, locations, possible backstories. And each evening, I'd come home to Denise, sinking into our shared life as if nothing else existed.

No more than ten days into this renewed fixation, an email from work disrupted my careful scheming. The corporate office was expanding into Phoenix, and I'd been handpicked to oversee the setup of the new branch. At first, disappointment churned in my stomach. There was something unfinished in my life here in Minnesota, a grand plan that had barely begun to take shape.

But then it hit me: this wasn't a setback—it was a gift. After all, my last victim had been written off as a freak hunting accident, a stray bullet that had tragically found an unintended target. Even so, a second suspicious incident would surely raise eyebrows, no matter how meticulous I was.

That's how serial killers get caught: they repeat the same pattern in the same location until the evidence stacks up against them. I couldn't risk that, not when I was so close to perfecting my methods. Better to take this new opportunity and disappear into the desert sun. Start fresh.

Shutting the lid on my laptop, I reminded myself that Phoenix offered a clean slate. A place where I could lie low or, if the urge demanded it, execute the perfect plan on brand-new terrain with zero ties to my old life. The thought sparked a sense of exhilaration in me, a validation that my compulsion could be carefully curated no matter where I went. Just one more time, I repeated in my head, echoing a silent oath to no one but myself.

One more time—and then, maybe,

I would allow myself to be free.

WE SETTLED IN AHWATUKEE, a quiet suburban pocket nestled against South Mountain, about fifteen miles south of downtown Phoenix. Our new home sat at the end of a cul-de-sac, perched on a slight hill that overlooked the valley. The desert air was different from Minnesota's humid summers—dry, crisp, and filled with a kind of openness that made the world feel larger, yet somehow emptier.

The neighbors were welcoming, the kind of people who brought over homemade cookies and invited us to block parties. I played along, smiling at their hospitality, letting them believe I was just another corporate transplant settling into a new life. Denise thrived in the sunshine, and for a while, everything felt disturbingly smooth. A new job, a new city, a new routine. Yet beneath the surface, the itch never faded. I had brought my mind with me, after all, and it never stopped calculating.

By Memorial Day weekend, I was restless. Denise and I planned a short getaway to Lake Pleasant, a sprawling oasis just north of Phoenix, where the water was a striking contrast to the surrounding desert. On Friday evening, we packed up the car and made the easy drive, arriving just before sunset. The lake shimmered under the fading light, its surface rippling with the movement of boats and jet skis.

Lake Pleasant was more than just a picturesque getaway—it was a social hub, a living, breathing entity that transformed with the sun. During the day, pontoon boats drifted lazily across the shimmering water, their decks teeming with families, fishermen, and sunbathers basking in the golden warmth. Laughter carried across the lake, mingling with the distant hum of outboard motors and the occasional splash of a fish breaking the surface. It was a place of serenity, where time seemed to slow.

But as the sun dipped lower and painted the sky in hues of burnt orange and deep violet, the lake took on a different character. I noticed something peculiar. Some boaters weren't returning to shore. Instead, they anchored in quiet coves, tying up to weathered wooden posts, their lights dimming as they settled in for the night. Others sought more remote locations, places where the water was deep and the shoreline hidden beneath thick clusters of trees. There, under the cloak of darkness, the lake became a playground of indulgence—low murmurs of seduction carried over the still water, punctuated by gasps and moans swallowed by the night. Bodies entwined in the moonlight, the gentle rocking of boats disguising the rhythm of lovers lost in the moment. The scent of spilled alcohol mixed with the dampness of the lake air, a heady cocktail of desire and secrecy. This was Lake Pleasant after dark—a sanctuary where inhibitions dissolved as easily as the starlight reflected on the rippling water.

We set up our campsite near the shore, the sand cool beneath our feet as the last traces of daylight disappeared beyond the horizon. Denise laughed, kicking off her sandals and dipping her feet into the water, the ripples distorting the perfect reflection of the rising moon. I smiled with her, life was perfect and yet my mind was fighting to be somewhere else. The lake was vast, its depths unknown, its hidden alcoves like the folds of some ancient secret.

The boats, scattered across the water, were more than vessels of leisure—they were sanctuaries of secrecy. Inlets swallowed sound, rocky alcoves devoured the echoes of laughter and whispers alike. Anonymity was easy here. And in the thick of the night, when even the stars seemed hesitant to bear witness, anything could happen beneath the still, black waters of Lake Pleasant.

By Sunday evening, as we packed up and started the drive home, my thoughts buzzed with new clarity. The lake offered the kind of cover I'd been searching for. The way boats drifted, the ease with which someone could slip into the water unnoticed—it was almost too convenient.

Hunting accidents. Drownings. Boaters vanishing in the night. It happened all the time.

A slow smile curled at the edges of my lips.

This would be my next spot to calculate and plan. The next time I returned, it wouldn't be for a weekend escape.

It would be for something much more deliberate.

MOVING INTO THE NEIGHBORHOOD, it didn't take long for me to meet John. He was the kind of man everyone knew, the unspoken leader of the community. If there was a gathering, he was hosting it. If someone needed a favor, John had the connections to make it happen. He had the biggest house, the newest gadgets, the fastest car, and a backyard that looked like something out of a luxury resort brochure. His presence was loud—always talking, always moving, always at the center of attention. He had a way of drawing people in, making them feel like they were part of something just by standing next to him.

His wife, Lea, was his complete opposite. Where John thrived in chaos, she was the quiet stability that kept everything running smoothly. You could see it in the way she moved through a party—always a step ahead, catching things before they spiraled, gently redirecting John when his energy got the better of him. She wasn't overbearing, just… steady. Grounded. It was obvious that she was the one who kept their life in order while John played the role of the reckless, good-time guy.

John took an immediate liking to me. Maybe he saw something familiar in me—a quiet intensity beneath the surface, a detachment that made me a good listener. Or maybe he just liked the way I didn't compete for attention. Either way, we clicked.

At first, our friendship was casual. He'd invite me over for beers in his garage, show off his latest toy—a jet ski, a high-end smoker, a new custom-built rifle he'd never actually use. Small talk turned into longer conversations. Soon, we were meeting up after work, sitting on my back patio with a six-pack, watching the desert sky fade into darkness. Our wives would call it a night, leaving us outside with our drinks and the low hum of crickets filling the silence between words.

John talked a lot. He liked to tell stories, to brag, to unload things he wouldn't say in front of anyone else. And for some reason, he trusted me. Maybe he sensed something different in me, something darker. Or maybe he just needed someone who wouldn't judge him. Either way, I listened.

It wasn't long before he started telling me things he probably shouldn't have.

One weekend, John organized a guys' trip to Lake Pleasant. A handful of his closest friends, boats packed with coolers, enough liquor to drown out whatever stress they were running from. It was meant to be an escape—just another weekend of indulgence.

For me, it was something else entirely.

Lake Pleasant was a contradiction. By day, it was a postcard-perfect getaway—families grilling along the shore, kids splashing in the shallows, couples lazily drifting on paddle-boards. But at night, it transformed into impromptu floating parties where single men prowled, scanning for women drunk enough—or reckless enough—to follow them back to their boats. Some succeeded, some didn't. Others had better luck offering another round, another hit of something that blurred the lines between inhibition and regret.

By midnight, the hierarchy was set. The families were gone. The responsible ones had made their way back to shore. What remained were the ones looking to disappear into the night—boats tied off in the more secluded inlets, shadows flickering against the water as bodies moved in secret.

They thought they were invisible.

They weren't.

I watched. I listened. And slowly, the pieces of a bigger plan began falling into place.

The lake was a perfect hunting ground—isolated, unpredictable, and filled with people who made mistakes. A place where someone could vanish with barely a ripple on the water. A drunken slip. A wrong turn. A body sinking into the depths before morning.

This wasn't just a weekend trip. It was research.

John had no idea, of course. To him, this was just another night of excess, another chance to push boundaries and wake up with a story to tell. But to me, it was an exercise in observation, in understanding how things worked when the world stopped paying attention.

And soon, I would put my knowledge to use.

Over the next few months, John and I grew even closer. The casual beers turned into full-blown confessions, his guard lowering bit by bit. And one night, after just the right amount of alcohol, he let it slip.

He was having an affair.

He told me like it was nothing. Like it was just another story. Another thing he could control.

I was indifferent to it. Lea was nice, but she wasn't my concern. I wasn't the type to judge. People had their secrets, their temptations, their weaknesses.

And while John was busy indulging his, I was refining mine.

I spent my days working, my nights with Denise, my weekends filling time with errands and distractions. Anything to keep my mind from circling the inevitable.

For a brief moment, I considered getting help. Therapy. A professional to talk to. But the thought unraveled before it could take shape. What would I even say? What could they possibly do?

No, this was something I had to manage on my own.

So I worked. I planned. I calculated.

And then, on a quiet Thursday evening, John unknowingly handed me the final piece, a gift.

"*Can you cover for me this Saturday night*?" he asked, his voice casual, as if he were asking me to grab him a beer. "I*'m going out with my... "friend". Just need an alibi for the night. If Lea asks, we were together, went camping, you know—a guys-only trip.*"

He thought I was doing him a favor.

I met his gaze, a hint of a smile on my face.

"*No problem, of course*" I said.

And just like that, the door opened.

John thought he was slipping away unnoticed, wrapping himself in another secret. He had no idea that while he was off with his affair, I would be setting something else into motion.

I told Denise we'd be out camping, a group of neighborhood guys taking off for the night. She, in turn, invited Lea over for wine and a movie, locking our wives into a perfectly airtight alibi. No questions. No loose ends.

At precisely 4:00 P.M. on Saturday, I walked out the front door, the sound of their laughter trailing behind me.

I set out for Lake Pleasant, my heartbeat steady.

Tonight, everything would change.

THE ARIZONA HEAT CLUNG to the air, thick and dry even as the sun began to set. By late June, boating season was coming to a quiet end—crowds thinning, the night belonging only to those who truly wanted to be out there.

I had scouted the area meticulously, pinpointing the perfect location: Cottonwood Creek, a mile and a half south of Fireman's Cove. A known gathering place for those looking to disappear into the night, where the main patrols wouldn't bother checking too closely, if ever.

I realized that Arizona wasn't a hunting hotspot, at least not in the way the Midwest or the deep woods of the Pacific Northwest were. This area was secluded but a gunshot would raise eyebrows, and I couldn't afford that kind of attention. That thought had led me to an idea—a way to control the noise, to ensure precision without unnecessary risk.

I had spent the past few days constructing a makeshift suppressor. It wasn't sophisticated, but it was surprisingly simple to find on the internet and it was functional. Using PVC piping, super glue, cotton and layers of masking tape, I had fashioned a crude yet effective device. It wouldn't last long, but it didn't have to. Just one use, one shot, and it would serve its purpose. The key was execution—quick, silent, and efficient.

As I ran my fingers along the assembled pieces, I felt a steady calm settle over me. Every detail had been accounted for. Every possibility weighed. The lake, the isolation, the fleeting nature of the crowd—everything was aligning exactly as I had envisioned.

Now, all I had to do was wait for the right moment.

I exhaled slowly, I was ready.

THE LAKE STRETCHED OUT before me, dark and endless, its surface broken only by the occasional shimmer of reflected moonlight. The heat of the night was thick, clinging to my skin, making every breath feel slow and heavy. A few boats dotted the water, distant silhouettes barely visible against the horizon, but I needed one to come closer.

I didn't have to wait long.

At 8:45 P.M., two boats glided into the cove, their engines humming low, their movements deliberate, careful. They were slipping into the shadows, unseen by everyone—except me.

I stayed perfectly still on the hillside, my body pressed low against the rocky terrain, watching as they maneuvered into position. The first boat, a sleek pontoon, dropped anchor first. The man onboard, young and dark-haired, moved with easy confidence. He set the mood, dimming the lights, putting on soft music, and lighting three large candle lanterns that flickered against the black water.

Moments later, the second boat arrived, a small cabin cruiser with an elevated helm. A man and a woman were on board, their bodies moving in relaxed, sun-drenched familiarity. He was tall, clean-cut, and in shape, his tan suggesting a life spent outdoors rather than in an office. She, however, caught my attention instantly.

She moved with effortless confidence—long, dark hair spilling over bare shoulders, her body wrapped in a small bikini that seemed barely necessary. She was young, 20 at most, and the way she carried herself told me she was aware of exactly how much power she held in her curves, in the way she leaned against him, laughing, brushing her fingers over his arm.

The two boats tied together, the connection between them seamless, unhurried. There was no awkwardness, no hesitation. This wasn't the first time they'd done this.

I knew that taking a shot with three people onboard wasn't an option, so I stayed silent, watching. At first, it was nothing more than idle curiosity—a group of friends letting the night carry them beyond reason, laughter and liquor guiding their movements under the dim glow of deck lights.

But then something shifted.

The music pulsed softly over the water, a slow, rhythmic beat that seemed to set the tone. She was dancing between them now, her body swaying with an easy, liquid grace. The younger man's hands hovered near her waist, testing the space between them, while the older man stood just behind her, his gaze dark, contemplative.

I could feel the shift in the air, the charge of something unspoken passing between them.

I blinked, watching as she moved closer to the first man, tilting her face up toward him. Their mouths met, slow and teasing, her fingers trailing along his chest. A lazy laugh slipped from her lips, her body turning just enough to acknowledge the second man. Her hand brushed against his arm, her fingers tracing the length of muscle there, an invitation made without words.

He took it.

Her head turned, and then she was kissing him, just as slowly, just as deliberately. His hand slid up her back, fingers threading into her hair as he pulled her closer.

The first man's hands were on her thighs now, thumbs pressing into smooth, sun-warmed skin, tracing slow, knowing circles. She made a sound—soft, breathless—and like an unspoken signal, all three of them moved at once, standing together in the flickering light of the candles.

She was between them, her body open, offering something unstated but understood. There was no hesitation anymore, no uncertainty in the way she leaned into them, her body molded against one while her lips sought the other.

I swallowed, my pulse hammering in my ears.

Her bikini top came undone, sliding from her shoulders and pooling onto the deck. The older man's hands found her, cupping her as her mouth moved against the younger man's. Their movements were unhurried at first, as if savoring the novelty of it, but as the warmth of their bodies pressed together, something deeper took hold.

Alcohol had burned away inhibition, leaving only need, only curiosity.

Hands roamed, bodies fit together as naturally as if they had done this a hundred times before. The boat rocked gently beneath them, the water cradling them in a rhythm as old as desire itself.

I couldn't look away.

Something about it was maddening—the ease of it, the surrender. Watching them dissolve into each other, lost in the moment, feeling the weight of something I couldn't touch. It wasn't just lust, though that was part of it. It was the way they gave in completely, how they moved as if the world didn't exist beyond the space between them.

I should have left.

But I didn't.

I stayed, rooted to the earth, the warm night breeze carrying pieces of their world to me—soft gasps, low murmurs, the rustle of bodies shifting against fabric.

The night wrapped around them, hiding them just enough to make it feel like a dream.

I sat there for 90 minutes, waiting for them to finish, unwilling to move, unwilling to break the spell.

Eventually, they pulled away from each other, the spell lifting, replaced with soft laughter, whispered words of gratitude. She hugged both men, her bare skin still glowing under the candlelight, as if the night itself had touched her.

Then, something unexpected.

As the pontoon's engine rumbled to life, the girl didn't return to the cabin cruiser. She was leaving with the younger man.

I frowned, reasoning that they must have been together all along, that the older man had simply been part of the game for the night. It made sense, but something about the way the older man lingered, standing alone on his boat as they drifted away, struck me as… odd.

He wasn't leaving.

He hadn't pulled up his anchor.

I narrowed my eyes, the hairs on the back of my neck prickling with awareness.

Looks like I was going to get my shot after all.

HE DISAPPEARED BELOW DECK for only a moment. When he returned, a glass of whiskey glinted in his hand, a cigar perched between his fingers, its tip already smoldering. He took his time settling in, lowering himself onto the back of the boat with the kind of ease that came from years of indulgence. The soft glow of the running lights flickered off the water against his face, casting shifting shadows over his features.

He was reflecting. I could see it in the way he exhaled slowly, watching the dark water stretch endlessly around him. Maybe he was replaying the night, savoring every moment of it. Maybe he was reliving her touch, her taste, the feel of her skin still lingering in his mind.

Part of me admired him. The other part resented him.

There was something calculated about him, something too smooth. Men like him didn't have to try. He had the boat, the lifestyle, the charm. He didn't earn moments like tonight—he expected them. Something in my gut told me this wasn't his first time, that he had perfected this game long before tonight.

He thought he was untouchable.

As he took another slow sip of his drink, I raised my rifle, easing him into my sights.

I could feel the weight of the trigger beneath my finger.

I steadied my breathing, heart rate slowing, muscles loose and relaxed. The shot would be perfect. The air was still, no wind to account for, no obstructions. Nothing between us but open space and inevitability.

My pulse quickened—not with nerves, but with exhilaration. My mouth went dry, then wet again as I swallowed, salivating at the chance to take the shot.

He was no more than 300 yards from me, this was it.

I exhaled, letting my body settle. My finger curled slightly—just a whisper of pressure. And then…

A realization slammed into me like ice down my spine.

This angle left me exposed.

I blinked, my focus sharpening beyond the tunnel vision of the scope. They would know exactly where the shot came from. No wind, no sound cover—too easy to pinpoint my location.

And worse… I had been here for almost two hours.

Two hours of sweat, of movement, of subtle shifts in position. Had I left a trace? A footprint in the dust? A single strand of hair on the rocks?

The high in my chest burned cold.

Instinct kicked in.

I inhaled deeply, pulling back, recalibrating. He wasn't going to stay out here forever. At some point, he would leave.And when he did, he was mine.

Patience.

I let my heartbeat slow, let the hunger simmer beneath the surface instead of boiling over. He was enjoying his last drink—let him have it.

And then, as if he had read my thoughts, he stood.

This was it.

He moved with slow precision, taking his final sip before setting the glass down. Then, with practiced ease, he reached for the anchor line and began pulling it up. A sign.

He was leaving.

My grip tightened. My body coiled with the certainty of what came next.

I had my chance now—a moving target meant sound cover. The churn of the throttle, the low hum of the engine—it would swallow the shot, mask any way to trace it back.

He circled the boat, making his way toward the helm.

I flipped the safety off.

The crosshairs settled on his chest.

He was mine.

THE MOMENT BEFORE A SHOT IS THE LONGEST. Time stretches, thick and slow, wrapping itself around me as I steady my breath. My pulse is calm, measured. I should feel hesitation. Maybe even doubt. But instead, there's something else—a dark exhilaration that coils deep in my gut, warring against whatever is left of my restraint.

He has no idea.

That's the part that grips me the hardest. He moves like he has forever—completely unaware that his world is seconds away from vanishing. He doesn't flinch, doesn't turn, doesn't even pause to wonder if someone is watching. Because why would he?

Death is an abstract concept to people like him, something that happens to someone else, somewhere far away.

But I'm here. I'm close. I have already decided his fate.

And yet…

Something tugs at the edge of my mind, a whisper of hesitation, a ghost of a question: *Do I really want to do this?*

It's not guilt. It's not remorse. It's something quieter, something deeper. A moment of stillness before the plunge. The last chance to step away, to disappear into the night without changing the course of this man's life and possibly mine forever. Maybe it's the goodness I still believe I am or the love of Denise who is my everything.

But then I watch him—watch how he stands, how he moves, how his chest rises and falls in steady, oblivious rhythm. He has no idea.

And that thought alone sends a sharp, electric thrill through me. More powerful than the others.

I own this moment in a way he never will. I hold the power here. His life is still his, but only because I haven't taken it yet.

And that's the real rush, isn't it?

Not the shot itself. Not the impact. But this.

The space between decision and action.

The moment where I can still turn away but won't….I can't.

My finger tightens around the trigger, and my breath slows. This is it.

The last second of his life.

And he still doesn't know.

I see his eyes through the scope, the dim glow of the boat's running lights catching just enough light to reflect back at me. He has no idea. The crosshairs are tight on his torso, rising and falling with his easy, untroubled breaths. I time it—wait for the exhale. One second of stillness. One heartbeat. One soft pull.

Pop.

The suppressed shot is nothing more than a muffled crack, barely louder than a branch snapping underfoot. For a brief second, he's still there—upright, moving, alive. Then he isn't.

He crumples instantly, a hollow marionette cut free of its strings. His body folds awkwardly, slumping forward over the boat's controls, but there's no struggle, no noise. No gasp, no last words. He's just… gone.

Perfect.

I stay motionless, heart steady, ears straining against the silence, waiting—listening.

Nothing.

No screams. No shouts of alarm. Just the soft chorus of night creatures, the quiet ripple of water against the hull of his drifting boat. The world doesn't even flinch.

I exhale slowly, watching as the boat, now driverless, begins to glide forward. He had just engaged the throttle before the shot. Now, with no one to steer, it drifts lazily up the channel, back toward the open lake, a ghost ship carrying its final passenger.

I couldn't have planned it any better.

Better than Owen could have planned.

It was perfect.

The thought settles into my chest, warm and satisfying. A deep, visceral certainty—one I've never felt before. I was complete.

I stay there for another minute, watching the boat grow smaller in the distance, letting the stillness settle over me. Then, without a sound, I turn away, slipping silently through the darkness toward my car.

RATHER THAN SPEND THE NIGHT out I decided to drive home to be with Denise.

I pulled into the driveway just after 1am. The house was dark, quiet, familiar. Denise wasn't expecting me. I slipped inside, the scent of our home wrapping around me, grounding me, telling me I was where I belonged.

She was in bed, fast asleep, curled into the blankets like she always did when I wasn't beside her. She had no idea what I had just done.

She would never know.

I had my story prepared: *The guys got too rowdy. Too much beer, too much noise. I left early because I wanted to be with her, not them.* A believable excuse, and one that would make her smile.

But as I stood in the doorway, watching her, something inside me shifted.

I wasn't just coming home.

I was alive.

More alive than I had ever been.

The thrill of it still hummed in my veins, electric and undeniable. My hands, steady on the rifle, now ached for something else—for her.

I stepped forward, shedding my clothes in the quiet, my eyes never leaving her.

She stirred at the sound, her expression softening as her eyes met mine. A slow, knowing smile spread across her face, as if she could sense the shift in me, as if she recognized the hunger in my eyes before I even touched her.

I slid into bed, pulling her body into mine with a quiet, commanding force. She knew this side of me. She welcomed it.

But tonight was different.

Tonight, I wasn't just taking control. I was claiming something.

She gasped softly as I kissed her, as my hands moved over her, peeling away the layers between us. I wasn't thinking about what I'd done—I was thinking about what I had watched.

The girl.

The way she had moved between them, fearless, uninhibited.

The way she had let herself be devoured by pleasure, no fear, no shame.

That was what I wanted.

And as I touched Denise, as I took her the way she had always craved; we gave into each other.

It was unlike anything we had ever shared before—urgent, deep, raw. Not just passion, but power. Not just love, but something darker, something primal. She felt it, responded to it, let herself be carried by the force of it, gasping against my lips as she surrendered completely.

I had never felt closer to her. Never felt more complete.

And when it was over, when we lay together, tangled and breathless, her body soft against mine, I finally understood.

This was it. I was free.

I was complete.

The past was behind me now. The hunger, the chaos, the restlessness—it was over.

We could start fresh. We could move forward.

Denise stirred against my chest, sighing softly in her sleep, completely at peace.

And for the first time in my life, so was I.

Chapter 7

ECHOS IN THE MORNING

MORNING BROKE WITH THE WARMTH of sunlight spilling across my face, the golden glow creeping through the curtains, bathing the room in quite serenity. Everything felt different.

The house was awake, humming with a renewed spirit, alive in a way I hadn't felt in a long time. I lay there for a moment, taking it in —the softness of the sheets, the stillness in my chest where unrest had once lived. The demon was gone.

A new sense of purpose stirred inside me, a clarity I hadn't known before. I was free.

There was a rich, inviting scent of coffee drifting through the house, coaxing me from bed. Denise had been up for a while, no doubt in the kitchen, moving through her morning ritual—brewing coffee just the way she liked it, folding eggs into soft, buttery curds with the effortless touch only she had. Thinking about her famous scrambled eggs was enough to get me moving.

I stretched, my body still heavy with the remnants of last night—of her. The scent of her lingered on my skin, my hands, a quiet reminder of the way she had let me come home and take her, completely. The memory sent a slow, satisfied hum through me, anchoring me in the certainty that this was more than just a morning.

This was a new beginning.

As I reached for the glass of water on my nightstand, my eyes caught Denise's journal, its worn cover resting beside her lamp.

I knew I shouldn't. But after last night, after she wrote first thing this morning, I *had* to know.

She never shared what she wrote, never let me into the world she poured onto those pages. I had always respected that. Always left it alone.

But not this time.

My fingers hovered over the leather, tracing its edges. A pause. A breath. A silent apology.

Then—before I could stop myself—I opened it.

The ink was still fresh. Guilt pressed in as my eyes moved over the words. And still, I read.

> ***Journal Entry*** *– Late Night Return*
>
> *I woke to the sound of the front door closing softly—him. No stumbling, no drunken clumsiness, just quite intent. He was home earlier than expected. That made me smile.*
>
> *He stood there in the dark, watching me, the air between us charged with something I couldn't name. When he slid into bed, I felt it—control, possession, hunger. His hands, his breath, his body against mine—he took me in a way he never had before.*
>
> *It was raw. Unrestrained. Consuming.*
>
> *I didn't ask why, didn't question the shift in him. Whatever had awakened tonight, I felt it too.*
>
> *For the first time in a long time.*

I closed the journal and set it back on the nightstand. Her words only affirmed what I already knew—we were turning the page together.

I JOINED DENISE DOWNSTAIRS, the warmth of the morning following me as I stepped into the kitchen. The scent of freshly brewed coffee mingled with something richer—butter, citrus, something sweet.

She had set the table beautifully. Not just a casual breakfast, but something more intentional—an experience. A bottle of champagne sat in an ice bucket, two delicate flutes waiting beside it. Fresh fruit, warm pastries, and her awesome scrambled eggs were plated with the kind of care that told me this wasn't just another morning.

This was something special.

Denise turned as I entered, a soft, knowing smile spreading across her lips. She was radiant in the morning light, wearing nothing but a loose satin robe, her hair still slightly tousled from sleep. But it wasn't just how she looked—it was the energy between us.

Something had shifted.

Reading her journal entry, feeling the way she had poured herself into this morning—it confirmed once agin she felt it too.

We were in a new place.

A better place.

And yes, it had come at a price—but t*he ends always justified the means.*

The love and passion that had once been effortless between us had dulled in recent months, not lost, just buried. The move, the stress of new jobs, settling into a new neighborhood, navigating new friendships—it had taken its toll. For a while, we had been going through the motions, caught up in the mechanics of life instead of truly living it together.

But last night had changed everything.

Last night had reminded us of who we were.

She handed me a glass a mimosa, her fingers brushing mine in a way that sent a slow, deliberate heat through me.

"*Hungry?*" she asked, her voice light, teasing.

I didn't answer right away. Instead, I stepped closer, letting my fingers skim over her wrist, my touch lingering before taking the glass from her hand.

Yes, I was hungry.

For this. For her. For us.

As we sat down together, toasting to something unspoken but understood, I knew with absolute certainty: this was a new beginning.

The morning felt effortless. Light streamed through the kitchen windows, casting a golden glow over the table as we lingered over breakfast. The soft clinking of silverware, the occasional laugh, the warmth of champagne spreading through us—it all felt right.

The television was on in the background, playing the morning news—the usual fluff. Stories about upcoming community events, a feature on a local bakery, a lighthearted segment about a rescued dog. The kind of news that made the world feel small, predictable, safe.

I reached for the champagne bottle, tilting it over Denise's glass, watching as the bubbles danced up the sides. Calm. Controlled.

Then, the tone of the broadcast shifted.

A subtle pause. A tension in the anchor's voice that hadn't been there before.

"*After the break, we have a developing story—breaking news about a murder that took place at Lake Pleasant last night.*"

The words cut through the air like a blade, sharp and unexpected.

My hand froze mid-pour, the bottle hovering just above my glass, the soft fizz of champagne the only sound filling the silence between us.

Denise turned her head slightly, her expression still relaxed, but there was curiosity in her eyes.

"*Oh wow,*" she murmured. "*Lake Pleasant? We were just talking about going back there.*"

She took a sip of her champagne, unconcerned.

I swallowed, my heartbeat steady—but beneath the surface, something twisted.

I felt it crawl up my spine, that strange, intoxicating contrast between normalcy and chaos. The perfect morning, the warmth of breakfast, the smooth taste of champagne—and the knowledge that this moment was only perfect because of what had happened last night.

Denise didn't know, She couldn't ever know.

I set the bottle down carefully, glancing at the screen as the news rolled into a commercial break.

I already knew what they were going to say.

I just wondered how much they knew.

Across the screen flashed,

News Broadcast, Live Coverage from Lake Pleasant.

The news begins with an aerial shot of the lake. Boats are already on the water but there is one, further out from the rest, a single vessel surrounded by law enforcement.

The Anchor in the studio reports -

"Breaking news this morning—a homicide investigation is underway at Lake Pleasant after a man was discovered dead on his drifting boat overnight. Authorities are calling this a targeted attack and are asking for the public's help in piecing together the events leading up to the murder. We now go live to our field reporter, Jessica Caldwell, who is at the scene. Jessica, what do we know so far?"

Standing on the dock with the cabin cruiser in the background Jessica says, "*Good morning. What began as a routine patrol early this morning quickly turned into a crime scene when authorities discovered a boat floating unmanned in the main channel of Lake Pleasant. Upon boarding the vessel, they found the owner—deceased at the helm."*

"Law enforcement officials have confirmed that the victim—whose identity is being withheld pending notification of next of kin—was last seen late last night, anchored in a secluded cove on the lake. He was alone at the time, or so it was believed."

"However, in a surprising twist, authorities have also confirmed that a ***second person*** *was found on board—**alive.**"*

The cutaway to a Sheriff on scene, the reporter asked the Sheriff what they can share.

"*Upon searching the vessel, we discovered an individual who had been below deck in the hull of the boat at the time of the incident. They were unconscious when first located but were able to wake and communicate with officers once medical personnel arrived. At this time, we are treating them as a potential witness, not a suspect.*", the Sheriff stated.

The reporter Jessica continued - *"Sources close to the investigation say that the individual—a young woman whose connection to the victim remains unclear—had been heavily intoxicated and was likely passed out below deck when the murder occurred. Investigators are working to determine whether she may have seen or heard anything that could shed light on the killer's identity."*

"Investigators are now trying to reconstruct the timeline, working with forensic evidence and witness statements to determine exactly when and how the victim was killed—and whether the woman on board could have been in danger herself without even knowing it."

"As of now, authorities have not identified any suspects."

"The authorities are urging anyone who was out on the lake last night to come forward with any information. "The woman found on board is being questioned, though officials have not released any details about what she may—or may not—remember from that night."

As they cut to a commercial, I sat frozen, my champagne glass still in my hand, the condensation trailing down my fingers. My mind now racing, what have I done - *Someone else was on the boat.*

Not dead. Alive.

Denise sighed, shaking her head as she cut into her eggs. "*That poor girl,*" she murmured, completely unaware of the way my world had just tilted.

My stomach twisted. I had been meticulous. Precise. I had accounted for everything.

Except her. Who was she?

What did she see?

Chapter 8

A HAIRLINE CRACK

SPIRALING, THE NEXT FEW DAYS and weeks were pure torture. Every waking moment was a battle not to unravel, not to let the panic take hold.

What had I done? How could I have been so careless?

I had gotten away with the murder in Minnesota—clean, methodical, untouchable. So why had I rolled the dice a second time? Why had I let the hunger take over again, convincing myself I was untouchable?

The answer didn't matter. I had done it.

And now, the weight of that mistake pressed down on me with every breath.

I was now losing focus, the strain bled into every part of my life. At work, my mind drifted—missed deadlines, forgotten emails, conversations I barely registered. I blamed it on "*problems at home,*" let my colleagues assume I was another man in a strained marriage, drowning in domestic issues.

Denise didn't question my distraction. She was patient, warm—too trusting. Around her, I forced a facade, tried to be the husband she knew, the man she believed I was. But I could feel the cracks forming.

Every moment with her felt like a test. Would I slip up? Say the wrong thing? Would she notice the way my hands trembled slightly when I thought too hard?

I considered telling her. Not the whole truth, never the whole truth—but something. A controlled confession. The rifle, for example. That was something I could explain—something I needed to explain, before the police had a reason to ask about it themselves.

At any moment, they could knock on the door. It wasn't paranoia; it was logic. If they started canvassing the area, tracking down every hunter, every shooter within range of the cove, they might land on me. Even if they didn't suspect me outright, it wouldn't take much to justify a search.

Better to prepare Denise, plant a seed of doubt, a reason for her to believe I had nothing to hide.

The silence was worse than the noise. The news had gone quiet. No reports. No updates. No leads.

It didn't bring me comfort. Silence was worse. It meant something was happening behind closed doors.

Had the girl spoken? Had she identified the other couple in the cove? Even if she had been too drunk to participate, she might have remembered their faces from earlier in the day—might have been able to name them. And if the police found them, they could place them at the scene.

More importantly, they could place me.

Even if they didn't know my name yet, they'd know someone was there—someone had taken that shot. And the moment they pinpointed the location, it wouldn't take much to find me.

Six weeks had passed, but this was Arizona. No rain had washed away my presence. No crowds had trampled over where I had lain for hours, watching, waiting. That hill was as untouched now as it had been the night I pulled the trigger.

This was bad.

And I didn't see a way out.

I started considering the unthinkable, there were moments—fleeting, but persistent—where I thought about telling Denise I wanted a divorce.

It wouldn't make sense. It would blindside her. But maybe that was the point.

If the police came knocking, if they started digging, she'd be dragged into this. And Denise was my biggest liability. She knew my routines, my moods, my lies. She could hold up under questioning—for a while. But what if they pressed?

If I left now, made her hate me, pushed her away before the walls started closing in, she wouldn't have a reason to protect me.

Because if it came down to it, if they asked her whether I had been acting differently…

Would she lie for me?

Or worse—would she start putting the pieces together on her own?

AT SOME POINT, reason returned. The fear and paranoia hadn't vanished, but I forced myself to focus on what I could control. Panic wouldn't save me—action would.

I took a systematic approach, breaking everything down into a checklist of damage control. The first and most pressing issue: the rifle, it needed to go.

I took a day off work, claiming I needed a personal day—a strategic move. I didn't want any reason for someone to wonder why I was out running errands. Early that morning, I retrieved the rifle.

I had already prepared a small bucket of bleach, stashed in the trunk of my car. Bleach wouldn't erase everything, but it would eliminate the surface layer of DNA, fingerprints, and any residue that could be traced back to me.

Sitting in an isolated parking lot, I field-stripped the rifle, breaking it down into as many small pieces as possible. Each component went straight into the bleach, submerged and swirling in the chemical bath as I worked.

The small parts—the springs, pins, screws—were easy. As I drove through town, I tossed them one by one into random dumpsters. Tiny, unrecognizable, worthless as evidence. Even if someone found them, they'd think nothing of it—just scrap metal, junk, garbage.

But the barrel and stock were different. Even disassembled, they were unmistakably parts of a rifle.

The best option was to melt them down. But that required a furnace reaching at least 1,500°F, something I didn't have easy access to. The next best option? Destruction beyond recognition.

Using a grinder and saw, I cut the stock and barrel into unidentifiable chunks, jagged and useless. The pieces were then dunked in the bleach, ensuring no trace evidence remained. Over the next several hours, I repeated my earlier process—driving around town, scattering the remnants in countless dumpsters.

Even if one piece was found, it would mean nothing.

If the police somehow retrieved a scrap of it, they wouldn't be able to reconstruct the full weapon, wouldn't be able to retrieve ballistics, wouldn't be able to connect it back to me.

The rifle was gone.

With the weapon dealt with, I turned my attention to another problem—where I had taken the shot.

The rocky hillside where I had laid for hours was undisturbed, unvisited, and worst of all—untouched by weather. Arizona didn't have the luxury of frequent rain to wash away the evidence. My sweat, skin cells, hair follicles—all of it could still be there. And if the police had started surveillance, returning alone was too risky.

I needed a reason to be there.

The best cover? Denise.

I planned a picnic—an innocent weekend outing with my wife, one that would place us exactly where I had been the night of the murder. The goal wasn't to remove evidence. It was to contaminate it.

If my DNA was ever found there, Denise could truthfully say:
"*Oh yes, we were there together. He sat on those rocks. We had lunch there.*"

A plausible explanation, an airtight alibi.

Getting Denise to agree was easy. She loved spontaneous little outings. We drove to Lake Pleasant, taking the same route I had traveled that night, retracing my steps.

Above the rocky embankment where I had taken the shot, there was a small clearing. That's where we set up. A blanket, a picnic basket, a couple of sandwiches, and a bottle of wine. It was picturesque, normal.

After eating, I suggested we climb down to the water, using the exact same path I had walked that night.

As we descended the rocky terrain, I felt it.

The weight of what had happened here.

This had been my hunting ground.

And now, I was playing the part of a carefree husband, walking over the very spot where I had ended a life.

It made my skin crawl, I felt a little nauseous, but I stayed in character.

When we reached the exact location where I had fired the shot, I faked an injury—twisting my ankle.

We sat there for a few moments while I played up the pain, subtly contaminating the area with new DNA. I ran my fingers through my hair, letting a few strands fall. I rubbed my hands on the rocks, scuffing them with my palms.

Denise, ever the attentive wife, noticed. I made sure of that.

"*Are you okay*?" she asked, her brow furrowing.

"Yeah," I exhaled, putting a hand to my temple, "*just... lightheaded. Think I stood up too fast.*"

A small moment, innocent to her, significant to me.

She saw me there. She would remember being there with me. And if questioned later, she'd tell the truth.

"*Yes, we were at that spot. He sat right there. But...*"

That "but" would be my safety net.

After a brief rest, we continued to the lake, wading into the cool, reflective water.

For a moment, I let myself breathe.

I had done what I needed to do.

My DNA was now entangled with Denise's. If forensic teams ever searched, they wouldn't be able to distinguish between what was old and what was recent.

That night would be buried beneath a new memory, a different story.

As we dried off and made our way back to the car, I knew the goal for the day had been accomplished.

Denise saw a romantic picnic.

I saw insurance.

And for the first time in weeks, I felt like I was one step ahead again.

IT WAS APPROACHING EIGHT months when a local journalist, Robert Duncan, published an article titled *The Shot That Ended Summer*. It had been just over a year since the shooting at Lake Pleasant, and Duncan had crafted a compelling retrospective piece, one of those long-form, investigative deep dives that sought to breathe life back into a story that had faded from the public's memory.

I found it amusing—his version of the events so far removed from the truth.

According to Duncan, Brian McKay, the man killed, was portrayed as a devoted boyfriend, tragically gunned down while looking after his girlfriend, Brandi, who had had a little too much to drink that night. A protective, caring partner making sure she got home safe.

No mention of the threesome while Brandi was passed out below deck.

Still, Duncan's article did clear up some lingering questions that had been gnawing at the back of my mind.

Brandi.

The girl in the hull.

Her name was Brandi.

According to the article, she had passed out sometime around 3 P.M. that afternoon and had no memory of meeting anyone at the lake, let alone know how Brian was killed that night.

That meant she hadn't spoken to the police.

She hadn't identified the other couple.

She had no recollection of the events that led up to Brian's death.

She was a black hole of information.

A blank witness.

I let that realization settle, letting it soothe the last edges of my paranoia.

Duncan also revealed something else—the homicide had officially been labeled a murder.

The police had ruled out any accidental or self-inflicted theories. Someone had shot Brian McKay. That much, they knew.

But what they didn't know was who.

The leading theory? That Brian had pissed off the wrong person on the lake that day.

Apparently, he was known for being a bit of an asshole.

Loud music, obnoxious behavior, a boat that cut too close, a general disregard for personal space and common decency. He had made enemies before. The assumption was that one of them had followed him that night, confronted him at his boat, and shot him in a fit of rage.

A reckless confrontation gone wrong.

And with no suspect and no eyewitnesses, the case was officially closed.

Officially Closed.

The words hung in the air as I read them over again.

The case was officially closed.

It was over. I had made it.

I let out a breath I hadn't realized I was holding. A slow, deliberate sigh that carried months of tension away with it.

The weight of the world dropped from my shoulders.

I could breathe again.

I read the last line of the article once more, soaking it in, letting it fully register.

And then I reached for my phone.

I needed to celebrate.

There was only one person to call.

John, it was time for a neighborhood party.

And no one could throw one better than him.

THE REST OF THE YEAR rushed by in a blur of festivities, laughter, and the kind of warmth that only the holiday season could bring. November and December in the neighborhood were something special. Every house on the block transformed into a glowing spectacle of lights, wreaths, and garlands, each neighbor trying to outdo the next in a friendly, unspoken competition. Parties filled the calendar—Thanksgiving feasts, Christmas cocktail gatherings, New Year's Eve blowouts. The air was thick with the scent of cinnamon, roasted meats, and the crisp bite of winter nights warmed by fire pits and spiked cider.

By the time January arrived, it marked two significant milestones.

One: Denise and I were celebrating our anniversary.

Two: It had officially been three years since we moved to Arizona—the longest we had ever lived in one place together.

We had built a life here.

A real one.

For the first time in years, I felt grounded. Settled. The past was exactly that—the past. And for the first time since the moment I pulled that trigger at Lake Pleasant, I wasn't looking over my shoulder anymore.

We had deep roots now. Work was thriving for both of us, our social circle was full of friends who genuinely cared about us, and, for once, I wasn't fixated on what had come before. No late nights spent obsessing over every detail of my crimes, no creeping paranoia eating away at my mind. I was free.

Or at least, I had convinced myself I was.

Owen hadn't crossed my mind in months. I hadn't called him, hadn't even allowed myself to think too deeply about him. A part of me knew that reaching out—even just for a casual check-in—was like standing on the edge of a black hole. If I got too close, I might get sucked back in.

And why risk that?

Everything was perfect.

Denise was thriving. I had always been amazed at how effortlessly she balanced everything—her demanding job, our home, her friendships and her family—all without missing a beat. She had this rare ability to make the most mundane days feel intentional, meaningful.

Holidays were her specialty.

It didn't matter if it was Christmas or Valentine's Day, Halloween or St. Patrick's Day—Denise treated each one with equal enthusiasm. Our home was always meticulously decorated, filled with small, thoughtful touches that made each celebration feel unique, important.

It wasn't just for us. It was for everyone.

Her energy was infectious. Friends, neighbors, even people who weren't particularly into the holiday spirit couldn't help but get swept up in it. She made our house a home in a way that I never could.

And as I watched her, moving effortlessly through life, so unburdened, so untouched by the shadows that I had carried for so long…

I realized just how much I admired her.

And just how much I had to lose.

AFTER THE FIRST OF the year, two life-changing things happened. The first: Denise was offered a major promotion. It was the kind of opportunity that would set her up for the next stage in her career—higher salary, more responsibility, more influence. There was just one catch: it required us to move to Florida.

Denise hated the idea of Florida. The humidity, the hurricanes, the politics, and the over-commercialized chaos of it all. She had always loved the Arizona desert—the dry air, the wide-open landscapes, the sense of stillness it brought her. But me? I was intrigued.

We had spent three years in Arizona. We had done all there was to do, seen all there was to see. The thought of a fresh start, a clean slate, was appealing. More than that—it was necessary.

I had other memories here.

Memories I was happy to leave behind.

But above all else, I was in love with Denise.

For years, she had been my anchor. She had followed me wherever my job took me, never questioning, never hesitating, always supporting me. Now, it was my turn.

And the truth was, this move wouldn't just be good for her—it would be good for us.

Because the second, far more important thing that happened:

Denise was pregnant.

When she told me, I felt like the world stopped.

I had spent so much of my life focusing on control, on precision, on keeping everything in check—but this? This was something that truly mattered.

We were going to be parents.

And the timing couldn't have been better.

Our home in Arizona was nice, but not child-friendly. It had been perfect for parties, late nights with friends, the occasional reckless indulgence. But it wasn't the place to raise a family.

Florida offered something different.

We could find a quiet neighborhood, a family-friendly community, a place where we could step away from the chaos and step into the next chapter of our lives. A place where nobody knew us.

A fresh start.

So we listed our home, packed our things, and said our goodbyes.

Some of those farewells were harder than others—John and Lea, the neighbors who had become family. The weekend get-togethers, the late-night drinks on the patio.

But some goodbyes were easier.

The ones to the memories I was ready to bury.

Then, one afternoon, while finalizing paperwork with our real estate agent, something caught my attention.

A black SUV idled just across the street, its windows dark, its presence lingering longer than felt natural. I told myself it was nothing—a neighbor's guest, a service worker taking a break. But then, when I stepped outside to check the mail, the SUV pulled away.

I brushed it off.

A day later, Denise mentioned a detective had stopped by while I was at work.

"*Something about the investigation at the lake*," she said, barely paying it a second thought as she folded laundry. "*I told them we weren't out there much. You know, just the picnic that one time.*"

A picnic.

A perfect, well-placed alibi.

I nodded, keeping my expression neutral, my mind already working through what this meant.

It was nothing.

It had to be nothing.

And yet, as we packed up the last of our things and prepared to leave Arizona for good, I found myself checking the mirrors more often.

Watching for cars that lingered too long.

Telling myself that I was in the clear.

That I had won.

That I was free.

Even as a small, quiet voice in the back of my mind whispered:

Then why does it still feel like someone is watching?

Chapter 9

FLORIDA AWAITS

WE DECIDED TO MAKE the move to Florida a road trip. There was no need to rush—we had nowhere to be at any specific time, no strict deadlines, just miles of open road ahead of us. It felt symbolic in a way, the idea of easing into our new life, taking in the scenery, stopping wherever we wanted. A transition, not an escape.

The movers handled the heavy lifting—our furniture, our packed boxes, everything that made up the physical foundation of our home. What remained with us were the personal things, the irreplaceable items—the pieces of our life we weren't willing to trust to strangers.

The first leg of the trip took us as far as Texas.

Denise had been quiet.

She wasn't upset, wasn't distant—just content in her own world. She curled up in the passenger seat with a book in her lap, the soft glow of her phone occasionally illuminating her face as she scrolled through real estate listings in Florida, humming softly to herself now and then.

I told her I was just focused on the road. That was an easy excuse—one that didn't require much effort.

But the truth?

I couldn't stop thinking about the black SUV.

I had played it off, convinced myself that it was nothing. That if it were something serious, they would have pressed harder. That their question—*"Had we ever been out to Lake Pleasant?"*—was just routine.

But was it?

How did they find me?

Had Brandi, from the boat, remembered something?

Had she started piecing together fragments of that night—something she had seen, something she had overheard?

Or had it been the other couple? If the police had spoken to them, they would have known exactly where they were anchored. And if they knew where they were, they could have pinpointed where the shot came from.

And if they knew that, then they might know about me.

Had I left DNA behind that they had somehow recovered?

The thought made my stomach churn. It had been months. Arizona's dry climate didn't erase things the way rain would. No weather had swept over the rocky hillside, washing away any trace of my presence. If they had taken samples from that spot… if they had found anything…

Could that have been what led them to the house?

Or was it the rifle itself?

I had purchased it legally. Had they traced it?

Would they have run a background check on registered owners and stumbled upon my name?

That seemed less likely—there was no ballistic evidence unless they had recovered the bullet, and even then, it would have needed to be linked back to my rifle.

But still…

The possibility crawled under my skin, hollowed out my chest.

And then there was something else. Something I had never accounted for.

Hidden surveillance.

I had been so meticulous about my approach—choosing a secluded ridge, a location with no direct visibility from the main lake.

But what if there had been a camera I never saw?

Something small. Motion-activated. A hunting camera strapped to a tree or a long-range lens installed on a remote piece of property I hadn't noticed.

What if my car had been captured?

A license plate number. A vague description. Something just concrete enough to put me on a list.

No.

That was impossible.

I would have known.

Wouldn't I?

I gripped the steering wheel tighter, forcing my breathing to stay steady. I needed to stop this—this spiral, this obsessive loop.

If they had something on me, they would have acted by now.

That thought became a mantra.

If they had something, they would have acted.

If they had something, they would have acted.

And yet, my pulse wouldn't settle.

I stole a glance at Denise. She looked so calm, so unaware of the war raging inside me.

We were on our way to a fresh start. I had put the past behind me. We had a child on the way.

This can't be happening.

But the truth was, it already had.

Pulling into the hotel parking lot, the weight of the day settled over us. The drive had been long, the miles stretching endlessly beneath us, and by the time we reached the hotel, exhaustion clung to both of us, heavy and inescapable.

Denise let out a quiet sigh as she unbuckled her seatbelt, rubbing her temples as if trying to massage away the fatigue. I could see it in her posture—the quiet slump of her shoulders, the way her movements had slowed.

Neither of us spoke as we grabbed our overnight bags from the trunk, weaving through the dimly lit hallways toward our room. The silence wasn't uncomfortable—just the kind of quiet that comes from two people who don't have the energy for small talk.

The moment the hotel door clicked shut behind us, we both moved on autopilot—shoes kicked off, bags dropped haphazardly near the wall. Denise barely glanced at the room itself. It didn't matter where we were. All that mattered was sleep.

The bed was a welcome relief, the cool sheets crisp against aching muscles. We crawled under the covers, our bodies sinking into the mattress with the kind of exhaustion that made everything else—conversation, closeness, even the simple act of reaching for each other—feel like too much effort.

She turned to her side, said goodnight, and I did the same.

A half-hearted kiss—barely more than a brush of lips. A silent acknowledgment of each other before sleep claimed us.

The last thing I remembered was the hum of the air conditioner and the distant murmur of traffic outside, a lullaby of movement beyond these walls.

Tomorrow would be another twelve hours on the road.

And beyond that - a new life waiting for us in Florida.

DENISE HAD AN UNCANNY gift for finding us the perfect place to live. It didn't matter if it was our first tiny apartment, a temporary rental on vacation, or a home we planned to stay in for years—she always knew. She had an instinct for spaces, for energy, for neighborhoods that just felt right. So when she told me, *"I found the perfect home and neighborhood,"* I didn't question it. I knew it would be exceptional.

We settled in a small town on Florida's Gulf Coast—Sarasota. It had everything we wanted. A quiet, charming community with just enough space to breathe, yet close enough to the action if we wanted it. Tampa and Orlando were both an hour or two's drive away, giving us access to the city without being swallowed by it. It was, by all accounts, an ideal place to start our next chapter.

And the neighborhood? It was straight out of a Norman Rockwell painting.

A brand-new development with wide, sunlit streets, perfectly manicured lawns, and homes that looked like they had been plucked straight from a luxury magazine. Everything was pristine, uniform, a perfect blend of community and privacy. The amenities were endless —a community pool, a kids' waterpark, a state-of-the-art gym, walking trails, even a clubhouse that hosted weekly social events.

Our home was one of the model houses and it came fully furnished, a showcase property right at the entrance to the neighborhood—a prime spot. We had a front-row seat to everything. We were directly across from us was the community pool, the playground, and the splash pad for kids. Everything we'd need for a growing family.

But there was one unexpected detail.

As we began to meet our neighbors, I noticed something a little strange. Everyone had already been through our house before.

Being one of the most popular model homes in the development, our place had been open to the public for months before we moved in. People had walked through it, imagined themselves living there, pictured where they'd put their furniture—but in the end, we were the ones who actually got it.

It gave the house a weird familiarity.

It was ours, yet it wasn't just ours.

Because of this, we got to know our neighbors fast. Faster than we had in any other place we had lived. Our home stood out. People felt comfortable here, like they already knew it.

And that meant, almost immediately, it became the place to be.

Most evenings, happy hour ended up at our house. Neighbors would wander over with drinks in hand, sinking into the patio furniture like they had been coming here for years.

And Saturdays?

Without exception, they were spent at our house.

Pool parties, barbecues, long nights in the hot tub with the soft hum of conversation and laughter filling the air.

It felt effortless.

Like we belonged here.

Like this was always where we were meant to end up.

Every place we'd lived, we wasted no time networking the neighborhood and making friends. Some people kept to themselves, some were friendly but forgettable, and then there were the key players—the ones who truly ran the show.

In a neighborhood this size, there were really only two people you had to know.

Brian was the guy everyone liked. Easygoing, charismatic, the type who made you feel at home the second you met him. He had the kind of effortless confidence that made people gravitate toward him, the guy who always had a beer in hand, a joke ready, and the inside scoop on everything happening in the community.

He had the perfect-looking family too—an amazing wife, two adorable kids, and a life that seemed picture-perfect from the outside. His son was sharp as hell, the kind of kid who soaked up knowledge like a sponge, always a step ahead of the other kids his age. His daughter, a tiny thing with big blue eyes and a streak of pure mischief, had more personality than most adults. Cute as a button, but could hold her own in any conversation. She already knew how to roll her eyes like a teenager, despite barely being out of diapers.

His wife, Hailey, was a party animal. She loved to drink, dance, and be the life of every social event. She was the kind of woman who made every other wife both admire and resent her at the same time—effortlessly fun, undeniably attractive, and completely unapologetic about it. She and Brian were the couple that set the tone for the whole neighborhood. If you were in with them, you were in with everyone.

The other person you needed to know was Jorma, (soft J).

Although his name was Finnish, he was actually a Canadian. He had two daughters who were in that teenage phase of barely tolerating their parents but still close enough to home to be around. They seemed like good kids, smart and independent.

Jorma himself?

To this day, he's probably the nicest guy I've ever met.

One of those rare, genuinely good people. The kind of guy who would drop everything to help you, no questions asked. You needed something moved? He was there. Car broke down? He had tools in his garage before you could finish explaining. Got into a bind? Jorma had your back.

But for all the good Jorma had in him, he had one glaring problem.

His wife, Becky.

Becky, the one everyone tolerated, ….. was… a lot.

She was obnoxious, nosey, and constantly in everyone's business. If she wasn't trying to insert herself into conversations she didn't belong in, she was talking about someone else's problems. A neighborhood gossip mill in human form.

And the worst part?

She flirted with every husband in the neighborhood—except her own.

It was subtle at times—a lingering touch on the arm, a laugh that lasted a second too long. Other times, it was blatant. A hand across the ass that didn't need to be there, or a whisper into an ear that was far too intimate for a married woman.

But she never did any of this with Jorma.

That was the part that got to me.

I wasn't sure if Jorma knew or not, maybe he just didn't care.

Part of me believed he was aware but chose to ignore it, like a man who had made peace with the fact that his wife was just that way. Another part of me wondered if he did care but didn't know how to stop it.

And that… bothered me.

Jorma was a good man. The best kind. And yet, it seemed like he had no control over his own home.

I felt a strange pull—an urge to help him, to build him up, to get him to deal with Becky.

Not that it was any of my business.

But this was a new group of friends, a new environment, a new dynamic.

And with my recent resignation from my position, I needed a project.

Jorma would be it.

And my hunch?

Brian would help.

He didn't like Becky either.

THE MONTHS THAT FOLLOWED were a blur of wine -soaked conversations, hot tub confessions, and late-night strategy sessions. Brian and I had a mission—to build Jorma up, to give him the confidence to take control of his own life. It became a ritual, an unspoken agreement between us.

It happened over countless drinks, long nights in the hot tub, and more dinners than I could count at Joe's—the local Italian place that had become our second home. We knew the owner well, and he treated us like family. The normal patrons had no idea about the off-menu specialties Joe saved just for us and that made us feel all the more special.

Some nights, after the last customer had left, Joe would lock the doors, flip the sign to 'Closed,' and keep the wine flowing. It would just be us—Brian, Jorma, our wives—drinking, eating, talking until the early hours. Mama's homemade pasta, the kind that melted in your mouth, pizza fresh from the brick oven, cigars on the patio under the soft hum of late-night streetlights. Those nights felt untouchable, golden.

Life was good.

Denise was thriving at work. I was working odd jobs, enough to keep things comfortable. We weren't worried. The baby was coming soon, and everything felt like it was lining up perfectly.

Happy hours at our house had gone from a couple nights a week to almost every night. It didn't bother us at first. We liked entertaining.

We had the perfect house for it—the one everyone gathered at, the one people just showed up to, uninvited but always welcomed.

Denise was ready to burst. Any day now. The entire neighborhood was on edge, waiting. Cards and gifts poured in, filling the mantle, spilling onto the dining table—well wishes, congratulations, tiny clothes for the baby that hadn't yet arrived.

And then, just as everything felt settled… the past reached out.

It was just another afternoon, the Florida heat thick in the air, the sun glaring off the pavement like white fire. I grabbed the mail on my way in, flipping through the usual—bills, junk flyers, another baby card for Denise.

Then, I saw it.

The glow of my phone screen cast an eerie light against my face as I scrolled absently, my mind elsewhere. Then, a vibration.

A text.

No name. Just a number I didn't recognize.

I stared at it, my thumb hovering over the notification.

Spam? A wrong number?

But something in my gut twisted. Something felt off.

I tapped the message open.

Seven simple words.

"I know it was you in Arizona".

Everything stopped.

My chest went tight, breath catching in my throat as I read it again. And again.

Owen.

It had to be Owen.

We hadn't spoken in years. No calls. No messages. Not a damn thing.

And now?

This.

Why now?

How did he know?

Had someone contacted him? Had he figured it out himself? Had he always known?

More importantly—was he the only one?

What about the black SUV, could this be from them?

My pulse pounded in my ears, a brutal, steady thump, thump, thump. The edges of my vision blurred as I fought to stay calm.

Think.

Was this a warning? A threat? A game?

Has he or someone else become a liability?

Had the black SUV been him all along? Or something worse?

I was so deep in thought, I didn't hear her at first.

"*Babe?*"

A voice—soft at first, then sharper, panicked.

I looked up.

Denise stood at the doorway, barefoot, her face pale. One hand braced against the frame, the other clutching her stomach. Her breath came in short, uneven gasps.

She glanced at my phone, still in my hand, still illuminated.

I saw it, the flicker of something in her expression. A pause. A question.

Then—a sharp inhale. Her body tensed. Pain. Real pain.

"*It's time,*" she gasped.

Her water had broken.

The phone slipped from my grip, landing face-up on the table between us.

The text still visible, like a large billboard.

But she didn't say anything.

She didn't have time to.

The past didn't matter anymore.

The future, the baby.

It was happening……Now.

Chapter 10

RESENTMENT IS A SLOW POISON

WITH THE BIRTH OF our daughter Chiara, everything changed—in the most profound and beautiful way. The shift in our lives was immediate, all-consuming, and yet, oddly seamless. While both of us were overjoyed, Denise was in her element. Motherhood wasn't just something she embraced; it was something she had been destined for. From the very beginning, she was the kind of mother you read about—the kind that seemed to *just know*. She anticipated every cry before it came, every need before it surfaced.

We shared responsibilities, taking turns with late-night feedings, diaper changes, and the inevitable sleepless nights. But Denise? She excelled. She didn't just endure the exhaustion—she thrived in it, as if every moment, even the hardest ones, were a privilege. There was a deep sense of fulfillment in the way she held our daughter, in the way she whispered to her during those quiet hours when the rest of the world was asleep.

By the end of the first month, we had settled into a rhythm. The chaos had softened into something structured, something familiar. We were no longer just two people—we were a family. And with that routine came moments of stillness, small pockets of time where my mind wandered back to things I had momentarily set aside.

The text. The SUV.

Was it Owen?

I hadn't allowed myself to dwell on it before—not with everything that had happened. But now, in those quiet moments between bottles and baby monitors, it crept back in. I knew Denise had seen it. She never overlooked anything, never forgot a detail. It had been a concern for her the moment she read it—I could feel it in the way her expression had flickered, even briefly. But then, life had swept in like a tidal wave: her water breaking, the frantic drive to the hospital, the whirlwind of nurses, the long hours of labor. And after that, a blur of visitors, congratulations, and the sleepless, beautiful chaos of adjusting to our new reality of family life.

But for now, I needed answers.

I needed to know what was going on with Owen—what he knew, what he was trying to tell me. Was this a warning? A threat? Or something worse? The uncertainty gnawed at me, tightening its grip the longer I let it fester.

There was only one way to find out.

Reaching for my phone, I hesitated for just a second. It had been years since I last spoke to Owen. Our lives had drifted apart so naturally that it was almost as if we had silently agreed to leave things in the past. And yet, here he was, resurfacing with a cryptic message—one I couldn't afford to ignore.

I needed a reason to reach out. Something casual. Something that wouldn't tip my hand.

The baby.

It was the perfect excuse. A natural conversation starter. An easy way to test the waters before diving into the real reason I needed to talk. Denise was asleep, her breathing steady beside me, our daughter nestled in the bassinet near the bed. The soft hum of the baby monitor filled the quiet room, a stark contrast to the storm brewing in my mind.

I tapped out the message, keeping my tone light, measured—like nothing was wrong.

Owen, what's going on? It's been a while. Things here are good. I actually have some big news—Denise and I had a baby girl. Her name is Chiara. She's a handful but already the love of my life. We should catch up soon, man. Let me know what you've been up to.

I stared at the screen for a moment before hitting send.

And then, I waited.

Would he respond? Would he even acknowledge the message? Or was this the beginning of something I wasn't ready for?

I wasn't sure which answer scared me more.

I lay there in bed, staring at the ceiling, the glow of my phone screen fading as the minutes stretched on. Maybe an hour passed. Maybe ninety minutes. Time blurred in the heavy quiet of the night. Every so often, I reached for my phone again, refreshing the screen, half-expecting to see a reply from Owen, half-dreading what it might say.

But nothing came.

The silence was worse than uncertainty. If he had answered, at least I'd know where I stood. Instead, I was left with the gnawing weight of the unknown, replaying every word of my message, wondering if I had said too much—or not enough.

Eventually, exhaustion won. My body gave in, and sleep pulled me under.

THE FIRST THING I DID when I woke up was check my phone. Still nothing. The pit in my stomach deepened. I had told myself I wasn't expecting an immediate response, but the truth was, I had been.

Not hearing from Owen was worse than not knowing.

I dragged myself downstairs, shaking off the restless night. Denise was already up, curled on the couch with a cup of coffee, scrolling through her phone while the local news murmured in the background. She glanced up briefly when I walked in.

"*The baby's still sleeping,*" she said, matter-of-factly, taking a slow sip from her mug.

I nodded. A quiet Saturday morning. A rare moment of stillness.

I poured myself a cup of coffee and sat down across from her. For a moment, I let myself enjoy it—the calm, the silence, the feeling of just existing without anyone around.

But deep down, I knew it wouldn't last.

It never did.

The front door swung open, and just like that, the peace was shattered.

"*Morning, party people*!" Brian's voice boomed through the house before I even saw him.

Saturday meant volleyball in the neighborhood. And before volleyball, it meant mimosas at our place. Baby or no baby—some things never changed.

Brian strolled in like he owned the place, juggling three bottles of champagne in his arms. His grin was wide, carefree—completely oblivious to the fact that we had a newborn and barely any sleep.

"*Jorma and his wife are on their way,*" Brian announced, kicking the door shut behind him. "*They've got the OJ and cranberry juice. Let's get this started*!"

I turned to Denise, expecting—hoping—for some kind of reaction. Annoyance. Frustration. Something. A sign that maybe, just maybe, she was as fed up with this as I was.

Maybe it was the stress of the SUV. Maybe it was the mysterious text still lingering in the back of my mind, gnawing at me. Whatever it was, it had pushed me to the edge, my patience unraveling in real-time.

Deep down, I knew these were my friends. I enjoyed their company. But in this moment, something snapped—a crack in the control I had worked so hard to maintain. Suppressed emotions clawed their way to the surface once again, hot and unfiltered.

And yet, when I looked at Denise, all I found was calm.

She didn't meet my anger with her own. No frustration, no concern. Just a slow glance over the rim of her mug and a small, knowing smile.

I knew what it meant.

Time for mimosas.

Don't get me wrong—I loved the Saturday volleyball games. They were an escape, a way to stay connected, to hold on to something normal. A few hours of friendly competition, banter, and good-natured ribbing.

But the rest of it? That was becoming a problem, and in this moment, now more than ever. My mind was secretly racing out of control.

It wasn't just Saturdays anymore. Somehow, "a few nights a week" had turned into almost every night. What started as a small group gathering three to four times a week had ballooned into a near-daily event, and our house had become the permanent hosting spot.

And Denise? She didn't seam to mind.

She cared, sure, but not in the way I did. It didn't weigh on her like it now did on me. It didn't irritate her to the point of resentment.

But me? I noticed.

I noticed that it was always me cooking and cleaning up afterward.

Me making sure there was enough food, enough drinks, enough space for people who never once considered hosting themselves.

For over a year, we had played the role of the perfect hosts—the ones who never said no, who never asked for anything in return. And not once—not once—had any of them offered to take a turn.

It was expected now.

Our house. Our money. Our time.

And I was done. And just like that, the anger twisted into something else.

Something darker.

Brian popped the first bottle of champagne, grinning. "*Alright, who's ready for a drink*?"

I gritted my teeth, setting down my coffee.

Denise got the glasses

THE REST OF THE DAY PLAYED out exactly as expected—because it always did.

The games were intense, the competition fierce, but the real event wasn't the volleyball. It was what came after. Like clockwork, everyone migrated back to our house for drinks, food, and hours of conversation that stretched long past what anyone would considered polite.

I cooked. I poured the drinks. I kept the music going. I played the host.

Denise, as usual, took care of Chiara, balancing a baby on her hip while our "friends" lounged in our backyard, shooting hoops in the pool, drinking alcohol, eating, and stretching the night into something that belonged to them instead of us.

Baby went down at 7 p.m.. Guests finally cleared out at 11p.m..

Two more hours of cleanup. Two more hours of them lingering. Of pretending this arrangement wasn't one-sided.

Denise, rightfully, was exhausted. The second the door shut behind the last guest, she was ready for bed. I told her I'd handle the cleanup. I wasn't even tired, strangely enough. Maybe it was the constant motion of the day, or maybe it was something else, something deeper. Something restless, something unsatisfied that was not triggered.

She kissed me softly and whispered, "*Thank you for a perfect day.*"

I watched as she disappeared down the hallway, oblivious.

Once the dishes were done, I stepped outside with a final glass of wine, seeking a moment of peace that never seemed to last.

The night was still, thick with heat, the crickets chirping in the distance the only reminder that the world still turned without demand. The pool water trickled softly over the rock wall, a rhythmic hum that might have been calming—if my thoughts weren't racing.

I should have felt lucky. I had everything. A beautiful wife, a perfect daughter, a home people envied.

And yet, all I felt was resentment.

It crept in, like a slow poison, curling around the edges of my thoughts. The realization that we were being used. That every single one of them—Brian, Jorma, the entire damn neighborhood—knew exactly what they were doing.

They had made our home theirs.

The worst part? We had let them.

The more I thought about it, the angrier I became. I could feel it building, pressing against my ribs, curling into my fists.

Before I even realized it, my mind had drifted somewhere darker. Somewhere dangerous.

Revenge.

Something to teach them a lesson.

Something they wouldn't forget.

I swirled the wine in my glass, staring into the deep red like it held the answer. Maybe it did.

Who would I target? We had met almost everyone in the neighborhood and on any given Saturday there would be 10 to 15 people at our place. At this point I had contempt for all of them so who to single out? Maybe a random act, an accident that mysteriously happened to one of them. Not decided by me but by chance, by the choice they made. Yes, that was the plan. I'd construct a series of "*if - then*" and who ever took the bait would be punished untimely because of the bad choices they made, not me directly. A comfort came over me. A relief that once again I would take control of the situation and return balance to the scales. Now I could go to bed. The details of the plan to be worked out later, tonight I could rest.

As I rinsed my glass and placed it in the dishwasher, my phone buzzed against the counter. The sudden vibration cut through the stillness, startling me. The house was silent now—just me, the hum of the appliances, and the weight of my own thoughts.

The white glow of the screen illuminated the dim kitchen. A text.

I frowned. 12:30 A.M.. Who the hell was texting me at this hour?

Brian. That was my first thought. Was he looking for one last nightcap? A drunken excuse to swing by because he "left something" here?

I grabbed the phone, half-ready to ignore it. But it wasn't Brian.

Owen.

A slow, uneasy breath left my lips. He had responded.

The message I sent days ago, the one I had nearly convinced myself would remain unanswered—here it was.

I hesitated, thumb hovering over the screen before I opened it.

"*Eric, Congratulations! I'm so happy for you and Denise. I can only imagine how on top of the world you both are. Sorry for the delay in returning your text. I have a new job and have been busy. We need to catch up soon, it's been too long.*"

I exhaled. The tone was warm. Inviting. Genuine.

Not at all what I was expecting.

No cryptic phrasing. No tension hidden between the lines. Just Owen.

I hadn't realized how much I'd built this moment up in my head. How I'd envisioned something darker—a warning, an omen, something to confirm that the past was never really buried. But this? This was just two old friends reconnecting.

A welcome relief.

Almost without thinking, I typed back:

"*Great to hear from you. Yes, things are going well—sounds like for you too. We do need to catch up. Life just got away from both of us, I guess. It's late, just getting ready for bed. I'm on baby duty tonight LOL.*"

I hesitated for a second, my fingers hovering over the screen. This should be the end of it. A friendly exchange, a reconnection, nothing more.

But I couldn't stop myself.

Before I even realized what I was doing, I typed the question that had been sitting in the back of my mind for awhile now.

"*Hey, real quick—this has been bugging me for a while. I have to ask. What was with that cryptic text you sent me? Some kind of joke?*"

The second I hit send, my heart pounded.

My breath hitched in my throat, my palms damp against the cool surface of the counter.

I had finally asked.

The question I had buried, ignored, reasoned away—it was out there now.

Good or bad, I needed to know.

Seconds passed. Then minutes.

The screen stayed empty.

My eyes locked onto the phone, watching. Waiting.

Then, the three dots appeared.

He was responding.

Why was it taking so long?

A chill crept over my skin, despite the warmth of the house.

Was he about to apologize? Laugh it off? Maybe he'd explain everything, make me feel like an idiot for even asking.

The dots flickered. Paused. Then flickered again.

I swallowed hard, pulse hammering in my ears. Something didn't feel right.

And then— The screen lit up.

I pulled the phone closer.

"*What message?* It wasn't me.

This is the first I've reached out to you in three years. Let's not make it another three before we catch up.

Semper Fi."

I stared at the words. They didn't make sense.

My mind struggled to process them, to fit them into some kind of logic.

What message?

A cold weight settled in my chest.

The text—the one that had haunted me for over a month—the message that started all of this…

Owen hadn't sent it.

I felt something tighten in my throat as I scrolled up.

I needed to see it again. The original message. The number. Something to prove that I hadn't imagined it.

My thumb swiped, eyes scanning. Once. Twice. Three times.

Nothing. It was gone.

I stopped breathing.

I checked again, this time searching for Owen's contact, for any trace of the conversation.

No record of the message. No number I didn't recognize. Nothing.

Like it had never been there at all.

A shiver ran down my spine.

I hadn't imagined it. I *knew* I hadn't.

So then... where the hell did it go?

Chapter 11

DRAWN BY CHANCE

AFTER A SURPRISINGLY RESTFUL night's sleep, the morning sunlight crashed through the blinds, slicing across my face and pulling me from the depths of unconsciousness. I blinked against the brightness, disoriented for a moment before reality settled back in.

Denise was already downstairs—I could hear the faint murmur of voices drifting up through the floorboards. Another morning, another invasion.

I let my head sink back into the pillow, willing myself to stay in bed just a little longer. Just long enough to think.

My mind drifted to Owen—to our brief exchange, to the warmth of his response, so ordinary, so normal.

And then there was the message—the one that had haunted me for nearly a month—was gone. *"I know it was you in Arizona"*

I had scrolled and searched for it again, swiped up, refreshed, checked my logs. Nothing. No trace, no proof it had ever existed.

Maybe I had imagined it. Maybe my subconscious had conjured it, a manifestation of guilt or paranoia. Maybe I wanted to believe in a warning because deep down, I knew what I had done and what I was still capable of doing.

After-all, text messages don't just disappear.

And then there was Denise. If there was a text then she had seen it when it first arrived—I was sure of it. She never overlooked details, never forgot anything. If there had really been a message, she would have asked. She would have confronted me by now.

But she hadn't.

Which meant… what?

I exhaled slowly, pushing the thought away. It didn't matter anymore. Real or not, the message was gone. And as far as I was concerned, that meant I had no reason to think twice about it anymore.

I sat up, stretched, and ran a hand over my face. I had just started to shake off the haze of sleep when I heard it.

A voice. Shrill, grating. Familiar.

Becky, "The Mooch".

Without even looking, I knew it was her. The woman had an uncanny ability to materialize the second food or drink was being served. No doubt she was standing in our kitchen at this very moment, holding out her empty mug, expecting it to be filled like some neighborhood stray too cheap to go to Starbucks but perfectly content drinking our coffee.

I clenched my jaw. Of course it was Becky. It was always Becky.

And then came more voices.

Louder now.

Within minutes, I heard Brian's booming laugh, followed by Hailey's obnoxious chatter, and then the unmistakable deep rumble of Jorma's voice. Their kids, screaming and running around out by the pool.

It was 9 a.m. on a Sunday, and my house was already overrun.

Suddenly there were two unfamiliar voices that cut through the mix —Anne and Steve?

Who the hell were Anne and Steve?

I scrubbed a hand down my face. Becky. That had to be her doing. She had a habit of dragging in new people, expanding our ever-growing circle of freeloaders without so much as a second thought. It didn't matter that we barely knew them. It didn't matter that this was our home, not some goddamn community center.

And no one ever asked. No one ever stopped to think that maybe we were tired of it.

I sat at the edge of the bed, my fingers curling into my thighs as I tried to compose myself. But the resentment was already building.

A slow, creeping fire that had been smoldering since the night before, maybe subconsciously longer.

And yet, there was something strangely comforting in the thought of revenge or retribution for all of this. The idea of finally tipping the scales in my favor. It settled me, soothed the irritation clawing at my chest.

Soon.

I would have my moment. A day of reckoning.

And none of them would see it coming.

I inhaled deeply, rolling my shoulders back, forcing myself to relax. This was all still in the planning phase, after all.There was no need to rush. A good plan required patience.

And I had plenty of time.

I stood, grabbed a pair of shorts, and pulled them on.

A faint smirk played on my lips as I descended the stairs, slipping effortlessly into the role they all expected me to play.

Time for mimosas.

THE NEXT FOUR MONTHS became an obsession. Every spare moment, every quiet thought, every sleepless night was consumed by the meticulous construction of my revenge. It wasn't just a plan anymore—it was a necessity.

And every single intrusion—every uninvited guest, every thoughtless demand, every early morning voice echoing through my home like they owned it—only fed the fire.

Every cup of coffee stolen from my kitchen. Every bottle of champagne popped without a second thought. Every plate left behind for me to clean.

They had no idea.

With each new offense, my resolve hardened. Their entitlement would be their undoing.

And soon, one of them would pay for all of it.

Through all of this time, not once did I stop to consider the consequences.

My mind was consumed by one thought, and one thought only—to kill.

At first, I tried to rationalize it. I attempted to self-analyze, to dissect my own psyche like an outsider peering in. Was this normal? Was there a logical explanation for the compulsion that had taken root inside me?

Or had this always been who I was?

Part of me insisted that this was nothing more than a social experiment, a test of fate. Just like the others before, it was a matter of wrong place, wrong time—but of their own choosing.

This was no different.

Whoever was to suffer, would do so because they were meant to.

Their own choices would seal their fate, not mine. I was simply the architect, the silent hand guiding the inevitable.

That thought alone should have been enough to keep my conscience clean.

But if I was being honest—truly honest—I knew that wasn't the whole truth.

I wanted to believe that this was a statement. An unconscious, symbolic act.

A lesson.

A warning.

That greed and excess should not be extorted from others. That taking without giving, without gratitude, had a cost.

That it was time for balance to be restored.

I convinced myself that this was about my family. That I was doing what ***was necessary*** to take back our home, our lives, our control.

And maybe, in some way, that was true.

But beneath that justification, beneath the layers of self-rationalization, there was something deeper.

Something darker.

In unfiltered reflection, I saw the truth staring back at me.

This wasn't just about restoring order.

This was about power.

Control.

This was about the undeniable high that came with knowing, in that moment—in the act of execution, in the final step of delivery—I was in control.

I was God.

I decided fate.

I chose who lived and who died.

And that realization? That intoxicating sense of power? It was blinding. It overpowered everything else in my life.

It wasn't a means to an end anymore.

It was the end.

The mystery text—the one that may or may not have existed—was no longer a concern. Owen's involvement, his intentions, whatever game I thought he might be playing… none of it mattered anymore. Denise knew nothing. Of that, I was convinced. There were no sideways glances, no quiet interrogations, no signs of suspicion. She was oblivious, just like the rest of them.

And so, my only focus—the singular obsession that now anchored my every thought—was crafting a perfect, masterful act of vengeance.

One person. That was all it would take. A single casualty. A single sacrifice. Done correctly, it would shift the dynamic of the neighborhood instantly and permanently.

The trick was execution.

I had always been trained to handle problems with precision. Distance, control, efficiency. But this was different. No rifle. No vantage point. No clean escape. This would be up close, personal.

And it had to have an element of chance.

That was important.

I didn't just want to take someone out. I wanted them to choose their own fate. I wanted a game of fate—one where the unsuspecting victim unknowingly walked into their own demise, one where their own greed, their own entitlement, was the thing that killed them.

And what better moment than Halloween?

It was September when the idea fully took shape.

Denise and I were known for our outrageous parties. They were events we both enjoyed to do but —one's we had unwittingly allowed to feed the very culture of entitlement that had taken over our lives. Every year, the neighbors swarmed our house like locusts, drinking, eating, and staying long after the festivities should have ended.

And every year, they expected more.

They expected a spectacle.

The next party, I would give them one.

At the height of their indulgence—when they were at their most arrogant, their most entitled, their most unaware—

that's when I would strike.

DURING COLLEGE, I HAD four roommates. One of them was a guy named Jon.

We weren't close—just acquaintances from high school who happened to each need a place to live for the same year. Jon was different from the rest of us. While we were caught up in the usual college nonsense—parties, relationships, future careers—Jon's world was rooted in something older, something established.

He came from a big Greek family—one that ran the best Greek restaurant in our hometown and all of his siblings worked there, fully invested in the family business. Jon, however, wasn't.

Jon had chosen a different path, chemistry.

Chemical Engineering, to be exact.

I remember watching him breeze through coursework that left the rest of us struggling. Chemistry, physics—it all came easy to him. He didn't just understand formulas and reactions; he respected them. He knew how to manipulate them.

And that was why, during our junior year, Jon decided to make cyanide.

I still remember the night he brought it home from his lab. A clear liquid in a tiny vial. A lethal dose, so simple, so unassuming. He had done it not out of malice, but out of curiosity.

That moment has always stuck with me.

Thinking about it now, I had realization of a simple truth:

Everything—harmless or lethal—is just a chemical composition.

This would be the key.

I wasn't going to use a gun or a knife. This wasn't a crime of passion this would be a crime of chemistry.

For the next month, I buried myself in research. I spent hours at the local library, old bookstores, obscure online forums. I needed to understand poisons—their potency, their stability, their detectability.

I studied the classics—arsenic, strychnine, botulinum. Too complex. Too traceable.

I learned about obscure plant-based toxins, most too difficult to extract. Too unreliable.

I needed something simple. Something effective. Something that wouldn't raise suspicion but would still be lethal in the right dose.

And then I found it.

The answer had been right in front of me the whole time.

Castor beans.

The very thing that made ricin.

It was perfect.

- Easily acquired.

- No complex chemical reactions.

- Very stable in hot/cold environments.

- And most importantly—rarely tested in an autopsy.

There were a number of articles about individuals like myself that had recently made exactly what I was looking to make at home, in the kitchen and garage. Minnesota, London, South Carolina, Georgia, all had documented cases where someone had attempted it but failed—not because the toxin wasn't effective, but because they had been lazy, careless. They had made mistakes.

I wouldn't.

I would be thorough.

I would be invisible.

And when the night came—when the neighbors filled my house, drinking, laughing, stuffing their faces with the very things I had prepared for them—one of them would make a choice.

And that choice would be their last.

HALLOWEEN SEASON HAD ARRIVED, and with it, the perfect cover for what I was about to do.

Every year, regardless of where we lived, Denise and I hosted the most anticipated party in the neighborhood. It was tradition—extravagant decorations, over-the-top costumes, a massive haunted house, and endless supply of food and drinks. And this year? This year would be no different. If anything, it would be our grandest celebration yet.

And none of them had any idea it would also be the stage for something far darker.

Brilliant in its simplicity.

First, I needed the raw materials.

Castor beans.

They were easy to obtain. A few searches led me to multiple local suppliers. They were sold as novelty items, organic curiosities, and even garden plants. No red flags. No suspicions and perfectly legal to own.

The next step was turning them into something lethal, not so legal.

I had assumed this would be the most complicated part—extracting and making the ricin, isolating its deadly properties is done via process called chromatography. Surprising, the process wasn't as difficult as it sounds. In fact, it has been fully described and in plain sight for decades.

A quick search led me straight to a 1957 patent—US3060165A.

There it was. Step-by-step instructions on how to process castor beans into a deadly compound.

Filed. Documented. Preserved.

In the same way a cookbook teaches a person how to bake bread, this document detailed exactly how to create one of the most potent poisons known to man.

They had made it too easy.

I read through the patent, memorizing the process and took notes, studying the necessary conditions, understanding the basic chemistry behind the process.

It wasn't difficult. No elaborate lab required. No rare chemicals. Just patience, precision, and the understanding that maintaining the correct temperature was the single most important element.

Ricin is highly lethal when inhaled in small amounts. Ingested, I would need slightly more, I estimated about 20 milligrams.

The final step was the most crucial—how to administer it without detection - the delivery.

Denise, as always, had already given me the answer.

Every year, without fail, she made jello shots. It had become a staple of our parties, a tradition so ingrained that I knew without even asking she would be making them for this one.

She'd start them the day before, carefully preparing each batch, pouring the liquid into tiny plastic cups, lining them up in neat rows, and placing them in the fridge to chill overnight.

That would be my opportunity.

Once she was finished and the shots were tucked away, waiting for the party, all I had to do was slip in unnoticed and lace one with ricin.

It was flawless in its simplicity.

Neither Denise nor I ever drank jello shots. We were wine drinkers, and everyone knew it. Skipping them wouldn't raise suspicion.

Even better—Denise made them with vodka, a liquor she despised and never touched. That meant the risk of her accidentally taking the poisoned one was nonexistent.

Midway through the party, after the costume contest, Denise would grab a friend, and together they would weave through the crowd, offering shots to the guests.

And somewhere in that moment—amid the laughter, the toasts, the mindless indulgence—one person would make a fatal choice.

It was so perfectly innocent. So unexpected.

And so easy to manipulate.

A single poisoned jello shot—that's all it would take.

One moment. One choice.

A single, fatal mistake.

Whoever ate it would never know what hit them.

Ricin had no smell. No taste. No immediate symptoms. It was the perfect silent killer.

By the time the poison began its slow, agonizing work, the party would be a distant blur.

Three, four days later, when they finally collapsed—body failing, organs shutting down—no one would think to connect it back to a party from days ago.

The brilliance of it wasn't just in the method—it was in the randomness.

It wouldn't be my decision.

Fate would choose.

Their greed, their entitlement—the very things that had fueled my resentment for so long—would be the reason one of them died.

No one would suspect me. Why would they?

Besides, I had done nothing. Not directly.

Denise made the shots. She handed them out.

I had merely presented an opportunity—one that someone willingly took.

And when the night ended, as our guests staggered home, full, drunk, and consumed with the thrill of the evening, one of them would unknowingly be carrying their own death sentence.

And that thought?

That was the most satisfying part of it all.

THE DAY OF THE PARTY had arrived, and everything was executed exactly as planned.

Our home was completely transformed—inside and out, top to bottom, a spectacle of eerie elegance. Cobwebs stretched across chandeliers, flickering candles lined the tables, and animatronic ghouls lurked in dark corners, waiting to startle unsuspecting guests. Outside, gravestones littered the lawn, half-buried skeletons clawing their way from the earth, their bony hands reaching for passing trick-or-treaters. A low-lying fog machine kept the yard suitably ominous, while motion-activated cackles and ghostly moans drifted through the night air.

But the centerpiece of the evening?

The haunted house.

I had spent weeks constructing a seven-room labyrinth of horror inside our three-car garage. It was the only way into the party. Each guest had to make their way through it first, winding through dimly lit corridors, disoriented by strobe lights, eerie whispers, and unexpected jump scares.

Each room had a distinct, nightmarish theme—a fog-drenched graveyard, a blood-splattered butcher shop, a demented circus complete with an animatronic clown, and even an exorcism room where a possessed girl writhed on a bed, her body jerking unnaturally. Denise had laughed when I first pitched the idea, but now? She was in awe.

This wasn't just a party. It was an event.

To complete the transformation, we hired two bartenders from a local restaurant we frequented—a pair of young, attractive women who always caught our attention. They arrived dressed as Vivian and Kit from *Pretty Woman,* and they looked incredible.

Julie, who came as Vivian, had crafted her costume down to the smallest detail—even pinning her boots with safety pins just like in the movie. Her tall, lean figure commanded attention, and she liked the attention.

Denise and I had put effort into our own costumes as well.

This year, I was a Roman soldier, complete with traditional armor and a sword strapped to my waist. Denise, ever the center of attention, was a stunning empress, draped in a long, form-fitting, low-cut dress, her golden bracelets jingling with every movement. Her blonde hair was piled high, her headdress adding an extra air of regality.

She looked breathtaking.

But more than that—she was completely in her element.

With the in-laws taking Chiara for the night, Denise was able to fully let loose—no midnight feedings, no early morning wake-ups. Tonight, she was the queen of the party.

And I?

I was waiting.

By 9:15 P.M., the house was packed, the energy infectious.

The DJ, perched in the corner of the patio, had the crowd moving—bodies swaying, costumes flashing under the dim, pulsing lights. The music pulsed through the floorboards, blending with the sound of laughter, clinking glasses, and the occasional shriek from a guest stumbling out of the haunted house.

The food was a hit, the drinks were flowing, and the buzz of conversation filled every inch of the house. Costumes ranged from classic horror to pop culture, superheroes to blood-soaked monsters.

It was exactly what I had envisioned.

At 9:30 P.M., the judges lined up for the costume contest, making their rounds before unanimously selecting Dee, a new neighbor, dressed as Cruella de Vil.

A well-deserved win. She looked unbelievable—bold, seductive, and commanding, just like the character. The crowd erupted in applause as she strutted forward to claim her prize.

At 9:45 P.M., as expected, Denise grabbed Hailey, and the two of them lifted the trays of jello shots, weaving through the party with playful grins.

I stood across from the DJ, my fingers curled around my drink, my pulse steady, my eyes tracking their every move.

And for the first time in months, I felt completely calm.

No hesitation. No doubt.

I had done exactly what I planned—prepared the ricin, poisoned a single jello shot, and shuffled them before placing them back on the tray.

Even Denise and Hailey had unknowingly helped me by rearranging them as they placed them onto the serving platters, eliminating any possibility of even me tracking the poisoned one now.

There was no way to know who would take it.

And that was the beauty of it. Somewhere in this house, a decision would be made, my excitement was almost overwhelming.

As Denise and Hailey playfully encouraged guests to grab a shot, laughter and cheers erupted. Some took two. Some downed them quickly, licking the remnants from their lips.

My heart didn't race. There was no fear. No second-guessing.

Just a cold, steady anticipation.

Denise walked over to the bartenders and handed one to Julie.

She was young, so beautiful, with here whole life ahead of her.

She tipped her head back, swallowing it in one gulp. Then she licked her lips, frowning slightly.

Julie looked up at me with a smirk. "*What'd you put in these, rocket fuel? Tastes a little bitter, Mister*" she teased, winking at me.

The words lodged themselves in my brain.

She quickly just shook it off, grabbing another shot and handed it to Amber, her friend. The two of them laughed, completely unaware.

I watched, detached, I felt nothing as they continued to walk the room.

Not for Brian, who had become my closest friend in the neighborhood.

Not for Jorma, who I had once considered my own personal project.

Not even for the bartenders, who I both secretly had admired from a distance.

By 10 P.M., both trays were empty.

It was done.

I took a slow sip of my drink, the ice clinking softly against the glass, condensation cool against my fingertips. Around me, the party roared on—laughter, music, the rhythmic pulse of conversation—but it all felt distant, like background noise in a scene I was no longer part of.

Somewhere in this house—amid the dancing, the drinking, the celebration—someone was already doomed.

The poison was in them now. Floating through their bloodstream. Seeping into their cells. Counting down the hours until they became nothing more than a story whispered over next year's drinks.

And I was the only one who knew, the one who orchestrated it all.

I turned slightly, my gaze drifting toward the darkened window beside me. Beyond the glass, the yard was bathed in deep shadows, the fog creeping low over the grass, swirling beneath the glow of string lights.

But I wasn't looking at the outside world.

I was looking at my own reflection.

And for the briefest moment, I didn't recognize the person staring back at me.

The man in the glass wasn't the host of this party. He wasn't the friend, the neighbor, the devoted husband or protective father.

His eyes were too steady. Too unreadable.

A faint smile curled at the reflections lips—except I didn't remember smiling.

A strange sensation crawled over my skin, an unnerving awareness of just how much I had changed.

Or maybe… this was who I had always been.

I exhaled slowly, the moment slipping away as the world around me lurched back into focus. Someone clapped me on the back, laughing, dragging me back into the party.

I let them.

Because tonight,

I had played my part perfectly.

Chapter 12

NO ONE IS INNOCENT

BY MIDMORNING, everything was getting back to normal.

We tore down the Halloween decorations, stuffed them into bins, wiped away the remnants of the night. The floors were sticky with spilled drinks, the air thick with the last traces of sweat, alcohol, and something else—something unseen.

The only evidence left behind was the stack of crumpled paper cups, stained with traces of jello. I gather them up counted them and made sure the bag made it to the curb for the trash pick up that was coming later that morning. No proof. No questions.

The neighborhood was quiet. The kind of silence that lingers before something terrible happens….or after.

Day two came and went. The world hadn't shifted, hadn't cracked under the weight of what I'd done. Everything was exactly as it always was.

No hushed rumors, no texts about someone getting sick, no whispers of consequences. I should've heard something by now. I should've *felt* the ripples.

Doubt clawed its way into my head. Had I miscalculated? Had the mixture been off? Maybe storing it in the refrigerator had compromised it. Maybe I hadn't used enough.

Had I failed?

The hose dripped onto the pavement as I washed my car in the driveway, my mind cycling through the possibilities, dissecting the what-ifs.

Then Brian showed up.

He clapped his hand against mine in a sharp high-five, his usual energy grating against my nerves. "*Dude, what an epic party. You gotta hook me up with your bartenders, man, they were next level.*"

I nodded, forced a smirk. We stood in the driveway, reliving fragments of the night—the music, the chaos, the shots passed around in flimsy paper cups. And then, I saw him.

Jorma.

He was walking toward us, slow and deliberate, his face carved with something tight and unreadable.

Brian greeted him with his usual enthusiasm. "*What's up, man*?"

Jorma barely acknowledged him. His gaze landed on me instead.

"*Eric…*" His voice was flat, controlled. "*Did anyone from the party reach out to you? Say anything about feeling sick? Maybe food poisoning*?"

My chest tightened.

This was it. The moment I had been waiting for.

The moment of discovery.

I kept my breathing steady. My expression neutral. My heartbeat was a steady drum against my ribs, but outwardly, I gave him nothing.

I tilted my head, let just the right amount of concern slip into my voice. "*No, why do you ask*?"

Jorma exhaled sharply, rubbing his temple. "*It's Becky. She's bad today. Can't get off the toilet. Vomiting nonstop. I don't know, maybe it's just a bug. Probably not from the party, but figured I'd ask.*"

Becky.

Becky was the one.

A slow, cold wave of satisfaction washed over me, but I smothered it beneath a carefully placed frown. I nodded, muttered something vaguely sympathetic, pretended to care.

But inside?

Inside, I was watching the first thread unravel.

And it was beautiful.

THE NEXT DAY THE neighborhood had settled back into its usual rhythm—cars pulling out of driveways, sprinklers hissing over manicured lawns, the distant sound of children playing down the street. It was a picture of normalcy, a lie wrapped in the illusion of suburban peace.

I was at the mailbox, sorting through the usual pile of junk—bills, grocery flyers, an invitation to some pointless neighborhood event—when I heard the distinct click of heels against pavement.

Linda.

The gossip queen of the neighborhood, always orbiting where she didn't belong, her little dog trotting at her side as if he, too, had stories to tell.

"*Hey*," she called out, her voice dripping with the kind of excitement that only comes from bad news. "*Have you heard about Becky*?"

I wanted to say yes, I'm the one that fucking did it to her.

I wanted to say of course I've heard—I've been waiting for this moment.

But I didn't.

Instead, I glanced up from my mail, forced my brow to crease just enough, and asked with a feigned curiosity, "*No, what now*?"

Linda practically *vibrated* with the thrill of information. She lived for moments like these—when she could be the first to deliver news, to watch reactions, to feel important in a way she never really was.

"*She's in the hospital,*" she said, lowering her voice as if we were sharing something sacred. "*I ran into Jorma last night—he was taking her in. They think she has liver failure.*" She let the words settle, gauging my reaction.

I gave her nothing.

She pressed on, eager now. "*Weird, right? I mean, sure, she drank a lot, but other than that, I thought she was pretty healthy.*"

Her words barely registered. My mind had already pulled away, working through the details, the science, the slow collapse happening inside Becky's body.

Her organs were shutting down. One by one, systems refusing to function. The liver first—predictable, given the toxins it was forced to filter. Next, the kidneys and spleen, a chain reaction leading to systemic failure. And then? *Then it would be over.*

If they didn't find the cause soon—and they wouldn't—death would come in a matter of a day, two at most.

Linda was still looking at me, expecting something. Sympathy, concern, maybe even a bit of shock.

I nodded, exhaling just the right amount of breath, a performance of subtle distress. "*No, I hadn't heard.*" I made sure my voice was *measured*, my expression carefully constructed. "*Please give my best to Jorma if you see him. I'll let Denise know so she can send flowers.*"

Linda beamed, pleased to have delivered something worth spreading. She tugged at her dog's leash, already eager to move on to the next house, the next conversation.

As she walked away, I stared at the mail in my hands.

The game was almost over.

And I had won, again.

As I watched Linda walk away, the edges of the mail blurred between my fingers, dissolving into nothing.

And then it came.

The **hunger**.

Not just a whisper, not just a flicker of something dark curling at the edges of my thoughts—but a force, pressing against my ribs, wrapping around my lungs like a second breath.

I had felt it before.

In Minnesota. In Arizona.

Before this. Before Becky.

Back then, the hunger had always retreated after I had satisfied it. A single act. A single moment of execution. And then, relief. A clearing of the mind. A settling of the storm inside me.

But this time?

This time was different.

Stronger. Heavier. Insatiable.

Even before Becky was officially gone, it had already begun to creep back in—not fading, not relenting, but expanding.

The knowledge that her body was shutting down, that I had set it in motion, should have extinguished the embers.

But it didn't.

It did the opposite.

It stoked them. Fed them.

They spread, licking at the edges of my mind, crackling, growing hotter, brighter, hungrier.

And for the first time, I understood something I hadn't before.

The hunger wasn't just for the act.

It wasn't just for the kill.

It wasn't even about the power—though that, too, was intoxicating. No

—this was more.

Something deeper. Something primal.

I exhaled slowly, steadying my pulse, my mind a tangle of thoughts I had once toyed with, entertained in the quiet hours of the night—only to push them away, dismiss them as fleeting curiosities.

But this?

This wasn't curiosity anymore.

This was inevitable.

I turned from the street, stepping back into the house, closing the door behind me with a soft, controlled click.

The hunger followed me inside.

And I knew then—it wouldn't stop.

Not now.

Not ever.

THE AIR INSIDE THE CHURCH was thick—grief, perfume, lilies and polished wood, all pressing down like a weight.

I sat among them, motionless, watching. The rituals played out as expected—Jorma hollow-eyed at the front, his voice cracking through a eulogy he barely had the strength to finish. Murmurs of sympathy, nods of understanding, the occasional sob muffled into tissues.

It was all so predictable. So easy to disappear into.

And then, I saw him.

A man in the back of the room.

He stood apart from the others, shifting from foot to foot, eyes downcast but restless. Dressed in black, like the rest of us, but something was off. He wasn't like the neighbors, who cried in careful, public displays of sorrow. He wasn't like Jorma's coworkers, who clutched their wives' hands and whispered about how *unfair* it all was.

He was alone. Uncomfortable.

And he didn't belong.

I watched him without watching him. He never approached Jorma, never acknowledged the mourners in the pews. He didn't immediately move when people trickled outside after the service.

While Denise went to pay her respects I walked out into the sharp afternoon sun, I spotted him again—hovering near the parking lot, hands shoved deep into his coat pockets.

I took my time approaching. Not too eager, not too curious. Just casual.

"*Did you know Becky*?" I asked, my voice quiet, careful.

The man turned to me slowly, his face blank—no recognition, no immediate attempt to fill the silence between us. He just studied me, as if weighing something in his head.

For a moment, I thought he wouldn't answer.

Then, finally: "*Yeah.*"

That was it. No elaboration.

I tilted my head slightly. "*From work*?"

A pause. The kind of pause that lasted just long enough to make me suspicious. Then:

"*...No.*"

The answer was too short. Too restrained. His fingers twitched at his sides. His throat bobbed like he was swallowing something down.

And just like that, I knew.

I didn't need him to say it. I didn't need proof.

It was in the tension in his shoulders, in the way he refused to hold eye contact for too long, in the way his jaw tightened when I said her name.

This guy, this was Becky's secret.

And her secret would be a way out should I need it.

If the police ever came knocking—if they ever started asking the wrong questions, digging in places I didn't want them to—I had a theory ready.

A lover. Someone no one knew about. Someone with a reason to hurt her. Someone with more motive than I could ever have.

The perfect red herring.

I gave the man a slow nod, as if I understood something he hadn't said. "*Yeah,*" I murmured, exhaling softly. "*She was something else.*"

He hesitated, shifting on his feet. Then, without another word, he turned and walked off.

I watched him go, my mind already piecing together the story I would tell, if I ever needed to.

A secret affair. A scorned lover. An unfortunate ending.

And just like that, Becky gave me one last gift.

An alibi.

AFTER THE FUNERAL, the four of us—Denise, Brian, Hailey, and I—gathered back at our house. The night had a strange stillness to it, the weight of the day pressing down like a thick fog. Funerals had a way of doing that—sucking the air out of a room, leaving behind something empty and uneasy.

Denise poured a bottle of wine, and for a while, we talked about anything *but* Becky. Small things. Meaningless things. The wine helped loosen the tension, but there was something beneath it, something unspoken hanging between us.

I hadn't told Denise about the stranger. Not yet. Not until I had a better read on it myself.

But by the time we opened the second bottle, I let it slip.

I closed my eyes, exhaled, and before I could second-guess it, the words were out.

"*Hey, I don't want to speak ill of the dead, but... I have a question. Did any of you know if Becky was having an affair*?"

The moment the question left my mouth, I felt the air shift.

Brian and Hailey exchanged a glance—not one of surprise, but of quiet confirmation. The kind of look people give each other when they've already had this conversation before.

Hailey dropped her gaze, studying her wine glass like it held the answer to something deeper. Brian, on the other hand, sighed, running a hand through his hair before looking me straight in the eye.

"*What makes you ask*?" he said.

I shrugged, keeping my voice casual. "*Nothing specific. I just noticed a guy at the funeral. Didn't recognize him from the neighborhood, and he stood out to me*."

Brian held my gaze for a beat longer, then nodded, as if that answer made perfect sense.

I felt Denise stiffen beside me.

Neither of us spoke at first. Not because Becky had been unfaithful —people cheat, marriages fall apart, secrets exist. It wasn't that.

It was the fact that we hadn't known.

That the neighborhood—the same people who gathered on warm evenings for barbecues, who smiled and waved on morning walks, who stood around in driveways chatting like we all understood each other—had been keeping this unspoken truth just beneath the surface.

And we had been completely blind to it.

Denise finally spoke, her voice softer than usual. "*How long*?"

Brian shrugged. "*A while. Maybe a year? Maybe longer.*"

I stared at him, processing. My mind reeled, piecing together the past with this new information, finding gaps, filling in the blanks.

Had Becky's lover been at the funeral today? Had he been in the back of the church, lurking just out of reach? Had I spoken to him without even realizing what he truly was?

I swirled the wine in my glass, watching the dark liquid cling to the edges.

The night stretched on, conversation moving in and out of Becky, of Jorma, of the strange and tangled lives people lived beneath the surface.

But in the back of my mind, something sat there, cold and unmoving. A thought. A realization. An opportunity.

If Jorma had known about the affair, then I had another out, a better one.

If the police ever questioned me—if anyone ever suspected foul play —there was already a much cleaner, much more believable narrative just waiting to be told.

A scorned husband. A marriage built on lies. A slow-burning resentment that finally snapped.

Jorma was the perfect suspect.

And if it ever came down to it?

I would make sure he took the fall

Chapter 13

THE KNOCK

IT DIDN'T TAKE LONG for things to get back to normal in the neighborhood.

If you could even call it that.

The morning dog walkers still strolled the sidewalks, their leashes taut, eyes forward, offering tight-lipped nods to passing neighbors. Lawn mowers hummed every weekend like clockwork, kids rode their bikes up and down the street, and porch lights still flickered on at dusk.

Becky's passing? Not even a topic of discussion.

The usual gossipers had moved on, their curiosity snuffed out quicker than a dying flame. No murmurs in hushed tones at the grocery store. No speculative glances at our house. It was as if she had never existed.

That was the thing about people. Their lives kept moving forward, even when someone else's had come to a sudden, violent stop.

It had been exactly two weeks since the party when it happened.

The knock.

Sharp. Hard. Deliberate.

I froze mid-step. The rhythmic tapping of the baby's swing metronome in the background, an eerie contrast to the silence that stretched through the house. But Denise wasn't home—she was out running errands with the baby. She must have forgotten to turn it off before she left.

That thought quickly left me.

I exhaled, shaking off the tight coil of dread in my gut. It's fine.

Then I passed the front window.

Two police cars in the driveway.

One more parked just beyond the mailbox.

A cold bolt of adrenaline shot through me, spreading like ice in my veins. Too many. This wasn't a casual follow-up. This wasn't some officer making rounds, asking generic questions.

I felt my heartbeat in my throat, a steady thump-thump-thump that almost matched the knock still echoing in my ears.

Check mode.

My mind raced through everything at once, flipping through details like a frantic stack of flashcards:

- The shopping—nothing suspicious.

- Any online activity—clean. Nothing tied to me.

- The cleanup—perfect. No loose ends.

- The last two weeks—played it normal. Calm. Forgettable.

There was no way this could be traced back to me. No way.

So why did it feel like it was?

A bead of sweat slid down my back as I forced my feet forward. My hand hovered over the doorknob for half a second too long before I curled my fingers around the cool metal.

Breathe.

I turned the knob and pulled the door open.

Two officers.

And a detective.

Standing there, staring at me like they already knew.

Like they had been waiting.

The two officers looked to be in their early thirties, their uniforms crisp and perfectly pressed. They stood slightly behind the detective, positioned just enough to suggest protection—or intimidation.

The detective, however, was different. She was composed, confident. Sharp. A woman in her forties, striking in a way that made her presence even more commanding. Dressed with an almost effortless professionalism, she didn't fit the usual image of someone working out of a beachside precinct.

Her eyes locked onto mine the moment I opened the door.

"Eric Sutton?"

Her voice was calm but carried the weight of expectation.

I swallowed, keeping my expression neutral. *"Yes."*

"We'd like to ask you a few questions. May we come in?"

I hesitated—just for a second—then glanced across the street.

Linda. Walking her dog. Of course. She slowed her pace just slightly, the telltale sign of someone pretending not to eavesdrop. Perfect. This would be the next piece of gossip spreading through the neighborhood like wildfire.

I turned back to the detective, forcing a casual nod. *"Yes, by all means, come in."*

I led them to the front room. It felt smaller with them inside, like the walls were pressing in ever so slightly. I offered them something to drink, but Detective Foss—the woman in charge, clearly—declined with a polite but firm shake of her head.

"We don't have that much time, thank you."

Her words should have put me at ease. If they didn't have time for a drink, they wouldn't be staying long. And if they weren't staying long, this wasn't an investigation into a murder.

At least, that's what I told myself.

She pulled out a small notebook and flipped it open with practiced ease, her pen already poised. Her gaze flicked to me.

"Is Denise home?"

"No," I said smoothly. *"She's out running errands. Should be back in about an hour."*

Detective Foss nodded, making a note before glancing at the officers beside her. Then, her attention returned to me.

"My name is Detective Foss. This is Sergeant Council and Staff Sergeant Sullivan."

I gave a slight nod, acknowledging them but keeping my focus on her.

Then, the question.

"Did you host a Halloween party on October 30th?"

The air in the room seemed to shift, an almost imperceptible drop in temperature.

"Yes," I answered, keeping my tone even. *"We do one every year. Is there a problem?"*

She didn't answer. She didn't even react. Instead, she simply moved to the next question, as if my response was expected, irrelevant even.

"Did you supply all of the food and drinks at this party?"

There it was.

Becky.

They were here for her. I knew it now.

I forced a casual shrug, as if the question didn't send a flicker of unease down my spine. *"Well, yes and no,"* I said carefully. *"I purchased all the drinks, but we hired two bartenders to serve them. As for the food, I provided most of it, but a number of guests brought side dishes and desserts. We just put them out for everyone."*

She jotted something down, her face unreadable.

Then she lifted her eyes again, studying me in a way that made my skin crawl.

"Did any guests mention feeling sick the next day?"

I exhaled, forcing a smirk to ease the tension.

"No—unless you count the hangovers," I said, offering a small chuckle. *"There was a lot of alcohol served."*

She didn't smile.

Didn't blink.

Just kept writing.

And for the first time since they walked in, I felt it—a subtle, creeping sense of unease.

They weren't here on a fishing expedition.

They already knew something.

And they were waiting to see if I'd slip.

Detective Foss fired off her next question without so much as glancing up from her notepad.

"I'm going to need the contact information for the bartenders and a list of anyone who may have brought food to the party."

I nodded smoothly. *"Of course. My wife, Denise, can get all of that for you."*

I tried one last time to get a read on them. To see through them.

"Is there a problem?" I asked again, keeping my tone measured, though I could feel the weight pressing down on my chest.

Detective Foss studied me for a moment before answering.

Her voice was even, calculated.

"We're investigating the homicide of your neighbor, Becky Forester."

The words landed like a physical blow.

Homicide?

Not liver failure. Homicide?

I barely registered the way my breath hitched—too sharp, too telling. But I couldn't stop it, couldn't control the slight widening of my eyes or the way my grip on the armrest tightened ever so slightly.

"Oh," I managed, forcing the word out. *"We just... we just attended the funeral. I—"* I swallowed, shifting in my seat. *"We were told it was liver failure. No?"*

Foss didn't flinch. Didn't blink.

"I'm not at liberty to discuss the details of an ongoing investigation," she said smoothly, her tone cool and practiced, *"but the autopsy suggests she was poisoned."*

Poisoned? Autopsy?

The room felt suddenly smaller, the air thick, heavy.

I kept my gaze on the wall behind them, locking onto an imperfection in the paint. I didn't trust myself to look at them, not yet. Every nerve in my body screamed at me to stay still, to control the instinctive reaction curling in my gut.

Poisoned.

A long silence stretched between us, only broken when Foss and the officers moved—all three of them standing at once. A quiet, deliberate signal that the conversation was over.

I followed, forcing my body to move, to keep up.

Walking them to the door felt surreal, like I was moving through mud, each step slow and deliberate. And yet, I could feel it—their eyes on me, watching, assessing. They weren't just leaving. They were measuring me, weighing every twitch, every breath, every flicker of emotion I failed to suppress.

Shock.

Guilt.

Confusion.

I tried to balance them all. Just enough of each to appear convincingly blindsided.

Then, just as I reached for the door, Foss turned back to me.

Her expression remained unreadable, but something about the way she paused, the way she tilted her head just slightly, sent a ripple of unease through me.

"Would you be open to a search of your home and property?" she asked, voice casual—too casual. *"I'm happy to get a warrant, but I thought I'd ask first. Save us all a lot of time and effort."*

Everything inside me went still.

For the first time since they arrived, I saw Foss differently. Not as an attractive woman who happened to be a detective, but as a hunter. A predator. A relentless investigator who was prepared to follow every lead, every shred of suspicion—to me.

I caught my breath, forcing myself to look at her without hesitation.

If I said no, they'd come back—with more questions, with a warrant, with even more suspicion.

If I said yes… I was opening myself up to scrutiny, exposure, risk.

A ridiculous decision from a legal standpoint. I knew that.

But I also knew something else.

I had been thorough. Meticulous. There was nothing in this house, nothing that could tie me to Becky, nothing they could find.

And on the off chance there was something?

They wouldn't be able to trace it back to me.

I exhaled slowly, let my lips curve into a small, cooperative smile, and met Foss's eyes with something that I hoped looked like sincerity.

"Of course," I said. *"No need for a warrant. If we can help in any way, by all means—search the home."*

A flicker of something passed through Foss's expression. Mild surprise? Amusement? Distrust?

It was gone too fast to read.

She nodded once.

"Appreciate it. we'll be in touch"

Chapter 14

UNDER WATCHFUL EYES

GRABBING THE MAIL on Wednesday, I caught movement out of the corner of my eye—Brian.

He was pedaling down the street toward me, effortlessly weaving between parked cars, his usual boyish energy on full display.

"Dude! Hailey's working late—let's grab a drink!" he called, skidding to a stop just before my driveway.

I exhaled through my nose, letting a slow smirk tug at my lips. Brian's presence was exactly what I needed. Loud. Distracting. Effortless.

Besides, with Becky out of the picture, so too were my annoyances with the neighborhood.

Her sacrifice had been a pardon for everyone else—at least for now.

"Sure," I said, tucking the mail under my arm. *"I have a few new bottles of wine to try."*

He grinned. *"Wine? Fancy. Let's do it."*

We headed to the back patio, Brian plopping down into a chair with the relaxed sprawl of someone who had never had to second-guess anything in his life. Meanwhile, inside, I could hear Denise in the kitchen, feeding Chiara. The clink of a spoon against a bowl, soft murmurs, the occasional baby giggle.

It was all so normal.

And then Brian broke the illusion.

"So, what's new? I heard you had a visit from the police," he said, laughing as he swirled his glass.

The words were so casual, so effortless, but they landed like a rock in my stomach.

I looked at him, my expression unreadable. *"Who'd you hear that from?"*

He snorted. *"Who do you think? Linda."*

Of course.

Brian rolled his eyes, lifting his glass in a mock toast. *"Don't sweat it, man. They came to everyone's place. It's not just you."*

"Oh yeah?" I said, keeping my tone neutral.

"Yeah. What'd you think of Detective Foss?" He gave me a knowing look. *"Smoking, right?"*

Brian had a way of doing this. He was the kind of guy who always pointed out the *pretty women* in a crowd, testing the room, gauging reactions. It was juvenile—like something from a frat party or a bad high school habit he never grew out of—but because it was Brian, it was expected.

Even the wives barely batted an eye anymore.

"Yeah," I said, shrugging. *"She was cute."*

But in my mind, I saw Foss differently now.

Not an attractive woman. A threat.

Brian took another sip, then leaned back with an easy grin. *"So when's your search?"*

My grip tightened on my glass, though I forced myself to keep my expression neutral.

"Search?"

"Yeah, they're searching our place Monday."

A slow, creeping tension curled in my gut.

"Wait. They're searching your house?" I asked carefully.

Brian laughed. *"Yeah. Anyone who brought food to the party is getting searched. They wanna make sure no one slipped something into the food, I guess."*

My mind reeled. This was new information.

"What'd you tell them you brought?" I asked.

He grinned, taking another sip of wine. *"Told them I brought my killer ribs—but they didn't think it was funny."*

I didn't laugh.

"Yeah, I can't imagine they would."

Just then, the sliding door opened. Denise stepped out, cradling a glass of wine, her eyes flicking between us. She sat beside me, crossing her legs under her, completely unbothered.

She and I had already gone over the police visit. We knew they'd be back.

Brian kept talking, completely unaware of the weight pressing down on me.

"I'm not sure when they'll get to our place, but I'm guessing they'll hit all the houses the same day," I said.

He nodded absently, while my mind was running through everything again.

The cleanup? Flawless.

The supplies? All disposed of properly.

The party? No lingering traces.

I had gone over it a thousand times, and yet, I did it again.

As Brian rambled about work and Denise chimed in, I kept checking, reviewing, confirming.

And when Brian finally headed home, and Denise and I started preparing dinner, I felt it—a calm certainty settling over me.

I was clean.

There was nothing for them to find.

But the real question wasn't what they would find.

It was what they already suspected.

BY MONDAY MORNING, the neighborhood was unrecognizable.

A once a quiet, predictable place where people kept to themselves, it had become a spectacle—a three-ring circus of police cars, unmarked investigation vehicles, and a growing crowd of onlookers.

The news had caught wind of the searches.

Neighbors who normally wouldn't have stepped outside without a purpose were now standing in driveways, lingering at mailboxes, pretending to do yard work. Others leaned over fences, whispering behind coffee cups, watching.

Everyone wanted to see something—to be part of the story without being in the spotlight.

And, of course, Linda was out front, front-row seat, coffee in hand, soaking it all in like the nosy parasite she was.

I watched her from the window as I sipped my own coffee, my stomach a cold knot of tension.

1:30 P.M..

The knock came. Sharp. Hard. Purposeful.

Right on time.

I took a slow breath, placed my mug down, and made my way to the door.

I already knew what to expect, but seeing them there—Detective Foss and the two officers standing in formation on my porch—sent an involuntary spike of fear through me.

Foss was in the center, unwavering, unreadable, while the other two flanked her.

They didn't come here hoping to find something.

They came expecting to.

"Eric Sutton?" Foss's voice was even, devoid of anything that could be considered warmth.

"Detective Foss," I greeted with a polite nod.

"We appreciate your cooperation," she said. It was a statement, not gratitude.

I stepped aside. *"Of course. Come in."*

The second they crossed the threshold, Foss nodded to her officers.

And just like that—the search began.

I stepped back just enough to give them space but stayed close enough to observe them.

I kept my posture loose, my expression carefully arranged into something that looked like mild concern—not fear, not defensiveness. Just a reasonable man letting the police do their job.

Foss didn't move right away.

She stood just inside the doorway, hands clasped loosely in front of her, eyes tracking every detail.

She wasn't looking for physical evidence yet. She was reading the room. Reading me.

The two uniformed officers, Sargent Council and Staff Sargent Sullivan, took different routes.

Sullivan surveyed the living room first. He ran his eyes across the bookshelves, the side tables, the mantle. He didn't touch anything yet—just looked, taking in the layout, the décor, the atmosphere. Looking for something out of place.

Council, meanwhile, went straight for the kitchen, moving with the kind of silent efficiency that only came from experience.

I remained in the front room, body loose, expression neutral—but my senses stretched toward every sound coming from the kitchen. The soft clink of glass bottles shifting in the fridge. The dry whisper of paper as he sifted through the stack of unopened mail on the counter. Nothing too deep yet—nothing invasive.

But it was coming.

A faint *zip* as he unsealed a bag of swabs.

I didn't have to see him to know what he was doing—I could picture it perfectly. The slow, deliberate swipe across the countertops, the careful press of a cotton swab against the grooves of the dishwasher handle. The metallic clatter as he checked the inside of the sink, then leaned lower—running another swab along the rim of the garbage disposal, down into the unseen depths where traces of the past might still cling.

I exhaled slowly, pressing my thumb into the palm of my hand—a grounding trick, a reminder that I had been thorough.

Then came the shift—the barely perceptible change in air as Council moved again. The creak of a cabinet. The snap of a glove being adjusted. A pause. Then the faint squeak of the door to the garage door swinging open.

Of course.

I didn't follow him, didn't move, but I could see it in my mind—the way he would scan the space first, eyes sweeping over tools, storage bins, shelves. Then, the methodical repetition of it all—more swabs, more silent cataloging of spaces that had long since been scrubbed clean.

I let my gaze flick to Foss, still seated, still watching.

She hadn't said a word in a while, but I could feel her eyes on me.

Waiting. Measuring.

I met her stare evenly, offering a polite, almost amused look. "*Thorough, aren't they?*"

Foss didn't blink. Didn't smile.

She just kept watching.

Foss finally moved, her gaze landing on me as if she'd been watching my reaction this entire time.

"Do you mind showing me the rest of the house?"

It wasn't a request.

"Of course," I said, my voice smooth. *"Right this way."*

I led her down the hallway, stepping aside at each room like she belonged there.

The master bedroom. The guest room. The nursery.

She barely glanced at the crib, moving with precision, eyes sweeping over every surface, every detail.

She wasn't looking for obvious things—she was reading the gaps. The missing links.

I kept my breathing steady, my steps slow and measured.

I had nothing to hide.

But I still felt hunted.

Finally, after what felt like an eternity, Sullivan and Council returned.

"We're done, nothing," Sullivan said simply.

Foss didn't react. Not outwardly.

But I saw it—the smallest flicker in her eyes. A calculation.

She had expected this.

Of course, she had.

After all, whoever had killed Becky Forester wouldn't be dumb enough to leave evidence sitting around their home.

Foss turned back to me, her gaze lingering half a second too long.

Then, she nodded. *"Alright. Thank you for your cooperation."*

I exhaled the perfect blend of relief and concern. *"I hope this helps. Anything we can do to assist, of course."*

Foss held my gaze for half a beat longer before stepping past me toward the front door.

"We'll be in touch."

And then, just like that, they were gone.

The door shut with a quiet click.

I stood motionless, listening to the sound of car doors opening and closing, the engines put into gear, and tires rolling down to the next home.

Then—silence. I

had been right.

They found nothing.

Because there was nothing to find.

And yet—deep in my gut, something twisted.

Because while they may have left empty-handed, Foss wasn't finished, no.

I'm thinking she had just begun.

I TURNED FROM THE door, my breath still steady, my hands loose at my sides, my face—neutral.

Denise stood at the entrance to the hallway, watching me.

She hadn't spoken a word the entire time the police were here.

She didn't ask questions now, either.

She just stood there, holding Chiara against her hip, the baby's small fingers tangled in her sweater.

Her expression was unreadable, but I knew her tells as well as she knew mine.

"*Well,*" I said lightly, breaking the silence that had settled between us. "*That was painless.*"

Denise didn't respond. She stood near the window, her grip on Chiara loose but instinctive, as if holding onto her kept her rooted in the moment.

Her gaze flickered toward the street, where the last of the police cars had disappeared beyond the curve of the road. A normal person might have sighed in relief, might have made some offhanded remark about how ridiculous the whole thing was.

But Denise wasn't a normal person.

Finally, she spoke.

"*They didn't ask about a gun.*"

Her voice was soft. Measured. But the weight behind the words was unmistakable.

A test.

I stayed perfectly still. Kept my expression neutral, controlled. But something inside me shifted, tightening like a knot in my chest.

"Because there was no reason to," I said smoothly, my voice even, deliberate.

Denise turned her head just slightly, eyes locking onto mine. She held my gaze for a second —long enough to make me wonder if she already knew more than she was letting on.

Then, without another word, she nodded. Adjusted Chiara against her hip. Turned, and disappeared down the hallway.

I let out a slow breath, steadying the rhythm of my pulse. I should have felt relief.

Instead, I felt something else.

Something cold.

Something unsettling.

Not being watched by Foss.

But now being watched by Denise.

And that was far more dangerous.

Chapter 15

CERTAINTY WITHOUT PROOF

IT HAD BEEN TWO WEEKS since Detective Foss had visited Eric and Denise. This morning, she sat in her unmarked car just two blocks down from the Suttons' house, engine off, coffee long since gone cold in the cupholder. The morning air outside had the filtered hush of suburbia—neatly trimmed lawns, sprinklers ticking away, a jogger passing by with their AirPods and oblivious. Foss watched the quiet street like it might betray a secret if she stared long enough.

She'd already been told to let it go.

No solid evidence. No motive that held water. But something about Eric Sutton lingered in her brain like a splinter under skin—subtle, irritating, impossible to ignore.

It wasn't what he said—his answers were polished, perfectly inflected, not a word out of place. No, it was the way he listened. Too carefully. Most people—grieving neighbors, distressed spouses—tripped over themselves trying to be helpful. Sutton didn't. He observed. Calculated. Like he was silently conducting an interview of his own.

Foss flipped through her notebook for the third time that week, pages soft from use, ink smudged in the margins. She stared at Becky Forester's photo, the candid one from the Halloween party. A blur of motion, smile half-cocked, plastic cup in hand.

It hadn't been random.
It hadn't been emotional.
It felt like Becky had been selected.

Foss exhaled slowly and let the photo drop to her lap.

Jorma Forester had motive. That part was straightforward now.

The affair was confirmed—text messages, late-night calls, a single hotel charge on Becky's credit card just ten days before the party. Foss hadn't told Jorma yet. She wanted to watch his face when she did. He had the motive. He had the temper. And he was unaccounted for during a crucial thirty-minute window that night—long enough to spike a drink. He claimed he went outside for air. No one saw him leave. No one saw him return.

It fit.
Too easily.

And still...

Eric Sutton.

There was something about him that clung to her thoughts. That unnerving calm. The way his eyes never flicked too far in either direction. During questioning, he'd been gracious. Polite. Almost... soothing. Said he barely knew Becky—just a neighbor, someone from the occasional BBQ.

But in her notes, there it was again:
"*She had more than her fair share to drink that night, huh?*"

It wasn't concern.

It was judgment.
Clinical.... Studied.

Like he'd been watching her.
Like he'd been waiting.

Now the ME's report was confirmed. Foss had read it three times, each pass tightening the knot in her gut.

Ricin.

Not something you find in a medicine cabinet. Not something you stumble across. Ricin had to be extracted, refined, carefully administered. It was invisible until it was too late. And once ingested, there was no undoing it.

She closed the file slowly and stared through the windshield at the Suttons' pristine home. The breeze rustled the palm fronds overhead. A new white bike leaned neatly against the garage. Perfect.

Ricin wasn't a weapon of passion.
It was a tool of control.
Clean. Quiet. Calculated.

Jorma had plenty of reasons to want Becky gone. But he didn't seem disciplined enough to do it this way.

Eric, though?

He struck her as the kind of man who scrubbed his search history. Who wore gloves in his own garage. Who could slip poison into a party drink and smile through a conversation while the woman across from him died in stages.

Foss flipped to a clean page in her notebook and wrote one word:

Premeditated.

Below it, she listed two names:

Jorma.
Eric.

This time, she circled the second one. Hard.

SHE SAW HIM BEFORE she heard him.

The Suttons' garage door rumbled open, slow and mechanical, like the opening note of a well-rehearsed performance. The silver SUV backed down the driveway and paused at the curb—just long enough to make her wonder if he saw her—then turned the corner and disappeared.

Eric was gone.

Foss waited until the tail-lights vanished, then quietly opened her door.

No partner. No clipboard. No badge showing.

Just Foss, in a gray sweater and black jeans, walking up the Suttons' front walk with the steady certainty that sometimes the truth didn't knock politely. Sometimes it let itself in.

She rang the doorbell.

Denise answered, apron still tied around her waist, hair swept back, a fine dusting of flour on her sleeves.

"*Detective Foss... I wasn't expecting—*"

"*I know,*" Foss said gently. "*Just a few follow-ups on Becky's case. Timeline stuff. Do you have a moment?*"

There was a hesitation. A flicker of something behind Denise's eyes. But then the door opened wider.

"*Sure. Chiara's at daycare. I was baking.*"

The Sutton home still looked airbrushed for a real estate catalog. Too clean. Too curated. Foss wondered whether that was Denise... or Eric.

In the kitchen, Denise offered coffee. Foss declined. She set her phone—recording, silent—on the counter, and opened her notebook like it was just another routine check-in.

"*I wanted to go over the Halloween party again,*" she said. "I*t was a big night. Lots of people. Easy to miss small things*."

Denise nodded, folding her arms.

"*You said you and Eric were hosting most of the night?*"

"*That's right.*"

"*And Becky? How long was she here?*"

"*A couple hours, maybe? She bounced around. She and Jorma had that little argument by the fence, she may have left after that.*"

"*Did Eric talk to her?*"

"*I don't know. Maybe? I wasn't keeping track.*"

Foss scribbled something meaningless, then looked up.

"*He told me she seemed pretty drunk that night.*"

Denise blinked. "*He said that?*"

"*Mmhmm.*"

Denise glanced toward the sink, thoughtful. "*She had a few drinks, sure. But I don't remember her being sloppy.*"

"*Neither does anyone else,*" Foss said.

A silence settled. Not heavy, but tense.

Denise shifted her weight.

"*Did something new come up?*"

Foss smiled—warm, polite, unreadable. "*Just revisiting a few details. Covering all angles.*"

She let the silence breathe.

Denise looked down, then past Foss, like she was searching for the right response—or debating whether to give one at all.

She opened her mouth, closed it again.

Then, quietly: "*Eric's been... different lately.*"

Foss didn't move.

Denise hesitated, the words forming slowly, like they weren't meant to be spoken out loud.

"*Not bad. Just... distant. Disconnected. Like he's in the room, but not really with us. Like something's always on his mind.*"

Foss made a small note in her head, not on the page.
Emotional distance. Subtle withdrawal. Change in routine.

She'd heard it before—different words, different cases. It was the shape of guilt trying to fold itself into daily life.

She offered nothing back.

"*Did he talk about Becky at all? Outside the party?*"

"*No. Not really.*" A pause. "*He did say something once... that she was messy. That she played too loose with people. I just thought he was being judgmental.*"

Foss nodded, pen moving silently across the page.

Becky didn't threaten Eric with chaos.
She offended him with it.

She closed the notebook gently, then looked up at Denise with that calm, unreadable expression.

"*Thank you,*" she said. "*This helps.*"

As she moved toward the door, Denise asked quietly, "*Do you think Jorma did it?*"

Foss paused, turned back.

"*I think someone planned it. Someone smart. Someone who didn't want to leave a mess.*"

Denise opened the door.

Foss stepped out into the morning light and pulled out her phone.

Digital records. "*Ingredient purchases. Lab access. Anything.*"

She didn't need certainty.

Not yet.

She just needed the cracks to widen.

FOSS STOOD OUTSIDE the judge's chambers, her warrant request clutched in one hand like a fuse she wasn't allowed to light. It was tight, targeted—digital activity only. Search history. Purchase records. IP logs. No surveillance. No taps. Just a crack in the facade.

A window into whatever the hell Eric Sutton had been doing in the weeks before Halloween.

Judge Mallory flipped through the file without urgency, the pages whispering like dry leaves. His mouth was a straight, unimpressed line. Foss had dealt with him before—prickly but fair, a man who weighed everything in ounces of logic. He liked his cases airtight and his paperwork spotless.

This case was neither.

"*You've got no motive,*" he said, barely glancing up. "*No confirmed link between the suspect and the victim outside of neighborhood proximity.*"

"*I've got behavior,*" Foss replied, voice flat. "*Inconsistencies. A pattern of calculated responses. A documented awareness of the victim's condition that no one else mentioned.*"

Mallory didn't look up. "*That's not probable cause.*"

Foss leaned in. "*The toxin was ricin.*"

That got his attention. A flicker in the eyes.

"*That's not just rare,*" she added. "*It's engineered. Whoever used it didn't act on impulse. They planned. You don't stumble into ricin. You don't panic and poison someone with it. You research it. You build it.*"

Mallory exhaled slowly, then said, "*So go after the husband. Motive's there. Timeline's messy. They had a public history.*"

"*I am,*" Foss said. "*But I'm also looking at the man who was obsessed with Becky that night. Who noted her alcohol intake. Who had the temperament to use a silent, undetectable poison and make small talk while she died by the glass.*"

He raised a brow. "*You're asking me to sign off on a warrant based on a feeling.*"

Foss's jaw tensed. "I*t's not a feeling. It's a pattern. He's too polished. Too measured. It reads like a man who's done this before.*"

Mallory closed the file and handed it back.

"*When you've got something that holds up in court, bring it to me. Until then—*"

He didn't finish. Just turned back to his monitor.

Dismissed.

Foss lingered a moment, said nothing, then turned and walked out with the file still in hand. It felt heavier than when she walked in.

SHE DIDN'T RETURN TO the precinct. Instead, she slid into her car and sat in silence, watching the rain gather in tiny rivers along the windshield. The wipers moved sluggishly across the glass. A damp kind of stillness settled in the vehicle.

If she couldn't get in through the front door legally… she'd have to find a side window.

She started with the Langleys. The neighbors just down the street from Eric and Denise.

Retired. Friendly. Predictably bored. They welcomed her in with smiles and the smell of fresh baked cookies.

"*Oh, that Halloween party was such a lovely time,*" Mrs. Langley said, her voice light as she poured tea. "T*he Suttons really go all out. Eric made the mulled wine—it was to die for.*"

Foss smiled politely. "*You spoke with him that night?*"

"*Oh yes. He helped us with the chairs when it started to drizzle. Such a gentleman.*"

Foss jotted down the answer, her pen silent on the page.

"*And Becky Forester?*"

Mrs. Langley's smile dimmed, just slightly.

"*She was... complicated. Not rude, exactly. But never warm. She always needed something. Borrowed our leaf blower last spring and never brought it back.*"

Foss nodded, collected her napkin-wrapped cookies, and moved on.

Across the street, the Bensons gave her more of the same. Young couple, baby toys on the floor, golden retriever curled at the foot of the couch.

Eric? "*Salt of the earth.*" Denise? "*Absolute rockstar. PTA president. Organizes everything.*" Becky? "*Bit of a flirt. Honestly? She thought she was too good for the rest of us.*"

"*She always needed something,*" Mr. Benson added. "*Used Denise for babysitting and never once offered to return the favor. People noticed.*"

"*Did you see her argue with anyone that night?*" Foss asked.

He shrugged. "*She and Jorma had a moment by the fence. But nothing out of the ordinary.* "

Foss nodded, pen barely moving. She went to four more houses after that. Same script. Different voices.

When she finally slid back into her car, her notebook read less like an investigation and more like a neighborhood resume for the Suttons.

Eric fixed sprinklers. Eric gave Christmas gifts. Denise brought homemade chicken noodle soup to anyone with the flu.

Becky? Took advantage. Rubbed people the wrong way. Didn't belong.

Foss closed her notebook and leaned forward, resting her forehead against the steering wheel. Her breath fogged the inside of the windshield.

It wasn't just that no one suspected Eric. It was that everyone had already decided Becky was the kind of woman bad things happened to.

The entire block had rallied to defend the Suttons—and the worst part? Eric hadn't asked them to. He didn't need to. He had built the kind of life that defended itself.

She sat there a while longer, the rain now only a whisper.

Then, slowly, she flipped to a fresh page in her notebook and wrote:

No one suspects him. Which is exactly why I do.

FOSS SAT STIFFLY IN front of Captain Morales's desk, her back straight, her hands resting on the case file she'd fought too long to keep open. Across from her, Morales flipped it shut with the kind of finality that didn't need words. The heavy folder thudded gently against the desk—quiet, but absolute.

"*That's it,*" he said. "*DA won't move forward. Not with what we've got. The tox report's vague. Timeline's soft. Sutton's record is spotless —no priors, no red flags, not even a parking ticket. No motive. No weapon. No witnesses.*"

Foss didn't flinch. "*I don't need motive,*" she said evenly. "*I need opportunity and access. He had both.*"

Morales leaned back in his chair, arms folding across his chest with the weariness of a man who'd had this argument before.

"*Then you should have brought me something real. Physical evidence. A traceable order. A receipt. Hell, I'd take a fingerprint on a wine glass. But right now?*" He tapped the closed file like it annoyed him just to look at it. "*You've got posture and tone. Body language. Vibes. That doesn't make a case.*"

"*It's not a hunch,*" Foss said, voice like ice. "*It's pattern recognition. He fits.*"

"*He fits a dozen dads in Sarasota,*" Morales fired back. "*PTA volunteer. Soccer coach. Charms the neighbors, mows his damn lawn every Saturday. You really want to walk that into court? Watch the DA fumble it on day one because the guy owns a spice rack and smiles too politely?*"

Foss clenched her jaw. Her pulse thudded in her neck, slow and deliberate.

"*You want the real answer?*" Morales continued, softer now but firmer. "*Close the case.*"

She didn't move.

"*Or,*" he added, tone sharpening, "*find another unit. Because if you push this past today, you're not doing it from my department.*"

Silence filled the room like static. The low hum of a printer echoed from the hallway, a mundane soundtrack to the moment her case died.

Foss stared at the folder a second longer. Then she stood, slow and measured.

"*We're not closing it,*" she said.

Morales didn't blink. "*We're not continuing with it either, not with what we've got*"

And that was that.

She picked up the file—not as a tool, but as a reminder—and walked out without another word.

She didn't drive home, but decided to drive down by the pier.

She sat behind the wheel of her cruiser in the marina parking lot, the soft shush of ocean wind pressing against the windows, the briny scent of salt and diesel in the air.

She pulled out her phone, thumb hovering over the screen for just a moment before typing:

If you're free, I'd like five minutes. Public place. No badge. Just a conversation.

She hit send.

The message sat there, unsent for less than a breath—and then it was gone.

Foss leaned back against the headrest, eyes fixed on the drizzle trailing down the windshield. A slow minute passed. Then another.

She had just started to wonder if he'd ignore her.

And then the reply came.

THEY MET AT A COFFEE shop by the docks—weathered wood siding, gulls drifting overhead, the sea breeze lifting the corner of the awning like a whisper. It was midday. Casual foot traffic. Bright light. Neutral ground.

Eric arrived alone.

Blue polo. Aviators. The kind of wardrobe that whispered trust. He looked like the cover of a lifestyle magazine—handsome, composed, designed to be forgettable.

Foss was already there. No badge. No notebook. Just a black coffee and the quiet weight of knowing.

"*Appreciate you meeting,*" she said as he slid into the chair across from her.

He smiled like he'd just been asked to sponsor a bake sale. "*Always happy to help law enforcement.*"

She nodded, leaned in just enough to close the space between casual and deliberate.

"*I was told to close the case on you.*"

He didn't blink.

"*Too many missing pieces. Too many clean hands. No one wants to gamble on a trial that might fall apart before opening arguments.*"

He sat still, pleasant, unreadable.

"*But here's the thing,*" she said. "*I'm not done. Not really.*"

She let it sit.

"*There are always loose ends. Tiny details people forget to account for. And I'm going to keep looking for them.*"

Now she met his eyes fully, nothing coy or performative in her gaze.

"*I know you had something to do with Becky's death.*"

A long pause. The smile didn't disappear, but it hardened. Like a painting drying into permanence.

"*I don't know how you got the ricin. I don't know where you made it. But I know it wasn't Jorma. It wasn't an accident. And it sure as hell wasn't random.*"

Eric didn't speak right away. His smile lingered, just slightly too long. Not warm. Not amused. Like someone politely tolerating a tedious dinner guest.

"*That's a dangerous allegation to accuse someone without proof.*"

Foss took a sip of her coffee, unshaken.

"*It's not a charge,*" she said quietly. "*It's a courtesy. I want you to know I see you.*"

And then, for the first time, a real smile. No mask. No attempt at charm. Just acknowledgement. One predator to another.

"*That's sweet, Detective.*"

They sat for a beat in the low murmur of espresso machines, ceramic clinks, distant boat horns.

Foss stood first.

"*Enjoy your day, Mr. Sutton.*"

"*I always do.*"

AS DETECTIVE FOSS WALKED out of the coffee shop, I didn't move.

I just sat there, calm, stirring my coffee in slow, measured circles. Watching the swirl fade like smoke.

She'd finally said it. Not with handcuffs. Not in a courtroom. But with certainty.

She knew. Or thought she did.

But knowing and proving?

Two very different things.

She came with no badge. No backup. No warrant. Just instinct. Suspicion. A gut full of conviction and nowhere to put it.

She was told to close the case.
And now she has.

That's the thing about conviction—it breaks quietly.
When no one's looking.

She expected guilt. A crack. A slip.

But I gave her nothing.
Just enough stillness to remind her she'd lost—
And enough calm to make sure she remembered it.
I took a slow sip. Let the bitterness rest on my tongue.

I wasn't lucky.

I was careful. Calculated. Exact.

And Foss?

She wasn't wrong.
She just showed up too late.
But as I watched the door swing shut behind her, something shifted.

She was closer than I'd like.

Closer than was comfortable.

Time to throw her off the trail.

And I already knew exactly where to start.

Every neighborhood had one—the self-appointed historian, collector of whispers, always ready to serve the next rumor with cream and sugar. I just needed give the right nudge.

Not a push.
A suggestion.

Let them connect the dots. Draw the map. Be the one to say it out loud, in the right voice, to the right ears.

By the time Foss came sniffing again, the trail would point straight back to Jorma.

And away from me.

Chapter 16

THE ART OF MISDIRECTION

WHISPERS SLITHERED THROUGH the neighborhood like a slow-moving fog.

At first, they were harmless speculation, passed between neighbors like half-baked theories over coffee and fences. But once the news broke—poison, not an underlying health issue—everything changed.

Everyone was a suspect.

And the party? Ground zero.

Gone were the carefree neighborhood gatherings, The volleyball games and the lazy weekend barbecues where kids ran wild through open backyards. Now, everyone looked at each other with quiet suspicion, sizing up old friends like potential killers.

Denise and I felt it too.

The weight of the stares. The shift in conversations when we walked the neighborhood with Chiara.

I didn't like it.

I had always worked in shadows, letting my obsessions remain mine alone, far removed from my family, my home. But now, they were in the crosshairs.

That wasn't acceptable.

I needed to redirect the whispers, reframe the narrative—make sure that if the neighborhood needed a suspect, it wouldn't be me.

My first instinct was to reach out to Detective Foss. I could tell her about the man I'd seen lingering at the back of the funeral, that cold, heavy stare of his. But that wouldn't work.

He wasn't at the party.
He had no access to my house.
No way to connect him.

No, it had to be one person and one person only.

Jorma.

He was the only logical choice—connected enough to be a believable suspect, but distant enough that no one could tie his downfall back to me.

But I couldn't be the one to plant the idea.

That would be too obvious.

I needed a carrier pigeon—a messenger, someone eager to spread the word but too self-absorbed to question where it came from.

And I knew just the person.

Every day, like clockwork, I retrieved the mail at 3:00 P.M..

And every day, Linda was there.

She took her daily stroll with her yappy little dog, always orbiting where she didn't belong, absorbing bits and pieces of conversations to hoard and redistribute at will.

She was the perfect pawn.

Thursday afternoon, I watched her from the window, waiting. As she made her way down the block, I stepped outside at the perfect moment, timing it so we would meet just as she passed my driveway.

"A lot of excitement in the neighborhood, huh?" I said, casual but baiting.

Linda perked up immediately. That was the hook.

Her eyes lit with familiar hunger—the thrill of being the first to share the next big story.

"Yeah, crazy," she responded, her voice eager, but I could see it—she was waiting.

Waiting for me to offer something first.

I stayed quiet. Letting the silence force her hand.

It didn't take long.

"So... what was the verdict? Anything from the party?" she asked, pretending at casual curiosity but fishing for intel.

I gave her exactly what she wanted.

"Yeah, they came and searched our place. Obviously, nothing was found," I said, letting my voice dip into something contemplative. *"Crazy to think someone would want to poison Becky, though. I mean... what would be the motive?"*

I left the space open—just enough.

And she took it.

Linda's face shifted, excitement flickering behind her eyes. She had a theory. She just needed someone to give her permission to say it out loud.

"Well," she said, leaning in slightly. *"I can only think of one person who'd want to hurt Becky."*

I barely held back my smirk.

I tilted my head, playing along. *"Really?"*

She paused dramatically, glancing up and down the street before lowering her voice like she was about to unveil a state secret.

"Jorma."

There it was.

Inside, I was laughing, but outside? I gave her shock, intrigue, disbelief—just enough to fan the flames.

"Jorma?" I repeated, furrowing my brow. *"But... why?"*

She nodded knowingly. *"Oh, you haven't heard?"*

I shook my head.

Linda lived for moments like this.

"Becky was having an affair. It's been rumored for months. And I think Jorma found out and finally had enough. Maybe he just wanted to scare her, maybe it got out of hand—but it makes sense, doesn't it?"

I let the thought marinate before responding.

"Wow," I said, exhaling as if I were just now connecting the dots. *"Have you told the police?"*

She hesitated for half a second, then that gleam returned—that smug, self-important look of someone about to be the center of attention.

"Not yet."

But I knew she would.

She wanted credit for cracking the case, and I had just handed her the perfect opportunity.

I took a step back, shaking my head in feigned amazement.

"Linda," I said, lowering my voice. *"If you're right, and you solve this mystery for the Sarasota Police Department, well... you'll be a legend."*

And that was it.

The final push.

Linda lit up—smiling as if I had just crowned her queen of the block.

"Oh, I'm not doing it for the fame," she said, waving a hand as if she wasn't thrilled by the idea. *"I just think we all have an obligation to be good citizens."*

"Well, you're definitely one of the good ones, Linda," I said smoothly.

And with that, she continued her walk, her mind already spinning with how she would deliver the theory to Detective Foss.

I watched her go, then turned back toward the house, the satisfaction blooming inside me.

It was done.

The stone was cast, and Jorma was about to have his hands full.

I smiled to myself as I stepped inside, grabbing a nice bottle of wine from the counter.

For Denise, it would be a better-than-average bottle of wine on a Thursday night.

For me?

A celebration of deception.

DECEMBER SETTLED OVER THE neighborhood like a fresh coat of paint, covering everything—the whispers, the suspicions, the unease—with a thin veneer of holiday cheer.

And no one embraced the facade more than Denise.

If Halloween was the neighborhood's grand spectacle, Christmas was her masterpiece.

By the first week of December, our house looked like a Hallmark movie exploded inside it. Garlands draped across every doorway, red and gold ornaments hung in perfect symmetry, and a Santa Claus sat in every room, their painted smiles unblinking.

And the trees—so many trees.

One in the front window, another in the dining room, a third upstairs in the hallway—each one color-coordinated, meticulously designed, perfect.

Denise was relentless about it.

Every spare moment she wasn't with Chiara, she was wrapping presents, rearranging decorations, filling every empty space with something festive. She hummed along to Christmas music in the kitchen, orchestrated gift exchanges with friends, baked cookies with Chiara on her hip.

She was fully immersed in the season—or at least, she was pretending to be.

Because no matter how much tinsel she strung, no matter how bright the lights, there was one thing she hadn't done.

She hadn't mentioned the gun again.

It had been weeks since she said it.

Since she stood in the hallway, watching me with that unreadable expression, and dropped those six careful words:

"They didn't ask about the gun."

I had been waiting for her to bring it up again.

Denise never let things go.

She was methodical, sharp, a force when she wanted to be—like me, but more patient.

If she had something to say, she would say it when she was ready.

And yet, she hadn't.

And that was what bothered me the most.

I was learning to suppress my demons now, too.

I had felt them stir, felt them awaken after Becky, but I had pushed them down—for Denise, for Chiara, for the illusion of normalcy.

I was playing the part.

I helped string the lights outside, kissed Denise on the cheek when she pulled me under the mistletoe, drank mulled wine at dinner parties.

I smiled when I had to.

And yet, there was always that underlying tension, simmering just below the surface.

Between me and Denise.

We moved around each other now, careful and calculated.

She didn't press. But she was watching.

And I didn't ask. But I wanted to.

There were moments—small, fleeting moments—when I'd catch her staring at me, her eyes lingering a little too long.

When I'd walk into a room and feel the weight of her gaze, as if she was trying to solve something in her head.

When she'd mention Becky in passing—casually, delicately—just enough to see how I'd react.

And I gave her nothing.

Because I wasn't sure what she already knew.

BY MID-DECEMBER, Detective Foss was a ghost.

I hadn't heard from her in weeks, and with every day that passed, I took it as a sign that I was in the clear.

The story had been erased from the headlines, replaced with holiday fluff—local Christmas markets, charity drives, human-interest pieces designed to make people feel good.

The reporters had stopped trolling the neighborhood, their cameras no longer flashing through car windows.

The rumors still lingered—dark corner conversations, whispered theories over glasses of wine at neighborhood parties—but there was no substance.

And that was what mattered.

The world was moving on.

On December 17th, Brian invited me over for drinks.

The drive to his place was quiet, the streets lined with glowing lights, inflatable reindeer swaying gently in the evening breeze.

As I turned the corner, my foot hesitated slightly on the gas pedal.

Jorma's house.

A newly posted "**For Sale**" sign stood in the front yard, its white post stark against the dead winter grass.

I slowed as I passed, my fingers tightening around the steering wheel.

He was leaving.

I pulled into Brian's driveway, exhaling slowly, the tension curling in my chest.

I knew Jorma wasn't guilty of anything—he was just a convenient scapegoat.

Maybe there was something I didn't know or maybe the pressure had become too much, it didn't matter now.

Because soon, he wouldn't be here at all.

I stepped out of the car, smoothing my expression, preparing to play the part once more.

And just before I knocked on Brian's door, I let myself smile.

Because Christmas had come early this year.

Brian met me at the door with a drink already in hand, his usual carefree grin in place. I took it, downed a sip, and didn't waste time.

"Did you see Jorma's house?" I asked, my voice casual but direct.

Brian frowned. *"What about it?"*

"The 'For Sale' sign. He's moving."

Brian blinked in surprise, shaking his head. *"Didn't even notice. Must be new."*

We finished our drinks, poured another, and without much discussion, decided to head over.

Jorma hadn't been around much since the funeral. In fact, no one had really talked about him—not his grief, not the police visits, not the endless questioning. Only the whispers on the streets.

And I knew why.

Jorma opened the door after the second knock.

The house was staged, stripped of the personal touches that once made it a home. No warmth. No Becky.

The absence of her was more than just physical—it was in the air, in the emptiness of the walls, in the hollowness in Jorma's eyes.

Still, he seemed genuinely surprised and happy to see us, his brows lifting slightly before he gestured for us to come inside.

I considered some small talk, but Brian—predictable, unfiltered Brian—jumped right in.

"You jumping ship? Leaving the hood?"

Jorma exhaled heavily, dropping his gaze for a moment before nodding. *"Yeah. It's not the same here anymore."*

The words stuck with me.

Not the same?

I did him a favor.

Becky didn't love him—she would've left him, drained half his bank account, taken the house, and disappeared into the arms of her lover.

He should be thanking me.

I forced concern into my voice. *"What do you mean, it's not the same?"*

The obvious answer—the one any grieving husband would say—was "*Because I'm alone. Because Becky is gone.*"

But Jorma didn't say that.

Instead, his expression hardened, a flicker of something dangerous behind his eyes.

"Don't act like you don't know," he said, his voice sharp. *"Everyone in this fucking neighborhood thinks I poisoned Becky."*

He let the words sit between us, watching for a reaction.

"I hear the whispers. I see the looks. I'm not blind. Between that and everyone talking about the affair she was supposedly having, I can't live here anymore."

His voice cracked slightly on the last part, but he steadied himself.

"I'm moving back to Michigan. A fresh start. For me and the kids."

Brian, ever the good guy, jumped in with reassurance.

"Come on, man, it's all in your head. No one's talking."

"Give it another month," I added, nodding along, keeping my voice even. *"You'll see—it'll all go away."*

But deep down, I knew that was a lie.

Because I wouldn't let it go away.

Jorma leaving was perfect.

It reinforced the rumors, planted him deeper in people's minds as the guilty man running away from it all.

Even if Foss didn't suspect him, the neighborhood would make sure his name stayed tied to Becky's death.

Only guilty people flee.

Jorma had made his decision. We could see it in the way he stood, the way his hands flexed and curled at his sides, like he was barely holding something in.

So we wished him the best, turned toward the front door, and that was supposed to be it.

But just before we reached the door, Jorma called my name.

"Eric—hold up a minute."

I turned back, keeping my expression neutral.

Jorma barely looked at Brian. Instead, his eyes were locked onto mine, his face set like stone.

"I need to share something with you."

Before I could say anything, Brian—blissfully unaware of the tension curling between us—gave a small shrug.

"I'll wait for you outside."

He stepped out.

Jorma closed the door.

And when he turned back to me, his expression had changed.

For the first time since Becky's death, I saw something real in his face.

Not grief.

Not anger.

Certainty.

He stepped forward, his voice dropping into something cold, something unshakable.

"I've spoken to the police. Numerous times."

I said nothing.

"They have no physical evidence," he continued. *"No theory that makes sense. Just wild speculation. They know it wasn't a random accident, but they can't prove anything."*

A pause.

Then his voice dropped even lower.

"But I know this."

His eyes bore into mine.

"I had nothing to do with it."

My jaw tightened, but I kept my posture loose, unbothered.

"I knew about her affair," he said, voice steady. *"And she knew I knew."*

That caught me off guard.

"I didn't care." He let the words sink in. *"We made it work for us. It wasn't anyone's business."*

I didn't react, didn't blink, didn't flinch.

But inside, something curled in my stomach.

Jorma leaned in slightly, his next words almost a whisper.

"Eric, I know you had something to do with this."

Silence.

The air between us stretched tight.

"I don't know why," he continued, his voice calm, too calm. *"Or how."*

A small pause.

"But I know. Deep down, it was you."

The moment hung there.

The weight of it pressed against my ribs, my lungs, my throat.

But I was prepared for this.

I let my lips part slightly, just enough to feign shock, confusion—hurt, even.

"Jorma—" I started, but he cut me off with a sharp shake of his head.

"I don't need you to lie to me," he said.

And that was the part that sent a shiver down my spine.

He wasn't asking.

He wasn't guessing.

He was certain.

I took a slow breath, keeping my voice measured.

"I'm sorry you feel that way."

That was all I gave him.

Jorma held my gaze for another long moment, searching my face for something. Anything.

Then, finally, he let out a breath—one that sounded like it had been sitting in his chest for weeks.

"I just needed to say it out loud."

With that, he stepped aside, pulled open the door, and let me out.

Brian was waiting on the sidewalk, oblivious, swirling the last of his drink in his glass.

"All good?" he asked, grinning.

I forced a smile. *"Yeah. All good."*

And as we walked away, the weight of Jorma's words settled in my mind.

He knew.

But he had no proof.

And that meant he may be a loose end waiting to be tied up.

Chapter 17

TIME TO TALK

DENISE NEVER LET things go. That was something I had always admired about her—her ability to latch onto something, turn it over in her mind, and wait until the exact right moment to bring it back up.

But the gun comment?

That had been weeks ago.

And she hadn't mentioned it since.

I had expected a confrontation, a follow-up, something.

Instead, she had buried it beneath Christmas decorations, wrapped herself in the season, played the role of the perfect wife and mother—as if she wasn't waiting.

But I should have known better.

Denise wasn't the kind of woman who forgot.

She was the kind of woman who waited.

It started after dinner.

Chiara had gone down early, and Denise had disappeared into the kitchen, wiping the same spot on the counter over and over again—a nervous tick I had come to recognize over the years.

I watched her from the doorway, the hum of Christmas music in the background, the scent of pine heavy in the air.

"What?" I finally asked.

She kept wiping. *"We should talk."*

I already knew where this was going.

She led the way to the garage, flipping on the overhead light. The air was colder out here, sharp with the winter chill sneaking through the cracks in the door.

She wrapped her arms around herself, but I knew it wasn't from the cold.

She was choosing her words.

"You never asked me what I meant," she said finally.

I leaned against the workbench, feigning confusion. *"About what?"*

She let out a sharp laugh, shaking her head. *"Don't do that."*

"Do what?"

She turned to face me fully, her expression unreadable.

"The gun, Eric," she said. *"You never asked me what I meant when I said that after the police were here. And that's not like you."*

I shrugged, keeping my voice light. *"I figured if it was important, you'd tell me."*

Denise let out a slow breath, as if she had expected that answer, but still found it disappointing.

"Funny," she murmured. *"That's what the police in Arizona said about you, too."*

Everything stopped.

My body didn't react, but something inside me went very, very still.

"The police?" I echoed, my voice carefully measured.

Denise nodded, stepping closer, closing the space between us.

"They called me," she said. *"A few weeks ago, maybe a month or so. Said they were following up on an old record. A firearm purchase made under your name."*

I exhaled slowly. There it was.

"A rifle," she continued. *"Purchased in Minnesota."*

She was watching me now, waiting for any tell, any break in my face, any flicker of something that confirmed what she already knew.

I kept my posture easy. Controlled.

"And?"

"And they wanted to know if you still had it."

My jaw tightened, just slightly. *"What did you tell them?"*

Denise's lips curved into a small, humorless smile.

"That I had no idea you ever bought a gun."

Silence settled between us.

I had never told Denise about that rifle.

Because she was never supposed to know.

It had been a clean transaction, a throwaway purchase from a time in my life when I had been testing the boundaries of control with Owen. A rifle, bought in Minnesota, with cash.

A ghost weapon.

But now, the police were looking for it.

And Denise knew.

"Eric," she said, tilting her head slightly, soft, but with an edge. *"Why did you buy it?"*

I let out a slow breath, shaking my head. *"Does it matter?"*

"It does to me."

Her voice was quiet, but there was something heavy behind it.

"Listen, I didn't tell them anything," she continued, watching me closely. *"Because there's nothing to tell them right?"*

I studied her for a long moment, weighing my next move.

Denise had always been smart.

But this was different.

This was calculated.

"You're really good at keeping secrets, Eric," she murmured.

I let out a short breath, pushing off the workbench, straightening.

"And you're good at finding them."

A small smile. Sharp. Knowing.

"I didn't find this secret," she said. *"They did."*

We stood there, the cold creeping between us.

A new game had started.

And Denise was playing.

She turned toward the door, pausing just before stepping inside.

"You know," she said lightly, too lightly, *"I don't think the police care much about an old gun purchase."*

I narrowed my eyes. *"No?"*

Denise glanced back, eyes lingering on mine.

"But I do."

Then, without another word, she disappeared inside, leaving me alone in the garage.

And for the first time, I felt it.

The weight of someone else's hand tightening around the pieces of my game.

I slept on the couch that night, telling Denise it was because I wanted to be closer to Chiara, but the truth was, I needed space—and time.

Time to think, time to calculate, time to fix the mistake I hadn't even realized I'd made until now.

My mind was racing, flipping through every detail, every small misstep, not from the night of the killing, but the aftermath—where things always fell apart.

I remembered something Owen had told me once:

"Try a decent crime, and you've got fifty ways you can fuck it up. If you can think of twenty-five of them, you're a genius."

I had thought of forty.

But not all fifty.

And that was coming back to haunt me now.

I should have told Denise about the gun years ago. Planted the seed, given it a story, made it an afterthought. Then, when the time was right, I could have "lost it," reported it stolen—erased it from existence before it ever became a problem.

But now? Now the police knew about it.

And if they asked for it, what the fuck was I supposed to say?

I could claim I sold it—maybe to Owen. But then the police would want a bill of sale, a paper trail, proof.

And I didn't want Owen to have to lie for me.

Not yet, at least.

I clenched my jaw, forcing myself to slow down. Breathe.

This wasn't something I could fix tonight. Too much wine. Too little clarity.

But by morning, I needed to come with a plan.

And that started with Denise.

Denise took Chiara to daycare early. I sat at the kitchen table, coffee untouched, watching the steam curl into the air.

I had made a decision.

I would tell her. At least part of it.

Not about Arizona. Not about Minnesota. Not about Owen.

And definitely not about Florida.

Not yet.

The question wasn't if Denise could handle the truth. It was how much of it she could take before she shattered.

What if I told her everything?

What if I told her I wasn't going to stop?

That I wanted to kill again. And again. And again.

Would she understand? Would she stay?

Or would she do what a normal person would do—run straight to the police?

I knew what I wanted to believe.

We were madly in love, bonded in a way most people wouldn't or couldn't understand.

We had promised each other—countless times—that nothing could ever break us apart.

But this?

This was beyond the scope of marriage vows and quiet compromises.

I had to be smart.

I had to tell her only what she needed to know—enough to make sense of things, enough to calm the storm in her mind, but not enough to make her afraid of me.

And more importantly—not enough to make her leave.

WHEN DENISE WALKED IN, I greeted her with my most loving voice.

"I made a fresh pot of coffee. Join me for a cup?"

She didn't answer right away.

But I saw it in her eyes—she knew.

She knew I was ready to finish the conversation from last night.

And she also knew I had spent the time in between crafting a lie.

She knew me too well.

The only real question was—would she let it die, or would she keep pushing?

I poured the coffee, kept my movements calm, measured.

Then I began.

"Love, you know what I did in the service, right?"

"Of course," she said, eyes steady.

I nodded, as if coming to terms with something in my own head.

"Well... I'd been thinking about it a lot. And when we moved to Minnesota, I decided to buy a rifle. For target practice. Something to help me relax. Maybe even go hunting with the guys one day."

Her expression didn't change, but I felt her pulse quicken in the space between us.

I exhaled slowly, carefully adding regret into my voice.

"I never told you because I knew you wouldn't like it. And that's why I paid in cash—I didn't want you to see it on a bill or statement and get upset."

She said nothing.

"Looking back, I should've told you," I admitted, adding just a touch of self-condemnation, a touch of weakness—something to make her believe it. *"I should have never kept it a secret. But at the time, I thought it was best."*

Denise took a slow sip of coffee.

"Where is it now?" she asked, her voice too neutral.

"Gone," I said immediately.

"Gone?"

"Yeah. When we moved to Arizona, when we started talking about a family, I decided to get rid of it. I didn't want it in the house. Didn't want it in my life."

I could see the wheels turning in her head.

She wasn't sure whether to believe me.

But she wanted to.

Denise nodded slowly. *"Well, great. Then I can call and let the police know that we talked, and that you confessed to buying a gun but have since sold it."*

That word.

Confessed.

My mind latched onto it, turning it over, feeling its weight.

I stared at her for half a second too long before speaking.

"You can't do that."

Her eyes snapped to mine.

"Why?"

I forced a slow breath, let my voice drop slightly, just enough to make it sound like I was being carefully honest.

"Because I didn't sell it."

Denise's grip tightened around her coffee cup.

"I tossed it out."

Her expression flickered, panic rising in her eyes.

"Eric..."

"If I tell them I sold it, they'll want a bill of sale. A transfer of registration. I don't have any of that."

The tension thickened, stretching between us like a thin, cracking wire.

Denise's lips parted, her breathing unsteady.

And for the first time, I saw it. Fear.

Not just suspicion. Fear.

But then something changed.

She inhaled sharply, clenched her jaw—and I watched the fear morph into something else.

Something stronger.

"Well, then," she said, voice steady but thin. *"What are we going to do?"*

My mind immediately relaxed.

My breathing slowed.

And just like that—I knew, *I had a partner again.*

There was no tension in the morning, and few words were spoken.

Denise and I had reached an understanding, whether spoken or not. From where I stood, the discussion—at least the one regarding the gun—was over.

I ran out to wash the car, stopped by the store for a few things, then headed home.

It was a beautifully strange day.

Everything felt sharp, like I was seeing the world through a new lens. The sky seemed bluer, the air crisper, the people I passed so unaware, so fragile.

I felt good. No, I felt alive.

The energy inside me buzzed, coiled tight like a wire sparking at the edges. I knew what it was. The afterglow of a plan executed perfectly. The undeniable satisfaction of control.

Becky was gone. Because I had made her gone.

But this time, the fire inside me wasn't the same.

It wasn't like Minnesota—that first taste, that quiet, controlled precision.

And it wasn't like Arizona—a kill that still pulsed in my veins, still called to me in ways I didn't fully understand.

This was different.

Stronger.

More than a craving now. More than a need. It was a hunger.

And I wasn't sure I had a limit anymore.

That thought alone should have scared me. It did scare me. But not in the way most people would think.

I wasn't afraid of getting caught. I had been too careful. Too calculated. That was never the concern.

No—what scared me was that I wanted to know how far I could take this.

I had always thought of killing as an exercise in control, a way to prove to myself that I could plan, execute, and erase a life without a second thought. A test of my discipline, my ability to stay three steps ahead.

But now?

Now my mind was shifting—testing boundaries I hadn't even realized existed.

It wasn't about the service anymore. This wasn't some leftover instinct, some psychological byproduct of war.

And it wasn't just about proving to myself that I could do it. I had already proven that.

So what was it now?

I thought about that as I drove home, let my mind wander into places it shouldn't go.

- How many ways could I kill?
- How much pain could a body endure before shutting down
- Could I push a person to the brink of death, let them taste it, then pull them back—only to do it again?
- Could I make someone beg for it?
- Could I take more than one life at a time?

The thoughts came easily, flowing through me like an inevitable truth, like they had always been there—waiting.

How far would I take this?

I didn't know.

And that was what scared me most.

I was back at the house by 11 a.m. The day was still, the kind of oppressive Florida heat that made the world feel heavy, sluggish. Denise and I worked in silence, putting dishes away, our movements routine. A life carefully maintained.

Then came the knock.

Not rushed, not aggressive—just *deliberate.*

I froze for half a second, fingers tightening around the rim of a glass. Denise, midway to the cabinet, hesitated too. We exchanged a glance, a flicker of silent understanding.

I already knew.

The confirmation came as I passed the window and saw the car in the driveway. The shape of her standing just beyond the glass.

Detective Foss - I opened the door, keeping my expression neutral, giving nothing away. She stood alone—no officers, no backup. Just her. That, somehow, was worse.

"*Detective Foss*," I greeted, my voice smooth, carefully level.

She didn't step forward, didn't smile. Just watched me with that same unreadable expression, the one that made my skin prickle. The kind that said she wasn't here *just* to deliver news.

"*I came back to let you know we're closing the case*," she said. No preamble. Straight to the point.

A slow breath left my lips, as if I had been holding it. As if relief had finally found me. I let my features soften just enough, controlled but natural.

"*Lack of substantial evidence*," she continued. "*Nothing that would hold up in court. Whoever did this... really covered their tracks, well, on this one.*"

That last part—it lingered. The weight of it settled between us.

Something too practiced in the way she shrugged. Too intentional in the way she phrased it.

"On this one."

My brain caught on those three words, and suddenly, the air around us felt different. Like she had set a trap and was waiting to see if I'd notice.

Did she know something? Something more?

I forced the thought away, focused on keeping my body relaxed, my voice steady.

"*So that's it*?" I asked.

"*For now,*" she said.

But the way she said it—the way the silence stretched between us—it wasn't a dismissal. It was a warning.

Then, just as I was about to thank her, she shifted her weight, adjusting the strap of her bag.

"*Oh—one more thing*," she added, almost offhandedly. "*The Phoenix Police Department will be in touch with you soon.*"

The words were too casual. Slipped in like an afterthought.

But I felt them hit their mark.

Inside, something coiled tight, a reflex, a gut-deep awareness that the ground beneath me had just shifted.

I didn't flinch. Didn't let my breath change, didn't let my shoulders tense. But my mind was already moving, calculating.

"Phoenix?" I echoed, my voice as smooth as ever.

She nodded, slow and deliberate. Amusement? No—something sharper than that.

"*Yeah. They reached out to my department. Apparently, they have a few questions for you.*"

She let the words settle. Then, without another glance, she turned and walked away.

I watched her go, my mind a storm behind calm eyes. The hum of her car faded into the distance, but the weight of her presence didn't leave.

Behind me, Denise shifted. I could feel her watching.

"*Eric?*" she asked, her voice barely above a whisper.

I shut the door. And for the first time in weeks,

Becky wasn't the problem. Phoenix was.

Chapter 18

WHAT SHE KNEW

SLEEP HAD BEEN RESTLESS, fractured by the weight of unfinished business. By the time I opened my eyes in the morning, one thing was clear—I had loose ends to tie up.

Not in Florida. That was done. Even my thoughts about Jorma had faded after Foss confirmed the case was closed. It would take new evidence to reopen it, and that would never happen. Even if Jorma had suspicions, it was a dead-end. Nowhere to go.

Sorry, Jorma. I won. Enjoy Michigan.

Arizona was the real problem now.

If they had something, they'd need proof. Witnesses, forensics—something that could hold up. I had been careful. No weapon was available to run tests on, there was no solid motive. Without those, there was no case.

Still, doubt crept in. A nagging sense that I couldn't ignore.

And then there was Owen.

Minnesota. The girl near Lower Lake.

Unexplained, unresolved. A loose thread of its own.

If the walls started closing in, I needed a fallback. Leverage. A way out.

Owen was smart, but not careful enough. He was the only person alive holding the key piece of evidence in that case—the barrel that was actually used. If it came down to it, I could serve him up.

Ballistics wouldn't lie. If they tested his rifle with that barrel, it would be a close enough match to the bullet that tore through that girl's body. Owen would have no defense. No alibi. It would be his word against mine, and in a jury's eyes, the evidence would speak louder than either of us. At the very least, it would muddy the waters enough to create reasonable doubt and that would be all I needed.

So, that would be the contingency plan.

But Arizona still needed immediate attention.

First step: get rid of the rifle. "Officially". Report it stolen.

The question was *how*—and *why now*?

It had to make sense. Seem plausible. No sudden panic moves, nothing that would raise suspicion.

I needed to think.

And I needed to move fast.

ARIZONA WAS THE immediate problem, but I didn't have all the facts. And that bothered me.

Denise had mentioned the Phoenix police contacted her, but she never fully disclosed the details of their conversation. She told me they had asked about the gun, and I had handled that with Denise. But what else? What had they really pressed her on?

And why wasn't she telling me?

The text—*the* text—hadn't come up since she first saw it. That wasn't like her. Denise wasn't the type to let things linger, to ignore unanswered questions. If she had truly forgotten about it, I might have believed it was insignificant. But she hadn't forgotten. She was choosing not to bring it up.

Then there was the black SUV.

It wasn't paranoia. I had seen it too many times now. Always in the periphery, just close enough to be noticed, just far enough to make me doubt whether it was real or imagined.

They were watching. That much I knew. But why now?

What had changed? What had triggered them to show up outside the house?

Those were the things I needed to clear up.

And then there was Denise.

The thought had been festering for days, maybe weeks. I had ignored it, dismissed it as intrusive paranoia, but the longer I let it sit, the more it took root.

Could I still trust her?

I wanted to believe I could. But that feeling—the space between us—had been growing for a while. It wasn't just the lack of intimacy, the absence of the kind of passion that once defined us. That part I had blamed on Chiara, on a newborn, on stress. But maybe it wasn't any of those things.

Maybe she was keeping her distance for a reason.

Maybe she was working with them.

If that was true, I wasn't just looking at a betrayal. I was looking at a test. The ultimate test.

Denise wasn't just my wife—she was the only person who had ever known me fully. The only person who had seen me at my worst and stayed. The only person I had ever let close enough to understand who I truly was.

But if she had turned against me… if she had flipped…

It meant she must know something and she also would know exactly what I was capable of.

The thought left a hollow ache in my chest, something sharp and unfamiliar. I had killed before. Calculated. Necessary. But this—this was different.

This was Denise.

The woman who shared my bed. The mother of my child.

Could I actually do it?

If it came down to protecting myself—*really protecting myself*—could I take her out?

It would be the ultimate act of survival. The final proof that I was untouchable, that no matter what, I could adapt. Cut ties. Move on.

This wasn't just about eliminating a threat.

This was about her.

And what she knew. I had to know.

I could sit Denise down and have an open conversation. That was an option. But it was a weak one. A reckless one. In a direct conversation, she would have the advantage—controlling what she said, what she revealed, and what she knew or didn't know. I couldn't afford to go into that blindly. Not now. Not when the difference between truth and deception could mean life or death.

This was about survival.

I kept telling myself it wasn't possible. That she wouldn't, *couldn't*, betray me. That even if she didn't know everything, she still had my back. That our family was still her priority.

But doubt had a way of sinking its teeth in.

She had been different lately. A fraction of a second too slow to meet my eyes. A hesitation in her touch that hadn't always been there. The way she spoke about Phoenix—brushing over the details, keeping the conversation light. Too light.

She hadn't told me everything.

And that terrified me more than anything else.

The thought of Denise not being the woman I believed she was? The thought of her turning on me? That would be the death of me.

And if it came to that…

It would be the death of her, too.

I didn't want to think about that possibility, but I wasn't naive. If Denise had flipped, if she had sold me out—then this wasn't just about what she had done. It was about what I would have to do next.

I wasn't there yet. Not mentally. Not emotionally.

But I needed to be prepared.

The only way to know for sure—the only way to see inside her mind without manipulation, without deception—was her journal.

Denise wrote everything down. She always had. It was her way of processing, of making sense of the world. And if she had been talking to them, if she had been lying to me, it would be there. Somewhere in those pages.

I would wait until she left for work.

Once she was gone, I would take the journal and read every word.

Because if there was even the smallest hint that she was working with them, that she was setting me up—then everything between us changed.

But if it wasn't there, if she was still mine, if we were still in this together…

Then I could breathe again and the plan would change.

My heart was pulling for that answer. For the woman I loved to still be the woman I believed in.

As much as my mind was consumed with what Denise knew or didn't know, with what the Phoenix Police Department suspected or dismissed, my body ached for something else.

I ached to kill again.

TO ANYINE READING THIS, I know it makes no sense. I had killed three times—three separate lives taken—and for all intents and purposes, I had walked away clean. No real suspicion. No evidence. No consequences.

And yet, the urge never left me. It never faded. If anything, it grew.

It was a hunger, a need that felt as natural as breathing. A force that wasn't external, wasn't imposed on me by trauma or circumstance. It had always been there, buried beneath the surface, waiting for its moment.

I wasn't an addict—not into alcohol, not into drugs. I never sought escape through those vices. But I understood now, in a way I never had before, what it meant to crave something beyond reason. The unrelenting pull, the quiet but persistent voice whispering that nothing else would feel as right, as pure, as *necessary*.

For the first time in my life, I felt a glimmer of sympathy for those who struggled with compulsions. The alcoholics, drug addicts or the sex addicts, the people whose urges defined them despite their best efforts. Maybe we weren't so different. Maybe we were all just wired a certain way, not because of some defining tragedy, but because it was simply who we were.

I had spent years convincing myself I was in control. That my actions were choices, not inevitabilities.

But I was starting to see the truth.

This wasn't about choice.

This was who I was or maybe who I was becoming.

And I was on the verge of accepting that.

Not with shame. Not with resistance. But with the quiet understanding that some people are built differently. That society conditions us to believe we should feel guilt for the things that make us whole. That we should seek help, correction, normalization.

But who decides what is normal?

Morality shifts. Laws change. People evolve. What is condemned today is accepted tomorrow. And what is celebrated now was once considered monstrous.

Help, real help, would mean conforming.

And I had no interest in conforming.

Instead, a new thought had taken root. A justification. A path forward.

What if I could balance both worlds?

What if I could be the perfect husband, the loving father, the good neighbor—and still *feed* this part of me?

Maybe, just maybe, I could turn this obsession into something righteous.

A vigilante.

Someone who corrected the failures of the justice system, the overlooked crimes, the people who deserved to disappear. After all, wasn't there a worse kind of monster? The ones who went unpunished, the ones protected by loopholes, by money, by blind eyes?

I wasn't convinced yet. Not fully.

Because I knew the truth.

I was searching for a single answer—one excuse, one reason—to justify what I already knew I wanted to do.

To justify what I was becoming.

Because the reality was, I was already at the doorstep.

And now that I was here, staring into the abyss of what I was, what I always had been…

I didn't care.

DENISE HAD TO GO to Tampa for the night—some work function. I barely registered the details. All that mattered was that I'd have the house to myself.

And I already knew what I was going to do.

Before she even walked out the door, I had decided. The second Chiara was asleep, I would find her journal.

Guilt? Guilt was a wasted emotion at this point. I needed answers. I needed to know where I stood. Where we stood.

Thursday morning came, and by 8:15 a.m., she was ready to go. Her suitcase by the door, keys in hand. She had decided to drop Chiara off at daycare on her way out of town, which meant I had the house to myself even sooner.

I pulled her close before she left. Held her tighter than usual. And then—before she could react—I kissed her. Deep. Slow. Intentional.

She smiled against my lips, maybe a little surprised, maybe just assuming I was in a rare sentimental mood. She didn't realize that, in my mind, it could have been our last.

She turned, grabbed her bag, and walked out the door.

I waited.

An hour later, she called me, her voice casual. *Traffic was terrible on the Skyway Bridge.*

Perfect. She was safely gone.

I hung up, exhaled, and went hunting.

The journal was exactly where I expected it to be—tucked in her bedside drawer, beneath the novel she had been reading. She never hid it. She never thought she had to.

I pulled it out, feeling the worn leather against my palms, the familiar weight of her thoughts, her secrets.

And then, without hesitation, I started flipping through the pages.

I didn't care about the small things—the day-to-day frustrations, the meaningless details. I needed to go back.

Back to Minnesota.

Because that's where it all started.

Page after page, entry after entry, the same routine thoughts, the same passing emotions. Nothing important. Nothing that mattered.

Until I found it.

The entry from the day we left Minnesota.

I stilled, my eyes locking onto her words, my pulse hammering just a little harder.

This. This was what I had been looking for.

> ***Journal Entry*** *– Leaving MN behind*
>
> *Something changed in Minnesota.*
>
> *Eric wasn't distant—he was alive. Sharper. Restless, but not with frustration—with energy.*
>
> *And the way he touched me... it wasn't just casual. It was more. A hand at the small of my back, fingers trailing over my arm. That night, he pulled me to him like he couldn't get close enough. Desperate. Hungry. Like something had woken up inside him.*

I don't know what shifted, but I loved seeing him like this.

Whatever happened, I just want it to stay.

She was happy. That much was clear. And she had sensed that I was happy too. But what she didn't know—what she couldn't have known—was why.

Something had changed in me, and she felt it. But she didn't understand it.

I kept flipping through the pages, searching for something meaningful. Something deeper.

Then I found it. The night I had gone to the lake. With the guys in Phoenix.

Journal Entry – *Night out with the Guys*

Eric's different today. Not distant—just ***somewhere else****.*

He went to Lake Pleasant last night with the guys. Just beers, stories, nothing unusual. But today, he's quieter. Preoccupied.

When I asked about it, he gave me the usual rundown, but it felt rehearsed—like he was saying what I expected to hear.

And the way he keeps staring off... not distracted, but calculating. Like he's replaying something.

Maybe it's nothing. Maybe I'm overthinking.

I kept flipping, my fingers moving faster now. The journal was a breadcrumb trail, leading me deeper into her mind, into the space where her doubts and loyalties lived side by side.

I reread it, taking in every word. She sensed something was off. She knew I had been different, that something inside me had shifted. But she hadn't pressed—not really. She had let it go.

Or at least, she thought she had.

I turned the page, scanning for something more, something that would tell me if she had ever truly moved past it.

And that's when I saw it.

The latest entry.

> ***Journal Entry*** – *Police Visit*
>
> *Police showed - out of nowhere. They asked about Eric.*
>
> *"Did your husband ever go to Lake Pleasant?"*
>
> *It caught me off guard, I said "Yes, he went with the guys sometimes why?"*
>
> *They didn't answer just stared at me like I should know something.*
>
> *They were looking for something. Asked me about a gun that was purchased but I told them I didn't know anything about a gun.*
>
> *I should tell Eric, maybe I'll wait and see if he has anything he want's to share, I'm sure he has his reasons. for not telling me about the gun. and the black SUV is back today. Why would they be watching us or the neighborhood?*

My pulse slowed.

They had asked about the gun.

I had handled that.

But she is hesitating. She was still waiting for something from me?

The black SUV.

She had seen it, again.

I traced the words, reading them over and over, my pulse steady but my thoughts turning.

She had witnessed it, too.

And she never told me.

Why?

Was it because she didn't want to worry me? Because she thought it was nothing—just some random car, some coincidence?

Or was it something else?

Did she keep it to herself because she was protecting me—or because she was protecting herself?

I kept reading, searching for an answer, some insight into why she had chosen silence over honesty.

And then I saw it.

> ***Journal Entry** – Black SUV*
>
> *I saw it again today. The black SUV. It wasn't the first time, but I had convinced myself it was nothing. That maybe I was just being paranoid. Not anymore.*
>
> *It was parked down the street, just far enough to seem innocent, just close enough to feel intentional. I told myself it must belong to one of the neighbors. But it never stayed long. And it was always there when Eric wasn't. Whoever they are, they aren't watching us—or watching him.*
>
> *I should tell Eric, but what if I'm wrong? What if I'm making something out of nothing?*

I turned the page, knowing it would either confirm my worst fears—or reassure me that I was still in control.

Then I saw the next entry.

And I knew.

> ***Journal Entry*** *– I Don't Care*
>
> *I laid awake tonight, listening to his breathing. For the first time in weeks I feel calm.*
>
> *Eric is my husband, my family. Whatever happened or whatever they think they know, I believe in him.*
>
> *That's all that matters.*

I exhaled.

That was what I needed.

Whatever doubts she had, whatever questions still lingered in her mind, she had chosen me.

She wouldn't betray me.

Not now. Not ever.

I closed the journal, my fingers lingering on the worn leather before setting it back exactly where I found it. Denise was still mine, still blindly devoted to the life we built. But blind devotion was dangerous—it made her predictable, made her easy to manipulate. She wasn't a threat, not now, but she also wasn't a shield. If they came for me, she wouldn't see it coming.

That meant I had to stay ahead of this. Arizona. Owen. The rifle. Loose ends, waiting to unravel.

I exhaled slowly, steadying my thoughts.

This house. This city. It was already starting to feel temporary.

Maybe it was time to move before

I no longer had the choice.

Chapter 19

EXIT STRATEGY

DENISE LOVED OUR HOME but had never been a big fan of Florida—the humidity, the snakes, the alligators, the politics, the way everything seemed to move just a little too slow for her taste. But what had once felt like a place we could settle in was quickly becoming something else entirely.

Beyond the drama of Halloween—the rumors, the sideways glances, the feeling that people were still watching even if they weren't saying anything—the neighborhood itself was changing.

The streets that had once felt welcoming now felt neglected, tired. Cracked sidewalks left un-repaired, overgrown lawns where there used to be pristine landscaping. Even the community center, once a hub of weekend gatherings, barbecues, and neighborhood parties, looked worn down, its paint peeling, its doors quieter than they used to be.

And then there were the For Sale signs.

One after another, houses were being listed, longtime families cashing out while the market was high. The ones moving in? They weren't the same.

They didn't know the history. They didn't know us. They didn't fit in.

The small-town charm that had drawn us here was fading. That sense of belonging we once had was gone.

And if we no longer belonged—if we were now just another pair of strangers in a neighborhood full of outsiders—then what was keeping us here?

That's what made the conversation with Denise so easy.

She still loved our home, but she could see the change too. She could feel it.

And with everything else hanging over me—Arizona, the police, the loose ends—I knew it was time for a move.

CHIARA WAS GETTING OLDER, and I wanted stability for her before she started school. A place where she could grow up without whispers, without the weight of Florida hanging over us.

I also wanted to get as far away from Florida as I could.

Denise and I had always loved the beach, the water, the air. In our younger days, back before marriage, before Chiara, we had spent long weekends in California, escaping reality for a few days at a time. There was a small Southern coastal area, known as the "South Bay" we used to meet in, tucked along the Pacific, before life got complicated.

We'd stay at this rundown little motel called The Sea Sprite, right on the sand. Every day, we'd wake up early, grab coffee from a hole-in-the-wall shop that probably doesn't exist anymore, and walk the Strand—the stretch of pavement running through Manhattan Beach and Hermosa Beach, where surfers, runners, movie stars, corporate exes and beach bums all blended into the same easy rhythm.

The weather was always perfect. The vibe felt like us—relaxed, detached, just far enough from downtown LA to avoid the drama, but close enough to still feel connected.

It felt like a logical choice now.

A fresh start. A clean break.

Denise was thrilled at the idea of moving to the West Coast. She already had a few friends out there, people she could reconnect with. And the lack of bugs, snakes, alligators and suffocating humidity? That alone was a win in her book.

For Denise, the move would be easy. She typically worked from home conducting meetings via Zoom and Teams calls, but if she need to go in, her company had an office downtown that was a short commute from the SouthBay. For me, the move was something else entirely.

Because it wasn't just about leaving Florida.

It was about cleaning up loose ends.

I needed to get rid of the rifle, and this move provided the perfect opportunity.

I planned it carefully. We'd pack most of the house ourselves. We had done it before—organized, labeled everything, handled our own logistics. It wouldn't seem strange.

Then, once we arrived on the other coast, I'd report a few missing items. A couple of smaller things, easily replaceable. And one not-so-small thing—the rifle.

The beauty of it was in the logistics.

The moving company had already helped me without realizing it—they had told us they would need to move all the boxes and furniture mid-route, and switch it to another truck, for the cross-country trip.

That was all I needed.

I'd make sure the right boxes were left open, accessible, making it easy to claim that somewhere in the shuffle, a few things never made it to California.

No red flags. No questions. Just a lost item in a cross-country move.

It was simple.

And best of all, I knew it would work.

I decided to bring Denise in on it, not because I needed her approval, but because I wanted to put her mind at ease—to eliminate any lingering doubts she might have about the missing rifle.

Denise had never been one for lies. She didn’t like them when I told them, and she sure as hell couldn't tell them herself. But this? This was different.

This wasn’t some elaborate deception—it was cleaning up a mess, erasing a loose end that was already gone.

I kept my voice casual, my tone reassuring when I laid it out for her.

"Look, the rifle's gone. It's not like I can turn back time and do something different with it. Reporting it missing with the move is the only logical option now."

She hesitated, but I could see the way her mind worked through it, the way she wanted to believe me. To trust that I had everything under control.

I sweetened the deal, offering a compromise.

"I'll submit an insurance claim against the moving company," I said. *"Make it official. That way, it's documented, and we're covered if anyone ever asks."*

That seemed to settle her. It was a paper trail, something real. Something she could point to and say, *See? It wasn't hidden, it wasn't suspicious—it was just lost in transit.*

She agreed.

And with that, the plan was set in motion.

One more piece wiped clean. One less thing to worry about.

And Denise? She didn’t bring it up again.

Because as far as she was concerned, the problem was solved.

THE EXCITEMENT OF MOVING —the packing, the goodbyes, the chaos of transition—took its toll on us. It was exhausting, draining, but in a way, it also saved me. It gave my mind something else to latch on to, a distraction from the darkness that had been steadily consuming me.

Because before all of this, before we started preparing for a new life, my entire being had been overtaken by one singular, all-consuming urge: to kill again.

There had been no noble intentions. No delusions of vigilante justice or some higher calling. That was all bullshit.

No, this was something deeper. Darker.

The hunger had grown into something almost physical, like a sickness burrowing inside me, a parasite demanding to be fed.

It became all I thought about. I stopped pretending it was something I could control and started studying it instead. I devoured books, films, and case studies about serial killers—not for admiration, not for psychological analysis, but to learn. To understand what had been done, what the possibilities were, what limits existed.

And more importantly—how far I could push past them.

Because I had already accepted it: I would keep killing.

I would chase this need, explore it, perfect it, until one of three things happened.

One: I got caught—unlikely, given how careful I was.

Two: I grew bored with it—also unlikely, because the thrill hadn't diminished; if anything, it had sharpened.

Or three—the only real possibility.

I walked to the very edge of myself.

I found the limit.

The one thing I wouldn't do. The one act that would force me to stop—not out of fear, not because of morality, but because it was something I physically or mentally could not bring myself to do.

Once I found that threshold—once I discovered my absolute boundary—only then could I walk away.

Only then could I find peace.

But sitting here now, in the middle of half-packed boxes and the sound of Denise on the phone making arrangements, I realized something.

That limit?

It was unimaginable today.

And that single thought didn't scare me.

It excited me.

The packing and move went off without a hitch.

By the time the movers loaded the last box onto the truck, it was just the three of us—me, Denise, and Chiara—standing in the hollowed-out remains of what had once been our home. The rooms echoed now, empty and unfamiliar, stripped of everything that had made them ours.

But I didn't feel sentimental.

This place had served its purpose. And now, it was just a house we used to live in.

With our remaining personal items packed into our vehicle, we hit the road. Once again, we decided to make the drive an adventure rather than a chore. A final cross-country trek before we settled into our new life.

The drive was uneventful, and by nightfall, we made it as far as New Orleans.

We hadn't planned to stop long, but there was something about the city—its decadence, its old-world energy, its casual acceptance of sin—that made us want to linger. So we did, spending two nights in the French Quarter, eating, drinking, blending into the steady pulse of life on Bourbon Street.

Denise was already working with a realtor in Hermosa Beach, narrowing down places for us to live.

She had always had a knack for finding the perfect place. And just like so many times before, she had done it again.

A quiet street called Lyndon, just a block from the beach. A modern but comfortable house, open, airy, full of light—everything about it sounded exactly like the fresh start we needed.

I didn't even have to see it to know it was perfect.

Everything was falling into place.

Better than we could have hoped.

After New Orleans, we made a quick overnight stop in Texas, just long enough to rest before continuing west. Denise was exhausted, too drained from the drive to do anything but order room service and collapse onto the hotel bed.

I, on the other hand, needed a drink.

After hours on the road, my body was restless, my mind wired, and the thought of sitting in that stale hotel room, flipping through the same five channels, didn't appeal to me.

So, I stepped out.

There was a saloon across the street—one of those places that looked like it had been there forever, its wooden exterior weathered from time and heat, neon beer signs buzzing faintly in the windows.

The moment I walked in, I knew exactly what kind of bar this was.

A real cowboy bar.

The kind with a huge dance floor, mechanical bull in the corner, and elevated cages above the crowd—empty tonight, but I could picture them on a packed Friday or Saturday, filled with young women in Daisy Dukes and cowboy hats, dancing for tips while cowboys threw back whiskey.

But tonight? Tonight, it was slow.

Just a handful of good ol' boys at the bar, country music twanging from the jukebox, the low murmur of conversation between them. Familiar. Comfortable.

I never had a problem walking into a bar alone and striking up a conversation. I grabbed a seat a few stools down from two guys and ordered a Lone Star—because, well, when in Rome…

I had barely finished my first beer when the guys next to me pulled me into their conversation.

By the time I ordered my second beer, they were arguing.

Not a fight—just the kind of heated, half-drunken debate that only happens in places like this, where people drink cheap beer and solve the world's problems in the span of a few rounds.

The topic?

Ghost guns.

I had no idea what the hell they were talking about, and when they turned to me and asked my opinion, I admitted it.

"*Never heard the term before,*" I said, taking a sip of my beer. "*What are you guys talking about?*"

They laughed—like I had just told them I didn't know what a revolver was. Bill, the older one, smacked the bar and shook his head before finally breaking it down.

"A *ghost gun is a firearm that you can build at home,*" he explained. "*You can 3D print the parts or order a kit online. Costs less than 300 bucks, and here's the kicker—no license, no background check, nothing.*"

That got my attention.

I leaned back, playing it casual, but my mind had already shifted into calculation mode.

I let a beat pass before asking the most important question—the one I needed the answer to.

"*Is it traceable?*"

Bill smirked. "*Nope.*"

His buddy clapped his hands together, as if that was the best part of the whole deal. "*That's why the feds are losing their damn minds over it.*"

I stayed quiet for a second, nodding slowly, carefully measuring my next words.

I always tried to be cautious with what I said, even in places like this. You never knew who was listening. You never knew who might remember a conversation and bring it up later, if it ever mattered.

So I took the backdoor approach.

"*What's the controversy about?*" I asked, as if I was just some outsider, mildly curious about the debate.

That was all it took to start them up again.

They launched into another round of arguments, and this time, I listened—really listened. Taking mental notes.

The cost, the lack of regulations, the ease of assembly—all of it was intriguing. But there was one detail that sent my mind into hyperdrive:

100% untraceable.

And that was why the government wanted them gone.

They called them "do-it-yourself murder weapons." No serial numbers. No paper trail. No way to tie them to a buyer or a seller. A gun that didn't exist on record.

A ghost.

To me, it wasn't about the politics. I didn't give a damn about gun laws or government oversight. What mattered was the utility of it.

Because now, for less than $300, I could have something invisible.

That changed everything.

OUR NEXT DESTINATION WAS Phoenix, where we planned to spend two days catching up with old friends from our neighborhood.

It had been years, but stepping back into their world felt effortless. The conversations picked up like no time had passed, filled with familiar faces, inside jokes, and just the right amount of gossip.

People kept telling us we should stay—that Phoenix was still home.

But it wasn't. Not for us. Not anymore.

California was waiting.

While in Phoenix, Denise and I made time for a night out with our closest friends, John and Lea.

It was good to see them still together. Given the way things were when we left, I half-expected John to have finally walked away—or for Lea to have buried him in the backyard by now.

But there they were, same as ever.

We met at a low-lit bar downtown, the kind of place we used to frequent before life got complicated. The girls headed outside to the patio, their laughter spilling through the open doors as John and I grabbed drinks at the bar.

John had always been the kind of guy who stayed ahead of the curve. Whether it was tech, trends, or underground markets, if something existed, he knew about it.

So I figured if anyone could give me the real scoop on ghost guns, it was him.

We ordered our drinks, and I didn't bother easing into it.

"*Hey, what are your thoughts on ghost guns?*"

John turned to me with that all-too-familiar smirk, the one that meant he already had a story to tell.

"*What do I think of them?*" he repeated, pausing just long enough to let the anticipation build. Then, with a casual shrug, he said, "Are you kidding? *I have like four of them. I think they're great. Need to buy them now before the government makes them illegal*"

I took a slow sip of my drink. "*Yeah?*"

"*Yeah. Why do you ask?*"

I shrugged, keeping my tone light, uninterested. "*No reason. I was in Texas, listening to a couple of guys talk about them. Figured it might be fun to put one together—something to do, a hobby. Maybe some weekend shooting.*" I glanced over toward the patio, lowering my voice just a notch. "*Not that Denise would ever go for it. You know how she is with guns.*"

John chuckled, nodding. "*Yeah, she'd lose her shit.*" Then, without hesitation, he added, "*Dude, no problem. I've got two brand-new kits at home, still in the boxes. Haven't even opened them. I'll give you one when we get back to the house.*"

I raised an eyebrow. "*Seriously?*"

"*Yeah, man. Take it. I got them for next to nothing.*"

I pulled out my wallet, offering to pay him, but he waved me off.

"*Nah, you cover drinks tonight, and we'll call it even.*"

Felt like a fair deal.

Besides, knowing John, he probably expensed them through his company or picked them up on the street for half the price. Either way, my problem was solved.

Finding one in California would have been a pain in the ass—probably impossible.

But now?

Now I had exactly what I needed.

WE ROLLED INTO Hermosa Beach just past 7 P.M. on a Thursday night, the last stretch of our cross-country exodus finally behind us.

Denise had handled everything ahead of time, and when we pulled up to the house on Lyndon, it was perfect.

The key was waiting for us under the mat, just like the realtor had promised. Inside, a bottle of wine and two glasses sat on the counter—a welcome gift, a small but thoughtful touch after so many hours on the road.

At the corner of the street, we spotted a small pizza shop, the kind of place that felt like it had been there for decades. By 8 P.M., Chiara was asleep in her new room, and Denise and I sat on the rooftop patio, sharing pizza and wine, listening to the waves crash just a block away.

For the first time in weeks, it felt like we could breathe.

With the moving truck not scheduled to arrive until Sunday, the next few days were spent exploring.

We stocked up on groceries, wine, and essentials, getting familiar with the neighborhood, finding the best spots for coffee, breakfast, and late-night drinks. We walked The Strand, retracing old memories, letting the feeling of being here settle in.

The ocean air, the laid-back rhythm of the town—it felt different from Florida. Better.

By the time the moving truck pulled up on Sunday morning, we were ready.

Denise and I have always been obsessive about setting up a home, and this time was no different. While some people let their boxes sit for weeks, we worked nonstop—unpacking, organizing, arranging furniture.

By Tuesday, the house was completely in order. Pictures and artwork were hung, bookshelves were filled, everything was in its place.

To anyone walking in, it looked like we'd been there for months.

But this wasn't just a house. It was a reset button.

And something was coming.

Chapter 20

RED LIGHT

JUST AS WE HAD FINISHED unpacking, but before we had met a single neighbor, Denise got a call.

She was needed in Amsterdam for a Global Conference, replacing a co-worker that had a last minute emergency. It was to be four days of meetings, with a formal reception the first night—one where spouses were invited.

I could tell she was already debating whether to ask me to go.

Before she could even frame it as an option, I told her, *"We should do it."*

And I meant it.

Not just because I wanted to be by her side, to play the role of supportive husband, shaking hands with her colleagues.

No.

This was about something else entirely.

Amsterdam.

The city itself had always fascinated me—something about its rhythm, its shadows, the way it seemed to hold secrets just beneath the surface. The chaos and indulgence, the way it blurred the lines between decency and depravity—but one place in particular had lived rent-free in the darkest corners of my mind for years.

The Red-Light District.

I had spent time imagining it, weaving together a fantasy so vivid that I could practically feel it.

And now, I wasn't just going to Amsterdam.

I was being given the perfect cover.

A conference. A respectable event. Legitimate reason to be there. No questions.

By the time our flights were booked, my mind was already orchestrating an entire event of my own.

I knew exactly what I wanted to do and how it would unfold.

Once again, my mind shifted into tactical mode.

Every time an opportunity like this arose, I felt it—a shift, a sharpening of focus. The world around me narrowed, the noise faded, and all that remained was the plan.

I had never been to Amsterdam before, never walked its winding streets, never stood beneath its neon glow. My only exposure came from pictures, movies, books, but that only made it more exciting.

The unexpected, the unknown—most people feared that.

I thrived on it.

The uncertainty didn't make me hesitate; it fed me. It filled my mind in a way that was almost obsessive, each blank space in my knowledge begging to be filled, each logistical question waiting to be answered.

What were the busiest nights in the Red-Light District?

Where were the darkest alleys? The quietest exits?

What time did police presence peak—and when did it fade?

How much attention did people really pay to who walked in and out of those windows?

This wasn't just about fulfilling a fantasy—that was too simple. Too easy.

This was a chance to push myself further.

To expand my boundaries.

To see what I was truly capable of.

And for the first time, I had a completely different playing field.

A city where vice was celebrated, not hidden.

Where pleasure and indulgence walked hand in hand with temptation, darkness, and opportunity.

I wasn't just planning a night out.

I was planning an evolution.

DENISE WAS CONCERNED I'd be bored. She knew how these work trips went—long, tedious meetings, hours of networking, industry jargon that meant nothing to me. She'd be tied up for most of the day, and she worried I'd feel trapped, waiting around with nothing to do.

But I reassured her.

"I'll make a day of it," I said casually. *"Hit a few museums, check out the local pubs. And yeah... maybe I'll stop by a 'coffee shop.'"*

That part made her laugh.

She knew I wasn't a smoker, but in Amsterdam, marijuana and hash weren't just legal—they were a culture.

The city's famed coffee shops were nothing like American dispensaries—no sterile waiting rooms, no security guards checking IDs. Instead, they were laid-back, dimly lit bars that served beer, cocktails, and an extensive menu of cannabis products—all out in the open, no stigma, no hiding.

A fully immersive vice experience.

I had no real interest in getting high, but I liked the idea of sitting back with a beer, watching the world drift by in a haze of smoke and sin.

Denise rolled her eyes but smiled.

"Just don't go full stoner on me," she teased.

I chuckled, playing along.

"Don't worry. I'll keep it classy."

But in the back of my mind, I knew the coffee shops, the museums, the pubs—they were all just a distraction. A smokescreen.

I had something else planned.

And Denise had no idea.

Denise's parents were to fly in on Tuesday to watch Chiara. We were booked and ready to leave first thing Wednesday, returning on Monday. Now, everything was taken care of.

Four days in Amsterdam.

Four days to indulge.

STRAIGHT OUT FROM AMSTERDAM Centraal, the city's main train station, the streets stretched out like veins, bustling with trams, cyclists, and the hum of life. Just past the famous floating flower market, where vibrant tulips spilled from vendors' stalls in every direction, lay the Keizersgracht Canal—one of the most picturesque and historic parts of the city.

Denise had found us a small Airbnb tucked neatly on a corner, its tall, narrow facade blending seamlessly into the row of classic Dutch townhouses lining the canal. The location was perfect—walking distance to everything: the museums, the Anne Frank House, the legendary Bulldog Café, and, of course, the Red-Light District.

Denise's company spared no expense for the event that first night. It was held in an opulent venue, a mix of modern elegance and old-world charm, with massive chandeliers hanging from vaulted ceilings. The room buzzed with conversation, the open bar flowing freely, live entertainment adding a polished atmosphere, and food stations strategically placed so no one had to fight the crowd.

Even as an outsider to this world of corporate handshakes and industry jargon, I had to admit—it was impressive.

But the night wrapped up early. With the conference kicking off the next morning, most of the attendees left before the real drinking could start.

Denise and I took it as an opportunity to wander the city.

We stepped out into the cool Amsterdam night, walking the quaint, cobblestone streets hand in hand. The city had an energy to it—something unlike anything back in the States.

There were hidden squares, tucked between buildings, where street musicians played for gathered crowds, the warm glow of cafés spilling onto the pavement. Every side street seemed to hold its own secret world—tiny bars, bustling terraces, and the clatter of bicycles as locals zipped past ringing their bells at tourists walking in the bike lane.

Even on a Wednesday night, the city was alive—not in the loud, reckless way of an American party town, but with an effortless vibrancy, a pulse that seemed woven into its history.

It was both intimate and electric, charming yet unpredictable.

And as we wandered through its maze of streets, taking it all in, I felt it settling inside me.

This city was more than I expected.

More than I'd imagined.

And I knew—this was only the beginning.

DENISE LEFT AT 8AM sharp for the conference, disappearing into a world of business attire and professional formalities.

I took my time. Moving slowly.

No urgency. No rush.

I made a cup of coffee, letting it linger on my tongue as I stood by the window, watching the city wake up. Then, I set out—beginning what would become my daily ritual in Amsterdam.

The walk.

I started north, making my way past Vondelpark, once infamously dubbed Needle Park due to the rampant drug activity that consumed it throughout the late '70s, '80s, and early '90s. The city had cleaned it up since then, but there was still something haunting about the place.

A lingering ghost of indulgence and excess.

From there, I wandered through the open-air market, nearly a mile of fresh fruits and vegetables, meats, cheeses—some of which I had never seen before. The scent of spices and grilled meats hung thick in the air, mingling with the crisp morning breeze.

I circled through the fish and seafood market, taking in the gleaming rows of freshly caught eels and shellfish, before stopping at the Hard Rock Café for a beer—a quick warm-up, something to loosen the edges.

And then, my final stop.

The windowed wonderland, the Red-Light District.

WALKING INTO THE RED-LIGHT District, the first thing that greets you isn't just the neon glow or the murmurs of passing strangers—it's the giant pink pig perched above the entrance of Casa Rosso, Amsterdam's oldest erotic sex-show venue.

Inside, the performances never stopped.

A relentless, all-day, all-night carousel of live sex acts played out in front of eager, wide-eyed audiences. The small, dimly lit theater pulsed with low music, the scent of sweat, alcohol, and something more primal hanging thick in the air.

The acts rotated seamlessly—each one designed to fulfill every possible fantasy.

A man and a woman, locked in an intimate, explicit sexual act.
Two women, tangled together in an erotic ballet of teasing and indulgence.
Two men and a woman, a dynamic shift of power and pleasure, a women the center of it all. And at times two women and a man, surrendering to both.

There were no boundaries. No taboos.

Each performance was a carefully choreographed display, blending raw lust with practiced control.

For the audience, it was more than just voyeurism.

It was indulgence. A front-row seat to the kind of pleasure most wouldn't dare experience outside the glow of flickering red lights.

Here, behind closed doors, they had it all.

But Casa Rosso was only the gateway—a mere appetizer to the feast that lay beyond.

The district unfolded like a maze, a labyrinth of alleyways, bridges, and narrow streets, where sex wasn't just advertised—it was on display.

Here, the air carried a scent that was uniquely its own—damp stone, hash smoke, flowers and perfume, an odd mix of vice and history, something that had existed here long before I had ever stepped onto these streets.

The red glow from the windows cast a strange, artificial warmth over the cobblestones, making everything feel surreal, like stepping into a dream where morality didn't exist.

The laughter of passing tourists mixed with low whispers in Dutch, German, English and more.

Money exchanged hands in dark corners.

The clink of glasses, the distant hum of music, the tap of stiletto heels against wet pavement.

Every sense was alive, heightened.

This place didn't just sell sex—it sold indulgence, without consequence.

Rows of three-story buildings, each lined with glass-walled rooms, stood like a living catalogue of flesh.

Each window was a stage.

Each woman, a performer.

And behind those glass walls, bathed in red light and desire, the real show was just beginning.

Inside the small, sterile rooms, there was nothing but a bed, a sink, and a girl. Some, their red curtains drawn—an indication that they had a customer inside. Others stood behind the glass, curtains remained wide open, their lingerie-clad bodies bathed in neon light, an open invitation to passing men that they were available.

The girls moved, swayed, touched their bodies, dancing to unheard music. Some teased, rolling their hips, arching their backs, fingers tracing along bare skin. Others simply stood there, staring through the glass, their gazes meeting yours in a way that was neither shy nor timid.

It was transactional. An offer, not a seduction.

To say there was something for everyone was an understatement.

A quick scan revealed women of every ethnicity, every body type, every age—from barely twenty to what had to be at least sixty-five.

Short, tall, thin, voluptuously curved.

Exotic, familiar. Some with the polished, airbrushed beauty of an escort, others with the rough, street-worn edge of someone who had been doing this too long.

And the customers?

Men. Couples. Some young, some old, some walking with a kind of quiet reverence, others laughing and pointing, treating it like a theme park attraction.

But none of them judged.

They walked past the windows like they were shopping at a mall, browsing a display of goods, their eyes scanning over bodies the way someone might appraise a luxury car or a designer watch.

It was both disturbing and lyrical.

And I knew, in that moment—

This was the perfect hunting ground.

IN THE HEART OF THE Red-Light District, nestled between the neon glow of sex clubs and the flickering red bulbs of the windows, there was a small pub that caught my eye.

The Old Sailor.

It was an English-style pub, dimly lit and comfortably worn, the kind of place that felt like it had been there for centuries. The bar was just the right size—intimate enough to be a hideaway, yet busy enough that someone could blend into the background, unnoticed.

That's what drew me in.

But what made it my home away from home over the next few days was the view.

From a small corner table, nestled next to a large window, I had a perfect line of sight to six—sometimes eight—windows in the alleyway directly across from the pub.

And behind those windows?

A live display of seduction.

It was still early afternoon, slow for this part of the city. But it didn't take long before I caught the attention of three of the women.

Each had her own way of drawing me in.

First, the brunette—a seductress.

She was young, barely mid-twenties, with the high cheekbones and long, toned body of a runway model.

Dressed in delicate black lingerie, she moved behind the glass like a dancer, her hips rolling slow, deliberate, her hands grazing over her body in a way that was both playful and intimate.

Whenever my eyes met hers, she'd blow me a kiss, then lift a single finger, curling it toward her in a silent invitation.

Come inside.

Stay a while.

I watched as she licked her lips, just slow enough to make sure I noticed.

She knew exactly what she was doing.

Next, a redhead—I called her the temptress.

She was strikingly pretty, the kind of classic Irish beauty that was impossible to miss.

Long, copper-red hair cascaded down her back, catching the light, contrasting against the emerald-green bikini she wore—one that was covered in tiny rhinestones that glittered as she moved.

But what really got me was her smile

A slow, knowing smirk, like she already knew the effect she had on me. She leaned against the glass, her fingers tracing the strap of her bikini, shifting it just enough to make me wonder if it might fall.

It never did.

She was a tease, but a good one.

Then there was a blonde—a definite party girl.

She looked to be pure Dutch—tall, blonde, with ice-green eyes and pale, flawless skin.

She didn't move like the others. She wasn't delicate or calculated. No, she had an energy, a wildness, that made it clear she was here to have fun.

She tapped the glass, locking eyes with me, then pointed to the bar.

"Buy me a drink?" she mouthed.

I smirked, shaking my head.

She pouted, exaggerated and playful, rolling her eyes before turning to her reflection, adjusting the lace-trimmed bra barely covering her breasts.

She was trouble, and I kinda liked that.

I knew I wanted to get closer to her. I needed to.

I wanted to know her story, to understand what lay behind those unreadable eyes. But more than that, I needed to decide if she was worth it.

Worth the time. Worth the effort.

Worth becoming my next victim.

I stayed for another hour, lingering, observing, playing my part.

I continued to flirt, casually, effortlessly, exchanging smirks and teasing glances with the women who had already marked me as an easy sale. The brunette with the slow, deliberate sway. The redhead with the glittering green bikini and playful smirk. The blonde with the wild streak, who pouted whenever I ignored her.

It was all just a game, one I had mastered long ago.

But then—a shift.

Out of the corner of my eye, I caught movement.

A different girl.

She was up on the third floor, barely visible, tucked away in a spot most wouldn't bother looking. But I saw her.

And once I did, I couldn't look away.

She was taller than the others, her long, sculpted legs leading to a body that was striking—lean, toned, but with enough curve to make a man forget himself.

Her hair, a light brown cascade, wasn't thrown up haphazardly like the others—it looked professionally styled, sleek, framing her face in a way that made her beauty even more dangerous.

And her face—

Exotic. Sharp. Defined.

A jawline so perfectly structured it could cut glass, cheekbones high and dramatic, lips full but unreadable.

She was maybe twenty-five, her skin smooth, unblemished, a shade that could belong to any number of nationalities.

She wasn't Dutch.
She wasn't French, Italian, Russian.

She was just… her.

And what made her different?

She didn't look at me.

Not once.

While the others flirted and played, she sat in her glass room with detached elegance, crossing her long legs slowly, deliberately, her body leaning back against the glass as though she had all the time in the world.

She wasn't selling herself.

She wasn't working the room.

She didn't need to.

She knew she was desired.

She knew every man walking by wanted her.

And that was the problem.

She didn't need to call for attention.

She already had it.

That's what made her dangerous.

Because the ones who don't play the game?

They're the ones who make you desperate to win.

I left the pub, the blonde party girl still fresh in my mind, her playful glances and teasing lips lingering like a cheap perfume.

But in the back of my mind, something else was brewing.

Something darker.

THE NEXT MORNING, after Denise had left for the conference, I repeated my same routine.

Same walk.
Same stops.
Same slow build of anticipation.

But by the time I reached The Old Sailor, my corner table was taken.

I settled for a seat at the bar—not quite the same vantage point, but still good enough.

I ordered lunch, and before it even arrived, the girls had already noticed me again.

But this time?

It was different.

The brunette, the redhead, the blonde—they weren't just flirting now.

They had the look of recognition.

The kind of look that said:

"He's back."
"He came yesterday. He's watching. He'll come to me today."

A silent expectation in their eyes, a hint of hunger in their movements.

And yet, up on the third floor, the mystery girl remained unchanged.

She still hadn't looked at me.

Not once.

Not when I walked in.
Not when I lingered.
Not when I stared at her long enough to make damn sure she noticed.

There was something undeniable about her—something that went beyond desire, beyond the cheap, transactional lust that filled the air in this district.

I couldn't explain it.

It wasn't just sexual, though she was beautiful, and the thought of being alone with her had certainly crossed my mind.

The way she sat there, effortlessly untouchable, made it feel less like she was selling herself and more like she was waiting for someone worthy of her time.

But I knew I wouldn't go to her.

Not for the reasons most men would avoid it—guilt, morality, shame. Those things didn't hold me back.

No, my reasons were far more practical.

WHILE I SAT AT THE BAR, a group of tourists came in—Texans, by the sound of their voices.

Denise and I had always joked that Americans stood out like a sore thumb in foreign bars. Texans even more so.

It was easy to tell who was new to the Red-Light District.

They all had the same curiosity, the same list of questions.

And Charles, the bartender at The Old Sailor, had all the answers.

He rattled them off like a well-rehearsed script—something he had probably repeated a thousand times before.

"The girls are all independent, no pimps. Licensed by the city."

"They rent the space—250 euros for an eight-hour shift."

"They set their own prices. Most charge between 50 to 100 euros for 30 minutes, but you can negotiate."

"Cameras aren't allowed—client and worker privacy."

"And the real kicker?" He chuckled, taking a sip of his drink.

"A surprising number of them are married. This is just...their day job."

I absorbed every word.

The final details.

The last pieces I needed for my reconnaissance.

Because this wasn't just a curiosity trip.

This was a hunting ground.

And I had just learned all the rules of the game.

I paid my bill, taking my time, letting the weight of the moment settle.

Then, I turned, my eyes drifting back to the party girl, the one who had been the most persistent, the most playful. The blonde with the wild streak, the one who had spent the last hour trying to pull me in with teasing glances and exaggerated pouts.

She was watching me, leaning against the glass, her body framed in neon light, her lips slightly parted as if she was already anticipating my next move.

I didn't break stride as I met her gaze—steady, deliberate—and gave her a slow wink.

A promise.

A silent message.

I'll be back.

Her lips curled into a smile—a knowing smile.

She bit her lip just enough to make sure I saw, then gave me a slow, lingering nod.

And I walked out, leaving her there, waiting.

Knowing that next time... she'd be expecting me.

Chapter 21

A DANGEROUS GAME

DENISE WAS EXHAUSTED when she got home, the weight of the day pressing down on her like a slow suffocation. She barely made it through the front door before kicking off her heels, rolling her neck from side to side, and exhaling the kind of deep, weary sigh that said, I'm done.

It had been a long day of "being on"—smiling, engaging, making small talk with people she didn't really know but had to charm regardless. I knew exactly what she needed.

A glass of wine.
A short foot massage.
And bed.

I played the part of the attentive husband effortlessly. I poured her wine, kneaded the tension from her feet, kissed her forehead, and tucked her in beneath the sheets. She was asleep within minutes.

"*I'll be in soon,*" I whispered, brushing my hand over her hair. "*Just going to clean up and finish my wine.*"

But that was a lie.

I wasn't tired. Not in the slightest.

I sat alone in the dimly lit apartment, the quiet wrapping around me like a cocoon. The room felt still, but inside my head, my thoughts twisted and turned, relentless.
The Party Girl was all I could think about.

How sexy she was.

How fun she seemed.
How alive she made everything around her feel.

And yet, despite that, I already knew she would most likely be my next victim.

The realization didn't unnerve me. It didn't make me hesitate.

If anything, it excited me.

I let my mind linger on her for a while—the way her lips moved when she spoke to me, the way her body fit so perfectly into that black lace, the way she commanded attention with just a look.

But then, something shifted.

Another image forced its way into my thoughts. The Mystery Girl.

I hadn't even spoken to her. She hadn't flirted with me, hadn't tried to pull me in like the others.

And yet…

She was still there. Still lingering in the front of my mind, refusing to be ignored.

Why?

Why was she still on my mind?

Why had she captivated me more than expected?

I hated questions I didn't have the answers to.

And this one—this one was bugging me.

There had to be a reason. A logical explanation. Something beneath the surface pulling at me.

I sighed, drained the last of my wine, and pushed myself up from the chair.

In the bedroom, Denise was breathing evenly, her body relaxed in the depths of sleep. I slid into bed beside her, settling against the pillows, turning off the light.

But sleep didn't come.

I stared at the ceiling, my mind still racing, still chasing the elusive answer—until it slammed into me like a speeding train.

I knew who she was.

She reminded me of the girl from the boat in Arizona.

A shiver ran through me, a flicker of something dark and electric.

The free-willed, uninhibited girl who had given herself over completely, her body a playground for two men who worshiped her. The girl who had no shame, no hesitation. She had let herself become their toy, their pleasure, their everything.
This was her all over again. Older. Slightly different. But the same.

The same exotic beauty.

The same undeniable presence.
The same aura of untouchable indulgence.

My mind was spinning at a hundred miles an hour now, reliving that night in Arizona

The way their bodies tangled on the boat, limbs intertwined, sweat glistening in the moonlight.

Clothes discarded in a pile on the deck.

The men taking turns, exploring her, pleasing her. And she let them. She wanted them to.

I closed my eyes, and the Mystery Girl now replaced her.

Now, she was the one on that boat.

I imagined her standing there—head tilted back, lips parted, waiting.

I saw her between them—hands roaming, bodies pressing, pleasure unfolding at her demand.

The image ignited something in me, something that burned.

Something consuming.

And as I lay there, breathing slow and steady beside my sleeping wife, I knew one thing. The subliminal attraction to the mystery girl was solved.

THE MORNING STRETCHED LAZILY into the afternoon, the city waking up slower than usual under the hazy weight of a weekend in full swing. Denise had an extra-long day ahead—meetings, networking, a team dinner that would likely stretch late into the night.

8 P.M., maybe later.

I kept my response casual, but inside, I felt a pulse of anticipation.

More time. More freedom. More opportunity.

I delayed my usual walk, taking my time, letting the sun climb higher. The morning chill burned away, replaced by the kind of crisp, comfortable air that made a slow stroll through the city almost meditative.

I followed my usual path—Vondel park, the market, a slow beer at the Hard Rock Cafe—before finally making my way to the Old Sailor around 2 p.m..

And the moment I stepped inside, I knew.

Saturdays were different.

The energy had shifted, the air electric with something wilder, something heavier.

The usual patrons—locals, businessmen, those who wandered in alone or in pairs—had been replaced. Tourists flooded the streets. The kind who had just stepped off a short flight from elsewhere in Europe, weekend warriors looking to indulge. The kind fresh off a cruise ship, stumbling through the Red-Light District with wide eyes and wallets ready.

And the girls knew it too.

They were different today.

Today wasn't about flirtation. Today was about money.

The outfits changed.

The attitudes sharpened.

Today was the day they turned fantasy into cash, and they moved like they knew it a golden opportunity.

My favorite corner table was open, waiting for me.

I ordered an Amstel, let it settle in my palm, and leaned back.

And then, like clockwork, the show unfolded before me.

The Seductress was first—wrapped in a sheer, pink robe that did nothing to conceal the white thong beneath it, tiny red hearts stamped over the delicate fabric.

She moved like silk, slow and deliberate, scanning the crowd with a gaze that promised sin. She wasn't hunting just anyone—she was selecting. Marking her target, weaving a web with nothing more than a tilt of her head.

Whoever she chose wouldn't stand a chance.

Then came the Temptress—and she had upped her game too.

Green cowboy boots, a sequined white thong, and silver tassels barely covering her large, heavy breasts.

A matching cowboy hat sat low on her head, a playful wink at anyone watching. She moved with an exaggerated sway, hips rolling, shoulders back, as if she was waiting for a man who could actually handle her.

She was here to give someone the thrill of their life.

By now, both of them had pegged me.

I wasn't a customer.

Not today, not yesterday. Not ever.

And they had already moved on, focusing their attention on the men whose wallets were open, who would fall under their spell.

But then—there was the Party Girl.

And while the others turned up the heat, she set it ablaze.

Everything about her screamed confidence. Competition. A refusal to fade into the background.

She had dressed for war.

Black stiletto heels—tall, sharp, the kind that made a woman's legs look impossibly long.

Matching black lingerie—lace-trimmed, delicate, but structured, holding her in place in all the right ways.

Thigh-high stockings, the sheer fabric giving just enough of a tease, held up by a glistening garter belt.

She looked like something straight out of a Victoria's Secret fantasy.

And she worked the crowd like she owned it.

Her movements were slower, more calculated today. Less playful, more controlled.

A predator with a smile.

And then—she saw me.

The sultry gaze softened, the smirk turned genuine—a silent greeting between familiar strangers.

Without hesitation, she mouthed the words through the glass.

"*Bring me a drink.*"

I tilted my head, amused, let my eyes run over her, then glanced at the empty chair beside me.

Without a word, I pointed to it.

"*Come sit with me.*"

She hesitated for half a second, then grinned—a smile filled with wicked promise.

And just before she turned back to the crowd, she gave me a look.

A look that said, *maybe.*

I ordered a second beer, and my eyes were drawn to the third floor, the Mystery Girl.

The curtains were drawn.

That simple, heavy fabric separating me from her sent a slow pulse of excitement through my veins. My mind immediately went to work. What was she wearing? Who was she with? What was she doing, stretching out lazily on the narrow bed, or was there a man in there with her, their bodies tangled in the dim glow of the red light? Was she working? Was she choosing to be with someone? Was she capable of wanting anyone?

The unknown drove me insane.

I took a slow sip of my beer, barely tasting it, my gaze flicking up every few moments, waiting—aching—for those curtains to part.

More than twenty minutes passed.

Based on what Charles had told me about how things worked here, she had to open the curtains soon. A girl didn't rent out a window just to keep it hidden. It was bad business. Bad business meant no money. No money meant no reason to be here. She was still in there. She had to be.

Still, I kept waiting. Kept watching.

So much so that I didn't even notice when the Party Girl left her booth. The curtains were open, the light was off.

Her shift was over.

Just like that, she was gone. Her performance finished, her stage now empty. No doubt heading toward the train, slipping back into her normal life, her identity shifting from seductress to someone else entirely.

I exhaled, a little disappointed—whether in myself or the situation, I wasn't sure.

I turned back toward the mystery girl's window-the curtains still shut.

I forced myself to break away, glancing down at my beer, telling myself to let it go, to stop obsessing.

The curtains were still shut.

I watched them one last time, feeling the burn of impatience creeping up my spine—and that's when I felt it.

A tap on my shoulder.

My body tensed.

For a split second, I felt like a peeping tom who had been caught, busted staring into someone's bedroom.

But as I turned, already preparing some excuse, some casual deflection—

I was met with a smile.

A knowing, wicked, dangerous smile.

It was Party Girl.

I'M SURE MY FACE gave me away for a moment—just a flicker of surprise before I caught myself and shifted into a welcoming smile.

"*Join me for that drink?*" I asked, my voice easy, smooth.

She didn't answer right away, just held my gaze with that same playful smirk before finally sliding onto the stool beside me.

"*I thought you'd never ask?*" she murmured, flagging down the bartender with a casual wave.

Now that she was up close, out of the neon haze of the window, I saw her differently.

Gone were the black stilettos and lace-trimmed lingerie—replaced now with a pair of well-worn, frayed jeans that hugged her hips in a way that didn't need to try and a soft white cotton sweater that fell loose around her shoulders, dipping just enough to tease a glimpse of the skin beneath.

Her heels had been swapped for classic white Converse, scuffed and broken in, like they had carried her through years of untold stories.

But what really caught me off guard—what completely undid me—was her face.

With her "work" makeup wiped away, she wasn't just pretty—she was beautiful.

Without the dramatic eyeliner and bold red lips, she looked softer, untouched by the life she led behind the glass. Her skin was smooth, flawless, kissed by just the right amount of natural color, and her eyes—.

They were still the same, striking and full of mischief, but now, without the heavy shadow and liner, they carried something deeper.

Something real.

I barely noticed when she took her drink, turned toward me, and placed her hands on my thigh.

Her fingers were warm, light, but confident.

She leaned in, tilting her chin just slightly, looking at me in a way that made it clear—she was studying me just as much as I was studying her.

Her lips parted, her voice a lazy purr.

"*So... what's your story?*"

She held my gaze, her fingertips pressing just a little harder into my legs.

I exhaled slowly, feeling the heat of her touch, the weight of her curiosity.

And for the first time in a long, long time—

I wondered how much of my real story I wanted to tell.

It's surprising how instantly we connected, like two lost friends reunited at a familiar watering hole. There was no awkward small talk, no cautious hesitation—just an effortless back-and-forth that felt natural, comfortable. It was the kind of easy chemistry that didn't require explanation.

She didn't carry herself like a woman who had just spent the last eight hours seducing strangers behind glass. There was no false bravado, no forced flirtation. Instead, there was a quiet confidence in the way she carried herself—relaxed, playful, like she belonged here just as much as I did.

I made it a point not to ask about her work, how she got there, or what the long-term plan was. Part of me didn't care. But another part of me—one I wasn't entirely comfortable acknowledging—was seeing her differently. Not as a lady of the night. Not as a product in a window.

But as a girl that, under any other circumstances, I could have fallen for. And fallen hard.

In my mind I was thinking that it is amazing how easy it is to gain someone's trust—to put them at ease. Deep down people *want* to be vulnerable. They *want* to believe in connections, even if it's fleeting. Even if it's built on nothing but whiskey and well-placed words.

She traced the rim of her glass with her fingertip, slow, absentmindedly. Not a nervous habit—something deliberate, something meant to be seen. Her eyes flicked up to mine, and I caught the flicker of amusement there, the way her mouth curved, like she knew something I didn't. When she finally spoke, her voice was lower than before—softer, warmer, as if the conversation had just shifted into something neither of us fully acknowledged yet. Then without me asking, she told me her name.

Lieke.

She was 28. Dutch, but she had an exotic air about her, a mix of something European with just a hint of something else—something I couldn't quite place.

She had high cheekbones, full lips, and a feline sharpness to her gaze, like she could read a man before he even spoke a word. Now, without the heavy makeup of the window, I could see faint freckles scattered across the bridge of her nose, a small beauty mark just above her lip.

She looked like the kind of girl you'd meet at a music festival, the kind who knew all the words to every song, who danced barefoot on the grass with a bottle of cheap wine in hand, laughing under the stars.

I felt obligated to respond in kind, to meet her openness with something of my own.

I told her my name was Nick.
That I was here for work.
And I'd be heading back to the States—to Boston—on Monday.

It was just enough to seem real. Just enough to put her mind at ease while still keeping the truth at arm's length. Nothing that could be traced back to me. Nothing that could leave a mark.

Lieke ordered another round of drinks, and then, without hesitation, two shots.

When they arrived, she reached across the table, took my hand in hers—not in a casual way, but deliberate, slow, teasing. Her fingers traced small circles along my palm, her touch featherlight yet intentional.

Then she grabbed her shot glass, lifting it with a knowing smirk.

I took mine, watching her carefully.

She locked eyes with me, her lips parting slightly before she spoke.

"*Op het leven.*" *(Op het LAY-ven!)* – "*To life!*"

We tossed back the shots, the burn rolling down my throat, warming my chest.

And in that moment, I knew.

I was in trouble.

For a split second, the balance shifted.
I wasn't the hunter anymore.
I was the one being watched. Being marked.

The realization sent a slow, electric shiver up my spine—something dark, something unfamiliar. I should have fought it. Should have tightened my grip, reclaimed control. But I didn't.

Instead, I let it settle inside me, let the weight of it press against my ribs like a loaded gun.

Because maybe—just maybe—this wasn't a weakness. Maybe this was an advantage.

A power I could twist into a justification.

Something I could use against her later.

It was approaching 4 p.m. when Lieke turned to me, her fingers toying with the condensation on her glass, and asked,
"*Would you like to grab dinner? It's been a long day.*"

Her voice was smooth, effortless, a suggestion that felt more like a certainty—as if she already knew my answer.

And she wasn't wrong.

I had all the time in the world. Denise wouldn't be home until at least 9 p.m., maybe later. I should have felt a flicker of guilt at the idea of spending my evening with another woman, but as I sat there, warm from the alcohol, electrified by the flirtation, all I felt was intrigue.

Excitement.

I took a slow breath, met her eyes, and smiled just enough to match her energy before saying,

"*Sure. Where would you like to go?*"

Lieke studied me for a moment, like she was deciding whether or not to tell me the truth. Then, with a playful smirk, she said,
"*I know just the place. Let's walk—it's not far.*"

AMSTERDAM WAS A PLAYGROUND of indulgence, packed with restaurants that catered to every vice. There were high-end spots where the elite sipped champagne over artfully plated dishes, and where a single meal could cost more than a flight home. As I pulled out my wallet to settle our bar tab, a thought needled at the back of my mind.

Had I just signed up for a six-hundred-euro dinner?

Champagne. Caviar. Overpriced decadence.

She could have picked anywhere.

That idea should have unsettled me, but instead, it made me even more intrigued. Was I playing her? Or, was she playing me?

The narrow cobblestone streets stretched before us, glowing beneath the street lamps as the late afternoon sun dipped lower. Lieke slipped her arm through mine, curling against me just slightly. It was subtle, too casual to feel like an intimate gesture—but still, it was there.

A part of me told myself to pull away.

But when I glanced around, I noticed we weren't the only ones.

Amsterdam had a different rhythm than back home. Strangers moved together easily here, with fluid familiarity. Couples walked with arms entwined, friends leaned into one another as they laughed. Closeness wasn't a question.

I let it happen. Let her hold onto me.

Any guilt I might have felt drifted further out of reach.

Then, just as I was beginning to suspect I was being led into something extravagant, she gestured ahead and said,

"*That's it. That's where we're going.*"

I followed her gaze, bracing myself—

Molly Malone's Irish Pub.

A wave of unexpected relief settled over me.

Not a five-star restaurant. Not a place where she could squeeze me for every euro in my pocket.

A pub.

A real one. Dimly lit, comfortable, the kind of place that smelled like old whiskey and good stories.

I glanced at her, curious. She could have picked anywhere. Why here?

She just smiled, reading my mind. "*What? You don't like Irish pubs?*"

I exhaled a laugh. "*No, I love them.*"

And that was the truth.

Inside Molly Malone's the pub smelled like sour beer and decades of late-night conversations. The walls were covered with faded photographs of Irish sports clubs, signed jerseys, and a weathered black-and-white photo of U2 in their early years.

It was loud but inviting. A band in the corner played acoustic covers of American songs, their voices melting into the hum of the crowd.

Lieke fit into the space effortlessly. She tossed her coat over her chair, her scent trailing after her—something sweet, warm, unmistakable.

Like suntan lotion in the heat of summer.

I wasn't expecting that. Not from her.

I let it sink in, the way the fragrance wrapped around me, deceptively innocent against the woman wearing it.

She was an interesting contradiction.

We ordered thick, juicy burgers & crispy fries, the kind of meal that soaked up alcohol and felt indulgent in all the right ways. She drank whiskey neat, no hesitation, like she had grown up on it.

We talked, we laughed.

And the longer we sat, the harder it became to convince myself this was still reconnaissance.

Because the truth was—I was on a date.

And I was enjoying myself.

AFTER DINNER, WE ORDERED one last nightcap. I let the whiskey burn slow, watching the way Lieke's fingers toyed with the rim of her glass, the way she leaned in when she laughed, the way her perfume lingered every time she shifted closer.

I glanced at my watch. It was almost 9 P.M..

I needed to go.

Denise would be home soon. I'd already stayed out longer than I should have and I didn't want to explain where I'd been. Didn't want to fill in the gaps with half-truths.

Lieke must have sensed my hesitation.

She tilted her head, studying me, then asked, "*Will you walk me to the train?*"

I shouldn't have.

But I did.

By now the city had settled into a softer hum, the energy of the day replaced by something quieter, more intimate.

We stopped at a bench overlooking the canal, the streetlights casting golden ripples across the water. The world felt slower here, removed from the pulse of the city.

For the first time all night, neither of us spoke.

She turned to me, her soft scent once again wrapping around me, as if she had been waiting for the right moment.

Then, she placed her hands on my leg—a slow, intentional touch—and looked me in the eyes.

"*Can I ask you something?*"

I nodded.

She hesitated for just a beat, then said, "*Why didn't you ever come to see me while I was working?*"

Her voice was different now—softer, quieter, almost… vulnerable.

Then, after a second, she added, "*Did you not think I was attractive?*"

There was something unexpected in the way she asked it. Not flirtatious. Not seductive. Just… searching.

For validation? For reassurance?

I exhaled a slow breath, held her gaze, and said,
"*Lieke, I think you're amazing.*"

A small smile curved her lips.

I went on. "*In fact, I think you're more beautiful tonight than any day I've seen you at work.*"

She didn't react right away. Just listened. Absorbed my words like she wasn't sure she wanted to believe them.

Then, finally, she asked, "*So… why?*"

I hesitated. Then, because I owed her at least some version of the truth, I said it.

"*Because I'm married.*"

She blinked slowly, then smiled—not surprised, not upset. Just… indifferent.

She tightened her grip on my leg with one hand.

With the other, she ran her fingers along my arm, slow, teasing.

Then, she leaned in, her lips grazing my neck, her breath warm against my skin as she whispered, "*I won't tell if you don't.*"

And then, just as softly, she bit my earlobe, her teeth pressing into me with just enough pressure to send a slow, liquid heat down my back.

Her hand slipped lower, trailing the inside of my thigh, and in that moment—

I thought about it.

About giving in.

About taking her somewhere dark and quiet, letting her pull me under, devouring her completely.

And then—killing her.

The thought of it ignited something inside me, something even stronger than lust.

Knowing that I had won her over.
Knowing that she had let her walls down.
Knowing that, in the end, I would be the one to take her life.

And that thought?

That thrilled me.

As she pulled back, I reached for her hand, threading my fingers through hers, feeling the warmth of her palm against mine. With my other hand, I slid around her waist, my fingers pressing gently into the small of her back as I pulled her in, close enough to feel the rise and fall of her breath.

There were no words.

No hesitation.

Her eyelids fluttered closed, her lips parting slightly—a silent invitation, an unspoken surrender. And then, we kissed.

It was deep. Wet. Unapologetically passionate.

Her lips were soft, even softer than I had imagined, her body was melting into mine as if we had done this a hundred times before. The faintest taste of whiskey warm and indulgent—lingered on her tongue.

She squeezed my hand, harder, tighter, like she didn't want to let go, like she wanted to anchor herself to the moment, to me.

I didn't want it to end.

I let the kiss linger, let it stretch into something almost dangerous. My fingers traced slow, deliberate circles against the small of her back, pulling her even closer, feeling the shape of her against me. She responded in kind, her grip firm, her body pressing into mine, her breath coming in short, unsteady gasps between kisses.

When we finally broke apart, our foreheads rested against each other for a brief second, both of us catching our breath, the air between us electric.

I opened my eyes first, my pulse still thrumming, and said in a voice that was low, deliberate, promising—
"*Maybe tomorrow.*"

The second the words left my lips, she sprung up, practically bouncing, a wide grin spreading across her face.

She didn't just smile—she beamed.

Then, with absolutely no shame, she threw her arms in the air and shouted loud enough for half the canal to hear—

"*I CAN'T WAIT!*"

A few late-night passersby glanced over, chuckling at her excitement.

I couldn't help it—I smiled too.

Just before she turned toward the train, she paused, glancing back at me with a wicked glint in her eye. She leaned in just enough for only me to hear, her voice dipped into a sultry whisper.

"*Oh, by the way...*" she dragged the words out, teasing.
"*Tomorrow is Sunday. My shift doesn't start until four.*"

The implication was clear.

I let my smile linger, tilting my head slightly as I held her gaze.

"*I'll see you tomorrow.*"

With that, she turned and walked toward the station, her hips swaying just enough to let me know she knew I was watching.

I exhaled slowly, watching as she disappeared onto the train platform, the warmth of her still clinging to my skin.

And then, the switch flipped.

PEOPLE ALWAYS THINK they're in control. Lieke believed she was leading the night, setting the pace, pulling me into her world.

But that's the real trick, isn't it? Let them think they're the ones making the choices. It makes it all the sweeter when they realize, too late, that they really only ever had one choice.

And just like that, the kiss that thrilled her was now the one that doomed her. She had no idea she had been claimed—not as a lover, but as prey.

As Lieke disappeared into the station, I turned toward the canal. The water stretched out before me, black and glassy, reflecting the soft glow of the streetlights overhead. It was eerily still, a perfect mirror—until the wind sent a slow ripple across its surface, breaking my reflection into fractured pieces.

For a moment, I didn't recognize myself.

Not the man Lieke had just kissed. Not the charming stranger who had bought her drinks, made her laugh, held her hand like a lover. No. What I saw in that water was something else entirely. Something I had seen before.

Florida.

That night of the party. When I stood in front of the sliding glass door, staring at the thing staring back at me. When I saw the monster for what he was—when I realized I wasn't just capable of killing, I was made for it.

And now, here it was again. A different city. A different life. But the same dark eyes staring back at me, waiting. Watching.

But this time?

This time, I smiled.

I saw what I had become, and for the first time, I didn't just accept it. I embraced it.

The reflection stared back, the water distorting it for a moment before settling again.

I turned my steps slow, measured, as I walked back toward the apartment.

No longer thinking about the kiss, her touch, her warm breath, or the way she had tasted.

I was planning.

The details.
The execution.
When and how I would do it.

By the time I reached my door, it was all laid out in my mind—the perfect ending to a perfect seduction.

And she had no idea what was coming.

Chapter 22

CHOICES

SUNDAY MORNING ARRIVED with an almost violent brightness, the early sun slicing through the windows and setting the small apartment ablaze in golden light. The orange-painted walls of the front room only amplified the intensity, turning the space into a blinding, glowing box that made it impossible to ignore the day's arrival.

Denise lay beside me, her breath slow and steady, still deep in sleep. She had come in late—far later than I had—and had slipped beneath the sheets without waking me. I listened to her quite inhales, her soft exhalations, and for a fleeting second, I envied the simplicity of her sleep, the way she could just exist without the weight of what I carried.

Lieke.

Her name alone sent a ripple of heat through me, a lingering pulse of something dangerous. My mind drifted back to the night before—the kiss, her scent, the warmth of her breath against my skin. Whiskey and sin. That's what she smelled like. Sweet, intoxicating, something that lured you in before you even realized you were trapped.

Her touch had ignited something in me. Not just lust—but something deeper. A hunger. A fascination. A pull toward her that I hadn't anticipated.

And yet, as I lay there, staring at the ceiling, I tried to convince myself that Denise had maybe experienced something similar last night.

A company event. Too many drinks. Maybe, for just a moment, she let her inhibitions slip. Maybe a colleague had leaned in a little too close, whispered something in her ear that made her laugh in a way she hadn't in years. Maybe there had been a stolen glance, a fleeting brush of hands.

Maybe someone had walked her safely to the trolley stop.

And maybe—just maybe—she had given in, just for a second. A meaningless kiss. A moment she would never tell me about, but one that would surface in the back of her mind at odd moments, a flicker of something exciting, something she would never fully acknowledge.

I needed to believe this had happened.

Not because I wanted her to cheat or wanted her to be unfaithful.

But because I needed to balance the scales.

I needed an excuse to wash away my guilt—not for what I had done, but for what I had felt. For the way I had wanted Lieke, not just as a conquest, but as a person.

I had stepped over the line last night and I knew it.

But by the end of today, none of it would matter.

By this time tomorrow, Lieke would be nothing but a distant memory.

And Denise and I? We'd be on a plane back to the States, returning to the illusion of our carefully constructed existence.

A normal life. A clean slate. A quiet lie.

Even as I wrestled with the guilt, my mind beat with anticipation.

I was aroused, not just by the memory of Lieke's touch, but by what the day would bring. By what I was on the verge of doing.

I slid out of bed, careful not to wake Denise, and made my way to the kitchen. I moved with deliberate normalcy, pulling eggs from the fridge, setting bread in the toaster, making coffee—going through the motions of a man making his wife a memorable breakfast.

And all the while, in the back of my mind, I was meticulously piecing together what was to come.

This was not going to be a distant kill with a gunshot from 400 yards. Not a quick, calculated execution.

Poison wasn't an option either. So what to do?

A knife crossed my mind—quick, efficient, intimate. We had learned in the Marine Corps that a single thrust into the voice box wouldn't kill a man instantly, but it would silence him. Mute the screams. Buy time to prolong the kill without the deafening wails that would alert the world.

That excited me, but a knife was messy.

And walking out of Lieke's private room covered in blood? More than suspicious.

No—if I was going to do this, it needed to be something else.

Something raw. Something primal.

Something that would make this a crime of passion that most likely, if investigated would lead to one of her regulars.

Strangulation.

Up close. Personal. The kind of death where you feel the life leaving them.

Where you watch the moment their body betrays them.

Where you feel their final, desperate struggle before everything goes still. Where you literally hold their life in your hands.

Yes.

That's how I would do it.

And just as I slid Denise's plate onto the table, my decision was made.

By tonight, Lieke would be gone.

DENISE STIRRED, stretching long and slow, her body arching against the sheets as she let out a soft sigh. The morning light cut through the window, slicing across the room in golden ribbons, and as she shifted, it hit her just right—illuminating her in a way that made me pause.

Maybe it was the emotions from the night before, or maybe it was the contrast of what I had done, what I was about to do—but at that moment, she looked more beautiful than I had ever seen her.

She slid out of bed, pulling on one of my shirts like she always did in the mornings, the fabric draping loosely over her frame. But as she moved into the light, the thin material became nearly translucent, revealing the soft curves of her body beneath it. It clung to her hips, traced the details of her body, and for the first time in longer than I could remember, I really looked at her.

Not just as my wife. Not just as a familiar presence in my life.

But as a woman.

A woman who was desirable. A woman who was still mine.

She ran a hand through her tousled hair, blinking away the last remnants of sleep, and made her way to the small kitchen table. Tucking her legs beneath her, she reached for her coffee, completely unaware of the effect she had on me in that moment.

Completely unaware of everything.

"*I feel guilty,*" she admitted, stirring a sugar cube into the dark liquid. "*We've spent no real time together here in Amsterdam, and tomorrow we're leaving.*"

There was sincerity in her voice, a quiet regret that tugged at the edges of her words. For a brief moment, I felt a flicker of something —remorse, maybe—but it was dull, fleeting, easily pushed aside.

I reached across the table, covering her hand with mine, my voice calm and reassuring. "*It's fine. I completely understand.*"

She exhaled, but I could tell she wasn't entirely convinced.

Still, she pressed on, pushing the guilt aside. It was habit for us, brushing past unspoken disappointments, filing them away for another time.

Reluctantly, she let me know that tonight was the final event of the conference—the closing ceremony, the last round of handshakes, obligatory smiles, and farewell drinks. She was required to go, and likely, it would stretch late into the night.

"*I'm sorry,*" she said, her eyes searching mine. This time, she meant it. There was a familiar look in her gaze—one I recognized from years of navigating this marriage together. It was the look of a woman who loved me, who missed what we had been. A look that said she wished things were different, but neither of us could do anything to change tonight.

I softened my expression, playing my part effortlessly. I leaned in, brushing my thumb over her knuckles.

"*Don't worry about it,*" I said smoothly. "*It's Sunday night. I'll make sure everything's packed for tomorrow morning. I might go out for a bit, grab dinner, have a couple of drinks with the locals... then I'll come back and try to wait up for you.*"

It was too easy.

The lie rolled off my tongue like second nature, my delivery flawless. And I knew—with the kind of certainty that only comes from experience—that she wouldn't question it.

Not because she didn't love me. Not because she didn't care.

But because she trusted me, and she was too preoccupied with the demands of her own day to spend any time wondering about mine.

She smiled, nodding, and took a sip of her coffee, accepting my answer without hesitation.

An hour, Denise was gone, disappearing into the rhythm of her conference, lost in a world of polite conversation and corporate obligations.

And I?

I had time.

Plenty of it.

I glanced at the clock. 10:00 A.M..

Lieke wasn't starting her shift until 4:00 P.M..

That left six hours.

Six hours to plan. To prepare. To savor the anticipation.

I poured myself another cup of coffee, letting the steam curl up toward my face as I leaned back in my chair.

I wasn't in a rush.

Not today.

Today, I was going to enjoy every moment of what was to come.

AT 5:30 P.M., I STEPPED out the front door, inhaling the crisp evening air, feeling the weight of the moment settle over me like an old, familiar friend.

I skipped my usual walk—no slow stroll through Vondelpark, no leisurely detour past the market. Tonight was different.My purpose was singular, my steps more deliberate than ever. The hum of the city around me felt sharper, more intense, every detail vibrating with clarity.

The scent of fresh flowers from a nearby vendor drifted through the air, mingling with the faint aroma of canal water and distant traces of warm pastries from a café down the street. The cobblestones beneath my feet, usually just a forgettable part of the journey, now seemed more defined, each uneven surface grounding me in the present. The buildings, old and timeless, stood against the soft glow of the fading sun, their facades whispering stories of those who had walked these streets before me.

Everything felt more alive tonight. More vibrant.

Sundays in the Red-Light District carried their own contradictions—a strange intersection of indulgence and repentance. Tourists clung to their last hours in the city, squeezing in one final taste of pleasure before boarding their planes in the morning. At the same time, locals drifted by, some heading later in the day toward or from mass at the old church near the canal, their hushed prayers colliding with the quiet murmurs of sin unfolding just feet away.

I walked into The Old Sailor, and the difference was immediate. The pub was thinner than usual, just a small mix of travelers and a few who called this place home, their voices overlapping in a blend of languages, laughter, and quiet conspiracies. Still the energy inside was heightened, almost electric, buzzing with a kind of restless anticipation.

I made my way to my usual table, letting my eyes adjust to the dim lighting as I took in every detail.

I wanted to remember this.

To burn it into the dark recesses of my mind, to recall it later when I needed to relive every single moment as it unfolded.

As I settled in, I turned my attention toward the window. Outside, the district was as it always had been—a living stage where desire, desperation, and commerce performed in perfect unison.

The Seductress was there, wrapped in something sheer and delicate, moving with the slow, calculated grace of a woman who knew exactly how to lure her prey. She scanned the thin crowd, searching for the right one, her body a web, waiting for someone to step too close.

The Temptress, dressed in crimson and gold, leaned into her role with ease. Tonight, she worked harder, the way a seasoned performer dials up the act when the audience is thin.

I glanced up.

And there she was.

Mystery Girl.

The curtains were drawn open, revealing her in a sheer, low-cut evening gown, the fabric draping over her body like liquid silk. The red glow from the room's walls refracted against the material, highlighting every curve, every line, every delicate shadow of her body.

She stood as she always had—legs crossed, poised, detached. A queen in her tower. Above it all.

She never looked in my direction. But tonight, there was a shift—something subtle. Something unspoken.

Tonight, I felt like she knew I was watching.

I let my mind wander, playing with the idea, the fantasy of her in place of the girl on the boat in Arizona. Her standing there, bathed in moonlight, untouchable yet completely surrendered to pleasure. My pulse quickened, a dark thrill threading through my veins.

And then—Lieke.

She stole my focus the second she appeared.

She was dressed in a short, black mini-skirt, a snug matching tube top hugging the curves of her body, and furry tan boots that only made her seem more effortless, more playful, more alive. But it wasn't her outfit that stopped me.

It was her face.

She had barely any makeup on.

She had remembered what I told her. She had listened.

She had taken it to heart—the way I said she was more beautiful without it, more real.

And she wanted me to see her that way again.

When she spotted me, she smiled—not a flirtatious smile, not an act for some passing stranger, but a genuine, knowing smile.

I stared at her, something in me momentarily softening. Without thinking, I lifted my hand and pointed to my face, acknowledging the change, letting her know I noticed, that I approved.

She was stunning.
And for the briefest moment, I let myself wonder—what if?

What if we had met under different circumstances?

What if I was someone else?
Would I have fallen for her?
Would she have fallen for me?
Would we have ended up somewhere far from here, living a life that wasn't built on lies and fleeting moments?

The thought unsettled me.

Because it was pointless.
Because it didn't matter.
Because by the end of the night, she wouldn't exist beyond my memory.

A beer slid across the table, pulling me back to reality.

Charles, the bartender, nodded at me before moving on to another patron.
I took a slow sip, steeling myself.

I was here for a reason.

These thoughts, these emotions—they had no place in what I was about to do.

The clock ticked past 8 P.M., and I could feel her eyes on me before I even looked up.

Lieke.

Her expression was different now—her lips parted just slightly, her head a silent invitation.

Come to me.

The look she gave me was pleading, wanting—the kind of look a woman gives when she wants to feel chosen.
I held her gaze for a moment, felt the weight of it settle in my chest.

I could still walk away.

I could still turn back.
I could still leave her untouched.

I wouldn't.

I pushed my thoughts aside, and order one last beer.

Because tonight was to be the night.

AT 9:00 A.M., I asked for my bill.

As I slipped a few folded bills onto the table, I drained the last sip of my beer, the bitter taste lingering on my tongue. The weight of what was about to happen pressed against my chest—not as hesitation, but as a slow, burning certainty.

I stood up, stretching slightly, my muscles tight from sitting too long, my body humming with a mix of alcohol, anticipation, and something darker.

From her window, Lieke saw me leaving.

Her eyes lit up, a large, knowing smile spreading across her lips as she watched me walk toward the entrance of the building. There was something undeniable in her gaze—a hunger, an expectation.

A desire to be chosen.

I opened the door to the building, stepping inside.

The hallway was a matrix of narrow corridors and winding staircases, leading to countless rooms, each holding a story, a secret, a transaction. The air inside was thick, stale, carrying a scent that curled around my senses like a ghost of pleasure and desperation.

Music could be heard playing louder than it should with soft moans coming from behind closed doors.

There was a smell of sin, layered over years, embedded in the walls, soaked into the sheets. A place where fantasies were fulfilled and forgotten in the same breath. It was a rancid combination of sweat, cheap perfume and urine.

I walked forward, my body set, my mind committed.

The excitement of the kill, the thrill of control, it should have been the only thing I was focused on. But Lieke was still in my head.

Her skin, soft and warm under my fingertips.
Her lips, eager, parting against mine with a moan that still echoed in my mind. Her body, the way it moved, the way it pressed into me like she wanted to melt into my skin, disappear into me completely.

She was everything—the kind of girl who didn't just exist in the moment but created it, shaped it into something unforgettable.

She wasn't just a body to use.

She was a memory waiting to be made.

And that thought unnerved me.

I reached her door, ready to negotiate, ready to step into a space where she would give herself to me completely.

And then—I stopped.

A flash of hesitation. A breath of clarity.

Like every other time before, when instinct and desire clashed in that single defining moment.

Did I really want to do this?

Take the life of a girl who had done nothing but trust me? Who hadn't played a game, hadn't made me a mark—just a girl looking for something real.

She had opened up, let me in. Kissed me like I was the only man in the world. Not for money. Not for business. Just for me.

And for one stolen moment, I had felt the same. That kiss—I never wanted it to end.

Standing in that dim, filthy hallway, my thoughts spun. Indulgence or secrecy? Control or surrender? Would I take her, taste her, ruin her—lose myself so completely that nothing else mattered?

For a moment, I almost let it happen.

But no.

Not to her.

Not to the girl who, in another life, might have been a love of mine.

That thought alone forced my hand.

Tight with decision, electrified with purpose—
I walked away from Lieke's door.

And knocked on the Mystery Girl's instead.

Chapter 23

BEHIND THE CURTAIN

BEFORE I COULD KNOCK a second time, the door swung open.

She stood there, framed by the soft red glow spilling from the room behind her.

Up close, she was even more striking.

Her eyes locked onto mine—dark, unreadable, yet filled with something… hypnotic.
I had been prepared for this moment, but for the first time in a long time, I was left momentarily speechless.

She held my gaze for a second, then with her lips parting, a soft whisper as she spoke.

In a tone that was"*very a matter of fact,*" she said, her voice smooth, even, practiced, "*it's 150 euros for 20 minutes… or 250 for the hour.*

And we can do anything you like…" she added.

Then she let the words hang for just a breath before finishing,

"*But you must wear a condom.*"

No emotion. No seduction. Just business.

Still caught in the magnetism of her presence, I barely registered the transaction.

I should have negotiated, played the role of the customer, but instead, the words came out without thought, without hesitation—

"*I want the hour.*"

Something flickered in her expression.

Not surprise. Not pleasure.

Something else.

Assessment.

She stepped aside, granting me entrance with a simple nod.

As I crossed the threshold, she moved to the window, reaching for the thick, velvet curtains.

The scraping of the metal rings against the rod sent a shiver through me, snapping me back to reality. A sharp reminder:

I was on the clock now.

The room was small, intimate, the red light enveloping everything, warping reality.

It softened imperfections, blurred edges, and created illusions. Not that she had anything to hide.

She turned back to me, her body at attention, deliberate, and gestured toward the bed.

"*Sit.*"

I obeyed, lowering myself onto the mattress. The sheets were crisp, freshly pressed, carrying the faint scent of detergent and something sterile, something clinical.

Then she sat beside me.

Her hands—warm, smooth—pressed against my shoulders, gliding down my back in slow, circular motions.

Not just touching.

Studying.

"*You're tense,*" she murmured, her breath warm against my skin. "*But that's why you're here, isn't it?*"

I didn't answer.

I didn't trust myself to.

Her voice was low, sultry—but it felt forced. Rehearsed.

A line she had used a hundred times before on a hundred other men, each one thinking they were different, special.

Like they mattered.

My jaw began to tightened.

Her scent hit me then, subtle, intoxicating, nothing like the overwhelming candy-sweet perfume of high-end strippers.

This was money—deliberate, refined.

Issey Miyake. Dior.

A fragrance designed not to scream, but to lure—a scent meant to stay on your skin long after she was gone.

She stood and moved in front of me now, her expression unreadable, her body inches away.

Then, with the same unhurried precision, she reached for the straps of her dress.

One.

Then the other.

She was in complete control now.

My stomach twisted.

My mind flashed for a moment.

Lieke had never tried to control me.

With her, there was something real, something genuine in the way she had touched me, the way she laughed, the way she looked at me when she thought I wasn't watching.

She hadn't been trying to sell me anything.

But this girl?

She was playing me, she was playing a game.

A game she thought she had already won.

And then, her dress slid down her shoulders, the fabric clinging, teasing, before it slipped lower, catching at her hips.

Her long, dark hair cascaded over her breasts, barely concealing them. My eyes were transfixed on her taking it all in. Then, without hesitation she let the dress fall to the floor in a whisper of silk.

She wore nothing underneath and stood in front of me deliberately giving me time to take it all in.

Her skin was flawless, smooth, a soft shimmer reflecting the red glow of the room.

I couldn't look away but my mind reminded me, this wasn't seduction. This was a performance.

She turned around slowly, giving me a full view, her hands running lightly down her sides as if to remind me—

This body is for sale.

I watched her, remembering the girl on the boat.

The way she owned her pleasure, the way she made men compete for the privilege of touching her.

Now, here she was.

Older. Wiser. More refined.

But still the same.

A woman who demanded to be worshipped.

Her body was sculpted, deliberately perfect.

But it felt… hollow.

She was calculating every move, every breath, every glance.

Because that's what she did.

That's what she had always done.

She thought she had power.

She bent at the waist, retrieving the fallen gown from the floor.

Her body stretched in front of me—perfect, inviting, framed by the dim glow.

She was a masterpiece, and she knew it.

Then she straightened, stepping forward.

Closer.

She reached down, tilting my chin up with two fingers, her nails dragging lightly along my skin.

She was studying me now.

And I realized something right then.

Something she didn't know.

Who I was. What I was. What was coming.

To her, I was just another man, another client.

Another fool willing to pay for her time.

The anger came slow, creeping, curling around my ribs like something thick and venomous.

I clenched my fists, forcing myself to breathe through it.

She looked at me, lips curving into a smirk, her fingers trailing along my shoulder, testing me, teasing me.

Then she bent forward, just enough that her lips were nearly at my ear.

Her voice was silk, honeyed and sweet—fake.

"*So... what would you like me to do for you?*"

I stared at her.

And I felt it snap.

Something inside me fractured, split wide open.

I hated her in that moment.

Hated the way she thought she owned this room, this moment, me.

Like she had power over me. Like she had power at all.

Like she wasn't just another thing waiting to be used.

She had spent her whole life turning men into slaves to their own desire.

She had played this game so many times she thought she was untouchable.

She had no idea how wrong she was.

My hands itched.

My breath slowed.

And in that moment, I knew exactly how this night would end.

I STOOD UP SLOWLY, letting the weight of the moment settle between us. The red light cast a warm glow over her skin, making her look almost surreal—a living painting, perfectly curated for display. I reached for her, I slid my hand to the curve of her lower back, drawing her in until the warmth between us was undeniable.

Looking deep into her eyes, I spoke in a low, deliberate tone. "*You take care of people all the time. Tonight, I want to take care of you.*"

Her expression didn't change, but I saw the flicker of curiosity in her gaze. She was waiting for the catch, the unspoken request, the inevitable demand that always came next. But I had no intention of giving her what she expected.

"*I don't want sex,*" I continued. "*No oral. No performance.*" I let my fingertips trace along the curve of her spine, slow, calculated, my voice dropping just a notch lower. "*I just want to give you a full body massage... for the remaining fifty minutes or so that we have.*"

A pause.

Her breath hitched slightly, and I could see the shift in her eyes—something unguarded, intrigued. It was subtle, but it was there.

She was considering it.

I waited, holding my breath just slightly, watching for any sign of rejection. This wasn't about seduction. This was about control. About shifting the power dynamic back in my favor.

And then, just as I had hoped, her walls came down.

She let out a small, indulgent sigh, stepping back just enough to let her body relax. My idea had worked—catering to her vanity, her self-worth, giving her something that made her feel valued beyond just a transaction.

"*That sounds nice,*" she finally said, her voice softer now. Then, with a teasing smirk, she added, "*Will you do my feet too?*"

I smiled, nodding. "*Of course.*"

She climbed onto the bed, stretching out like a cat, her body perfectly positioned beneath the dim light.

I watched her for a moment, taking in the way she moved, the way she let herself ease into the moment, as if she had already forgotten that I was a stranger.

Exactly where I wanted her to be.

Starting at the base of her neck I let my hands roam over her bare shoulders, the heat of her skin warming my palms. Soft. Almost too soft. There was no hesitation in the way she moved, no stiffness, no tension—just an easy, practiced compliance.

She sighed as I pressed into the delicate muscles along her spine, rolling her neck lazily, stretching beneath. A sound of satisfaction. A sound of pleasure.

My fingers traced the sharp curve of her shoulder blades, then drifted lower, following the elegant line of her back. The light in the room was dim, casting shadows that made her body look almost unreal.

My thumbs pressed into the dip of her lower back, kneading slow circles, feeling the firmness beneath the surface. She was toned, the kind of body that had been trained to be admired, to be touched, to be worshiped.

And she knew it.

Every sigh, every stretch of her limbs, every arch of her back—it was deliberate.

I moved lower, exploring the curve of her hips, the smooth swell of her thighs. Her skin was warm, almost unnaturally so. My fingers pressed deeper, working their way over the tight roundness of her ass, feeling the way it gave beneath my grip, then resisted.

She let out another sigh, tilting her head slightly to the side. "*Mmm... you're good at this,*" she murmured, her voice thick with something between amusement and arousal.

I didn't respond.

I just kept going, kept exploring, kept memorizing the feeling of her beneath my hands.

Her breath hitched as I squeezed a little harder, kneading into the fullness of her curves, the muscles beneath the softness. She shifted, adjusting her position, pressing back into my touch just slightly, just enough.

An invitation.

A test.

I knew how this worked. She was guiding the moment, controlling the rhythm, pulling me into the act without saying a word.

I hated it.

My contention was mounting.

Not enough for her to notice.

Not yet.

She thought she was leading me exactly where she wanted me to go.

I continued to let my hands linger on her lower back, pressing my thumbs into the delicate muscles along her spine, working slow, deliberate circles. She sighed into the sheets, her body melting beneath my touch, every ounce of tension and resistance draining from her.

"*Roll over,*" I murmured, my voice low but firm.

SHE HESITATED FOR JUST A FRACTION of a second, then complied, shifting onto her back with effortless grace. The movement was slow, teasing in a way that felt almost unintentional—but I knew better. This was second nature to her, the art of making even the simplest motion seductive.

Now, laid out beneath me, she stretched her arms above her head, exposing every inch of herself to me, completely at ease.

I started with her feet, lifting one gently, pressing my thumbs into the arch, feeling the way her toes curled slightly in response.

"T*hat feels so good,*" she murmured, her voice dripping with indulgence.

I smirked, gripping her ankle a little firmer, running my fingers along the sensitive pressure points, watching her expression shift between pleasure and relaxation.

Her other foot was just as responsive, her body sinking deeper into the mattress as I worked my way up, kneading the tension from her calves, tracing slow, methodical strokes along her toned legs.

Then, just as I reached the inside of her thigh, she shifted slightly—spreading her legs just enough for me to notice.

A silent invitation.

I kept my movements steady, my expression unreadable, my fingers pressing deeper into the muscle just above her knee.

Her breathing changed.

Slight.

But I noticed.

I moved higher, my hands grazing the soft skin at the top of her inner thigh. She parted her legs a fraction more, a calculated movement that sent a slow pulse of heat through the air between us.

I glanced up at her.

Her eyes were half-lidded, watching me, waiting.

Testing me.

I let my hands linger just inches from where she wanted them, my fingertips dancing along the sensitive skin, teasing without committing.

She let out a slow exhale, a lazy smirk.

I continued moving up, my hands gliding effortlessly over her stomach, feeling the way her muscles subtly tensed under my touch before melting back into relaxation. Her skin was impossibly smooth, a seamless expanse of silk, free of even the slightest imperfection. My fingertips traced along the gentle curve of her pelvis.

She was meticulously maintained, every inch of her body perfected—not just for herself, but for the endless rotation of men who paid to touch her. The thought sent a flicker of something sharp through me, something dangerous.

Still, I kept my touch slow, deliberate, pretending she was still in control.

I skimmed upward, feeling the dip of her ribcage, then higher, cupping her breasts, massaging them in lazy, synchronized circles. Her nipples hardened beneath my palms, reacting to my touch even in her half-conscious state. Her head tilted slightly to the side, her lips parting just enough to release the softest, most unguarded sigh—a sound so natural, so instinctive, that for a split second, I felt something almost human stir inside me.

Her eyes were closed now, her body fully surrendered.

She looked peaceful.

Almost innocent.

But she wasn't, not really.

I picked up her arm—it was limp, heavy in my grip, a stark contrast to how her body had clung to mine just moments before. I kneaded the muscles from her shoulder to her fingertips, massaging the delicate bones of her hand, gently tugging at each finger, pretending this was still just a game, still just an act.

I reached for the other arm, but the thought intruded again.

All the men she had been with.

The ones she had entertained, teased, played for money, not for passion, not for the moment, just for the transaction.

The anger started to build.

Slow, steady, like a storm forming on the horizon, quiet but inevitable.

We had just over fifteen minutes left.

Fifteen minutes before this hour would be up, before she'd rise from this bed, dress herself in that slinky little gown, and return to her window, ready to do it all over again with the next man.

I couldn't allow that.

I placed her arm back down, my fingers shifting, trailing up the column of her throat.

Her body was still relaxed beneath me, basking in the pleasure of my touch, completely unaware of what was coming. She had no reason to suspect, no reason to tense or resist.

Not yet.

She trusted me.

And that trust was her fatal mistake.

I let my fingers slide up, tracing the elegant curve of her collarbone, my thumbs ghosting over the delicate hollow of her throat. Her pulse was steady beneath my touch, strong and rhythmic, completely at ease.

I savored that moment.

The last second before everything would change.

HER PULSE FLUTTERED beneath my thumb.
Unaware. Unconcerned. Unprepared.

She looked up at me as if she was ready to make another insensitive demand. That was all it took.

And the storm hit.

At first, she barely reacted—a small furrow of confusion between her brows. Then, instinct kicked in.

Her body jerked, hands flying up, nails digging in, desperately trying to pry me off. I squeezed harder. She thrashed, her legs kicking wildly against the bed. A choked whimper escaped her lips, but no real sound followed. Her throat was already closing.

Her eyes went wide—fully awake. Fully aware.

Then came the panic. Raw. Animalistic.

Her fists pounded my chest, nails scraping at my arms, but it didn't matter. It wouldn't have mattered if she had a knife—her fate was already sealed. She fought hard at first, her body twisting, kicking, arching off the bed, trying to throw me off. Then weaker. Slower. Her strength faded as oxygen drained from her body.

Her mouth opened, lips trembling, trying to form words that wouldn't come.
Begging.
Not with sound—just her eyes.

Her face darkened, veins rising beneath the skin, lips parted in silent cries. Her hands—once frantic—slipped.
Her legs slowed.
Her chest heaved once, twice—then collapsed inward, desperate for air that would never come.

Then—nothing.

I slowly released her throat.
Silence. Stillness. Done.

I exhaled.
I'd done it, up close and personal.

I paused, waiting but nothing came.
No regret. No guilt. Just quiet. Just peace.

Then—

A gasp.

Not a sigh. Not a final breath. A ragged, lung-tearing wheeze as her body convulsed, sucking in air like a drowning victim breaking the surface.

I was momentarily stunned, but a slow, euphoric rush crept over me. I could do this again. I could take her life twice. A smile manifested itself on my face as her chest jerked violently. Fingers clutched at the sheets. Her fucking eyes opened.
Wide. Wild. Terrified. Alive.

She sucked in another breath, her body betraying her, trying to force itself back to life.

I let her.

I watched.

Let her believe, for the briefest moment, that she had survived.

That she would be okay.

That I would help her.

Then I covered her mouth, pressing my lips close to her ear. I softly said "*I'm in control here. Not you. Not ever again.*"

Her scream died against my palm.

Her body spasmed beneath me, thrashing, legs kicking—but my mind was determined.

I wrapped my fingers around her throat again, squeezing harder than before.
This time, I wouldn't let go.
Her body bucked, twisting, fighting with everything she had left.

Her eyes begged.

Not just for air.
Not just for mercy.
But for one more second.
One more breath.

I denied her.

I squeezed tighter, crushing the last bit of life from her.

Her limbs spasmed in weak, involuntary convulsions.

Her chest fluttered through its final, useless breaths.

Her eyes fluttered.
Then—
Stillness.

This time, I waited.
One minute. Two. Five.

No breath. No twitch.
No second chances.

She was gone.

A slow, satisfied smile spread across my face, the kind that came not from pleasure, but from purpose.

This wasn't just about the act. It was about what it meant.

I had done more than just take a life tonight—I had spared countless men from the game she played, from the manipulation, the false promises, the way she lured them in only to leave them empty. She was a predator in her own right, one who fed on vulnerability, not with a blade or a bullet, but with a smile, a touch, a lie.

And now, she would play no more games. I quickly justified and took solace knowing that her death would be a warning—a shift in the routine, a ripple in the cycle. That other girls would hear about her, and the unease would settle in, make them think twice before pulling another desperate man behind those curtains.

Better yet, maybe someone like Lieke would see it as a sign—a reason to walk away from this business before it was too late.

I sat with her for another five minutes. Then ten.

I wanted to.

I was savoring it.

Not the kill itself, but the absolute certainty of it.

She was gone.

Her body cooling, her once-perfect lips parted slightly, her eyes still open, staring at the ceiling in a vacant, eternal daze.

Only when I was completely sure—when I had used every last second of my hour—did I move.

Methodically, I turned off the red light, plunging the room into shadows. Then, with careful precision, I pulled back the curtains.

I knew the routine. When a girl finished her shift, she opened the curtains and turned off the light.

Now, she was just another girl who had closed up shop for the night.

THE STREET BELOW WAS STILL ALIVE with tourists, drunks, and wanderers. No one would think twice about her window being dark. The third floor wasn't that visible from the street, and no one would look close enough to see that the bed remained occupied.

Tomorrow, the next girl would come and the police would be called.

But by then? I would be gone.

On a plane, thousands of miles away, nothing more than a ghost in the night.

The room was covered in years of DNA from countless visitors, they'd have no where to even start.

Besides, by the time they found her, they probably wouldn't even care enough to investigate, this would most likely be nothing more than another tragedy in the Red-Light District.

A brief headline, a cautionary tale, a footnote in a city built on vice.

And I?

I would be untouchable, again.

As I stepped away from the bed, I locked the door from the inside, making sure it looked just as she would have left it. Then, moving with calm precision, I descended the stairs, each step taking me further from the scene.

I walked through the corridors, the stale air still thick with perfume, sweat, and cigarette smoke. I stepped into the alleyway, blending into the neon-lit streets as if nothing had happened and paid careful attention to not walk past Lieke's window.

Better she think I had gone home early.

Better she never know,

tonight, she had been the one spared.

Chapter 24

HOME SWEET HOME

I HAD JUST CRAWLED INTO BED when I heard the front door open. Denise was home.

Her heels hit the floor with a sigh, the unsteady rhythm of alcohol and exhaustion. She had been drinking. Maybe dancing. She loved to dance, especially when work and obligation loosened their grip for the night.

She moved through the bedroom, shedding clothes as she walked, leaving a trail from the doorway to the bed. When she slipped beneath the covers, her body was warm, pressing into mine like instinct. Like home.

I pulled her close, let my face rest against the scent of her skin, and for the first time in days, my mind was empty. No Lieke. No Mystery Girl. No memories of the night. Just this. Just her.

And I let myself enjoy it.

THE MORNING WAS chaotic.

We overslept.

The alarm blared an hour too late, throwing us into a mad scramble —rushed packing, a frantic cab ride, a sprint through the airport. We were the last ones to board.

Denise, was feeling every bit of the prior night's indulgence, the alcohol, the exhaustion, the endless corporate small talk that had drained her. She pressed her forehead to the window, asleep before we even left the ground.

As the plane lifted from Schiphol, I watched Amsterdam shrink beneath us. It looked different now. The excitement, the mystique—the electric pulse of the city—was gone.

It was nothing more than a skyline fading behind me. A place I would never return to.

Somewhere over the Atlantic, I let my mind wander.

I wasn't sure who I was anymore.

But maybe, for the first time, I knew exactly who I was becoming.

Amsterdam had been a contradiction—a collision of self. A transformation. A burial. A part of me had come alive there. And a part of me had died.

I felt guilty. I had betrayed Denise.

Maybe not in the way most would consider unforgivable. I hadn't had sex. I hadn't crossed that line. But I had explored.

My hands had roamed every inch of the Mystery Girl's body, tracing every curve, every breath, memorizing her like a collector studying a rare artifact. But it had never been about touch. It was a means to an end. A necessary prelude to the real thrill—her final breath, the moment of absolute control.

Not once, but twice.

The way she surrendered beneath me, the way her gasps became weaker, her body stilling—it had satisfied something inside me in a disturbingly effortless way. A way that felt more natural, more exhilarating than any physical pleasure I had ever known.

It was deeper than desire. Stronger than lust. The combination of control and inevitability. More fulfilling than sex itself.

And then, there was Lieke.

We had never gone further than that single kiss. A kiss that lingered, a kiss that did something to me I wasn't prepared for. We had barely touched, yet she had burrowed deeper under my skin than anyone else ever had. Our connection had been instant, raw, undeniable. A force I hadn't anticipated, hadn't invited—but one that forced me to check myself, to suppress the hunger, to do something I never did.

Protect.

With her, the temptation wasn't to take—it was to hold on. And that terrified me in a way no kill ever had.

I knew the emotional attraction was worse than sex. It would last longer. It would haunt me.

I turned to Denise, still asleep, still innocent in all of this.

I reached for her hand, threading my fingers through hers.

There were a lot of questions.

But one thing was certain.

I wasn't the same man who had arrived in Amsterdam.

AFTER A GRUELING 12-HOUR FLIGHT, all Denise and I wanted was to uncork a bottle of wine and unwind on our new rooftop, watching the California sunset bleed into the horizon. Denises parents were staying until Saturday to help with Chiara, which meant we'd have some time alone—something time to connect again.

As we pulled into the driveway, exhausted but relieved to be home, we noticed a pink envelope taped to the front door. Denise plucked it off with curiosity, flipping it over before opening it. Inside was an invitation to a neighborhood block party happening just up the street on Friday.

"*That's nice,*" she said, scanning the details. "*And for once, we're not the ones hosting.*"

That alone made California feel like a step up from Florida. A fresh start.

It happened while unpacking, quicker than I expected. Denise noticed scratches on my arm, her eyes narrowing as I reached up to put a suitcase on the top shelf.

"*What happened to your arm?*" she asked, pointing to the thin red marks that ran along my forearm.

I paused for half a second—just long enough to make it look like I had to think about it, not long enough to raise suspicion.

"*Oh—Ms. Jinte's cat,*" I said, adding a sheepish laugh. "*Remember her? The older neighbor from two floors down? Her cat got out while I was coming back from the bakery Sunday. It bolted down the hallway and she was panicking. I helped catch it.*"

Denise raised an eyebrow. "*And it attacked you?*"

"*I wouldn't say 'attacked.'*" I smiled, lifting the arm to show her again. "*It was scared. Clawed me up a little while I was holding onto it. But it's fine. Barely broke skin.*"

She looked at it again, her expression softening just enough before she shrugged. "*Well, you probably should have cleaned it.*"

I chuckled, kissed her on the forehead, and moved on to the next suitcase.

Crisis averted.

FRIDAY NIGHT WITH A BOTTLE OF WINE in hand, we walked three houses up to where the party was already in full swing. The hum of conversation, the clink of glasses, and the occasional bursts of laughter spilled onto the street, blending into the warm California evening.

As we turned and looked up the street, the scene unfolded before us.

Every house had its garage door thrown open, each one transformed into makeshift gathering spots, buzzing with energy. Groups of neighbors floated between driveways, drinks in hand, catching up on old stories, meeting new faces, or topping off their glasses before shifting to the next stop. It was like walking into a well-rehearsed play where everyone knew their lines, their places, their roles.

Except for us.

There were easily 45 to 60 people—maybe more—all comfortably settled into their familiar circles. Conversations carried the weight of years spent together, inside jokes exchanged with ease, stories that had been told a dozen times before but were still greeted with the same knowing smiles.

Denise and I, the outsiders, waded in cautiously, drifting between clusters of chatter, listening in on fragmented conversations that felt like a foreign language. But it didn't last long.

The moment people spotted us—the "new kids on the block"—the questions started pouring in.

"W*here are you from?*"
"*What do you do?*"
"*How's the new house?*"
"H*ave you met so-and-so yet?*"

It was a lot. A flood of names, faces, and rapid-fire introductions. Overwhelming, but undeniably welcoming.

And then we met Anthony.

Anthony was impossible to miss.

Older, with a larger-than-life personality that demanded attention, he moved through the crowd with the kind of confidence only someone who had lived there forever could. He had an energy that was infectious, a voice that carried effortlessly over the party, and a way of making everyone feel like they were his favorite person in the room.

Within minutes, we learned that he was the self-appointed, self-declared *Mayor of Lyndon Street*—a title he wore with pride. And after only a few minutes in his orbit, it was obvious why.

Anthony knew everyone. Every story. Every piece of history. Every bit of drama.

"*You guys are lucky,*" he said, slapping me on the shoulder with an exaggerated grin. "*This is a great street. You got the newlyweds at the end, the quiet ones across from you—don't expect much from them—and that guy over there?*" He motioned discreetly toward a man nursing a whiskey neat. "*He's got a real problem keeping his music down. But hey, if you like classic rock, you won't mind.*"

We couldn't stop laughing.

Anthony was a walking, talking neighborhood archive, and within minutes, we knew more about our street than we could have learned in a year on our own. From which houses had hosted the wildest parties to who had the best wine collection—he filled us in on everything.

From what we gathered, he was a single parent with two kids, both off at college. And though he never said it outright, there was something about the way he threw himself into the party—into the neighborhood—that hinted at a deeper loneliness beneath all the showmanship.

Still, we liked him instantly.

Anthony made sure we met *everyone* and, just like that, we were no longer outsiders.

The night stretched on, filled with stories, laughter, and the ease of slipping into something that, for once, didn't feel forced.

For the first time since moving, California didn't feel like just a new house.

It felt like home.

THANKS TO ANTHONY, we now knew nearly everyone on Lyndon Street—the chocolatier with a hidden whiskey collection, the production grip who had worked on more blockbuster movies than he let on, the former model who still turned heads, and even the actual Mayor of Hermosa Beach.

For the next few months, life on the block settled into a comfortable rhythm—new friends, discovering local hotspots, and a steady rotation of happy hours at different houses up and down the street.

It was the kind of neighborhood that felt picturesque, almost *too* perfect.

But, as with any place, beneath the charm and hospitality, there were stories. And not all of them were innocent.

One warm summer evening, Denise and I found ourselves at Robert and Cindy's for happy hour.

Robert worked in the production industry, the kind of guy who had stories about famous directors and actors but never name-dropped. Cindy, his wife, was a flight attendant for a major airline—effortlessly social, the kind of person who could make you feel like an old friend within minutes. They lived just two houses up from us, and what started as a casual gathering quickly stretched into hours of food, drinks, and neighborhood lore.

Then Cindy leaned in, lowering her voice just enough to make me sit up.

"*Have you guys heard about the house over here?*"

I was instantly hooked.

I loved urban legends, the strange and unexplained. The dark underbelly of suburban life fascinated me.

Denise, on the other hand, shifted in her seat, already uneasy.

Cindy didn't disappoint.

She launched into a story about an ex-football player who used to live on the street—a volatile relationship, constant fights with his girlfriend, until one night, he *ended* it.

Murder.

No hesitation, no second-guessing. He killed her.

Then Robert took over, adding another layer of horror.

"*A few years before that, a guy who lived in those apartments at the end of the street—his girlfriend broke up with him. He couldn't handle it. One night, he crawled through her window and strangled her in her own bed.*"

Denise's fingers tightened around her wine glass.

I could feel her discomfort, the way she was already deciding that maybe she *didn't* love living here as much as she had earlier in the evening.

I, however, felt something different.

Something twisted, something *electric*.

Destiny.

It was almost as if I had been meant to live here.

As the wine flowed and the stories darkened, Cindy hesitated before dropping the next bombshell.

Her eyes flicked toward us, then toward Robert, almost as if seeking permission.

"*I know you guys hang out with Anthony a lot,*" she said carefully. "*Has he ever told you about his wife—his former-wife?*"

Robert exhaled heavily, running a hand down his face as if he already knew where this was going.

He stood up, grabbed another bottle of wine, and uncorked it with a sharp *pop*.

His body language spoke for him.

Cindy shouldn't be telling this story.

But she pressed on anyway.

"*Well, I don't know if it's true or not,*" she prefaced, leaning in slightly, "*but rumor has it... Anthony killed his wife.*"

Denise let out a soft, incredulous laugh.

"*Anthony?*" she repeated, shaking her head. "*Our Anthony?*"

The same Anthony who played host to every party, who knew everyone's name, who made sure no one ever felt like an outsider? It was absurd.

"*People like that don't kill,*" Denise said dismissively.

I knew better.

I leaned forward.

"*Go on,*" I said.

Cindy didn't need more encouragement.

"*His wife, Laura, came home late one night,*" she continued, dropping her voice. "*Anthony told the police he thought someone had broken in... that he didn't recognize her... and he shot her.*"

Denise frowned.

"*But if that's true, why wasn't he arrested?*"

"*Lack of evidence,*" Cindy replied. "*Or at least, that's what they said.*"

Robert groaned, swirling the wine in his glass.

"*You shouldn't spread gossip, Cindy,*" he muttered. "*The police investigated. They came to the same conclusion. It was a tragic accident—but these things happen. That's why people shouldn't have guns in the house.*"

Denise nodded firmly.

"*I agree with that,*" she said, supporting Robert.

Cindy, however, wasn't convinced.

"*Yeah, but the police didn't know about the affair Laura was having,*" she added. "*Or the fact that she came from 'family' money. And guess who inherited all of it?*"

Robert sighed, leaning back in his chair, his expression unreadable.

"*You don't know if any of that's true,*" he said simply.

And just like that, the conversation ended.

The wine was gone. So was the energy of the night.

Denise and I said our goodbyes, stepping out into the quiet warmth of the evening, our house only a short walk away.

She talked about the food, the party, the decorations in Robert and Cindy's house.

I, however, was thinking about something else.

Something far more interesting.

Maybe I had found a new best friend in Anthony.

Chapter 25

MAYOR'S SECRET

DENISE AND I HAD more than settled in. Life in California had smoothed into a rhythm that felt effortless. We had friends, we knew the hot spots, and Chiara was thriving, her days filled with playdates and endless energy. Work was going great for Denise—better than it had in years—and our relationship felt stronger, more connected. Maybe it was the fresh start, the absence of old ghosts, or maybe we had just learned how to exist better in each other's worlds. Whatever it was, for the first time in a long time, things felt easy.

At the corner of our street was a small, unassuming shop. The kind of place you stopped by for last-minute essentials—eggs, bread, detergent—but it was also known for something far more enticing: its exceptional wine selection. It had become a regular part of our routine, an almost daily stop to pick up a bottle to enjoy on the rooftop, watching the sunset bleed into the ocean. It didn't take long for the shop owner to recognize us, and I was fairly certain we had become some of his best customers.

Walking to the store had its own perks. More often than not, I'd run into Ken—the *real* mayor of Hermosa Beach. His house was close to the shop, and he spent most afternoons outside, tending to his landscaping or loading his kids into the car for one of their endless sporting events. Ken had the kind of presence that made people take him seriously without him having to demand it. He was always friendly but carried an air of authority, a subtle reminder that beneath the casual neighborhood charm, he was a man used to power.

Just as often, I ran into Anthony.

Anthony had quickly become my closest connections, friend, in the neighborhood. He was always around, always in the mix, always moving. And, much like me, he was a regular at the corner store. While Denise and I had a fondness for wine, Anthony had an affinity for whiskey. The good kind. The kind that came with stories, with slow pours, with a quiet nod of appreciation after the first sip. The corner store had a decent selection, and he took full advantage.

One evening, as we walked back from the corner store together, the setting sun casting long shadows across the street, Anthony turned to me casually.

"*Hey, care to join me at the club tonight for a drink?*"

I glanced at him. "*What club, a strip club?*" I said half joking.

"No, *The Harbor Yacht Club,*" he said, as if it were the most obvious thing in the world.

That gave me pause. Anthony hated the water. Despite living near the ocean, he never talked about boats, never so much as mentioned taking a ride on a boat and given his lifestyle, was positive he didn't own a yacht.

Still, I played along. "*Sure, why not.*"

He grinned. "*Great. I'll pick you up around seven, and we can walk over. Tell Denise she's free to come too, if she likes.*"

I nodded, but I had already decided—I wouldn't mention that part to Denise. As much as she would have enjoyed going, this wasn't about a night out. I needed time alone with Anthony. Time to get the real story.

About his life. About his wife.

And, more importantly, about whether the whispers about him were just neighborhood gossip… or something more.

THE HARBOR YACHT CLUB sat right on the water, its exterior a blend of old money and aging charm. The wooden facade was weathered by salt air, the large bay windows framed a perfect view of the marina, and the glow of lanterns flickered against the dark ocean backdrop. Inside, the club carried the weight of time—polished brass fixtures, deep leather chairs, and an air of exclusivity that hadn't quite caught up with modern trends.

The place had a lived-in feel, but not in a way that suggested neglect. It was the kind of bar where the same men had been drinking the same whiskey for decades, where laughter was subdued, conversations were discreet, and no one asked too many questions.

Anthony walked in like he owned the place.

"Drinks here are *generous*," he said with a knowing smirk as we stepped up to the bar.

I let him order, deferring to his experience. He went for his usual—a double whiskey, neat. He ordered me my safe go to, a nice cabernet wine.

We grabbed our drinks and made our way outside to the deck, where the air was thick with the scent of saltwater and the faintest trace of cigar smoke. It was quieter out here, the hum of conversation fading behind the glass doors. The ocean stretched out in front of us, the rhythmic crash of waves against the pier setting a steady, hypnotic pulse beneath the murmur of the city.

For a while, we just talked. Small talk, the easy kind, about neighbors, local spots, the kind of surface-level chatter that fills time without really meaning anything. But Anthony had something on his mind.

I waited until the moment felt right, then asked, "*So what's your story? Ever been married? Dating anyone?*"

Anthony took a slow sip of whiskey. If the question caught him off guard, he didn't show it. Instead, he let the moment settle between us, the kind of pause that wasn't hesitation but calculation.

Then, finally, he exhaled.

"*You don't know?*"

I played it neutral. "*Know what?*"

He looked down at his glass, rolling it in his hand. The ice clinked softly against the crystal.

"*I was married,*" he said. His voice had lost its usual charm, the boisterous energy replaced with something quieter. "*She was amazing. I loved her more than anything.*"

His eyes were turning red, the telltale sign of someone on the verge of something they rarely allowed themselves to feel.

"*We had it all—a beautiful house, great vacations, two amazing kids. Everything.*"

I watched him carefully. This was a different Anthony than the one I'd come to know—the self-proclaimed mayor of the street, the life of every party, the guy who knew *everything* about *everyone* but never talked about himself.

I had never seen this version of him. Then, the shift.

"*Long story short,*" he said, voice tightening, "*I went out one night. Had too much to drink. Shouldn't have driven, but I did.*"

He stopped, running a hand through his hair, like he needed to physically shake off the memory before continuing.

"*I don't know if it was the booze or paranoia, but I felt like someone was following me. Couldn't shake it.*"

His fingers tapped against the side of his glass. A restless movement.

"*I got home, went inside, and immediately looked out the front window. Didn't see anyone, but then—*" He swallowed, shaking his head slightly. "*Then I heard pounding at the front door. Hard. Aggressive. Like someone was trying to get in.*"

The ocean breeze had cooled, but the story made the air feel heavier.

"*I panicked. Grabbed my gun from the case. Laura was already in bed, and all I could think about was getting to her before whoever was outside did. I went to the bottom of the stairs, gun raised, and the second I saw movement around the corner…*"

He trailed off.

I already knew how it ended.

"*I fired. Twice. Point blank.*"

Silence stretched between us.

He let out a shuddering breath, his fingers gripping the edge of the table. "*Then I turned the light on.*"

Another pause. Longer this time.

"*It was Laura.*"

I stayed still, watching him.

"*She had forgotten her key,*" he continued, his voice now a strained whisper. "*She was pounding on the door to get my attention, and when I didn't come, she used the spare we kept outside.*"

His eyes shimmered, the weight of it all still as raw as if it had happened yesterday.

I didn't see a man trying to manipulate me. I didn't see a liar.

I saw a man who had been drowning in guilt for over a decade.

Anthony wiped his eyes roughly, forcing himself back into composure.

"*No, I'm not dating anyone,*" he said. "*Never will. Laura was the only love of my life.*"

I felt an odd, unexpected discomfort. I had expected a confession, a reveal of some hidden darkness, but this? This was different. It was tragedy.

"*I'm sorry I brought it up,*" I said, unsure of what else to say.

"*It's okay,*" he murmured. "*How could you have known?*"

Then, he leaned back in his chair and exhaled, his eyes still glassy but his voice steady again.

"*I will tell you this,*" he added. "*There are a lot of rumors in the neighborhood. And I have no doubt at some point, you'll hear at least one or two versions of the story.*"

I nodded. "*Like…?*" I prompted.

Anthony smirked, but it didn't quite reach his eyes.

"*Oh, you know. That she was having an affair. That I did it for the money.*"

His gaze drifted to the water. "*The usual stuff.*"

I hesitated, then—without thinking—said, "*No truth to that, though, right?*"

He didn't answer right away. Instead, he took a slow sip of his whiskey, letting the silence work in his favor.

Then, finally, he looked up.

"*Well,*" he said. "*No truth to the money thing. I had plenty of my own from my copier business.*"

He paused.

"*But the affair…*"

Another long, measured silence.

He glanced around, scanning to see if anyone was nearby.

"*Listen,*" he said, lowering his voice. "*We had an open marriage.*"

I raised an eyebrow. "*Very Californian of you,*" I mused.

He chuckled dryly.

"*Yeah. She went out some nights. So did I. It wasn't anything more than an understanding.*" He shrugged. "*My guess? A neighbor saw her out, put two and two together, and, well—gossip spreads fast.*"

He took another sip.

"*But the joke's on them. I knew. And we were fine with it. With two teenagers at the time, trust me—that was the least of our issues.*"

I let his words settle.

It was unexpected. Messy. Complicated.

And yet, it still didn't quite *clear* him.

Not entirely.

Sensing the weight of the conversation, I changed the subject.

"*So what do you do now?*" I asked.

Anthony exhaled, like he was relieved to move on.

"*Not much,*" he admitted. "*Semi-retired. And you?*"

I shrugged. "*Just looking. Had some consulting work for a while, but that's drying up. Need something with decent pay and flexible.*"

Anthony's eyes lit up.

"*You should look into becoming a ride-share driver,*" he said. "*Great money, choose your own hours… and living this close to the airport? You'd never be short on work. Besides,*" There was a pause in his voice, "*you never know who you'll pick up*"

I nodded, considering it.

I had been searching for something.

And maybe, just maybe—this was it.

Chapter 26

UNKNOWN ROUTE

A RIDE SHARE DRIVER. In the moment, I didn't fully grasp the concept. Anthony tried to describe it as an on-call personal taxi—simple, convenient, just a side hustle. But the way he said it, the way his voice carried that slight edge of something unspoken, made it feel like more.

For me it wasn't about the money. It wasn't even about the flexible hours.

It was *the unknown.*

"You never know who you'll pick up."

That line stuck with me, lodged itself somewhere deep, where curiosity and something darker intertwined. He had meant it casually—maybe—but the words resonated. They pulled at something inside me I hadn't felt in awhile.

Denise wasn't thrilled.

The second I told her, she had that look—that mix of exasperation and concern that I had seen before when I did something she deemed reckless.

"*Seriously? You want to drive drunk strangers around LA? Have you lost your mind?*"

She had a point. Los Angeles at night wasn't exactly a safe place. The streets were unpredictable, the people even more so. And when I casually mentioned I planned to drive exclusively at night, her frustration hardened into something closer to anger.

"*Absolutely not.*"

The words were firm, immediate. No room for discussion.

I had to pull my "***Marine-Card.***"

"*Denise,*" I said, keeping my voice level, "*I was a sniper in the Marine Corps for six years. Who's going to fuck with me?*"

She sighed, shaking her head, rubbing her temples like she was physically restraining herself from arguing further.

I could see the battle happening in her mind—the worry versus the logic.

She knew I could handle myself.

But that wasn't what unsettled her.

It wasn't the danger that gnawed at her—it was *me*.

And maybe she was right to be worried.

Because something about this—the late-night drives, the random encounters, the opportunity for anonymity—was calling to me.

I just wasn't sure why yet.

There were a few ride-share companies to choose from, each promising competitive earnings, flexible schedules, and the chance to be my own boss. The sign-up process was surprisingly easy— almost *too* easy.

First, I had to download the app. From there, the requirements were basic: proof of a valid driver's license, a registered vehicle that met their standards, and insurance. That was it.

No interviews. No real vetting. Just a superficial background check, a quick look into my driving record to make sure I wasn't a reckless idiot behind the wheel. No deep dives into my history, no psychological evaluations. They weren't looking for good people—they were looking for available drivers.

I applied to three companies, filling out the applications in under an hour. There was no doubt in my mind that I'd pass whatever flimsy requirements they had. And sure enough, within 48 hours, my phone lit up with a series of near-identical messages.

"Congratulations! You're hired."

No phone calls. No personal interaction. Just a handful of automated emails welcoming me aboard, complete with links to training videos and "best practices" guides I quickly reviewed.

It was almost laughable how easy it was.

Within two days, I had full access to the platforms. I could flip my status to "Online" at any moment and start picking up strangers, driving them wherever they needed to go, no questions asked.

I had unlimited access to whoever got into my car.

And they had no idea who I was.

I DECIDED THAT THURSDAY NIGHT, 8 P.M. would be my first shift.

To be honest, I had no idea what to expect. I'd spent the last week preparing—reading through driver forums, watching videos about handling unruly passengers, even testing out the best routes to and from the airport. But no amount of research could prepare me for the reality of having strangers behind me in the dark, their presence just inches away, unknown, unpredictable.

The thought jolted me more than I expected.

That's when I reminded myself—I had a safety net.

John's gift.

The ghost gun had come from Phoenix, handed over in an unmarked box with nothing more than a knowing nod and the words, "*Enjoy*" He hadn't elaborated. He didn't need to. The weight of the case in my hands had said enough.

That morning, while Denise was on a conference call in the other room, I took the box into the garage and laid out the parts on the workbench. The gun was a modified .22—a compact but deadly piece, small enough to conceal, quiet enough to not draw attention.

I had never built a gun before, other than field striping my weapon in the Corps. But John had chosen this one for a reason. It was disturbingly easy to assemble.

Each piece clicked into place with a level of precision that felt natural. Satisfying.

By the time I inserted the magazine and racked the slide, only seventy minutes had passed.

The weapon was real. Loaded. Ready.

I turned it over in my hands, admiring its smooth, featureless surface. No serial number. No history. A phantom—like it had never existed.

Just like I would be.

"Thank you, John."

The plan: keep it in the armrest of the car. Not for show. Not as a threat.

A just in case.

Because you never know who you'll pick up.

Thursday night the city was alive, traffic lights flickering onto the streets, the hum of nightlife just beginning to pick up. I had promised Denise I'd text her every thirty minutes until she went to bed, reassuring her that I was OK and would only stay out as long as I was comfortable.

It wasn't that she didn't trust me—she just didn't trust the city. Los Angeles at night was an entirely different beast. A playground for the reckless, the drunk, and the desperate. But for someone who had been in the service, I had spent time in places around the world far more dangerous than L.A.

The first few days the rides were uneventful.

Airport drop-offs—businessmen too absorbed in their phones to even look at me. They slid into the backseat, rattled off a destination, and disappeared back into their digital worlds, emails and stock updates far more important than the stranger behind the wheel. Easy money. No conversation. No connection.

Night five, I had developed a routine. Stay near the airport for the easy fares. By week two, I had started to become bored and ventured closer to downtown. Once the bars started emptying. Drunk people tipped better. They slurred their words, laughed at nothing. They treated me like a friend, an ally in their mission to get home safely.

It didn't take long and I started noticing something, a pattern.

Subtle at first, but once I saw it, I couldn't unsee it.

Almost every single passenger who stepped into my car asked the same question:

"You're my driver right?"

At first, I didn't think much of it. Just polite confirmation, small talk. But the more I thought about it, the stranger it became. The ride-share app provided everything—a photo of me, the make and model of my car, even my license plate number. All the details were there, right in front of them.

And yet…

They didn't look.

They didn't check.

They just assumed.

Because people are too absorbed in their own worlds to pay attention to the things that really matter.

And just like that, from the dark corners, my mind started to open up again, something shifted.

I started to feel what this job could actually be.

A never-ending opportunity.

THEN SHE GOT IN.

She was pretty—late-twenties, maybe younger. Long legs that seemed to unfold endlessly as she slid into the back seat. Her skirt was so short I didn't have to imagine anything—her thighs were bare, smooth, and parted just enough that I could see all the way up. She didn't adjust. Didn't pull it down. Whether she was unaware or didn't care, I couldn't tell.

Either way, it was an invitation.

Her hair was tousled in that deliberately careless way—waves tumbling over one shoulder, strands stuck to her lip gloss. Her skin glowed from the heat of the night, a sheen of sweat highlighting her collarbones. Her dress—tight, damp in spots—clung to her curves like shrink-wrap. She smelled like tequila and perfume, uninhibited and wild.

A target?

"*Hey,*" she slurred, falling into the seat with a giggle. Her voice was soft, playful, the kind of tone that made weak men want to protect her. "*You're my driver, right?*"

Predictable.

"*I think I put the address in the app... Did I?*"

I glanced at my phone. An apartment complex. Fifteen minutes away. Nice area.

"*Yeah,*" I said. "*I've got it.*"

She let out a breath, melted into the seat like a puddle, head tilted back, legs still parted just enough to hold my attention in the rearview mirror.

"*You're awesome,*" she sighed. "*This night has been such a mess. My friends are idiots.*"

I pulled away from the curb, letting the city swallow us.

For a while, she didn't move. Her head rocked gently with each turn, eyes half-shut, lips parted like she was stuck between sleep and thought.

Then she spoke again.

"*You're, like… safe, right?*"

The question was barely a question. More like a passing cloud of concern. Her voice didn't even carry weight. But I saw her reflection —her gaze catching mine in the mirror. Glassy. Trusting. Empty of suspicion.

"*Yeah,*" I said with a smile I knew would settle her. "*Of course.*"

She nodded slowly. Content.

Her head tilted to the side again, neck exposed, pulsing lightly with the beat of her drunken heart. Her breathing slowed, the shallow rhythm of someone completely vulnerable.

She had no idea.

I could veer off course. Take a wrong turn. She wouldn't know until we were nowhere.

I could pull into a parking lot. A quiet street. Kill the engine.
I could climb into the backseat, press my hand over her mouth before the first scream, slide the seatbelt around her throat and squeeze until her pulse faded beneath my fingers.

The thought wasn't intrusive—it was comforting. Familiar. Like slipping on an old jacket that still fit perfectly.

And still, I didn't move.

Not yet.

Instead, I let it simmer. Let the possibility soak into the space between us like humidity. I imagined the weight of her body as it stilled beneath me. The silence. The peace. The *control.*

She shifted again. Her skirt rose even higher. "*I always do this,*" she muttered, half-laughing. "*Go out, swear I'll behave, and next thing I know I'm getting in a car with a complete stranger, hoping he's not a psycho.*"

She laughed again. A sweet, stupid laugh.

"*You're not a psycho, right?*"

I smiled into the mirror. A practiced smile. One that never failed.

"*Nah,*" I said. "*Not tonight, you're safe.*"

And she believed me.

She leaned against the window, her breath fogging the glass.

I watched her.

I was tempted.

The last turn came too fast. Her apartment complex loomed ahead, bright lights washing over the lot, flooding the safety of the familiar.

I slowed to a stop.

She stirred, groaning softly, fingers fumbling for the handle.

"*Thanks,*" she said, her words slurring at the edges.

"*Need help getting inside?*" I asked gently.

She shook her head, stepping out on unsteady legs, almost stumbling. Her heels scraped against the pavement as she caught herself on the door. I thought, for a second, she might look back. Say something. Ask me to walk her in.

But she didn't.

She gave a sloppy little wave, turned, and disappeared into the building. The automatic doors hissed shut behind her.

Gone.

I exhaled slowly.

Not tonight.

But the idea?
It lingered.

Longer than it should have.

And in that lingering, I knew—there would be another. There would always be another.

This new career.

A way to kill at will.

No forced entry. No break-ins. No struggle. Just an open door and an invitation inside.

A hunting ground disguised as a job.

And best of all?

They came to me.

FROM THE MOMENT SHE left my vehicle, it began, started slowly, as a casual thought. A fleeting idea with no weight, no immediate direction. But within the next few days, it had rooted itself deep inside me, consuming my every waking moment.

The feelings.
The memories.
The dark desires resurfaced.

Minnesota.
Arizona.
Florida.
Amsterdam.

Each place had left a mark. Each had shaped me, pushing me toward what I had always known—what I had always been meant for. ***A killer***. Not by accident. Not by impulse. By design.

By the end of the following week, it was no longer just a thought.

I was in full tactical mode now once again.

The old instincts returned—meticulous, calculating, cold. I wasn't just thinking about the *act* anymore. It was time to start thinking about covering tracks. Eliminating risk. Ensuring perfection.

Through all of this, I was also trying to maintain the balance of the home—Denise, Chiara, the neighbors, the rooftop wine nights, the spontaneous playdates. From the outside, everything looked effortless. Domestic harmony wrapped in California sun.

But inside… a dark storm was rising.
A quiet, gnawing hunger that no amount of routine could suppress.
It crept into the quiet moments—the pauses between conversations, the silences between Chiara's laughter, the spaces between Denise's kisses.
It whispered while I smiled.
It stalked me while I played the caring husband, the attentive father, the friendly neighbor.

The more I fit into this life, the more I felt the fracture widen beneath it. I was performing stability while something far more primal twisted just beneath the surface.

And that duality—being both the man Denise needed and the man I truly was—

That was the real weight.
And I could feel myself starting to crack beneath it.

THE RIDE-SHARE GIG was almost too perfect. Constant movement. Ever-changing faces. Random pickups across the city. No patterns. No immediate red flags.

But I knew better.

There were vulnerabilities. Weak spots and I needed to work them out.

First, LA is filled with cameras.

They were everywhere. Streetlights. Toll booths. Traffic stops. Even the ride-share app itself logged everything. Every route. Every pickup. Every turn. Every stop.

But there was a solution.

It took less than 5 minutes to search the web and find it.

A website, RadarBusted.com.

They sold something called invisi-plates.

A nearly invisible film that fit over your license plate. To the naked eye? It was nothing. To cameras? A ghost. The plate would be completely unreadable to traffic cams, speed traps, and automated surveillance.

The moment I saw it, I knew.

This would make my vehicle unidentifiable.

I could drive anywhere. Pick up anyone. Drop them off anywhere.
And if anything went wrong?

There would be no photographic record of my car ever being there.

I clicked 'Add to Cart.'

The next potential problem, cell phone.

Every phone is tracked. GPS data. App logs. Cell tower pings. If someone went missing, it wouldn't take much to cross-check where they were picked up and where they were supposed to be dropped off.

That meant I needed a workaround.

A way to scramble the trail.

I started researching.

Not just casually—not like someone Googling a new hobby—but with purpose. With obsession. Every thread I pulled led to something useful. Every rabbit hole gave me another layer of insight. And eventually, the answer revealed itself. It wasn't through hacking or technology.

It came in the form of a workaround.

LAX, like most major airports, had a designated lot specifically for ride-share drivers. It was a holding area—a purgatory of sorts—where drivers waited to be pinged for pickups. It was also where conversations happened. Quiet, passing exchanges between strangers who never expected to see each other again.

I started hanging out there between rides.

I made a few connections. Acquaintances at best—guys who talked too much, and others who barely made eye contact. But the ones who had been doing this a while? They were clever. Efficient. And a little shady.

That's where I first heard about the business card trick.

To avoid paying service fees to the ride-share companies, drivers would pass their personal cards to passengers. A casual gesture, "*Hey, next time, skip the app—just text me. I'll get you there cheaper.*" Simple. Harmless. Profitable.

But for me, it was something more.

It was the perfect workaround to the problem of digital tracking.

I went out the next day and purchased a burner phone—cheap, prepaid, cash only. No ID, no trace. Then I designed a small card—not a take-away, too risky for evidence—but something subtle. A printed message encased in a plastic sleeve and mounted discreetly behind the driver's seat headrest. Eye level. Impossible to miss.

"***Save money on your next ride—contact me directly.***"
A number followed. Just ten digits. No name. No logo. Just a number.

To anyone else, it was a smart business move. To me, it was the beginning of the perfect vanishing act.

If someone used the card, there would be no record of the ride. No GPS log from the app. No notification sent to their device. Just a text message. A pickup time. And a passenger who willingly stepped into a car they thought they could trust.

Of course, it didn't help with those still booking through the app. Not yet.

But I had a long-term plan for them, too.

Thanks to the girl in the short skirt, the one who got in drunk and alone, who never once noticed how vulnerable she truly was—that night had awakened something in me. She had shown me just how easy it was to gain someone's trust. How seamless it could be to slip beneath their radar.

She had sparked everything.

And now, I was building something calculated.
Something undetectable.
Something final.

One ride at a time.

Chapter 27

THE PARK

DENISE AND I —for better or worse—had fallen into a rhythm that mimicked normalcy. It wasn't love, not really, not anymore. It was routine. Familiarity dressed up as affection. We were co-managing a life. Her work consumed her—always one more meeting, one more pitch deck, one more late-night email. Our conversations had thinned into logistics: school schedules, grocery lists, calendar syncs.

To fill the gaps, we hired a live-in nanny—a college student with a clean face and a practiced smile. She exchanged free rent for responsibility and gave the illusion of balance. She picked up Chiara, made dinner, filled the house with a softness that let Denise pretend she was keeping it all together. It gave us space—manufactured time. Just enough to play the part of a couple still in sync.

We went out.
Held hands.
Smiled at the right moments.
It was all very charming.

Life on Lyndon Street had become a carousel of curated normalcy—birthday parties, sidewalk chats, afternoon barbecues. I waved to Anthony as he walked by each morning with the dogs, headphones in, sweat soaking through his cotton tee. Ken, was always knee-deep in landscaping or packing soccer gear into the back of his SUV. We exchanged pleasantries—weather, local sports, inflation jokes. Just two suburban men playing their parts.

Cindy's dog barked every time it saw Chiara, then wagged like an idiot when she got close. Robert would always ask if I'd finally tried that sushi place, grinning before I could answer because we both knew I hadn't. Everyone had a role. A reliable personality. A function to fulfill.

And so did I.

Friendly. Grounded. Funny, but not in a way that drew attention. The kind of guy you could trust with your spare key. The kind who asked about your mother, remembered your kid's birthday, offered to help move your furniture on a Saturday.

I knew how to listen.
When to laugh.
When to retreat.
When to draw people out just enough so they'd never think to look back in.
It wasn't an act anymore. It was instinct. Muscle memory.

They trusted me. They liked me.

And they would never, ever suspect what lay beneath the smile.

Not in a place like this.
Because monsters don't wear aprons and pass out barbecue and cocktails at block parties.
'*Until they do.*

And while the wine flowed and the dogs barked and the kids chalked rainbows on the sidewalk, something inside me tightened.

A pulse.
A heat.
A need.

Gone were the days I wasted wondering about the black SUV. Whatever shadow once lingered near our house, I'd convinced myself it was Foss's team—desperate, circling, hoping for something that no longer existed. Let them sit in their parked cars with their stale coffee and binoculars, digging through smoke. Her words—*"The Phoenix Police want to speak to you"*—also no longer echoed with dread. They had nothing.

At best, they suspected a gun that no longer existed.
And without it, they had no leverage.
No case.

They were chasing ghosts.
Unaware the monster had already walked right past them, and was now helping organize the neighborhood potluck.

And I was changing, evolving.

WHAT BEGAN AS A HARMLESS JOB—driving strangers home—had evolved into something else entirely. Something sacred. Each ride was a ritual. Each shift behind the wheel a ceremony. The moment I slid into the driver's seat, my mind sharpened. My breath slowed. The world became clearer, quieter.

Every ride carried potential.
A careless word. A smug tone. A flash of arrogance.

Letting of ones guard down
Some small tell sign that signaled permission.

I didn't always know what I was looking for until I heard it—until something shifted in the air. And then it was there. The flicker. The flame. The dark engine humming beneath my skin.

When I wasn't driving, I was imagining.
Plotting.
Rehearsing.

Sitting at dinner, listening to Denise talk about project budgets while my mind wandered back to a girl from two nights ago—mid-thirties, wine drunk, alone. She had lectured someone on the phone about a promotion she didn't get. She had rolled her eyes when she got in. She had *dismissed* me with a glance.

I had driven her home.

But I could've kept going.
Veered off.
Let the city swallow us.

I imagined it constantly.

It wasn't fantasy anymore.
It was premeditation.

There were nights I stood in the garage, staring at the armrest where the ghost gun rested. I would imagine her voice—shrill, stupid—followed by the click of the lock. The crack of the shot. The sudden silence. The warmth of blood against leather.

Not just a kill.
A cleansing.

This wasn't about rage.
It wasn't even about justice.

It was all about control. Control of the person, the event, the moment in time.

Total.
Absolute.
Control.

Because in a life of pastel-painted routines and potluck invitations and bedtime stories, control was the only thing that still felt like truth.

And I needed it.

Every mile I drove wasn't work—it was hunting.
Every passenger wasn't cargo—they were auditioning.

The first kill in this new life was near. I could feel it in my bones. Smell it in the air. Like a storm gathering, thick and waiting.

It wouldn't be impulsive.
It wouldn't be messy.

It would be deliberate.
Calculated.

Art.

And when it came, I wouldn't flinch.
Because by then—I'd know exactly who I was.
And I'd never question it again.

LOS ANGELES - THE EPICENTER of entertainment, culture, and chaos. On any given night, the city pulsed with life. The Forum. Crypto.com Arena. BMO Stadium. The Convention Center, SoFi Stadium. Venues designed to draw thousands. Tens of thousands. A constant flood of concerts, sports games, expos, comedy shows, award ceremonies… you name it, LA hosted it.

And when those events let out, people didn't think—they reacted. They just wanted to get home. Fast.
Drunk. High. Buzzing from the night. Phones nearly dead, apps glitching, wallets clumsy in their hands. Half of them didn't even have a ride booked.

I'd ease the SUV into position near the crowd—always on the edge, never too close to security, just close enough to be noticed. And within seconds, someone would step forward. Sometimes two or three. All of them asking the same thing:

"*Hey, you taking rides*? I'll pay cash."
No names. No questions. No digital trail.

It was perfect.

No app tracking. No GPS ping. No credit card transaction. Just anonymous cash-for-hire in a city that didn't care to look twice.

They never even so much as ask my name. They just climbed in.

And why wouldn't they? I had the right kind of vehicle—clean, professional, with the glow of LED lights in the footwells, a soft playlist humming through the speakers, and a polite man behind the wheel with a calm smile and a nod.

I was exactly what they were looking for.
Exactly what they *needed.*

It didn't take long for me to learn the rhythm.
Find the right exits.
Know where the foot traffic poured out first.
Which venues had enough chaos to let me blend in.
It became a system. Predictable. Repeatable. Efficient.

While everyone else was scanning their phones, panicking about wait times or surge pricing, I was already in motion—scouting, positioning, watching. A shark beneath the surface of their night out.

They never suspected a thing.

The best part? They handed me cash and climbed in willingly. They gave me everything I needed—time, trust, access—and thought nothing of it.

And once the door closed behind them, we were sealed inside our own private world.
I wasn't just a driver anymore.

I was a curator of moments.

A collector of lives.
A ghost behind the wheel.

And in that simplicity, I saw opportunity.
Endless.
Quiet.
Perfect.

THE SHOW HAD JUST ENDED, and the crowd spilled out in waves—loud, chaotic, glittered in sequins and sweat. Women in high heels wobbling across cracked sidewalks, men trying to look cooler than they were, phones glowing in their faces as they fumbled with ride share apps. The scent of booze, weed, and expensive perfume clung to the air like humidity.

I was already parked in the line of ride share drivers, my SUV idling, windows down just enough to catch the noise. But my app was off.

No GPS logs.
No digital trail.
I wasn't here—not officially.

It took less than ten minutes.

He came out of the chaos with two beautiful women, late 20's early 30's on either side of him, like a man who thought he was living a fantasy—until it unraveled.

He was Mid-50s. Stocky. Middle Eastern, maybe, with the kind of swagger that money gives a man who's never had to earn anything but always expects more. His designer jeans clung too tight to his thighs, his black button-down shirt open enough to show a chest too hairless, too smooth—like he was trying to freeze himself at 38 and failing. His hair was slicked back, but sweat betrayed him. Strands clung to his temples, greasy and wilting under the weight of whatever cologne he'd drowned himself in—something sharp, bitter, expensive, and desperate.

He had one arm hooked under each girl, herding them toward the curb like trophies. One a little too drunk to balance herself.

Both girls were Asian. Petite, stunning, young. One was tall for her frame—maybe 5'9" in heels—with legs that moved like they'd done this a dozen times before. Her top was sequined, tight and low cut, showing off curves that had clearly gotten them past VIP security earlier in the night. Her makeup was flawless—until you got close and saw the mascara bleeding beneath her lashes. Her expression was vacant but trained—a model in standby mode.

The other girl—the one he was really struggling to keep upright—was younger. Late twenties at most, but the kind of face that could pass for college if you didn't look too long. Her features were soft, delicate, almost cherubic under the streetlights. But she was gone. Not crying, not slurring—just... absent. Her head lolled against his arm, her body limp, her legs scraping along the sidewalk like she barely remembered she had them. Her sundress had ridden high on her thighs, the fabric bunched beneath her as if she'd given up trying to fix it. A thin strap had slipped off her shoulder, exposing smooth skin and the shimmer of sweat. Her mouth hung open slightly. Her breathing was slow, shallow.

She was somewhere between blackout and surrender.

The man looked pissed. Not concerned. Not protective. Just... inconvenienced.

He gave me that look.
The one that says: *I've paid for everything tonight—her cover, her drinks, her transportation to the show—and now she can't even get it together to show me a good time.*

He stepped up to my window, already holding a folded $100 bill between two fingers like a bribe.

"*Dude,*" he said, voice slightly hoarse from yelling over the music, "*can you take this trashed one home*?" He gestured toward the girl, barely upright. "*She's like, fifteen minutes from here. Los Feliz. This'll more than cover it.*" He shoved the bill through the window before I could even respond. "*It's, like, less than five miles.*"

I didn't ask questions. I didn't need to.

And just like that, they poured her into my backseat like forgotten luggage. He gave me the address - and the door clicked shut.

The other girl gave a half-hearted wave and a slurred "*Sorry, girl, call you tomorrow*" before linking arms with the man again, already moving away—already erasing the other from they're night.

Neither looked back.

I stared at her in the mirror.
She was sprawled across the seat, one leg bent, the other hanging off the edge. Her dress offered no modesty. Her breathing was slow and uneven, lips parted, makeup smudged like bruises across her cheekbones. She smelled like club smoke, dance sweat and something sweet—body spray, maybe. Artificial innocence.

She didn't stir when I put the SUV in gear.

Didn't open her eyes when I pulled away from the curb.

She was completely mine now.

I DROVE IN SILENCE down Hillhurst, then onto Vermont, the girl slumped in the back seat like a discarded coat. She hadn't stirred since we left the venue—her body slack, her breath shallow, the telltale signs of someone far beyond drunk. I pulled in front of her home in The Oaks and looked back at her.

Nothing.

Not even a flinch.

I sat there for a moment, watching her. Her head against the window, a faint fog marking the glass. She looked peaceful. Trusting. That fragile space between consciousness and nothingness. It was almost a shame.

Almost.

I glanced in the rearview mirror. The street was empty. Still. I checked the side mirrors, watched the soft pulse of porch lights blinking behind the hedges, then slipped the SUV back into gear and rolled past her driveway without another thought.

Ten minutes later, we were at Griffith Park, the moon low, shrouded by the kind of clouds that hold back the stars. I turned off the headlights and let the SUV coast into the lot near the old bird sanctuary—an abandoned relic that once housed hundreds of exotic birds before a fire turned it into a skeleton of rusted wire and cracked stone.

I waited.

No headlights. No voices. No interruptions.

Only the distant rustle of leaves and the faint, rhythmic click of the SUV cooling down.

Eventually, I stepped out and opened the trunk. Beneath the floorboard, the tools were waiting—neatly organized, unassuming. Not weapons, not overtly. Just the kinds of things anyone might carry for an emergency. Duct tape. Cargo straps. Roadside flares. A box cutter, small and silent. Objects that told no stories on their own.

I set everything inside the cage.

Then returned for her.

She didn’t resist when I opened the door. Her body slumped against me easily, like a child being carried to bed. I whispered something—meaningless, soft. Something that sounded kind. It was all she needed. She mumbled something in return, eyelids fluttering open for just a second before closing again. Sleepwalking.

The cage groaned under our weight as we stepped inside, its frame bending with memory.

I positioned her gently, the way you might guide someone to lean against a wall when they're too far gone to stand on their own. Her eyes opened once more, dazed, unfocused.

"Where… are we?" she asked, voice sluggish, confusion beginning to surface beneath the fog. "Who are you…?"

I didn’t answer. I didn’t need to.

Instead, I watched.

Her eyes flicked to the corners of the cage, to the dim, unfamiliar surroundings. She shifted—subtly at first—testing her arms. The moment her wrists met resistance, her breath caught.

That’s when I stepped forward.

The tape in my hand made no sound, but she saw it—felt it.

I pressed it over her mouth, slow and deliberate, smoothing it into place with the palm of my hand. Her final syllables died under it, warm breath fluttering behind the seal.

Then I stepped back.

And waited.

There it was. She was instantly sober now.

Then stillness. That tightening of the jaw. The wide, blinking silence as realization sank in.

The fear came next—not loud. Not panicked. But quiet. Heavy. A bloom behind the eyes, delicate and complete.

Beautiful.

Her panic was wordless, just the frantic tension in her arms and the desperate tug of her legs. I stepped closer, watching her chest rise and fall faster, her breath sharp now.

There would be no screams tonight.

Only the sound of the wind through the trees.

At that moment—the decision—settled over me like a second skin. Cold. Natural. Final.

She looked at me like I might change my mind. Like somewhere in the deep part of her, she believed the mask I wore in the car, the friendly driver with water bottles and a playlist designed to soothe.

But the mask was gone now.

And the man in front of her wasn't a driver.

He was something else entirely.

She trembled—subtle at first, just a shift in her legs, the soft clink of her bracelet against the rusted wire of the cage. Her eyes followed me now, locked in wide, unblinking horror, but she still didn't scream. She couldn't. The tape had done its job. But it was more than that.

She was trying to understand. Trying to rationalize.

That's the problem with hope. It dies slowly.

I stood just out of reach, letting her panic soak into the silence. The air was damp, the kind of damp that clung to the back of your throat and made everything taste like metal and ash. I could feel it press against my skin, could hear the low hum of the city far below, muffled by the trees. Up here, it was just the two of us.

I crouched in front of her.

Watched her body language—every twitch, every flinch. I didn't speak. I didn't touch her. I just watched.

People say the eyes are windows to the soul, but they're wrong. It's the silence that gives them away. The way it curls around the body, how the chest tightens, how the breathing turns jagged.

She knew she wasn't going home tonight.

I leaned in slowly, my breath just inches from her ear.

"*You were never in danger,*" I whispered. "*Not until now.*"

Her body jerked. Fight or flight. A primal pulse. Too late.

I stood up again, slowly, deliberately, and turned away—not out of mercy, but control. Let her feel the shift. Let her dread the return of my gaze. Let the moment drag its claws across her nerves until even the quiet was unbearable.

I walked a slow circle around the cage, fingers brushing the aged iron as I went. I remembered reading once that the birds who lived here had sung for days after the fire—singed feathers, blistered skin, still chirping while their lungs collapsed from the smoke. They hadn't known they were dying.

She was starting to.

I could see it in her posture now. The sag in her knees. The trembling in her shoulders. The breath catching just a second too long in her throat.

It was a beautiful thing to witness—transformation. The moment someone realizes they've slipped off the edge of normal life and into someone else's nightmare.

I didn't need to rush. Not tonight.

Tonight was about clarity.

Control.

Becoming.

She let out a muffled whimper.

It wasn't a cry. Not yet. It was that sound people make when they realize help isn't coming. That their breath, their voice, doesn't matter anymore. I tilted my head, listening to it like music.

I stepped back into view.

Her eyes locked on mine—pleading, wild, full of questions that would never be answered. Behind the tape, her mouth moved, desperate for meaning. I gave her none.

Instead, I reached into my coat pocket and pulled out a small pink box cutter, the metal shined under the faint moonlight.

Her pupils dilated. Her body sagged further.

"*I used to wonder if there was something broken inside me,*" I continued, speaking more to the night than to her. "*A switch that never flipped. But it's not broken. It's just different. And I've spent too long pretending otherwise.*"

I played with the box cutter in my hand.

Her body jerked violently against the restraints, the metal cage groaning as she struggled. A soft grunt—panic muffled by adhesive. Her feet scraped at the dirt. Her head thrashed.

It was instinct. Beautiful. Futile.

I stepped closer again and placed a hand over her heart. It pounded like a war drum beneath her skin—fast, erratic, confused. I closed my eyes for a second, just *feeling* it. It was intimate. Real. More real than any conversation, any connection I'd ever had.

When I opened my eyes again, mine were the only ones that were calm.

"*I'm not going to hurt you,*" I said softly.

A lie.

The blade clicked. A sound so small, so sharp, it cut through the trees like a gunshot. She froze, breath hitching hard against the tape.

I could feel it rising in me now—not lust, not thrill. Something colder. Cleaner. Like watching a storm roll in and realizing, for once, you're the one holding the lightning.

I traced her cheek with the back of my hand.

She stood barely conscious, arms bound, dress clinging to her skin, mouth sealed with tape. The cold of the night coiled around us both, but I barely felt it. Her breath, shallow and uneven, fogged in front of her face. Her eyes searched mine—confused at first, then slowly registering panic.

The box cutter felt small in my hand. Insignificant, almost. But in this moment, it held the weight of God.

I didn't touch her right away. Not yet. I stood in the stillness, letting her feel my presence, letting the silence stretch so thin it became suffocating. She began to shift, testing her restraints—first subtly, then more frantically. The cage clinked softly behind her, metal against tension, rust against skin.

She tried to speak through the tape. It came out a muffled cry. Maybe it was her name. Maybe it was a plea. Maybe it was just instinct, some primal scream clawing for survival.

I watched her chest rise faster, her body responding before her mind had fully caught up. Adrenaline. Terror. She knew now.

I stepped in and gently placed a hand between her legs. My fingers barely grazed her thigh—light enough that it could have been a shift in the wind, a trick of temperature. But I felt it. The soft, almost imperceptible bristle of fine hairs standing on end beneath my touch. Not shaved. Not groomed for the occasion. Natural. Unfiltered.

It was the detail most men overlook. But I didn't. I noticed everything.

The contrast between smooth flesh and that faint resistance—barely there, but enough to register beneath my palm like a whisper trying not to be heard.

That's the moment I knew she felt me.

Even if she didn't know what to feel yet. She froze.

It wasn't sexual— but it was erotic and intoxicating.

Her skin was soft and cool to the touch. I felt the her muscles twitch beneath my fingers, her legs stiffening as she tried to suppress a tremor.

My hand slid slowly upward.

She whimpered.

And then I whispered, "*It's not what you think.*"

Her eyes widened.

And in that exact moment—when she didn't know whether she was being violated or saved, when confusion held her hostage—I felt it again. That peace. That click inside me. The calm before the storm.

I leaned in close, my breath brushing her cheek.

"*You can stop being afraid,*" I said. "*It's already decided.*"

My hand continued to feel it's way up her inner thigh. When I got close to her groin I felt it, just inches from the silk undergarment she was wearing. It was an undeniable pulse, a thumb a beat so strong that it pushed my fingers away from her skin, her femoral artery.

Instinctually, the tip of the box cutter went in swift and deep, her body barely had time to react before it started to shut down from the lack of oxygen being carried to the cells. Blood was pouring out now in a gulping sound. It pooled on the cold ground and an eerie fog appeared and rose up.

She looked up at me in disbelief and the last thing she saw before the world went red… was me smiling.

I stood there maybe 5 more minutes, until the last of her blood had been drained from her body.

I leaned in close, touched her cheek with the back of my hand, and told her

she was the quietest one yet.

Chapter 28

COME UNDONE

THE HOUSE WAS STILL When I walked in.
Quiet.
Dim.
Normal.

Denise had left a single lamp on in the living room—her silent way of showing she was thinking of me without waiting up. She always left it on when I was out driving. A soft, warm glow cast across the hardwood floors, flickering just slightly with the movement of the fan overhead. I stood in the entryway for a beat too long, letting the stillness settle over me.

No one had followed.
No one had seen.
It had been clean.

I moved toward the bathroom with quiet, deliberate steps. The light above the sink buzzed faintly as I flipped the switch. In the mirror, I barely recognized myself—not because I looked different, but because I didn't. My reflection was calm. Steady. As if I had just come back from a jog, not from draining the life out of a woman in an abandoned bird cage.

Blood had soaked into the cuff of my shirt. A few flecks marked my neck. One, just one, had landed beneath my left eye—a thin red arc, almost like a tear.

I stripped slowly, folding each piece of clothing into a tight square before placing them into the laundry basket.

The water ran hot.
Steam bloomed against the mirror.
I stepped into the shower and let it burn.

As hints of blood spiraled down the drain, I found myself thinking about her—not her name, I hadn't asked—but her last look. The moment realization struck her. That sudden, pure clarity before the panic. It wasn't cruelty I remembered.

It was quiet.

The quiet that came after the struggle, after the fear, after the questions.
The quiet I had created.

It was… beautiful.

I lathered the soap into my hands, scrubbing until there was no trace left. Then I stood there for a while, letting the water hammer down on me. Not because I needed to feel clean.

But because I wanted to feel nothing.

When I emerged, Denise was asleep. Curled on her side, her breathing slow and even. The kind of sleep that only comes from routine, from safety, from trust. I stood in the doorway for a moment, watching her. The same way I had watched the girl in the cage.

But this was different.
This was… my life. The performance. The stability.

And that was the release. The freedom.

The truth.

I slid into bed beside her, careful not to wake her, careful to match the rhythm of my breathing to hers. My heart rate was already slowing. My thoughts, still and focused. I felt no guilt. No remorse. No conflict.

As my eyes drifted to the ceiling, listening to the soft creak of the fan overhead, I realized something unsettling: I had evolved—and was still evolving—into something unrecognizable. A beast. A monster with sharpened edges.

I was so far from where I began. Just a single, calculated shot on a quiet, forgotten road. I wanted to convince myself that it was still just fate, she decided to go out that night, to endure too much, the one decided to get in the car. I was just the ultimate and predictable end to the choices she made.

But now? I knew better. Each kill had become less random. More personal. More violent. A distant shot no longer satisfied. A subtle poisoning felt hollow. Even the slow, hands-on moment in Amsterdam—so intimate, so deliberate—hadn't filled the void.
Tonight was different. Tonight, I had crossed into something darker.

I hadn't just killed.

I had tortured.
I had enjoyed it.

Sadistic.
That's what I was now. A man who didn't just take life, but twisted it before letting it go.

And deep down, I knew this wasn't normal.
Not even for me.

It should've scared me.
And maybe it did.
But I closed my eyes... and smiled.

Because tomorrow, the sun would rise.
Chiara would run down the hallway.
The nanny would make coffee.
And Denise would kiss me good morning like nothing had changed.

Because nothing had.
Not in their world.

But mine?

Mine had just begun.
And for the first time…
I wasn't sure I could stop what was coming next.

DENISE WAS ALREADY UP when I came downstairs.
The scent of fresh laundry mixed with coffee and detergent hung in the air, warm and domestic—too clean for how I felt inside. She was standing in the kitchen, sorting through clothes, her hair pulled back in a loose bun, sleeves rolled up like it was just another Saturday.

I made a beeline for the coffee pot, still groggy from too little sleep and too much adrenaline lingering in my veins.

Behind me, I heard her voice—casual, but clipped.
"*Hon, did you cut yourself?*"

I turned. She held up my shirt— It was stained.

"*There looked to be blood on this,*" she said, watching my face more than the fabric.

I didn't hesitate. "*No. I spilled wine.*"
I forced a small laugh, dismissive, tired. "*Poured a glass after I got home, tried to unwind. Sloshed it. Tried to rinse it out, but I guess it set. It's an old shirt—if it doesn't come out, just toss it.*"

I turned back to my coffee, hoping that would be the end of it.

It wasn't.

When I looked up, she was staring at me—really staring. That familiar squint she gave when she was trying to read between the lines.
She set her cup down and crossed her arms.

"*Eric... you're different.*"

Her voice wasn't accusatory. It was concerned. But concern from her felt like pressure—like a weight I didn't want to carry.

"*Is everything okay? With this... new driving thing?*"

What could I say to that?

That I was slowly eroding under the weight of the mask I wore every day?

That the job she rolled her eyes at had become my religion?
That I felt more alive driving blackout strangers through the night than I ever did holding her hand at dinner?

Instead, I just nodded. "*Yeah. It's fine. Just adjusting.*"

A lie. Like every other one I'd told her lately.

My life was an endless maze of deception now—about where I went, what I did, what I thought. Even what I felt. There were no truths left between us, only performances. Rehearsed lines. Smile cues. Strategic silences.

Somewhere in my head, the lyrics to Robbie Williams played on loop:
"If I stop lying, I just disappoint you... I've come undone."

That was it, really.
I had come undone. Quietly. Neatly. Without a sound.

Whatever ties I had to family, friends, possible consequences... they'd all frayed into threads. My marriage, my fatherhood, my role in this picture-perfect neighborhood—they were all just placeholders. Props in a life I no longer lived in.

Because now? Now it wasn't about the thrill.

The euphoria of the first kill—the rush, the shaking hands, the giddy sense of invincibility—it was long gone. Replaced by something colder. Sharper. A hunger with no pulse, just a ticking metronome inside my chest, counting down until the next time I had to feed it. This wasn't excitement anymore.

This was addiction.

An urge not to feel good, but to feel anything at all.

And the only thing that did that... was the kill. And the more I did, the better I became.

So I smiled at Denise. I kissed her cheek. I grabbed my coffee and muttered something about needing to check email.

And just like that, I left the conversation behind.
Left her behind.
And walked straight back into the quiet, controlled lie of my life.

Because love might lie to protect.
But monsters?
We lie to survive.

IT WAS A JOGGER WHO found her.
A man in his late thirties, earbuds in, breath steady, trying to make good on a New Year's resolution already unraveling by March. He had taken a different path that morning—bored of his usual route, tempted by the early mist curling off the pavement and the quiet of the park before the city woke up.
He never made it past the old bird statuary.

At first, he thought it was a mannequin.

Something left over from a twisted prank or photo shoot. The way she hung—arms bound above her, head tilted to the side, hair matted to her face—it was too still, too posed. Like she'd been arranged.

When he stepped closer, the truth hit him.
The color. The smell.
The pool beneath her, now a congealed dark rust spreading out in uneven shapes across the cement floor of the cage.

He stumbled back, hands shaking as he dropped his phone twice before managing to dial 911.
His voice was calm, oddly restrained, as if his brain hadn't caught up to what his eyes had seen.

By the time the authorities arrived, the fog had thinned, but the silence still hung heavy. Crime scene tape went up quickly. They photographed the body from every angle. Measured the spatter. Collected samples from the surrounding dirt.

But there were no shoe prints. No fingerprints. No tire marks, I'd made sure of that.
No signs of struggle.
No defensive wounds.

Just her—bound, silenced, and bled out with surgical precision.

The EMTs couldn't move her right away. Not until forensics finished.
So she hung there, suspended in the cold morning light, a grotesque statue in the cage that once held birds.

They combed the area.
Canvassed the park.
Checked local security cameras—nothing. No footage. No witnesses. No digital breadcrumbs to follow. Whoever had done this knew the blind spots. Knew how to vanish.

The detective in charge didn't say much.
Just stared at the girl for a long time, jaw set, one hand on his hip, the other tightening around his coffee cup until it buckled slightly in his grip.
"*This wasn't rage*," one of the officers said. "*This was... planned.*"

And it was.

Down to the last detail.

But no one would find those details.
Not in the cage. Not in the woods. Not in the dark space between the start of the ride and the end of her life.

She was just one girl in a city full of them.
And I was already out again.
Already back behind the wheel.

Ready for the next.

Chapter 29

A WIFE'S INSTINCT

MORNING IN OUR HOUSE had a rhythm. Not perfect, but predictable.

Chiara was always the first to stir—padding down the hallway in her too-long pajama pants, dragging that faded giraffe behind her like it was part of her body. The poor thing had one ear half-chewed, the other barely hanging on by a thread. Chiara's hair looked like she'd slept in a tornado. She didn't say much—just grunted something about waffles or oatmeal, then curled up on the couch like a little storm chaser, watching cartoons from behind her blanket as if they were live weather reports.

This morning was no different.
The house was warm. Still. Safe.

I was in the kitchen before the coffee pot even finished its first sigh, flipping through a basket of clean laundry I'd pulled from the dryer. Warm socks. Folded dish towels. One of Eric's undershirts, creased just the way he liked them.

Then I saw it.

His gray button-down. The nice one—tailored, clean lines, the one he wore for higher-end fares or investor dinners. Folded too tightly. I shook it loose to hang it properly and that's when I saw it.

A faint, rusty stain just under the cuff of the right sleeve. Easy to miss. You'd almost have to be looking.

I rubbed it with my thumb.
It didn't smear.
Didn't fade.
Just stared back at me like something that wasn't finished.

Chiara asked for cocoa, and I moved on instinct, heating the milk, stirring the powder, watching it spiral like a tiny storm before it vanished. The smell of sugar and chocolate filled the room, but that shirt stayed in my peripheral vision like it was watching me.

When Eric came downstairs, the air smelled like cinnamon and clean cotton. He looked… fresh.

Rested.

He kissed the top of my head, murmured, "*Morning,*" and made a beeline for the coffee pot.
I watched him move—too fluid, too measured.

Not tense. Not tired.

Just… disconnected.
Like he was already somewhere else.

I picked up the shirt.

"*Hon,*" I said, keeping my tone light, "*did you cut yourself?*"

He didn't answer right away. Just stirred his coffee with that slow, methodical swirl. He didn't even turn. And when he finally did, he wore a face I'd seen a thousand times—pleasant, casual, controlled.

"*No. Why?*"

"*There's a mark on your sleeve,*" I said, holding it up between us. "*Looked like blood.*"

He glanced at it—too quickly. A flick of the eyes, then away.

"*Ah—no, that was wine. Last night. I was trying to unwind and I spilled a little. Tried rinsing it out but I guess it set.*" He gave a little shrug. "*It's old. If it doesn't come out, just toss it.*"
I nodded. Smiled. Said, "*Okay.*"

But something twisted in my chest.

Because that answer had come too fast.

Not thoughtful. Not uncertain.
Rehearsed.

Eric always hesitated when he lied. Just a beat. Just enough for me to catch the shift behind his eyes.

But this time?

Nothing.

The rest of the morning played out like it always did.
He scrolled emails at the dining table. Chiara watched cartoons.
I made a grocery list I didn't really need, just so I had something to do.

But I watched him.
And I *saw* it.

The way his eyes flicked to Chiara and lingered just long enough to feel like a checkmark. The way he cleared his plate with robotic precision. The way his movements—his *presence*—felt like an echo of who he used to be.

And suddenly, I couldn't stop thinking about that night. The party. The one with the PTA moms and the neighbors and the lights strung up like we were trying too hard to be festive. I'd been in the kitchen, pouring shots into those cheap plastic cups—the bright yellow ones, the ones Becky used to joke looked like "liquid sunshine."

Eric had walked in and said, "*Are you making jello shots again?*" I

laughed.

And I remember now—he didn't. He didn't laugh.
He just looked at me for a beat too long. Like he wasn't asking about the drink at all.

And then later, when I found him outside alone, standing by the pool, drink untouched... I kissed him. Pulled him into the bathroom. We didn't talk. Just hands. Heat. That animal kind of need that reminded me we were still us—at least in the moment.

But then two days later?
Nothing. Cold. Distant.
Like I'd dreamed it.

It had become a cycle. Passion like a wave crashing out of nowhere—then silence.

A touch so hungry I thought he still wanted me—followed by a week of nothing. No warmth. No connection. Just… withdrawal.

Sometimes I wonder if that's the most intimate he can be now—when he's pretending we're strangers.

I wiped down the counter and tried to shake it off. Thought about Foss again—her voice in Sarasota, calm and careful.

"*Has your husband been traveling more lately*?"
"*Does he come home ever smelling like bleach?*"
"*Has he been... different?*"

I had laughed. Told her we moved. New house, new routine. Adjustments. It was normal.

But now, it didn't feel normal.

Now it felt deliberate.

The locked glove compartment.
The extra set of keys.
The new gloves in the trunk.

The dreams are always the same. Mine—not his.

He stands at the foot of our bed in the dark, unmoving. Just watching. And in the dream, I never ask what he's doing. Because I already know."

Later that afternoon, I stripped the bed to wash the sheets. The sun was pushing through the windows, soft and golden, the way it only does in winter. But when I went downstairs to start the laundry, I saw the shirt again.

Still hanging where I had left it. Still there.

Waiting.

I picked it up again, slower this time.
Held it up to the light.

The stain had faded, sure. It wasn't red anymore.
Just a soft brown.
The kind of brown that blood turns when it dries and settles.
When it no longer wants to be cleaned.

I didn't cry. Didn't scream. I just went numb, convincing myself that everything was fine—until the quiet made it impossible to believe.

Then, I just folded it.
Carefully. Neatly.
And put it back in Eric's closet.

For now.

Because when things don't come out in the wash…
You have to start wondering what else is stained.

IT STARTED WITH THE keys.
I didn't plan it. There was no strategy. Just a moment—Chiara down for her nap, the house quiet, the laundry done. Eric was in the shower and the spare keys to the SUV, lying on the desk.

I stared at them for maybe five seconds before I took them. They felt heavier than I remembered.

Eric's SUV was parked in its usual spot, clean as ever.

Always clean.

Even when we lived in Florida, he vacuumed the floors like a rental return. Now in California, it gleamed like it had never been driven.

I opened the door slowly, half-expecting an alarm. None. Just the soft creak of leather and the faint, artificial scent of pine.

The driver's seat was pushed back slightly, like he needed extra space to breathe.

I sat down and closed the door.

It was ridiculous, I told myself. He's my husband. I was probably just being paranoid. Foss had gotten in my head.

The shirt was nothing.

The dreams were nothing.

The cold distance? Normal.

Still, my fingers were already moving.
Glove compartment. Empty, aside from the manual and a half-used pack of gum.

Under the seat. Nothing.
Side door pockets. Receipts, wrappers, a pen that didn't work.

I opened the center console.

Just coins. Sunglasses. A phone charger.

And then I reached for the armrest.

It was stiff—heavier than it should've been. Like it didn't want to open. I pulled a little harder and heard the latch give way with a soft pop.

Inside:
A folded cloth. Black. Clean.
A tiny bottle of hand sanitizer.
An unopened energy bar.
A clean, unused pair of gloves. Latex.

I stared at them for too long.

That's when I heard the garage door.
Not the big one—the side one. The one that led into the kitchen.

Eric.

I froze. The hair on my arms stood up before I even heard his voice.

"*Looking for something?*"

I spun around. He was standing just outside the driver's side door. Calm. Too calm. His hand was still on the edge of the doorframe, as if he hadn't decided whether to shut it or rip it off.

"*I—*" My voice cracked. "*I was just cleaning. Thought I'd grab the trash out of here.*"

He nodded slowly, eyes scanning everything.
My hand still on the open compartment.
The gloves.
The silence.

"*Trash,*" he repeated.

His tone wasn't angry. That made it worse.
If he'd yelled, I could yell back. If he'd looked shocked, I could apologize. But this?

This was a test.
And I didn't know which answer would pass.

"*You don't trust me,*" he said finally.

I swallowed. "*Eric, don't—*"

"*You're going through my car. My things.*"
He leaned in, voice quieter now. "*Do you know how that looks?*"

I wanted to say something. Anything. But the words sat like rocks in my throat. I couldn't lie. Not now.

"*I just...*" I shifted in the seat, my voice quieter now. "*I saw the blood on your shirt, and you brushed it off, and I—I don't know. Something about the way you said it, it just... didn't feel right.*"

Eric didn't speak.

"*I thought maybe there was more to it. That something happened, and you weren't telling me. And I was worried.*"
I turned toward him then. "*Not suspicious, Eric. Worried. About you.*"For a beat, he didn't move. Didn't blink. Then he let out a long, careful breath and leaned against the edge of the doorframe.

"T*here was more to it,*" he said finally. "*But not what you'd think.*"

He looked down at the garage floor as he spoke, as if conjuring the story from memory. "*A guy I picked up a couple nights ago. Drunk. Aggressive. One of those guys who thinks the world owes him something because he had to walk twenty feet to find the car.*"

He let out a soft, humorless laugh. "*Kept barking at me about the route, said I was scamming him. Then started getting weird—talking about Chiara's school sticker on the window. Like he was trying to provoke something.*"

My stomach turned.

"I pulled over and told him to get out. He wouldn't budge—just sat there, running his mouth, acting like he owned the ride. So I got out of the truck, walked around, and opened his door to get him moving. That's when he took a swing at me—caught me right in the chest. Hard enough to knock me back a step. I held up my hands, tried to de-escalate, just wanted him out and gone. But then he came at me again, full speed, like he was looking for a fight. And yeah—I punched him. Right in the face. I didn't have much of a choice. Could've been his lip or his nose, I'm not sure, but he was bleeding. He backed off after that, muttering something, and I got in the truck and drove home."

Eric looked up at me then. "*It wasn't serious. I didn't want to make it into a thing.*"

I stared at him, blinking. "*Jesus, Eric. Why wouldn't you tell me?*"

"*Because I knew you'd react like this,*" he said, gently. "*You already hate that I'm doing this at night. You'd start worrying every time I left the house.*"

He stepped forward, hands raised—not in defense, but surrender.

"*I wasn't hiding anything sinister. I just didn't want you to feel unsafe.*"

Something in his tone pulled at me. Soft. Honest. Measured.

He moved closer now, one hand lightly touching my arm.

"*I'm okay, Denise. It was nothing. I've let it go. You can, too.*"

I wanted to believe him.

God, did I want to believe him.

I stared down at the armrest I'd just searched, at the gloves, the gum wrappers, the nothingness that had felt like a secret. I nodded slowly, even as my chest still felt tight.

"*I just... you've been different.*"

His hand squeezed my arm. "*And you've been incredible. Moving here, taking care of everything, keeping us all sane. I'm just tired. That's all this is.*"

He kissed my forehead. Slow. Soft. Familiar.

"*Let's forget it, okay?*"

I nodded again.
But the truth was—I couldn't.

Because it was almost a good story. Almost perfect.

But I knew Eric. I knew the sound of truth in his voice.
And this?
This wasn't it.

"*I'm going to take a drive,*" he said at last. "*Clear my head.*"

He reached in and gently closed the console, then the door. He didn't slam it. Didn't touch me. Just walked around the front of the car, slid into the driver's seat, and pulled out of the garage like it was any other afternoon.

I stood there for a few seconds after he left. Still not breathing right.

The garage felt colder now. The air tighter. I could hear the dull rumble of his SUV as it backed out onto the street. No screech. No dramatics. Just a quiet pull away, like nothing had happened.

And maybe nothing had.
Maybe it really was some drunk asshole and Eric didn't want to worry me.
Maybe he just needed space. A release. A reset.
God knows I've wanted to hit someone lately.

I let out a breath I hadn't realized I'd been holding. My hand was shaking.

I walked back into the house.
Washed my hands.
Put the kettle on.
Sat down at the kitchen table and forced myself to check Chiara's school calendar, like any other day.

I didn't bring it up again.
Not that night.
Not the next day.

But the feeling stayed.

Like a window left cracked in a storm.

I DIDN'T DRIVE FAR. Just to the overlook above the canyon where the cell service drops out and the only thing you can hear is wind and your own breathing.

I put the car in park and let the engine idle.

She was smarter than I gave her credit for.

I thought I'd played it right—steady hands, calm voice, just enough detail to satisfy the instinct without feeding it.

But she saw something. Felt it. That stare of hers—too long, too still. Not afraid. Not angry.

Suspicious.

And that's worse.

It wasn't just the shirt. Or the gloves. It was *me*.
The version of me she's starting to sense under the surface.

And that's dangerous.

I used to think she was like the others—curious but easily redirected. Distracted by the details of life. PTA, bake sales, Chiara's play dates. And for a long time, she was.

Or maybe I just needed her to be.

But now she's watching. Noticing.
Connecting dots.

"She's not guessing anymore.
She's hunting.
And she doesn't even know it."

And it won't be long before she finds something I can't explain away with a drunken passenger or a stubborn stain.

Which means I need to be careful.

Not with her - Of her.

Chapter 30

THE STORM ARRIVES

SIX MONTHS, THAT'S HOW long it took for the lines to disappear —for the distance between who I was and what I've become to dissolve into something seamless. Natural. Pure.

In that time, the kills came faster. Cleaner. No hesitation. No remorse.

The girl at Griffith Park wasn't just the beginning.
She was the catalyst.
The ignition point that turned a flicker into an inferno.

Most of the kills were quiet—surgical acts of violence that barely stirred the surface of my daily life. They served their purpose. But some… some still echo inside me. Etched into memory. Burned into my bloodstream.

One of them began with an article I read in the *LA Times*.
It said that on any given day, the stretch between 104th and 92nd along Figueroa Street was home to hundreds of prostitutes. A lawless corridor of bodies for sale, minds for rent, and souls already sold. Johns parked with their headlights off. Gang members prowled. The Bloods and Crips waged their silent war in shadows. And drug dealers waited—vultures perched on corners, feeding on the weak.

It was a playground for predators.
But '*even predators have a hierarchy.*

One night, after I had just dropped a middle-aged couple off at *Perch*, one of downtown LA's rooftop hotspots.

On a whim, I drifted down Figueroa. At the corner of 101st, I pulled into *Tam's Burgers*, slid through the drive-thru, and parked in the back corner of the fenced-in lot. From where I sat, I had eyes on everything—a motel, a gas station, a vacant lot littered with broken glass and memories.

Girls walked the curb, dressed in nearly nothing, scanning every slow-moving car.

But it was the man standing beside an abandoned sedan in the vacant lot who caught my eye.

He didn't move. Not much. Just stood there, slouched, chin tucked into a hoodie. Every fifteen minutes or so, a kid on a bike would ride up, stop for less than a minute, and vanish into the night.

He wasn't subtle.
He was selling.
Feeding addiction, stripping people down from the inside out.

Maybe it was the way he stood there like a king.
Maybe it was the way he used others to carry his poison.
Or maybe I just wanted to remind someone that even monsters can be hunted.

I reached into the center console and rested my hand on the ghost gun.

I pulled out of the diner lot and coasted into the vacant lot beside him.

He didn't flinch.
White T-shirt. Baggy jeans. The newest Jordans—immaculate. Like he thought they made him bulletproof.

He took a few steps toward me, eyes glassy, skin twitching.
"*What the fuck you want?*" he barked.

I didn't flinch.
"*Fuck you got?*" I said.

That broke the ice. A slow smirk crept onto his face. He thought I was there to buy.

"*Bro, I got you,*" he said, eyes darting down the street. "*Whatever you need. Let's go.*"

He stepped closer. Pupils blown wide—coke, meth, maybe both. He was high on his own product, wired and buzzing with false confidence.

As he reached for the window, I raised the gun.

There was no time to run.

Only time to see the truth in my eyes before I pulled the trigger.

The sound was sharp.
A concussive pop that cracked through the night like a firecracker in a tomb.

The front of his face caved inward. The back of his skull exploded in a wet, chaotic burst—bone, brain, and blood misting into the air. His scalp split like overripe fruit, flaps of flesh peeling back as a thick arc of red sprayed the asphalt.

Chunks of gray-pink tissue slapped against a cinderblock wall. One long strand of brain matter dangled from a bent rebar like a grotesque decoration.

His mouth hung open, frozen mid-snarl. One eyelid fluttered—nothing more than static in the wires. His tongue lolled out, swollen and black with pooled blood.

And then the smell hit.
Copper. Burnt hair. Gunpowder.
And the sour stench of his bowels letting go.

His chest gave one final twitch. A death spasm.

And then—nothing.
Just the slow, wet drip from his nose.

There was no struggle. No screaming. No chaos.
Just a single moment. One pull of the trigger. And silence.

The kind of silence I'd been chasing since Amsterdam.

I watched him for a moment longer. Just to be sure.
Then I slid the gun back into the armrest.
Shifted into gear.
And drove.

No panic. No witnesses.
Just another drug deal gone bad in South Central.

He thought selling death made him untouchable.
He was wrong.

WITHIN THREE WEEKS, there were four more.

The first I baited in—not by force, not even with words, just a look. A subtle exchange outside a 24-hour diner in Echo Park.

He was twitchy, desperate, probably high. He saw me alone in the SUV and saw opportunity. I saw the same. I cracked the window, made eye contact, gave him the smallest nod. He approached like a stray dog sniffing for scraps. When he got close enough, I smiled. He never made it to the passenger seat. The ghost gun barked once, and the alley behind the diner swallowed him whole.

No one heard. No one cared.

That kill taught me how effortless it could be. No planning. No stalking. Just a moment—a micro-expression—and I knew. It wasn't improvisation. It was instinct. The cleanest kills weren't orchestrated. They were offered.

The second was bolder. A gangbanger—eighteen, maybe twenty—thought he'd make a name for himself by carjacking my SUV just off Florence and Crenshaw.

He yanked open the driver's side door, shouting commands, half-cocked bravado in his voice and a cheap pistol in his waistband. What he didn't know—what he couldn't know—was that I had been waiting for someone like him.

A test.

A challenge.

I needed to get out of the vehicle.

So I did—stepping out like I was surrendering to his will.

His gun never left his belt.

Mine did.

Two shots, center mass. He collapsed against the curb, twitching.

I didn't blink.

I stepped over him, closed the door, and drove away as blood pooled beneath the wheels.

There was no rush. No panic.

Just silence.

And the quiet satisfaction of control, reclaimed.

That one was about control. Reclaiming it. The power in preparation, the confidence in calm. He came at me with noise, and I answered with silence.

The third… well, the third was elegance.

A businessman headed to Australia—buttoned-up, polished, a man used to upgrades. He was late to LAX, sweating through his collar but still too proud to complain. I offered him a chilled bottle of water from the cupholder. He accepted it with a distracted "*Thanks, man,*" unscrewed the cap, and downed half of it before we hit the 405.

He never knew the water had been tainted. Tasteless. Odorless. Perfect.

He boarded his flight, took off into the clouds, and somewhere over the Pacific—between time zones and turbulence—his heart stopped. The coroner called it cardiac arrest. Stress, maybe. Travel fatigue. But I knew better.

That kill reminded me how beautiful *subtlety* could be. No blood. No scream. Just a single, irreversible sip. A whisper of death traveling 38,000 feet into the sky. By the time the body was cold, I was already home, brushing Chiara's hair out of her eyes as she watched cartoons.

Then came the woman. She was different.

Fresh off a flight from Bora-Bora, sun-kissed and self-assured, with three oversized bags and an attitude thick enough to cut through TSA. Santa Monica was her destination, a townhouse just four blocks from the beach. She'd spent the last six months globe-trotting on her ex-husband's dime—divorce settlement well spent.

She talked the whole ride about how men were leeches, liars, pathetic creatures who couldn't handle a strong woman. I listened. Smiled. Nodded at the right moments.

She didn't know I wasn't listening. I was studying.

Every word, every smug aside… she thought I was beneath her. A driver. A nobody.

When we pulled into her driveway, she turned and asked, "*Would you mind helping me with the bags?*" Her tone was sharp, entitled. Like I worked for her. Like I owed her something.

I didn't mind.

Not at all.

She was found two days later, naked in her bathtub. Water cold. A wine bottle tipped at the edge. A note, carefully written, full of regret and vague allusions to self-hate. Guilt. Exhaustion. The kind of suicide no one questions when the story fits the stereotype.

That one wasn't about rage. It was about erasure. A reminder that some people don't need to be killed loudly. Sometimes they just need to disappear in a way that makes sense to the world around them.

Another clean ending.

Another page turned.

There were never any headlines. No news specials. No candlelight vigils. Just a string of disappearances that never connected. That was the beauty of it—how easily people vanish when no one is looking closely.

I had perfected it.
Not just the kill—but the orchestration of it. The disappearance. The silence that followed.

I was no longer experimenting. I was executing.
No wasted motion. Just precision.

It stopped being improvisation somewhere between the business class flight and the bathwater suicide. Somewhere in there, I stopped asking myself if I could.

I just did.

Like breathing.

THERE WAS A TIME, NOT LONG AGO, when each kill required forethought. A spark of justification. A slow spiral of planning. I needed a reason. An angle. A crack in their façade that I could pry open and call motive. But not anymore.

Now, I barely heard the rationalizations. They were background noise. Static beneath a frequency I had already tuned past —I let go of hesitation. I no longer questioned if they deserved it. I stopped wondering if they'd be missed. I stopped weighing risk against reward.

Because the reward had become the act itself.

It was the way her handwriting curved in perfect, forged guilt. The way his heart failed quietly over the Pacific, so far from anything familiar. The way blood slicked the asphalt beneath that kid's sneakers, how it shimmered under the streetlight like oil on water. These weren't moments anymore.

They were movements.

A rhythm I had learned to follow. The beat of a second life I no longer had to hide from myself. Each kill was more than just a name erased—it was a piece of clarity. A flash of truth in a world addicted to lies.

I used to think the hard part would be the kill itself. The physicality. The logistics. The risk.

But I was wrong.

The hard part—the part that used to gnaw at me—was pretending it didn't feel right. Faking remorse. Manufacturing the illusion of guilt. Keeping the beast leashed when all it wanted was to breathe.

Now, I didn't fake it. I didn't need to.

I had evolved past the rules. Past the fear. Past the need to justify anything at all.

This wasn't improvisation anymore.

It was instinct.

And instinct doesn't wait for permission.

It feeds.

I came home just after 2A.M..

The house was still—silent in that curated, domestic way. The hum of the fridge. The soft tick of the hallway clock. A faint citrus-clean scent from the plug-in Denise always kept by the stairwell. Normalcy, wrapped in citrus.

But my mind hadn't left the bathroom in Santa Monica.

I could still see her—floating in lukewarm water, pale legs slack, hair fanned out like seaweed. Her skin had taken on that delicate, postmortem sheen—translucent, untouched. There was something almost holy in how still she was. A portrait of peace. Not in the poetic sense… in the clinical one. In the absolute stillness that only the dead get to claim.

She had been beautiful in that final moment. More beautiful than she was alive. The tension, the arrogance, the bitterness—all gone. Just a naked body, soft and serene beneath a film of scented bathwater and bubbles.

For a brief moment, I had stared longer than I should've.

Not with lust.

With awe.

I stood in that tiled room, forging the suicide note in her voice while steam curled against the mirror—and I remember thinking how strange it was… that death could look like grace.

I was still holding that image in my mind when I stepped into the hallway.

"*Daddy?*"

My body stiffened.

Chiara stood in the doorway of her room, one hand gripping the edge of the frame, the other rubbing her eye. Her voice was soft, laced with sleep, fragile as a matchstick.

"*I had a bad dream.*"

And just like that, the moment shattered.

I turned, slowly—my mask already back in place.

She was so small. Drowning in a unicorn pajama top two sizes too big. Her curls were flattened on one side, her cheeks pink from sleep. She looked like a question mark—unsure if she'd really seen me, or if she was still inside the dream.

I crouched and opened my arms.

"*Come here, baby.*"

She came without hesitation, bare feet whispering across the hardwood. Her arms wrapped around my neck. I lifted her easily—so light—and held her against my chest.

I could feel her heartbeat.

And mine, still slow from the kill.

She tucked her head beneath my chin.

I closed my eyes and exhaled.

Not because I felt guilt. Not because I had to shift gears. But because holding her was the only thing left in this world that still felt *pure.*

"*I'm here,*" I whispered into her hair. "*You're safe.*"

And she believed me.

God help her, she believed me.

I NOW LIVE IN A perfectly curated life.
The rooftop dinners.
The daddy-daughter playdates.
The neighborly barbecues and wine nights.

We waved at strollers, passed out cocktails at block parties, flipped burgers like suburban royalty. We belonged—woven into the fabric of Lyndon Street so tightly that no one would think to tug the thread.

The street was ours now.
Not legally. Not officially.
But in the way that mattered.

We were the couple people trusted with their kids, their house keys, their secrets. And beneath it all, the truth pulsed quietly—like a second heartbeat.

What no one would believe is how the killing brought Denise and I closer—not in conversation, not in confession, but in something more elemental. Desire.

It started with the shift in me.
The silence. The focus. The control.
I moved differently now—quieter, slower. Not reaching for control, but radiating it. It followed me like heat.

And Denise felt it.
She didn't ask questions anymore.
She didn't need to.

Whatever had eroded between us over the years—the small fractures of routine and obligation—sealed shut almost overnight. Maybe it was primal. Chemical. The way animals sense a change in the pack, an alpha rising.

She started looking at me the way she did in the beginning—curious, hesitant, hungry. Her touch lingered. Her eyes lingered longer. She leaned into me like she couldn't help it. Like whatever I was becoming had woken something in her, too.

Our intimacy returned like a storm.
Sudden. Unapologetic.
We didn't fall back into old patterns—we broke them.

We made love like strangers.
Like we were trying to memorize each other all over again.
It was rougher. Messier. Real.

She bit my shoulder one night. I liked it.
She liked that I liked it.
We didn't speak about it.

The routine of marriage—touch out of obligation, kisses out of habit—vanished. In its place was something darker, hotter. Something we hadn't touched since our early days.

She didn't ask why my grip had changed.
Why I whispered things I never had before.
Why I looked at her like I might devour her.

She didn't need answers. She just wanted more.

Maybe she thought it was therapy.
Maybe she thought it was healing.
Maybe she didn't care.

Whatever fire I was feeding in the dark, it had found its way into our bed, into our walls, into the breath between us when we weren't touching.

And Denise welcomed it.

Welcomed me.

Like she finally recognized the man across from her again.
Like she had been waiting for this version of me to return.

Somewhere between the loaded silence of a kill and the warmth of her breath in the dark, I stopped wondering if I could keep doing this.

I just did.
Like breathing.

And the same hunger that drove me to kill…
Was now the same one that made me reach for her in the dark.
And she reached back—without hesitation.

Denise had no idea what I'd become.
But she loved who I was now.
And that was enough.

Because sometimes intimacy isn't built on honesty.
Sometimes it's built on heat.
On power.
On the lies we never say aloud.

And in that space—between the silence of a kill and the warmth of her breath on my neck—I found rhythm. Balance.

A dual life.

And for now…
It was working.

Too well.

Sometimes I wonder if this is who I always was.
Or if something snapped along the way—quietly, irreversibly.

Not all monsters are born with blood on their hands.
Some learn to smile first.
To kiss their daughter goodnight.
To pay the mortgage.
To earn trust.

Some monsters wear wedding bands and drive hybrids.
And mean it when they say, *"Have a good night."*

I didn't ask for this darkness.
I just stopped running from it.
And when I did, the strangest thing happened.

Life made sense.

Not in the way it's supposed to.
But in a way that finally let me exhale.

Because behind every lie I tell…
Behind every body I leave behind…
Behind every time I reach for Denise in the dark—

I'm not searching for power.
I'm not chasing death.

I'm chasing peace.

And in this life I've built—
This carefully measured lie that feels more honest than the truth ever did—
I've found it.

Even if it came at the cost of my soul.

Maybe you judge that.

Maybe you should.

"Easy for you to judge me now. But one day, when the world finally asks too much of you—when the weight becomes unbearable—you'll remember this chapter. And you'll understand. Maybe not the blood. But the clarity.
And that's when the door opens."

But if you'd felt what I felt—
Just once—
You'd understand.

You'd understand why I keep going.

And maybe, just maybe...

You'd do the same."

Chapter 31

THE PARTS WE PLAY

THE CALL CAME just after three.

Chiara was upstairs, playing quietly. I'd been folding laundry in the kitchen, trying to stay busy, but my mind had been drifting all day. The towel in my hands had already been folded twice, unfolded, then folded again without me realizing.

Then my phone buzzed.

Unknown number. Florida area code.

I let it ring twice before answering.

"*Hello?*"

"*Mrs. Sutton?*"
The voice was calm. Unhurried.
"*This is Detective Foss.*"

I didn't respond right away. I shifted my grip on the phone and turned toward the kitchen window, heart already thudding.

"*I know it's been a while,*" she continued. "*And I know this is... unusual. I just—well, this isn't official. Not a report. Not an interrogation. Just a call. Off the record.*"

Something in her voice made me reach for the edge of the counter. Steady myself.

"*You said something to me last time we spoke. Back in Sarasota.*"

A pause.
'Eric's been... different lately.'

My chest tightened.

"*I remember,*" I said softly.

"*Back then, I didn't know what to make of it. But now?*" Foss's voice dropped, quieter. Like she didn't want anyone overhearing. "*Now I can't shake something. And I need you to hear it from someone who's been doing this a long time.*"

I said nothing.

"*I believe your husband was involved in what happened to Becky.*"

The kitchen felt smaller. The air, thinner.

"*We reexamined the toxicology. Ricin. That much we knew. But what didn't make sense was the delivery—no injection site, no abrasions. Which means it was ingested. We think it was a jello shot.*"

My throat closed. I couldn't speak.

"*You served them, didn't you?*" she asked, softer now. "*You and a friend, walking through the party?*"

I closed my eyes. I could still hear the music. See the lights. Feel the weight of the tray in my hands. The way we laughed. Julie and Amber flirting their way through the crowd. Becky—licking sugar from the rim of her cup.

I remembered the bitterness.
The one shot Julie wrinkled her nose at.
The one no one thought twice about.

"*Yes,*" I whispered.

"*I believe your husband poisoned one of those shots,*" Foss said. "*Not for Becky. Not for anyone in particular. Just... to see what would happen.*"

My fingers went numb. "*That's not possible.*"

"*No?*" she asked gently. "*Because I think you already know it is.*"

I tried to steady my breath. "*Why are you telling me this now?*"

"*Because I'll never be able to prove it—not the way it was done. It was clean. Smart. No prints. No witnesses. It's textbook sociopath behavior: calculated, impersonal, emotionally detached.*"

I leaned forward, resting my elbows on the counter.

"*I'm not asking you to testify. I'm not even asking you to agree with me. I'm asking you to trust your instincts. Because if he's capable of that—he's capable of worse.*"

Still, I didn't speak.

"*He didn't just kill a stranger, Denise. He killed someone in your home. At your party. Surrounded by people you love. And he did it knowing you were right there.*"

I pressed my palm to my mouth, holding everything in.

"*I'm not telling you to go to the police. I'm telling you to be careful.*"

She paused.

"*I'm sending you my personal number. Not the department's. No record. If anything feels wrong—off—text me five words:* ***I think we made a mistake moving****. That's it.*"

Another beat.

"*I hope I never hear from you again. But I'm not sure that's how this story ends.*"

A breath.

"*Take care of yourself. And take care of your daughter.*"

The line went dead.

A message followed seconds later. Just a number. No name.

I didn't delete it.
But I didn't save it either.

Because it was ridiculous.

Eric might be distant. Quiet. Secretive.
But a killer?

No.
Becky was his friend.
Brian—his best friend—was at that party. He would've risked killing him too.

And the bartenders, the ones he openly flirted with—Julie had winked at him right in front of me. He wouldn't put them in danger. Not when he was enjoying the attention.

It didn't make sense.

I set the phone down on the counter and picked up the towel I'd forgotten I was folding.

Then the front door opened.

"*I'm back!*" Eric called, cheerfully.

Chiara's voice echoed from upstairs. "*Daddy!*"

He was halfway up the stairs before I even turned.
She launched herself into his arms.
He spun her once, both of them laughing like nothing had changed.

I stood in the kitchen, watching. Watching the man I married. The man I built this life with.

Then he walked into the kitchen.

His eyes swept over me—then to the phone on the counter.

"*Everything okay?*" he asked casually.

"*Yeah,*" I said, smiling too quickly. "*Just laundry.*"

He glanced again. "*Someone call?*"

"*No,*" I said, too fast. Then softened. "*Spam number. I didn't answer.*"

He nodded, slow. "*Mm.*"

I kissed Chiara's cheek and turned to grab the towels.

"*I'll go put these away.*"

He didn't stop me. Just watched me go.

When I returned, he was sitting on the couch, smiling at something Chiara had drawn.

And for a moment, I believed all of it.

The sound of Chiara's laughter, the way Eric ruffled her hair, the soft warmth of the late afternoon sun slanting through the window—it all felt like the life we'd worked so hard to build. A picture-perfect moment. Calm. Familiar. Safe.

But then—
That flicker again.
Like the light shifting in a room, just enough to make you question what you're seeing.

I remembered Amsterdam.
The first night in the new house back from Amsterdam.
We were unpacking in the bedroom— the suitcase.

He was putting it away and I saw the scratches across his forearm, red and raw, like something had clawed at him. Not deep, but not superficial either.

"*What happened?*" I asked.

He didn't even look up.

Blamed it on the neighbors cat.

I hadn't pushed. I wanted to believe him then, too.

But now—layered on top of everything else—I could see it for what it was: a placeholder story.

Not a lie you fight to protect. Just one you tell and expect to be swallowed.

Then there was the shirt.
The gray one in the laundry.
The rust-colored stain tucked just below the cuff.
"*Wine,*" he'd said. "*Sloshed it while I was pouring a glass.*"

It had sounded reasonable. Casual.

But it had come out too fast.
Too smooth.
Too clean
And when I pushed, he tells me about a fight.

The explanations all left no gaps.

The moments that should've felt messier, more human, more flawed.

But Eric never faltered. Never fumbled. Just answered, smiled, moved on.

And now this.

The call.

Foss's voice still echoing through my head.

The things she said.
The things I didn't want to hear.

I looked at my phone, still sitting where I'd left it. The screen was dark now, but I knew the number was there. The message. The warning. The choice.

I hadn't deleted it.
And I couldn't. Not yet.

But something inside me was shifting.
Not enough to act.
Not enough to run.
Just enough to wonder.

Sometimes survival doesn't look like escape.
Sometimes it looks like silence.

And beneath the doubt—beneath all the carefully stacked reasons why none of this could be true—
something colder had begun to curl inside me.

Not belief.
Not certainty.
Just the terrifying possibility
that one day,
I might need that number.

- Downstairs -

Denise took the towels up the stairs, her footsteps soft.

I waited until she was out of sight. Then I picked up her phone.

Just curious.

Something she said hadn't sat right.

I tapped the screen.

The call log was still open.

Sarasota, FL.

I stared at it for a long moment.

Then, without a word, I placed it exactly where I found it, and walked calmly back toward the living room.

Chiara looked up and smiled.

I smiled back.

Chiara was giggling as she colored beside me, her tongue poking out of the corner of her mouth in perfect concentration. I kept my hand on the back of the couch, leaned in every so often to say things like *"That's beautiful"* and *"Should we show Mommy?"*—things I'd said a thousand times before, with the same gentle tone.

But my mind wasn't on the drawing.

It was on the phone.

The Florida number.

Sarasota.

She said it was spam.
Didn't answer.

But the call log.

If she was going to lie, she should've been smarter about it.

It wasn't a neighbor—she would've mentioned that. Some silly gossip, some ridiculous new PTA drama. It wasn't one of her sisters or her mother—those names would've shown on the screen. And it wasn't work.

So who was it?

There was only one person in Florida who made sense.
One name that explained her hesitation.
Her too-fast smile.
The way she left the room like her skin itched.

Detective Foss.

She must have called Denise.

And Denise didn't tell me.

I sat back slightly, resting my arm across the couch. Chiara held up her drawing and beamed. I smiled back and kissed the top of her head.

My pulse never spiked. My hands never shook.

But something inside me settled.

Not in relief. In confirmation.

The house was quiet again—laundry humming in the background, the faint clink of dishes upstairs. Normal.
But Foss was circling.

And Denise…

Denise was starting to ask questions.

Or worse—she was starting to get answers.

I glanced toward the stairs. I could hear her moving around. Folding towels. Changing sheets. Playing the role she'd always played so well.

But now I had to wonder…
Was it still a role?

I turned back toward Chiara and tucked a loose curl behind her ear.

"*Want to surprise Mommy with cocoa?*" I asked.

She nodded eagerly.

I stood, walked to the kitchen, and opened the cupboard with one hand. The other was already pulling up a note in my phone, logging the timestamp of the call:

3:04 P.M.. Sarasota.

Not for now.

Just in case it was needed later.

I stirred the cocoa slowly, the powder blooming into the milk like ink in water.

Chiara hummed behind me. Denise moved somewhere upstairs. The house carried on as if nothing had changed.

But something had.

I glanced down once more—at the timestamp, the area code. Sarasota. My finger hovered for a moment… then tapped lock.
This was what Denise didn't understand.

She thought she was being careful.

But lies don't survive in quiet.
They echo.

She'd heard a whisper of the truth.
Now she was deciding what to do with it.

And me?

I already knew how this would unfold.

Because we all have a part to play.
Denise. Foss. Even Chiara.

And mine?

Mine was written a long time ago.
All I'm doing now—
is playing it out.

Chapter 32

FINAL THOUGHT

YOU MAY HAVE BEEN to one of our parties.
Maybe an intimate dinner.
Maybe a casual happy hour.
Maybe you rode with me once, late at night, after a concert, too drunk to drive yourself home.
You don't remember it, do you?

But I remember you.

I always do.

See, most people assume danger comes loud—
A scream. A struggle. A headline.
But the real danger?

It's quiet.
It asks how your day was.
It adjusts the air conditioning for you.
It knows exactly when to speak… and when not to.

It waits until you feel safe.

And you did.
You always do.

Serial killers don't wear masks anymore.
They wear smiles.
They hold doors open.
They're your neighbor.
Your favorite barista.
The bartender you flirted with.

The food delivery guy.
Your Tinder date.

They blend in.

You know the name John Wayne Gacy, right?
Forty-five confirmed.
Buried beneath floorboards.

Hidden behind charm.

The worst serial killer in American history, they say.
But they're wrong.

By the time you finish this story—
By the time you turn this last page and check the locks on your doors —

I will have surpassed him.

Exponentially.

Quietly.
Cleanly.
Without a single scream.

You never suspected me.
Why would you?
I offered you comfort.
Convenience.
A ride home after a long day.
A piece of gum. A bottle of water...
Funny how trust tastes like peppermint, isn't it?

But choose carefully.

What you drink.
What you chew.
What car you get into.

Because I'm still out here.
And I'm still hunting.

I used to think the story ended when the killing started.
But some stories don't end.
They evolve.
And this one?
It's just getting started.

So keep in mind -

The next time your phone lights up,
The next time you glance down without thinking,
The next time those three words flash across your screen—

Just remember:

Your Driver's Arrived.

Printed in Dunstable, United Kingdom

78833450R00234